HIDDEN PREY

HIDDEN PREY

John Sandford

G. P. PUTNAM'S SONS

New York

This novel is a work of fiction. Names, characters, places, and incidents either are
the product of the author's imagination or are used fictitiously,
and any resemblance to actual persons, living or dead,
businesses, companies, events, or locales
is entirely coincidental.

G. P. Putnam's Sons
Publishers Since 1838
a member of
Penguin Group (USA) Inc.
375 Hudson Street
New York, NY 10014

Copyright © 2004 by John Sandford
All rights reserved. This book, or parts thereof, may not
be reproduced in any form without permission.
Published simultaneously in Canada

Library of Congress Cataloging-in-Publication Data

Sandford, John, date.
Hidden prey / John Sandford.
p.   cm.
ISBN 0-399-15180-X
1. Davenport, Lucas (Fictitious character)—Fiction.
2. Private investigators—Minnesota—Minneapolis—Fiction.
3. Minneapolis (Minn.)—Fiction.   I. Title.
PS3569.A516H54   2004   2004044351
813'.54—dc22

Printed in the United States of America
1   3   5   7   9   10   8   6   4   2

This book is printed on acid-free paper. ∞

HIDDEN PREY

THE TAG END of summer, in the very heart of the night.

Annabelle Ramford sat on a soggy piece of carpet, in a patch of goldenrod on the southernmost shore of Lake Superior, a huge butter-ball moon rising to the east. A bottle of New York pinot noir was wedged securely between her thighs. She was warm, comfortable, at peace, and a little drunk, bathed in the odors of dead fish and diesel exhaust, ragweed, and the rancid sweat of her unwashed cotton shirt.

Annabelle's friends, if they were friends, called her Trey. She had shoulder-length reddish-blond hair, which hung straight and close to her skull because of the dirt in it; a deeply weathered face with feral green eyes; a knife-edged nose; and a too-slender, square-shouldered body, with the bones showing through. On her chin she carried what she thought of as her identifying mark—as in "Police said the body carried an identifying mark."

The mark was a backwards-C-shaped scar, the product of a fight at the mission in Albuquerque. A bum named Buddy had bitten her, and when she'd gotten up off the floor, she was dripping blood and missing a piece of chin. Buddy, she believed, had swallowed it. She almost sympathized: when you're a bum, you get your protein where you can.

Like Buddy, Annabelle Ramford was a bum.

Or maybe a bummess.

A long and exceptionally strange trip, she thought, growing philosophical with the wine. She'd grown up well-to-do and thoroughly educated—had sailed boats on Superior, which was why she returned to Duluth in the summer. After private schools in St. Paul, she'd gone to the University of Minnesota, where she'd majored in sociology, and then on to law school, where she'd majored in marijuana and gin-and-tonic. She'd graduated, though, and her father's influence had gotten her a job with the Hennepin County public defender's office, interviewing gang-bangers at the height of the crack plague.

Crack. She could close her eyes and feel it lifting her out of herself. She'd loved crack as she'd loved no human being. Crack had cost her first the job, then all her square friends, and finally her parents, who'd given her up for lost. Even at the end, even when she was fucking the crack man, it had seemed like a reasonable trade.

When she finally woke up, four years after she went on the pipe, she had no life and three STDs, though she'd somehow avoided HIV. She'd been traveling ever since.

A strange trip, growing ever stranger . . .

STRAIGHT NORTH OF her spot on the working harbor shore, she could see the bobbing anchor-light of a sailboat, and beyond it, the street and house lights stretching along Minnesota Point, the narrow spit of land across the mouth of the harbor. Though the boat was five hundred yards away, she could hear the tinkling and clanking of hardware against the aluminum mast, and, every once in a while, a snatch of music, Sinatra or Tony Bennett, and a woman's laughter.

Overhead, a million stars. Off to her right, another million stars, closer, larger, more colorful—the night lights of Duluth, sliding north along the hill.

A dying summer, and cool. The breeze off the lake had teeth. The day before, Trey'd scored a Czechoslovakian Army coat at the Goodwill store, and she tugged the wool collar up around her throat. Superior's water temperature didn't get much above fifty degrees, even at midsummer, and you could always feel the winter in the wind. But with the coat, she was warm, inside and out.

She took a pull of the wine, wiped her lips on the back of her free hand, savored the thick grape flavor. *A month,* she thought.

Another month here and she'd start moving again. Back to Santa Monica for the winter. Didn't like Santa Monica. Too many bums. But you could freeze to death in Minnesota, no joke: get a skin full of whiskey and forget what you were doing, and the next morning the cops would find you in a doorway, frozen stiff, frozen in the L shape of the doorway. She'd seen it.

Still, for the time being, she had a good spot, a cubbyhole that was safe, obscure, sheltered, and free. Women transients had a tougher life than the men. Nobody wanted to rape some broken-down thirty-five-year-old bum with no teeth and a fourteen-inch beard and scabs all over him; but women, no matter how far down they'd gone, had that secret spot that some guy always wanted to get into, even if only to prove that he was still male, somehow, someway. To further prove it, half the time they weren't happy with simple rape; they had to beat the shit out of you.

Some women got so accustomed to it that they barely cared, but Trey wasn't that far down. Scrape away the dirt and she didn't look too bad. She still worked, sometimes, waitressing, fry-cook jobs, rent-a-maid stuff. Hadn't ever quite gotten to the point of selling herself. Not technically, anyway.

Here in Duluth, she had a nice routine. The morning bus driver with the route along Garfield Avenue—his name was Tony—would let her ride into town for free. There were good safe public bathrooms at the downtown mall, and after cleaning up, she'd get up to the Miller Hill Mall to do a little subtle panhandling, avoiding security, picking just the right guys: *Got a dollar? Got a dollar, please?* She'd perfected the waif look, the thin high cheekbones and starving green eyes. Some days she cleared fifty dollars. Try doing that in Santa Monica.

She took another pull at the wine, leaned back, heard the sailboat woman laugh again. Then, a little later, something else.

Somebody coming.

CARL WALTHER SAT silently, his back against the side of the building, his senses straining into the night, the pistol cold in his hand. He could hear the elevator inside, moving grain up to the drop-pipe, and the rush of it into the ship's hold.

He'd waited like this before, in the dark, on an early-morning deer stand, listening for footfalls, trying to pick movement out of the gloom. As also happened in a deer stand, when he'd first found his ambush spot, he'd been all ears and eyes. As the minutes passed, other thoughts intruded: he thought he could feel bugs crawling on him; a mosquito whined past his ear. He needed a new job, something that didn't involve food—six months in a pizza joint was enough.

He thought about girls. Randy McAndrews, a jock-o three-letter guy, had been talking after gym class, Carl tolerated on the edge of the conversation, and he said Sally Umana had been cooling him off with blow jobs in the backroom of Cheeney's Drive-In. The account was greeted with a half dozen groans and muttered *bullshits*, but McAndrews swore it was the truth. Carl had groaned with the others but later that day had seen blond Sally in the hallway and had instantly grown a serious hard-on, which he had to conceal awkwardly with a notebook as he hiked through the school.

And thinking about it now, waiting in the dark, began to feel the same effect; the idea of that blond head bobbing up and down . . .

He heard a voice on the deck of the ship; a distant voice. He shifted position and strained into the night. Where the fuck was he? He pushed up his sleeve and looked at his watch: jeez—six minutes since the last check. Seemed more like an hour. Same as on a deer stand, waiting for dawn.

He was not exactly tense; not as tense as when he'd killed his first dog. He still thought about that, sometimes, the black-and-white pooch from the pound, out in the woods.

"Why are you killing the dog?" Grandpa asked.

"Because it's necessary to condition myself against the shock," he said. The response was a learned one, like the responses for a Boy Scout rank, or a First Communion exam.

"Exactly. When you are working as a weapon, you must focus. No pity, no regrets, no questions, because those things will slow you down. All the questions must be resolved into trust: your committee instructs you to act, and you do. That's your highest calling."

"Okay."

"Remember what Lenin said: 'There are no morals in politics: there is only expedience.'"

"Okay." Enough Lenin.

The old man said, "Now. Kill the dog."

He could remember licking his lips, working the slide on the pistol. The dog knew something was going on, looked up at him, small black eyes searching for compassion, not that it had gotten much in the pound. Then the dog turned away, as if it knew what was coming.

Carl shot him in the back of the head.

Not hard. Not hard at all; a certain satisfaction uncurled in his soul.

That surprised him. The shock came a few minutes later, when they buried the dog. When he picked up the small body, it was still warm, but it was dead and there was no way to get it back. The dog was gone forever. He remembered looking back at the small grave and thinking, *Really?*

There'd been more dogs after that, and Carl's soul had hardened. He no longer dreaded the trips. He didn't enjoy it; he just didn't feel much at all.

Now he sat with his head down. Would a human be harder? He doubted it. He liked dogs better than he liked most people. And while the dog had been a test, this killing was absolutely necessary . . .

Then headlights played across the wasteland, amid the railroad tracks. A car bounced along a rutted track, then stopped a couple of hundred yards out. There was a light on the roof. A taxi. Carl slipped the safety on the pistol, felt the weight in his hand; kept his finger off the trigger, as he'd been trained.

RODION OLESHEV HAD been left in the dark.

The taxi turned away, the door locks snapped down, and it was gone, back to the hillside of light, back into town. Oleshev scowled at it: the taxi driver, a blockheaded Swede, according to his taxi license, wouldn't go any farther off-road. He might break a wheel in the dark, he'd said. He might fall in a hole. Fuckin' Swedes. The whole area was lousy with them.

Oleshev was a broad man in a black leather jacket, black denim jeans, and plain-toed military dress shoes. He hadn't shaved that morning and his two-day beard was a briar patch, chafing against his neck. He carried a black nylon briefcase. Inside were his seaman's papers, a digital camera, a pair of Razor sunglasses, and a laptop computer.

The night was pretty, with the thinnest summer haze over the cool water of the lake, and the moon coming up, and he could clearly see the lights of a building six miles down the shoreline. Ahead of him, closer, only two hundred yards away, the bulk carrier *Potemkin* sat in a berth beneath the TDX terminal. The deck of the ship was bathed in floodlights, as it took on durum wheat from North Dakota.

There was a lot of light around, Oleshev thought; there just wasn't any where he was. The whole area south of the grain terminals was a semi-wasteland of dirt roads, waist-high weeds, railroad tracks and industrial detritus, all smelling of burned diesel. The moonlight didn't help, casting hard shadows everywhere, making holes look like bumps, and bumps like flat spots. Oleshev felt his way toward the *Potemkin,* stepping carefully; saw a shiny, knifelike streak in the dirt ahead of him, reached out with his toe, felt the steel rail of the first set of tracks.

"Fuck this place," he muttered out loud.

Oleshev was an unhappy man, thinking about the satellite call he'd have to make back to Russia. Things were more complicated than anyone had expected. The Circle at the SVR had expected either agreement or rejection, had been prepared to react with either money, as a gesture of goodwill, or blackmail. What they'd gotten was . . . bullshit.

What'd the old man say? "It is impossible to predict the time and progress of the revolution. It's governed by its own more or less mysterious laws . . ."

Vladimir Ilyich fuckin' Lenin. Oleshev spat into the weeds, thinking about it. Bullshit and more bullshit. The people here swam in it. They were *Communists.* How crazy was that? Somehow, they'd been expecting *Russians,* and they'd gotten *Communists.*

Politics complicated everything. He tripped again, swore into the quiet of the night, and stumbled on, cursing, scowling, toward the waiting ship.

OLESHEV HAD JUST stepped into the light, onto the concrete pad around the grain terminal, when another man moved out of the shadows on the side of the terminal. The man stepped out backwards, and Oleshev saw that he was fumbling at his crotch, zipping up.

Taking a leak: the idea popped into Oleshev's head and he relaxed a half inch, enough that he wasn't ready. The man turned around and Oleshev saw the pink apple-cheeks and the blond hair and the thought flashed through his mind that the blond was a crewman, a member of the night watch who he'd not often seen coming across the Atlantic.

"Mr. Moshalov."

Not a crewman, not with those round, Swedish-sounding Os. The man's hand came up. Not to shake. He was holding a gun and Oleshev saw it and another thought flew through his mind, one word from his training: *Shout.*

Actually, what the manual said was *Try to relax but be prepared to move instantly. If you see that your captor intends to fire, shout at him, to distract him. Even if you are killed, perhaps your companions will gain from the edge you give them.*

A lot of horseshit, Oleshev had thought when he first read it. Let somebody else shout. Still, at the critical moment, he thought *Shout,* but before he could open his mouth, the other man shot him in the heart. Oleshev fell over backwards. His chest hurt, but his mind was okay for a few seconds, and his vision actually seemed better: there was lots of light now. Enough light that when the man stood over him and pointed the gun at his eyes, he could clearly see the O of the muzzle. He wanted to shout again.

Carl, who didn't know that he'd hit Oleshev in the heart, stepped forward and fired twice more, from short range, through the Russian's forehead. Unnecessary, but he didn't know that. He had the theory, but he didn't have the training.

TREY HAD HEARD Oleshev coming, stumbling through the weeds, muttering and grumbling.

There had been two or three people walking around the terminal in the past hour. She'd stayed out of sight in her hole with her bottle, invisible in the night, enjoying the lake. She yawned. When this one had gone up the ladder into the ship, she thought, she'd head back across the wasteland to the shack where she was crashing.

Her pad.

She'd found two whole rolls of bubble wrap in a Dumpster at the Goodwill store, and with a little duct tape, had made the most luxurious mattress out of it. Asleep on the bubble wrap, cocooned in an olive-drab army blanket, she could almost believe that she was back home. The best nights were the nights when it was raining, when the rain on the roof and the warmth of the bed made her feel cozy and snug. The problem with it was that when she was lonely, or bored, or stressed, she tended to pop the bubbles.

Now, sitting in her hole, she heard a man speak; and then a shot. She recognized the shot for what it was, though it wasn't loud. A *Bap!* like the noise made by a pellet gun. She stood up, thinking herself safe in the dark, her eyes just inches higher than the weeds around her.

A tall man, with fair hair, stood over another man, who was supine on the concrete slab. The tall man's face was turned toward her, and she registered his good looks. He pointed the pistol and fired twice more into the second man's head, bap! bap! The pistol had a bulbous barrel. A silencer? She'd only seen them in movies.

The killing had been cold, she thought. She shivered, lost her balance for a moment, caught herself. Stepped on piece of broken concrete, lost her balance again, and caught herself a second time. And made just enough noise to attract the attention of the killer.

His head came up, and he saw her—saw the light reflecting off her face—lifted the pistol and fired two quick shots at her. She saw the small flashes, but never heard the slugs go by, because she was already moving, running through the jumble of weeds and concrete along the bank, frantic to get away from the gun.

Moving just a fraction slower than she might have, had her hands been empty: but a bum and a drunk would never drop a half-full bottle of pinot, not if there was an alternative.

Behind her, a thrashing. Trey fell, saved the bottle by rolling, clambered to her feet, looked back, was shocked to see the killer only fifty feet away and closing. She ran, scrambling, heard him fall and cry out, ran some more, fell, smashed the bottle, cried, "Motherfucker," turned and saw him, still coming, even closer, saw him go down again, ran a few more steps, the darkness now closing down like velvet, looked back, saw him coming, thirty feet away, catching her . . .

He stopped and fired again, and she imagined that the slug went through her hair; fired again, and now he was so close that she couldn't imagine him missing her, but he did. Running and shooting was hard, and he wasn't trained.

But he was going to catch her. She went down again, felt the rocks under her knees, and he was right there. She dug in her pocket. A helpless Mexican bum in Los Angeles, selling the last thing he owned so he could buy a little food, had given her a six-inch switchblade with a curved yellow plastic handle, for six dollars. She'd carried it for two years, more as a comfort than as a weapon, but now she dug it out, nearly dropped it, pushed the button and the blade sprang out, turned, desperate, not ready to die . . .

The killer was there, three feet away, and he pointed the gun at her and pulled the trigger . . . and nothing happened.

He said, almost conversationally, "Shit."

Trey went after him with the knife. She didn't like to fight, but she wasn't bad at it. Not for a woman her size. She knew to shout, too. She screamed, "I'm gonna cut your fuckin' face off, motherfucker . . ." and she was right at him, slashing at him, and he put up his gun arm to fend her off and she slashed his arm, and he screamed and backed away from her, and she went for his face.

He looked around, backed away, then said, "I'll come and get you." He turned and half ran, half walked, into the dark, back toward the lights of Garfield Avenue.

A minute passed, then another. Trey could hear her own heart beating, hear her breath, harsh, grating as she gasped for air. A car started, out in the wasteland between Garfield and the docks, and she saw the taillights, tall and vertical, with smaller lights below, a scarlet exclamation point.

SHE LOOKED AROUND: she was only a hundred feet from the dock. Her flight had gone almost nowhere, with all the falls on the rough ground. Still trying to catch her breath, her body trembling with the adrenaline, she made her way slowly back to the dock. The knife was slippery in her grasp, and she thought it must be blood: she pushed the blade back into its groove with the heel of her hand, dropped the knife in her pocket, wiped her hands on her pants.

At the edge of the dock pad, she squatted in the weeds, looking around. No sign of anybody living, just the body stretched on the concrete. After a moment, scared, but powerfully tempted, she moved out of the weeds and then stole toward the body like a hungry cat looking for something to eat.

"Are you okay?" she called out loud. Stupid. The man in the leather coat was dead. She knew he was dead. She saw him killed. He lay unmoving, like a six-foot paperweight, like a leather-jacketed anvil, spread legged on the concrete.

She squatted next to him, groped under his hip for a wallet. There was a thickness there, but no wallet. Next she went into his jacket; and found a wallet, took it, shoved it into the briefcase that lay by the man's hand. She looked around again, stepped away toward the safety of the surrounding darkness, and felt again, in her mind, the sensation of thickness at the man's waist.

Looked around; a *nervous* cat.

Stole back, knelt again, fumbled at the dead man's belt buckle, unc-inched it, unzipped his pants, felt . . . there. Another strap, elastic. She pulled it through her hands. She couldn't see it, but she could visualize it—she'd once had a belt like this of her own, given to her by her father for a postcollege trip to Italy. She found another buckle, freed it, and pulled hard. The man was heavy, but the money belt was made of slip-pery nylon, and she felt it coming free . . .

Got it. She was surprised by the weight of it. Couldn't be money, must be papers of some kind. The ship was Russian . . .

She moved away, carrying the belt and briefcase, slipping back into the dark. She was forty yards from the body when she heard somebody call from the top of the elevator: *Hey. HEY!* An American voice, not a Russian. She kept moving, faster now, deeper into the dark, choking back the panic.

HER SPOT WAS in an abandoned shed off Garfield, six hundred yards from the grain terminal, across the street from the Goodwill store. The shed's door and windows were heavily boarded. Two months ear-lier, she'd walked around the place, interested, but unsure of how she could get in without attracting the cops.

Then she'd seen the loose concrete blocks in the foundation on the back side of the building. She'd levered the blocks out, pulled herself be-neath the shed, and found herself looking at the underside of a board floor. She'd gone back out, scouted the tracks until she found a conve-nient length of re-rod, and had come back and pried and pounded on the floor boards until she'd gotten inside.

Inside was perfect: empty, dry, and safe. Everything but a phone. The place smelled of creosote, like old railroad ties or phone poles, but she no longer noticed it.

. . .

NOW SHE PULLED her blocks out and crawled under the shed, up and inside. She had a pack, and inside the pack, an REI candle lantern. She lit it with a book match, then opened the wallet.

Holy shit. She fumbled the bills out, looked at them in wonder: tens, twenties, more than a dozen fifties. She counted: nine hundred and sixty dollars. She was rich.

She pried at other parts of the wallet, but it was full of cards in Russian, and a few photos, small color snaps of a dark-haired woman who looked like she came from a different time, from the fifties or sixties. But then, she thought, maybe that was what Russian women looked like.

And the money belt: papers of some kind, she thought.

She unzipped it and turned it, and thin bricks of cash began falling out. *Holy shit. Holy shit.* Hundreds. They were all hundreds, still in bank wrappers. She snapped the wrapper off one brick, and counted the bills in the pale yellow light of the candle. Fifty. She counted the bricks: ten. She had fifty thousand dollars in hundred-dollar bills.

She sat motionless for a moment. People would be coming. They'd want the money. But no fuckin' way. Finders keepers. Her jaw tightened: the money was *hers.*

Trey looked around at her snug little spot, suddenly unattractive in the flickering candlelight. She'd been happy enough here, but now she had things to do, places to go. This place was history. Somebody might have seen her, the cops might be coming . . .

But she could handle all that, if she had a few minutes. She was a lawyer, for Christ's sake; she'd *lived* with criminals, and she'd worked with cops. She knew what to do. She was cleaning frantically when, far away, a siren started.

Please God: Just a few minutes . . . just do this one thing for me.

2

FRIDAY AFTERNOON, a workday off, thunderstorms rumbling to the southwest, the lawn already cut, the soft, pleasant odor of freshly mown grass and gasoline and clean sweat lying on his T-shirt . . .

Lucas Davenport sprawled on the couch, at peace, his head propped on a foam pillow, a Leinie's on the coffee table. Letty West, his twelve-year-old ward, was canoeing with a school group; his nine-month-old son slept quietly in his crib at the top of the stairs; the housekeeper was out shopping.

He was alone, and he was doing something he did only secretly, with guilty pleasure—he was watching TV golf, his mind floating like a hummingbird in the dim space between sleep and the British golf-announcer's hushed voice. This was the kind of quiet, private place where one might feel comfortable giving one's nuts a thorough scratch.

. . .

H E   W A S   D O I N G that when his wife drove through the garage door: *WHANG!*

The impact jammed the house like an earthquake.

The initial *WHANG* was followed a half second later by the screech of tearing metal, a second, smaller impact, and a sudden, short-lived silence. Into the short-lived silence, Lucas said, aloud, the heels of his hands pressed into his eye sockets, "Jesus God, don't let it have landed on the fuckin' Porsche."

In the next half second, the kid started screaming from his crib upstairs, the phone began to ring, and all the pleasurable ambience, the golf, the odor of the grass and gasoline, vanished like a pickpocket in a subway station.

Given the sequence—the whang, the impact, the ripping noise, and the second impact, Lucas knew that his wife had just driven through the garage door, when the garage door was not entirely open. A few weeks earlier, he'd told her, "You keep coming in the driveway like that, you're gonna run into the garage door."

She sniffed: "I've got the reflexes of a surgeon." That was true, because she was one.

"Combined with the driving skills of an anteater," Lucas said. "You're gonna hit the garage door and rip it off the ceiling."

"Excuse me?" she said. "Why don't you worry about something real, like weapons of mass destruction?"

A s   T H E   K I D continued screaming and the phone continued ringing, Lucas launched himself from the couch and ran barefoot through the kitchen, ignoring both kid and phone, down the hallway to the garage access door. He burst into the garage and found his wife's Honda Prelude beneath the overhead door, which had come off the rails and dropped straight down onto her car. The Porsche, in the next stall, appeared to be untouched.

Inside the Honda, Weather was on her hands and knees, hands on the passenger seat, knees on the driver's seat, ass impolitely up in the air. The driver's-side car door was pinned by the wreckage of the overhead garage door, and she was trying to get out the passenger side. Lucas stepped around the green John Deere riding mower and pulled open the door. "Are you okay?"

Weather rarely cried. She considered crying an insult to the feminine mystique. But her lip trembled: "The door went up too slow."

Lucas had been married only a short time, but his history with women had been intense. He knew exactly what to say. He said, "Maybe there's a brownout or something, and there wasn't enough power. I was afraid you'd decapitated yourself. That you were hurt."

This, instead of screaming, "THAT'S BECAUSE YOU DROVE INTO THE DRIVEWAY AT FIFTY MILES AN HOUR, YOU FUCKIN' MORON."

WEATHER CRAWLED OVER the stick shift and out the passenger side. The phone stopped ringing and she turned her head toward the house, her eyes narrowing: "What's wrong with Sam?" They could hear the kid crying through the open door to the kitchen.

"The noise scared him. The whole house jumped when you hit the door," Lucas said. "He'd been sleeping fine."

A neighbor, a chubby balding man in cargo shorts and a golf shirt, came wandering up the driveway. He carried a brown paper grocery bag with a head of lettuce poking out the top, and a querulous look. "Jeez, hit the garage door, huh?"

"The door went up too slow," Weather said. "The garage-door opener didn't work right."

The neighbor nodded, and his eyes took on a duplicitous glaze:

"Sometimes the drive chain slips. You gotta watch out for it," he said. He'd been married for three decades. Then, to Lucas, "When I saw the door come down, I was afraid it'd landed on the Porsche."

"Oh, boy." Lucas looked at the deep green 911 S4 crouched in the next space. "Never crossed my mind until now."

The neighbor said to Weather, "Thank God you're okay," his eyes involuntarily drifting back to the Porsche.

"Thank God," Lucas agreed.

T H E C O L L I S I O N T O O K an hour to straighten out. One of Lucas's older friends, a narrow man named Sloan, came over to help. The Honda, they agreed, was probably totaled: every piece of sheet metal on the car had at least one ugly gash, dent, or nasty scratch. The garage-door rail guides had punched holes in the roof and hood.

The State Farm adjuster told them where to have the Prelude taken for an assessment. "Thank God it wasn't the nine-eleven," she said. The garage-door company, the original contractors, couldn't send anyone out until Monday, but promised to fix the door before Monday evening. "Happens all the time," the garage-door guy said. "Usually you're backing up, but the door doesn't get clear."

"Wasn't me, it was my wife," Lucas said.

"Always is," the garage-door guy said.

T H E P O R S C H E W A S eased out into the driveway, clear of the wreckage. Lucas brought tools up from the basement, along with a jack. He and Sloan jacked the door up off the Honda, pushed the car out of the garage, and took the damaged door the rest of the way down.

"I hope you didn't blame Weather," Sloan said.

"I know the rules," Lucas said.

"It was just a car and a door," Sloan said. "You got insurance up to your neck."

"She missed the Porsche by a foot," Lucas said.

Sloan winced: "Jesus."

WHEN THEY WERE done clearing the wreckage, they went inside for beer, and a subdued Weather, the baby on her shoulder, told Lucas, "There was a message on the phone. Rose Marie wants you to call back right away."

"Hmm." Rose Marie Roux was the commissioner of Public Safety, and Lucas's boss. The baby peered at him, and sucked at his thumb knuckle. He had Lucas's blue eyes, and lived in a cloud of odor, equal parts milk-burp, leaky diaper, and Johnson's baby powder. "Maybe it's something."

Weather said, "Something about a dead Russian in Duluth."

"That happened a couple of weeks ago," Lucas said. "The guy shot in the grain elevator?"

"Better than in the heart," Weather said. She considered herself a syntactical enforcer.

"Probably a spy," Sloan said, tipping his bottle toward Lucas. "You're probably going into espionage."

Lucas called Rose Marie. Behind him, he heard Weather say, "I don't know what happened. I hit the garage door opener, but it just didn't open fast enough."

"The chain slips sometimes," Sloan said. "Or maybe you had a temporary brownout."

"That's what Gene said, from next door. The chain thing. I thought he was patronizing me."

"No way," Sloan said. "That shit happens all the time. People call nine-one-one . . ."

"Really?"

. . .

ROSE MARIE ANSWERED her private cell phone: "Lucas? You know that dead Russian in Duluth?"

"Yeah," Lucas said. "He's a spy."

A moment of silence. Then, "How'd you know?"

LUCAS DAVENPORT WAS a tall, tough, rangy man, dark complected, blue eyed, and tanned with the summer. A few white scars were distributed around the tan—an old bullet wound in the throat, and trailing through an eyebrow and down one cheek, what looked like a romantic knife slash from the docks of Marseilles, but was actually a cut from a fishing-leader snap-back. And there were others, the hide punctures of a rambunctious life.

Lucas ran the Office of Regional Research at the Minnesota Bureau of Criminal Apprehension, after years of working intelligence and homicide in Minneapolis. His brief was to look at interesting and, usually, but not always, violent crimes, and to "fix shit" for the governor. He'd done well at it, in the six months he'd been in the job.

The horizon was not without clouds. He was forty-six and worried that he was too old to have an infant son, with a wife who was probably plotting another pregnancy; too inexperienced and not hard-nosed enough to handle his ward, Letty, who was fast becoming a teenager; that he was too rigid to relax into what was a late first marriage. As a cop, he still loved the hunt, but suspected that twenty-five years of contact with violent death and brutal criminals was beginning to corrode something essential inside him; the cynicism was rising like water in the basement. He'd seen it in other cops, always laughing at the wrong time, always skeptical about good deeds, suspicious of generosity. And as a longtime athlete, he could feel the years wearing on him: he'd lost a step.

Maybe, he thought, he should do something else. The trouble was, he couldn't figure out what that might be. Weather suggested that he go back to school, but he couldn't think what he might study, nor, from what he'd seen of educational bureaucracy, was he sure that he could put up with the bullshit.

He didn't have to work. At the height of the Internet boom, in the late nineties, he'd sold a small simulations software company for more money than he would ever need. He'd sold out because he wasn't a businessman, and the idea of beginning another business didn't interest him.

On the other hand, he couldn't sit on his ass. He wasn't made that way, and neither was Weather. If ever they had marital problems, he thought, it wouldn't be over the usual problems of sex or money, it'd be over work. They both worked all the time. He wasn't sure that either of them could stop.

So: he was hung up and they were talking about it.

At least he had a spy to think about.

LUCAS AND WEATHER and Letty and Sam, with Ellen Jansen, the housekeeper, lived on Mississippi River Boulevard in St. Paul, more or less halfway between the downtown areas of Minneapolis and St. Paul. From the master bedroom, on the second floor, Lucas could see the steel-colored surface of the Mississippi in the gorge that separated the house from Minneapolis.

The house was new. Lucas had worked out the design with an architect, had torn down his old house, and put up the new one. They all called it the Big New House.

After his brief chat with Rose Marie, Lucas went up to the bedroom, changed out of his T-shirt and athletic shorts into jeans, a golf shirt and loafers, and a light wool-knit sportcoat to cover the .45 clipped to his belt. From his house to downtown St. Paul was fifteen minutes;

the Department of Public Safety was located in a converted department store. A half hour after he spoke to Rose Marie on the telephone, he was walking down the hall to her office, trying to scrub a spot of garage-door guide-rail grease from his thumb.

HER RECEPTIONIST SAID, "I hear Weather ran through the garage door."

"Yeah. Door fell on her car."

"You gonna sue?"

"Sue who?"

The receptionist shrugged: "Gotta be somebody." She touched an intercom button. "Lucas is here."

ROSE MARIE ROUX was an old friend and boss; she and Lucas went back twenty years, in a couple of different jobs. She'd been the Minneapolis chief of police when a shift in administration impelled her into the state job. She'd convinced Lucas to move with her.

Rose Marie smoked too much and was known to take a drink and use coarse language; she despised exercise and guns. She was working with an assistant on a PowerPoint presentation for a legislative committee when Lucas stuck his head in.

"Come on in," she said. To her assistant: "I've got to talk to Lucas. Why don't you redo the pies on the rif and the restruck and I'll call you. Fifteen minutes."

Lucas dropped into a visitor's chair as the assistant gathered up his papers and left. "What the hell is a pie and a restruck?" Everybody in the department knew what a rif was—a reduction in force. Five percent across the board, the result of one of the occasional budget crises that struck between tax increases.

"Pie chart and restructure," Rose Marie said, moving around behind her desk. She had just turned sixty. Her hair was flyaway, and she was wearing a loose gray skirt and white blouse. A gray jacket hung in a niche in the corner. "These days, you don't know PowerPoint, you ain't shit. What're you up to?"

Lucas shrugged. "Got that thing down in Worthington. It's ninety-nine percent that the Carter kid did it, but his family covered him with an attorney. We can't even talk to him. Unless we come up with a witness, we're not going anywhere."

A wrinkle appeared in her forehead. "But he did it?"

"Yup. Michelle told a girlfriend that she thought she was pregnant, and that she'd told him so. He didn't want to deal with it, so he strangled her and threw her body off the bridge. But he was smart about it. He wasn't supposed to see her that night. He snuck out of the ball game and picked her up. All kinds of people saw him at the game, in the stands, under the stands, before, during, and after. Nobody can pin down any time that he was gone, and nobody saw him pick her up. She probably slipped out to meet him. So . . ."

"We're toast."

"Unless he has a conscience or somebody in his family does," Lucas said. "To tell you the truth, I think he's a little psychopath. Maybe even the family is fooled."

Rose Marie sighed. "Shoot. I would have liked to have gotten that one."

"If she really had been pregnant, we could have done a DNA on the fetus, and that would have given us some kind of motive, but . . ." He spread his hands, a gesture of frustration. "We can't even prove the pregnancy angle."

"What're you gonna do?" Rose Marie lit up—an illegal act—and blew smoke toward the ceiling, relaxing with the nicotine. "Maybe something will happen."

Lucas nodded. Sometimes, something did. A witness wanders in, the killer blurts out a confession to a friend, who goes to the cops.

"What else?" Rose Marie asked. She had a can of pencils on her desk, chose an unsharpened yellow one, and gave it an experimental twiddle.

Lucas continued: "Del is working the McDonald's thing. He hates it, he's running a forklift all day. We still don't know what the fuck is going on. The Bruins' auditors claim another thousand bucks went out the door last week, right under Del's nose, and he says it didn't, and they put him on the night shift, but there are only a few guys on the night shift and they'd all have to be in on it . . ."

"That could be," Rose Marie said.

"I don't know," Lucas said. "Anyway, we're working it. And Dannie's trawling for that pimp in the Brainerd festival killing."

"How's Del's leg?" Del Capslock, one of Lucas's investigators, had been shot in the leg a few months earlier, and a bone had been broken.

"Still hurts, still goes to rehab," Lucas said.

"Maybe he came back too soon," Rose Marie suggested.

"Nah, he's okay. He was going nuts, sitting on the couch."

Rose Marie twiddled the pencil for a few more seconds, then tried a tentative drumbeat with the eraser end. "I don't care about Brainerd so much," she said finally. "We'll get the guy, it's just a matter of time. But the Bruin family and their employees put thirty thousand dollars into the governor's campaign last cycle. If Del can break that . . ."

"He will, sooner or later. If there's anything really going on. I gotta wonder, what are the chances it's some kind of tax scam by the Bruins?"

"Ah, Jesus, don't go *there*," she said. "Besides, I talked to Elroy Bruin, and this is no tax scam. He was pissed."

"Okay."

"So what are *you* doing?" The pencil drumbeat picked up.

Lucas shrugged. "Spent some time down in Worthington, trying to figure out the Carter kid. Then, the feds are worried about stuff coming across the border from Manitoba; I've been talking to Lapham up in Kittson County about it. He doesn't want to spend a dime out of his budget. He wants to set up a task force, so we'd have to pay for it. I've been trying to put it off."

"Keep putting it off. We got no money for nothin'."

"Absolutely speaking, or relatively speaking?"

"Relatively. I'm not nearly stupid enough to be absolutely broke." More twiddling, and a couple of more drumbeats, then, "So I could get you free for a week or two—you personally?"

"For the spy?"

"We've got a Russian coming in," she began. "The State Department called the governor . . ."

THE DEAD RUSSIAN, she said, had been named Oleg Moshalov, according to his seaman's papers, but FBI counterintelligence had identified him as a Rodion Oleshev, once an agent for the Russian KGB. They'd spotted and printed him when he'd been stationed in Washington as a junior attaché in the late 1980s.

"The feds don't know what he was doing in Duluth, or why he was doing it. The Russians say he was fired during the big government layoffs in the nineties and he joined the merchant marine. He was supposedly the first officer on this ship," Rose Marie said. She snubbed out her cigarette, went to the window, opened it, fanned some smoke toward the opening. "The feds say that's bullshit. They say he was on an intelligence mission and somebody murdered him. They interviewed the ship's captain and crew, and they all said he really *was* the first officer . . . Well. Read the report." She stepped back to her desk and touched a file folder, and nudged it an inch closer to Lucas.

He didn't move. "Okay. What then?"

"Nothing much, for a while," she sat down again, heavily. "The Russians denied everything, and the case was being handled by some Joe Blow at their consulate as a routine misadventure. The investigation was a dead end. Then, out of the blue, two days ago, the Russians call up the FBI and start screaming for action. Turns out that the dead guy's father is a big shot in the oil ministry—it took them that long to figure out who Oleshev really was. The father talked to Putin and now their embassy is jumping up and down and the State Department's got the vapors. The Russians are sending an observer to see what the FBI and the Duluth cops have been doing. He's scheduled into Duluth on Monday afternoon."

"What's everybody been doing?"

"The usual workup, but the case isn't going anywhere," Rose Marie said. "It looks like a planned ambush. The feds, the local guys in Duluth, think it's Russian on Russian. And they don't care about the State Department. Not much, anyway."

"A cluster fuck."

"Exactly. Nobody knows who's doing what to whom. Mitford and I thought you could go up there. When this Russian arrives, take him on a tour of the crime scene and fill him in on what everybody's done."

"Mitford wants it fixed." Mitford was the governor's top aide, what the newspaper called his go-to guy.

"He wants everything made nice," Rose Marie said. "He wants people to cooperate with each other, and to shake hands and agree that this was a tragedy, and that what could be done, was done."

Rose Marie stopped talking, and for a moment, they examined each other across her desk: the years really *were* piling up, Lucas thought. Rose Marie had crossed the physical border that comes in the late fifties or early sixties, when people begin to look old. Not that she'd particularly worry about it. Like Lucas and Weather, she worked all the time.

"So you want me to do PR," Lucas said into the silence.

"Do me a favor," Rose Marie said. She nudged the file another inch closer to Lucas. "Go up and look around. See if you can figure something out. If you can, that's fine. If not, fuck it—just make us look good.

Right now, we look bad and everybody's annoyed. And we've got this budget thing on our back. The goddamned legislature . . ."

THERE WAS NO big hurry to the job. Lucas called Duluth from Rose Marie's outer office, talked to the cop who was covering the homicide, and made arrangements to meet him on Monday morning. Then he called the Minneapolis office of the FBI, left a message for the special agent in charge, who was, he was told, "in Kenora, discussing border problems with his opposite number in the RCMP."

"In an office or out in a boat?" Lucas asked. The SAC had been in the newspaper for taking a fly-fishing record for northern pike on one-pound tippet.

"I have no information about boats, nor would I rule boats out," said the fed who'd answered the phone. "I am simply designated to answer phone calls on a weekend when the temperature is eighty-four degrees, the skies are partly cloudy, and there is little or no wind to influence the flight of a golf ball. He'll be in the office Monday."

LUCAS AND WEATHER spent a quiet Saturday at home. The missing garage door was a constant irritant. The house looked as though somebody had punched out one of its teeth.

"Big New House looks hurt," Weather said, as they went out for croissants in the morning, leaving Sam with the housekeeper. Later, they spent an hour at a pottery show given by one of Lucas's old flames—Weather only cared what he was doing *now*, she claimed. So they looked at pots and had a nice chat with Jael, the flame, who was looking *very* good, and who made goo-goo noises at Sam. Sometime during the tour, it occurred to Lucas that maybe he was being shown off with a baby on his back . . . then he thought, *nah, Weather wouldn't* do that.

That afternoon, Lucas took Sam for a stroll. Actually, he took him for a five-mile run on the bike path that ran along the top of the river valley. Sam was tucked in a high-tech, big-wheeled, three-hundred-dollar tricycle stroller, designed, Weather said, expressly for yuppies. A few minutes after he got back, Letty called from canoe camp. Her school had an introductory week, involving four days of consciousness-raising in canoes, which is what you get from Episcopalian private schools, and said that her group was headed into the Boundary Waters the next morning, right after church.

LATE IN THE afternoon, Lucas read the file that Rose Marie had given him. The file had been compiled by the FBI, and included findings both by local FBI agents and the Duluth police. There was a narrative on the discovery of the body, and the search of the area around the dock, as well as interviews with the elevator worker who'd discovered the body and with members of the ship's crew. There were photos of the victim both at the scene and at the medical examiner's office.

The dead man had been shot three times and fragments of two hollow-point slugs had been recovered from the body, enough to establish the killer's weapon as a nine millimeter. The fragments were too badly damaged to match to a particular gun. One interesting note was that three shells had been found, and the shells were old—1950s vintage. They'd been polished: there were no prints.

A man was spotted running from the dock area just as the body was discovered by a worker at the grain terminal. The man was reported as wearing a long coat. A scrawled note by the Duluth investigator, on the edge of the typed report, said, "Kid? What was coat? Check temp."

The report noted that the dead man's body apparently had been searched. The Russian's wallet and papers were missing, and maybe a money belt from around his waist—the man's pants had been loosened, and the medical examiner found elastic-band marks in the skin around his waist that were not consistent with his underpants, and which might have been consistent with a money belt.

There were details: the Duluth cops had found a fresh trail through the weeds along the lakeshore, which showed signs of a number of falls, which they thought might represent a chase, which seemed odd, in what otherwise looked like an execution. There was no question that the dead man had been killed where he was found: there were bullet impressions on the concrete under his head.

Lucas mulled it all over: there was information to work with, which wasn't always the case. He began to put together a list of questions.

Saturday evening, they barbecued: Sloan and his wife came over, and Del and his wife—Del worked in Lucas's office and was investigating the McDonald's thefts. Sister Mary Joseph, wearing street clothes, showed up with a post-doc student in psychology, who'd wanted to meet Weather and talk about cranial-facial surgery.

Earlier in the summer, Lucas had met a white-haired Georgia man on a flight between Chicago and Atlanta. The man was wearing a burgundy-colored baseball cap that said *Big Pig Jig* on the front, and it turned out that he was a barbecue judge.

In the ensuing conversation, James Lever of Tifton, Georgia, recommended that Lucas try his special competition Pig Jig spareribs. Getting the ingredients together had been a pain in the ass, cutting the membrane off the bone with a dull knife had been a pain in the ass, marinating the ribs for two hours had been in a pain in the ass, and Weather had insisted that they go the whole route and grind their own spices, which had been interesting in its own way, leaving the kitchen redolent with garlic, fennel, ginger, oregano, basil, and marjoram. And though she'd insisted on going the whole way, Weather quailed at the idea of mixing the two cans of Coca-Cola with a bottle of Chianti, but Lucas, in his turn, had insisted.

Just before getting off the plane, Lever had said that the ribs should be accompanied by Miller Genuine Draft beer, "because if you drink some fruity Mexican beer with these ribs, you'll be fart'n' up a storm."

Lucas refused to drink Miller Genuine Draft on moral grounds, and so they made do with a case of Leinie's.

While Lucas was barbecuing, Weather roasted sweet corn, still in the husk, in the oven; at the end of it, the kitchen looked like Anzio Beach, but everybody agreed the food was wonderful.

SUNDAY WAS EVEN slower than Saturday, but still a great day: blue skies, cool enough to make your face and skin feel good. On Sunday afternoon, Lucas and Weather took a long walk down to a bookstore off Ford Parkway and along the way talked about what he should do.

"I like working for Rose Marie, but the governor . . . the governor. After a while, it feels a little like prostitution," Lucas said. "This is the first time I've felt sleazy. Chasing people down for political reasons."

"You're putting the same old assholes into jail," Weather pointed out.

"Yeah, but not because anybody gives a shit—it's because the politicians don't want the TV people talking about crime waves, or because some out-state sheriff fucked it up and we go bail them out so he'll owe us."

"If you go back to school . . ."

"Jesus, Weather."

"Listen, you've got a B.A."

"Yeah. Not worth the paper it's printed on."

"Sure it is, because it means you don't have to go through a lot of other shit to study something you're interested in. I was thinking: you really liked building the Big New House. That's the happiest I've ever seen you, when you were doing that. You drove everybody a little crazy, but look at the house. What a great house."

"Not that great. If I find the guy that sold me the front door, I'll cut his nuts off. And how in the hell . . . ?"

"Shut up for a minute. You loved doing it. Building the house. Have you ever thought about doing something in construction? Building custom houses or something?"

They walked along for a few seconds, and then Lucas said, "No, I never thought about it."

"You'd be good at it. And I think you'd be interested in it. You'd be . . . building something. Think about driving around town in your old age, looking at the neat houses you'd built."

They walked along a bit more and Lucas finally sighed and said, "Something to think about."

Weather said, "That's encouraging."

"What?"

"Ever since you've gotten into this mood, you've pushed away everything I've suggested. This is the first time you said anything remotely positive."

"Houses."

"Think about it."

BY SUNDAY EVENING, Lucas was ready to go. As the evening news ended, the FBI's special agent in charge called. "Got back from Kenora an hour ago, I just picked up my messages," he said. "You're heading up to Duluth?"

"Yeah. Whattaya got going up there?"

"That's what I want to talk to you about. Could you come by in an hour or so?"

"I'm leaving tonight . . ."

"Just need a few minutes. We've got a guy in from Washington who wants to hook up with you."

"It can't wait?"

"Not really."

"See you in an hour," Lucas said.

LUCAS HAD ALWAYS had an ambiguous relationship with the FBI. They were supposed to be the elite—and they *did* do some good work— and they acted that way. Even their offices reminded Lucas of their superior status. The offices were like spaceship interiors seen in the movies; sealed airlocks with only the initiated allowed inside.

The FBI's attitudes, their separateness, their secrecy, their military ethic, had filtered down to state and local cops, and eventually were taken for granted. Police stations, once relatively open, had become fortresses, places that people feared and that they hurried past.

But local cops weren't the FBI, and they didn't do what the FBI did. FBI agents worked in offices and did intricate investigations; they weren't on the street. But as cops began to develop FBI-like attitudes, and to build FBI-like fortresses, as they sealed themselves away in patrol cars, as they fended off contact with the public, they began to resemble a paramilitary force, rather than peace officers.

When Lucas was a kid, cops were part of his neighborhood, with jobs just like the mailman and the teacher. By the time Lucas had joined the Minneapolis cops, that old workaday attitude was disappearing— cops were creating their own bars, holding their own cop parties, picking up privileges that weren't available to outsiders.

That all began, Lucas thought, with the spreading influence of the feds, and he didn't like it. It was bad for the country and bad for cops, he thought. And he thought it again as he checked through the airlock and was buzzed into the FBI offices in Minneapolis.

. . .

CHARLES PEYTON WAS a small man, thin, blue eyed, wind-burned with chapped lips. He wore jeans and a long-sleeved outdoorsy blue shirt, with the sleeves rolled up over the elbows, the rolls held in place by a little buttoned tab on each sleeve; nobody ever called him Charley.

His feet, in expensive-looking leather ankle boots, were up on one corner of his desk. He stood up when Lucas was ushered into the office, said, "Lucas, how're you doing?" and reached across his desk to shake hands. Another man, heavier, lazy eyed, red faced, and blond, sat off to the right on a leather chair, and said, "Barney Howard," and lifted a hand.

Peyton pointed at a visitor's chair and asked, "Can I get you a coffee or a Coke?"

Lucas settled down in the chair and said, "No, thanks . . . What's going on?"

"Have you read the file? We sent a Xerox over to Rose Marie."

"Yeah," Lucas said. "Mostly forensics."

"We did what we could, on the technical end, but there wasn't much," Peyton said. "Nothing moving."

"How many investigators are working it?"

Peyton leaned back, as if chewing over what he was going to say, then leaned forward again. "Look, you're a smart guy. That's not moonshine, that's the fact of the matter, and you've worked with some of our big guys . . ."

"Louis Mallard," Howard chipped in. "He says you're a friend."

Lucas tipped his head: *Maybe. Then again, maybe not.*

"We've got some people up there. Some counterintelligence people," Peyton said. "They're working the case, but not as criminal investigators. They're not homicide cops."

"They work with you?" Lucas asked Howard.

"Yeah." Howard nodded, smiled, and showed large square teeth. "They're doing a lot of analysis, looking at people coming and going through the port, that sort of thing. Computer stuff. Looking at people we know who are close to the Russians. We've been keeping up with the Duluth police through the office here, in Minneapolis—but when we heard that you were going up there, we thought we'd talk to you directly."

"About?"

"About what you find, if anything. What you think. What you suppose. We're interested in speculation," he said. "We won't interfere with your investigation and if you catch the killer, that's fine. But if you find anything else that might suggest a Russian intelligence operation—if you find anything at all—we'd like to hear about it before the newspapers. For your protection and the protection of our people up there."

"Have your guys picked up anything on the murder?"

"We poke around and hear all this stuff," Peyton said. "We hear that the dead guy was an intelligence agent. We hear that he really *was* a sailor. We hear that he may have had a connection with the Russian Mafia, or that he was operating for his old man in the oil business. We hear all this stuff, and I'd give you even money that he picked up the wrong woman in some beer joint and got himself shot. But we just don't *know.*"

"The shells that Duluth picked up were older than I am," Lucas said. "That does sound like a beer-joint job."

"But it was one in the heart and two in the head, dead-on, and that sounds like a pro," Howard replied. "There was no heat-of-passion. He was ambushed. He was *hit.*"

"But if it was an assassination, why'd they roll him?" Peyton asked Howard. "Computer disks? What?"

"I don't know," Howard said. "Could be anything. But if they were planning to roll him, why'd they take him in the middle of the biggest lit-up area out there? The cab driver says he dropped him off in the dark, where that track ended. If they'd hit him there, they might not have found him yet. They could have rolled him in peace."

Silence.

Then Peyton said, "Americans didn't like nine-millimeter pistols in the fifties, back when the shells were made. I mean, there were war souvenirs around, Lugers and P-38s and so on, but not many Americans were buying nine millimeters as new guns."

"What does that mean?" Lucas asked.

"It means that if an American did it, it was an odd gun to have around. But the Russians had a lot of nines, especially after the war. Maybe one was stashed on the ship, but never used. The ship was almost as old as the shells. That makes some kind of sense to me," Peyton said.

"But the shells were American," Howard said.

"But the guy on the ship didn't hear any shots, which suggests the weapon was silenced, which suggests it was a pro job," Peyton said.

Lucas was amused. "You guys are arguing both sides of this," he said.

"We're confused," Howard said. "We keep going around in circles. This killing was weird. That's why it'd be nice if you'd stay in touch. We'd really like to know what's going on."

Lucas nodded. "Sure."

Another long pause.

"You don't sound enthusiastic," Howard said.

Lucas stood up, took a turn around his chair, jingling change in his pockets. "I gotta ask," he said. "What are the chances that your guys did it? You know, that the guy had the plans to the moon rocket taped to his dick and somebody in the CIA killed him, and pulled his pants down to get the plans. What I'm asking is . . . what if we did it?"

Howard shook his head. "We didn't."

"Boy Scout's honor?" Lucas asked skeptically.

"You'll have to take my word for it—but I checked," Howard said. "Our people don't really kill other people. And if we did, you're about the last guy we'd want investigating it."

Flattery, Lucas thought; makes you feel warm and fuzzy, unless it makes you feel manipulated and used.

"So I see these guys on TV, CIA guys, they've got M-16s and they're wearing these rag things on their heads . . ."

"We don't kill people. Not on this kind of deal," Howard insisted. "We have paramilitaries, you'd see them in Afghanistan or Iraq, everybody knows that. But we don't do murder. If somebody did, I'd know about it. You can't keep that kind of thing secret."

"Not even in the CIA?"

"Nowhere. They'd be shit-faced panicked and I'd get a *feel*, you know? All I got from this one was confusion. Nobody at the CIA even knew who this asshole was, until we told them. And *we* didn't pay any attention until the Russians called us up."

"Which makes it less likely that it's a big secret mission," Lucas said. "The Russians calling up like that."

"You'd think so," said Howard. "But Russia is so fucked up right now that their right hand doesn't know what their left hand is doing. Maybe the wrong hand is the one that's calling us up."

They thought about that for a moment, then Lucas asked Peyton, "Anything else?"

Peyton said, "We've got a young guy up there, named Andy Harmon. He's coordinating with a couple of our auditors. He's a book guy—but he can get to me or Barney in a hurry. If you need phone checks, or research, like that, we'd be happy to help. Something we can do on a computer. If it gets serious, then we can put some guys in."

"You got six zillion guys . . ." Lucas said.

"All but three of them are reading *Terrorism for Dummies* books. The whole goddamn bureau . . ." His voice trailed away; he didn't want to say it out loud. "Anyway, we don't have a lot of time for a small-change antique Russian operation."

Lucas shrugged. "Okay. I'll stay in touch."

"Our guy will call you when you get there," said Howard. "He'll give you some contact numbers. Good luck."

A whole lot of nothin' going on, Lucas thought, as he checked out of the place. Nothing but a murder. Small change.

Back home again, Lucas finished packing, kissed Weather and the baby, and talked to the housekeeper about dealing with the garage-door contractor. She told him not to worry.

At ten o'clock, as Weather was going to bed—she got up early every day that she operated, and that was almost every weekday—Lucas tossed a duffel bag on the passenger seat of his Acura truck, slipped an aging Black Crowes album into the CD player, and headed up I-35 for Duluth.

Spies, he thought.

3

CARL WALTHER WAS HUNTING. In black jeans, a Mossy Oak camouflage shirt, and a ball cap, he moved almost invisibly through the night, closing in on the woman as she trudged down West Fourth Street, pushing her shopping cart with a rattle-bang-bang-bang over the cracked sidewalk.

He liked the night: liked the cool air, the silence, the odors of foliage and damp soil that rose in the darkness. Liked the taste of salt in his mouth as he completed the stalk.

He remembered the knife, remembered the slash she'd taken at him. He could feel the tightness in his arm, the wound still healing. He told himself to run cool: but the fact was, he felt almost nothing. Grandpa still worried that he might become tense, that he might panic, that he might somehow be overwhelmed by his mission. Wouldn't happen. He listened to his heart. Seventy-two beats a minute. He might be watching the evening news; he smiled at his own cool.

There were a couple of girls at school who would be surprised to see him like this, swift, dark, deadly. He could *feel* how impressed they would be, if they knew. He had a little fantasy of a girl being told, saying, *Carl? Our Carl? There was always something about him, his eyes, like a tiger's . . .*

He pushed the fantasy away as he moved down under the row of yellow lights like a shadow on the wall, listening to the racket of the woman's shopping cart, *bang, spang, rattle and knock.* He'd spotted her earlier in the day. As soon as he saw the long coat, he knew he'd found her. He remembered the wool, the strange hairy feeling of wool on a warm summer's night.

Had to be right. Duluth was too small for two female bums in long woolen coats. He'd been patrolling the city every couple of nights for two weeks; had to be her. The woman turned the corner. He'd been waiting for that—if she was pushing up the hill, she was less likely to get away from him. He was in shape; she was a tramp.

He moved quickly now, took the nails out of his pocket, flicked out the wire. He was a good student, and Grandpa was a good teacher.

TWO WEEKS EARLIER, the teacher had had his first real test . . .

Grandma and Grandpa Walther lived in a gray two-bedroom shingle-sided house in Hibbing, Minnesota, an hour's drive northwest of Duluth. The house sat squarely on a postage-stamp lawn. The lean grass was neatly mowed, but struggling for life against the bad soil and limited sunlight.

In back, a freestanding one-car garage leaned to the southeast, away from the winter's wind. Inside the garage was a six-year-old Taurus station wagon with seventeen thousand miles on it.

Grandpa, at ninety-two, still drove, eyes sharp, his mind snapping up the landscape. Grandpa had a wreath of white hair around his wide head, but was pink and bald on top, with a few brown age spots. His nose was wide and short, genes from the steppe; his shoulders had been wide, but had narrowed since his mid-eighties. He had an old-man's ass and skinny legs. Losing it, he said.

Grandma, at ninety-one, was weaker both in mind and body. She spent her days in a wheelchair, only dimly aware of life. Her hands shook and her head trembled and the skin under her eyes had collapsed into loops that hung down into her cheeks. She'd had cataracts removed from both eyes, and though she could apparently see well enough, her eyes always had a distant look, as though she were peering into the past. Her arms were mostly skin and bone, and her she had no calves at the back of her legs.

In the morning, Carl would come over before school, and they'd move her into the bathroom, and Grandpa would close the door and take care of her, put her in her diaper. Then Carl would help seat her in her chair, and Grandpa would feed her. The rest of the day she sat in front of the TV; occasionally, she'd look at Grandpa and smile, and say something. Usually, whatever she said was unintelligible, and sometimes seemed to be in Russian.

While Grandma sat in her chair, waiting for death, Grandpa was almost always on the enclosed back porch, under the best lamp in the house, reading, or working problems on his chessboard.

But not this night.

This was the night that Moshalov—surely not his real name, but the only one that Grandpa had—would be eliminated.

This night, Grandpa waited by the front door, mostly standing, sometimes sitting on a bar stool. Sometimes breathing hard, remembering the days when he hunted through the streets of Moscow, no older than Carl, cutting down the enemies of the state. Back in action now: the action felt so good. A little extra piece of life, in a life gone gray.

When Carl Walther arrived in his Chevy, parking in the street, Grandpa turned his head to Grandma and said, "He's here." Grandma stirred, but said nothing. On the television, David Letterman was working over the president.

When Carl came to the door, Grandpa opened it, looked once up and down the street, pulled Carl inside, and shut the door. His face was pink with excitement: "How did it go?"

"As planned," Carl said. He added, "Almost." He was seventeen, blond, good-looking; long faced, round jawed. He wore an athletic jacket without a letter.

"Almost?"

Carl nodded, turned his face away, glancing out the front window. "I parked near the terminal, on a side road, and walked through the dark, maybe three hundred yards. Like you said: thirty yards, get down, watch and listen. Then thirty more, watch and listen," Carl said. He had ordered his thoughts: he'd been trained to report. "There were some people on the stern of the boat, one or two, but nobody coming or going. There was some light. Moshalov arrived right on time. He must have dropped the car at the airport, like he said, and come right straight back to the boat. I met him in the dark outside the terminal. I shot him once in the heart and then twice in the forehead, just as specified. Then . . . there was a woman."

"A woman." Grandpa tried to be calm, but his round rimless glasses glittered in the lamplight and gave him a frightening aspect, a skull-like harshness, and his old-man's hands trembled.

"She was sitting in the weeds along the bank. Drinking, I think. I never saw her or heard her before I shot Moshalov, and I'd been there for a while. Then she stood up, saw me, and started running. I went after her. I fired two shots and then the gun jammed." He was lying, now. He'd fired the gun wildly and had run out of ammunition too soon. He hurried on. "The gun misfired; I cleared it and tried to fire again, and got a misfire on the last round. She had a knife and slashed me with it; I had to decide. I left."

"You're hurt?"

"I got a bad cut," Carl said. "I need to get it sewed up." There was no visible blood—Carl was wearing a navy blue sweatshirt—but when he pulled up the sleeve, and peeled away the newspaper pack he'd used to cover the wound, Grandpa winced.

"We'll have to come up with a reason for that," Grandpa said. "For Jan."

"Mom doesn't have to know about it," Carl said. "She'd blab all over the place."

"In case she finds out," Grandpa said.

Carl nodded. "Okay. I was washing windows in your basement and I broke one and got cut. I didn't think it was so bad for a while," he said. "That's why we didn't come get it sewed up right away."

Grandpa nodded: "That should work. We'll break a window. I'll go with you to the emergency room."

Grandpa turned and looked at Grandma. "We're going to leave you for a while, Melodie. We have to go to the hospital."

She stared at the television.

"The random factor," Grandpa continued, his eyes drifting as he thought about it. "The woman. There's almost always a random factor. Somebody once said that few plans survive contact with the enemy."

"I didn't see her . . ."

Grandpa wagged a finger at him. "Don't apologize. You did well. You had to make a decision, and you made it. A conservative decision, but you were there, you knew all the factors. Now: Is there any way she can identify you? Other than the cut?"

"There was some light. She saw my face. But with the bad gun, and she had that knife, I thought it'd be better to go back later, if we had to. Get some new ammo, and take her out later." Carl had been nervous about the report, about the lying. He'd panicked, he thought. Not all his fault, he'd been surprised—still, better not to talk about it. He fished the pistol out of his pocket. "Should we get rid of this? I don't see how anyone could find us, but if they did . . ."

"We'll keep it for now," Grandpa said, taking the gun. He worked the action and a shell popped out. He fumbled it, and Carl picked it up off the floor and handed it to him. He looked at the primer cap, saw that it had been hit by a firing pin, but hadn't gone off. "We should have gotten new ammunition for it. But it worked okay in the woods . . . mostly."

"What about the woman?" Carl asked.

"Finish your report," Grandpa said. "Another five minutes won't make a difference with the cut."

CARL TOLD HIM the story in detail and described the woman. "She smelled like wine. She smelled dirty. She called me a . . ." He glanced at Grandma; but this was a professional matter. ". . . a motherfucker. She acted crazy."

"Not like she came off the boat?" Grandpa asked.

"No. I think she was a tramp. You know, a street person, like, you remember old Mrs. Sikorsky when she'd go around all messed up and pushing that baby stroller? Like that."

"Huh," Grandpa said. "If she didn't come off the boat, was there anyplace there she might have come from? When we looked at the place, I didn't see anything."

"Neither did I," Carl said. "There's nothing out there."

They all sat for a minute, then Grandpa said, "Well. We have to think about this. Let's go over to the hospital and get that arm fixed."

"It's still bleeding a little. If we go break the window now, I could drip some blood on it," Carl said.

"Let's do it," Grandpa said. Then, "You know, if we could find this woman, it might be useful to remove her."

"That's what I thought," Carl said. "If she's dead, she couldn't ever testify about me . . ."

"But if we send you out again, we take another risk—and how would she find you?" Grandpa asked.

"By chance. I might walk by her on the street someday. I can't stay out of Duluth. I'm probably gonna go to college at UMD."

Grandpa nodded. "Okay. If we can find her . . . but we wouldn't use the gun. Not the same gun. The police would match them with the slugs in Moshalov and tie them together. If she's a tramp she'd have to die a tramp's death. A fight, or something."

T H E Y W E N T D O W N to the basement, broke a storm window that already had a crack in it, and Carl squeezed some blood on the glass.

In the car, Carl driving, Grandpa brought up the woman again. "If we remove this woman, assuming we can locate her, it would be good training. We had to throw you at Moshalov because it was an emergency, and we had no choice. You did well, but that doesn't mean that you're trained. Your first target should have been easier. This woman . . . would do."

"Assuming we can locate her," Carl said. He could feel the *want* in Grandpa.

And a minute later, Grandpa asked, "So how do you . . . feel?"

Carl shrugged. "Fine."

"No, no, not so quick. How do you *really* feel? Think about it for a minute."

Carl thought about it and then said, "I was scared going in, and I was scared driving back. But I wasn't scared when I was doing it. Not even when the woman showed up. If the gun had worked, I would have eliminated her without a problem. I think . . . not having the best equipment was an amateur mistake. The gun is fine. We need new ammo."

"Yes, yes, yes, the technical details. We had no time . . . But that's not what I'm talking about. You don't feel . . . depressed, or morose, or sick? Sick in your heart?"

"No. No, I really feel fine, Grandpa. It was sorta a head rush, you know?"

"I don't know what that means," Grandpa said. "Head rush."

"It means I felt like I was doing something important, you know, like, for the *people*."

"That's fine—but you may later feel some sorrow," Grandpa said. "If you do, remember then what Lenin said. He said that some people are like weeds in the garden. They destroy the work of others, they make progress impossible—they make the harvest impossible. Therefore, like weeds, they must be destroyed themselves. We shouldn't be happy with this, with this mission, but it's a mission that must be done. You are like a fighter pilot in a war; and we are in a war."

"I know, Grandpa."

CARL WAS A high school senior; he'd been fighting the war since kindergarten. Grandpa had brought him along carefully, teaching him the history, using scenes from Carl's daily life as examples.

"Think about what you see around you," Grandpa had said. "Your mother works her fingers to the bone and she never gets anywhere. If you analyze what she does, you can see that she's forced herself into a servant job. They don't call them that, but that's what they are.

"Look around your city. You can be a cook, a waiter, a miner, a truck driver, a salesman, but do you really have a chance against the capitalist? Against the people who own the companies, who hire the cooks, the waiters, the miners? Open your eyes, look around."

Carl had looked, and he had seen what Grandpa saw. Later, when he was older, he got the hard stuff: Marx, Engels, Lenin, Stalin. People he could never name in school. All of it secret.

AT THE HOSPITAL, Carl had been sewn up, and the wound had healed cleanly. Three days after Moshalov was removed, Carl began patrolling Duluth, one night in his own beat-up Chevy, the next in Grandpa's Taurus, concentrating on the harbor areas, making nightly passes on the downtown saloons.

He and Grandpa agreed: he couldn't become a Duluth regular,

somebody seen driving by every night. He had to make his runs at odd times, when he was less likely to be seen by the same person twice, less likely to be remarked upon. Good training.

The care had paid off. He'd finally spotted the woman, tracked her, guessed where she was going. He felt the same excitement he felt during hunting season, when he saw a deer threading its way through the woods, toward his stand.

He parked on a side street, and when the woman walked by, at the bottom of the street, he fell in behind her. She never noticed, never looked, just rattled along with her shopping cart banging down curbs, occasionally talking to herself.

When she turned the corner, she triggered Carl. He stepped out, camoed and ready, the wire strung between his fingers, the big nails in his palms as handles on the garrote; the garrote had been built by Grandpa.

"NOTHING SPECIAL, all the parts can be thrown away, and be perfectly innocent. But it's deadly effective," Grandpa had said, snapping the wire under the bare bulb in the basement workshop. They'd had gourds growing on the fence behind the house. Grandpa got one, and Carl practiced slipping the wire over the gourd, and then snapping the noose tight. The wire slashed through the yellow gourd like a straight razor.

"Works the same way with a neck," Grandpa said. His eyes came to life as they worked with the wire. The idea of killing with the garrote was interesting—it was a traditional tool used by resistance groups and revolutionaries, Grandpa said, and that was what they now were: a resistance cell, living underground.

CARL TURNED THE corner and almost stumbled over the tramp. She saw him at the last minute, seemed to snarl, then to start away. "Run," she called, as though instructing her legs. "Runnn . . ."

He was moving fast and he threw the wire over her neck, put his knee in her back and pushed. He could smell her now, the same stink he'd smelled the first time they met. He bent her, felt the wire cut in, felt it tremble and sing. She didn't attack him as she had the first time. She flailed her arms, like a bird trying to fly, and they turned once or twice on the street, bumped into her shopping cart.

The cart jerked away and then began rolling slowly down the hill toward the intersection, bumping along, rattling, right through the intersection and on down the hill, picking up speed . . .

She was dead.

CARL FELT HER GO and for the first time this night, felt something, a cold little thrill, unrelated to the people's cause. He lowered her to the pavement, unwrapped the wire, had to pull it out of her flesh, like pulling a piece of sticky tape off a wall. He could smell the blood in the damp night air; and in the light of the single visible streetlamp, saw a reflection from the whites of her eyes. They were unmoving.

He stood still for a moment, listening, trying to see into the dark; heard cars at the bottom of the hill, and the cart still rattling down the blacktop toward the street below. Time to move. He walked fifteen feet to the corner, turned toward his car, glanced back once at the lump on the sidewalk.

Stuffed the garrote in his pocket, felt a wetness. When he took his hands out to look, found them covered with blood. An imperfect weapon still, he wiped the blood on his pants. The woman had been a fountain . . .

He moved on, quickly. Had to clean up. Had to get rid of the garrote and the clothes.

Had to report.

4

JERRY REASONS WATCHED Lucas slide four feet down a pile of broken concrete-block chips to the lake. Reasons was a cop and a muscle-man, with a broken nose and a crooked smile and a chipped tooth. He wore a black golf shirt that showed off his ball-bat forearms and Mack-truck chest; his jeans looked like they were painted on his perfect, sculpted butt. He had a Glock on a belt clip under his right hand, and a badge in a belt clip over his left pocket. He said, "I hate the fuckin' Russians."

"Yeah?" Lucas stood with one foot on a chunk of eroded concrete, the other on the lake bank, stooped and stuck his hand in the water. The day was unexpectedly warm and windless, but Superior was as cold as ever, the color of rolled steel. He'd been on the lake a few times, but had never been easy with it. Fall overboard in Superior, you had fifteen min-utes to get out before the cold killed you. He looked back up at Reasons. "Hate 'em, huh?"

They were at the end of a boat slip, one that must have been a half mile long and a couple of hundred feet across. The TDX grain elevator stood along one side of the slip, a series of off-white ten-story-high cylinders full of wheat, soybeans, and various kinds of agricultural pellets.

"Yeah. You ask them a question about one of their buddies bein' killed, and you can see them thinking it over, what to say. They're figuring out whether or not to lie. You see it all the time," he said. "You pick up a drunk Russian on the street, you ask, 'You been drinking?' and the guy thinks it over. He smells like a fuckin' distillery, he's got puke running down his shirt, he's got a bottle in his hand, he can't stand up, and he's thinking it over. *What happens if I say yes?* Fuckin' Russians."

"So you don't like Russians," Lucas said. He shook the water off his hand, patted his hand against his pants leg, and climbed back up the bank. They started back through the weeds toward the dirt track that led to the elevator. The ground was rough, hard to walk on. They'd followed what Reasons said was a chase path that had been crushed through the weeds, though there was no longer much evidence of the chase, if there had been one. Reasons thought that the victim had run from the gun, had taken a fall or two—the gunman may have fallen as well—and then, perhaps disoriented, he'd turned back toward the elevator. The gunman had caught him on the pad, and had killed him. Lucas thought that was possible, if a little strange. "You ever known one personally? A Russian?"

Reasons kept a toothpick in the corner of his mouth. Using his tongue, he switched the toothpick from the left side to the right side, cleared his throat, and said, "I married one."

Lucas grinned at him. "That's good."

"I don't know what I was thinking," he said. He scratched his neck. "Living with the bitch is like having a rock in your shoe. A big rock. Though I gotta say, she still turns my crank."

"You got nothing from the Russians on the ship?"

Reasons shook his head. "Nothin'. They didn't know a thing. They weren't sure the moon was gonna come up. Or go down, if it did come up."

Lucas nodded. "Listen: in the file, you had a note that said, 'Kid?' And then there was something about the coat and the temperature. What was that all about?"

Reasons turned and looked up at the elevator. "This guy Kellogg was what they call a grain trimmer. When it's time to load up a boat, he goes on board to supervise." He pointed at a long metal pipe, a foot or two in diameter, that dangled from the side of the building. "The grain comes down through that big pipe, outa the elevator and into the ship's hold. He'd just gotten done and walked over to the rail for a cigarette. He was standing right there." Now he pointed to a spot in the empty air at the end of the slip. The Russian ship had been sent on its way a week earlier. "That's when he saw the guy walking away from the body. He yelled at him and the guy runs. The guy was small, almost like a kid. He's not sure about that, because the perspective from up there is goofy—way high, looking down, in the dark. But he thought the guy was small."

"How about the coat?"

"He said the guy was wearing a long coat. I checked with the weather service, they said the temperature down at lakeside that night was sixty-one degrees. It'd been a hot day. I wondered about the coat."

"Kellogg never went after him, didn't try to find him."

Reasons shook his head. "No. He had to get help for the hurt guy, and all the cabins and the gangway and shit were all at the back of the boat, way back there . . ." He pointed again, to the far end of the slip. "Besides, he was scared shitless after he saw the blood."

"Have any thoughts?" Lucas had figured Reasons out during the ride between Duluth police headquarters and the grain terminal. Beneath an assumed cynicism, the muscleman was a fairly smart guy.

Reasons scratched his head, as though stirring up a few thoughts. "Not many. There was . . . You know about the Minnesota Rangers?"

Lucas touched his nose with his index finger, thinking. He had: "The militia guys?"

"Yeah. Skinheads. Some old Vietnam veterans, Gulf War veterans, bikers. They go around in long black coats, like in that *Matrix* movie. Even in the summer. Shave their heads. They think that America is a socialist hell and that we're all being turned into batteries."

Lucas showed a little skepticism. "You think one tried to prove his manhood by killing a Russian?"

Reasons shook his head: "No. I don't. This was too cold for a fruitcake. You'd maybe take a trophy, cut off an ear or something, but open his pants up and search him? I don't think so. The killer was after something specific. But . . ." He turned his hands palms up, an *I can't help myself* gesture.

"What?"

"One of our intelligence guys heard a rumor that the Rangers were taking credit. You know, like the PLO takes credit when they blow something up? I went out to see Dick Worley, he's the leader out there at their war grounds. He said nobody he knew had heard anything. I put some bullshit on him, but he said that, honest to God, nobody knew anything about it. They hadn't even heard the rumor that they'd done it."

"You believed him."

Reasons nodded. "Yeah, pretty much."

"What are the war grounds?" Lucas asked.

"One of those paint-ball places. They play capture the flag, and all that. War games."

Lucas looked up at the grain terminal. There was a tiny window at the top, with a man's face framed in it. He was looking down at them. "Bummer."

THEY MOOCHED AROUND the area again, and Lucas said, "The idea of a chase . . . that's a little odd."

"Maybe it never happened," Reasons said. "But that night, and the next morning, you could see where somebody had been beating through the weeds. Falling down a lot, too, or wrestling around. And it was fresh, like the weeds had just been broken. I think maybe they're connected. If somebody had another idea, though, I'd be happy to hear it."

"I got nothing." Lucas looked at his watch, took a last look around the murder scene, and then asked, "You want to meet another Russian? The guy'll be here in an hour. Or you could haul my ass back to the station, and I'll go get him."

"I'll go with you," Reasons said.

"Maybe you'll hate him."

"Probably. But I go back to the office, they're gonna have me chasing down bums."

"Yeah?" They started back toward the car, which Reasons had parked next to the terminal.

"Somebody offed this old lady last night, street person, kinda crazy. You know. Schizo. Strangled her with a wire, we think. That's what the doc thinks, anyway. Cut her throat with it. We got four guys going around interviewing winos—not my idea of a good day."

"Any leads?"

"Nothing. Her pushcart—she had a shopping cart—found it a block away, down the hill. It's possible that somebody tried to take it away from her."

"Killed her for a cart full of junk?" Lucas eyebrows were up.

"Hey, if it was another wino . . . but we dunno. Found her on the sidewalk, head cut halfway off, big puddle of blood. Whoever did it was a strong motherfucker, is what the ME says."

"You're a strong motherfucker," Lucas observed.

Reasons's brown eyes snapped over at Lucas, and he grinned: "Yeah, I am. Lift every day. It made me wonder . . . you know, if I know the guy. Wonder if he pumps a little iron?" He thought about it, then shook his head: "Nah. Probably another wino."

. . .

THE TRACK INTO the terminal was not much more than a long series of potholes and ruts. They bumped out of it, over a curb, and turned up toward the city.

The south end of Superior is shaped like a pocketknife blade, pointing down into Minnesota; the lake itself is sunken into the landscape, with steep hills and bluffs along the shore. On the east side of the tip of the knife point is Superior, Wisconsin; Duluth, Minnesota, is on the west side, built on the flats along the lake, up a long lakeside hill, and then onto the plateau west of the crest.

The main airport is on the west side, a twenty-minute drive from the lake. They took Garfield Avenue out of the terminal area, crossed the interstate, climbed the hill, and dodged traffic on the main east-west drag. Lucas knew a little about the town, but Reasons kept up a running commentary on the local attractions as he drove, and got Lucas oriented on the main business and governmental areas.

"Be a nice place if it wasn't so fuckin' cold," Lucas said.

"Ah, it ain't bad. When it gets really bad in January, we can always run down to the Cities and get a little sun."

"Very little sun," Lucas said. "The whole fuckin' state's a freezer."

"I kind of like it," Reasons said.

"Yeah, so do I."

THE AIRPORT TERMINAL building was a concrete-and-red-brick wedge. They parked in an open lot and went inside, showed their ID to security so nobody would get excited about their guns, and figured out where the baggage would be coming in.

"I can't remember a case like this Russian," Reasons said, as they walked to the baggage claim. "Sixty percent of the time, you know who did it two minutes after you arrive. Twenty-five percent of the time, you figure it out in the next day or two. The rest of the time, you look at it and you say, shit—we ain't gonna solve this one. And you don't, except by accident." He turned and stared out one of the windows, brooding a bit: "This one's like a hybrid—a lot of dumb-fuck stuff, and the rest of it is 'Uh-oh, we ain't gonna solve it.' "

"Planned, cold, probably for business or political or money reasons—maybe even espionage reasons—but with an old gun and crappy ammo and he almost breaks a leg running off into the weeds," Lucas said.

"Don't know it was an old gun," Reasons said.

"Who'd put fifty-year-old ammo in a new gun?" Lucas asked. "You pay four or five hundred dollars for a gun, and you're not gonna pay ten bucks for a box of nines?"

Reasons nodded: "Won't argue with that."

THE NORTHWEST FLIGHT was only ten minutes late. When they'd confirmed the arrival time, they wandered off, both bought copies of the *Duluth News Tribune*. Lucas turned to the sports to see what, if anything, had happened with the Twins. They'd lost to Baltimore, 6–1; the story didn't try to make the game sound exciting.

The front page was dominated by a hard-news story and a sidebar, a weeper, about the murdered street person:

Mary Wheaton was a thin, round-shouldered woman who pushed a shopping cart full of treasures she collected daily from the gutters and alleys of Duluth, a familiar figure to downtown store owners. They were shocked when they heard of her murder.

"She wasn't quite right, but there was nothing bad about her," said Bob Anderson, of Five Corners Hardware. "She'd come in most days and get a dollar from somebody. The folks at the Burger King'd always give her a burger and fries.

That's about all she needed to keep herself together. I hope to God they get the animal who did this . . ."

The rest of the story was in the same vein. A file photo showed Wheaton pushing a shopping cart along a downtown street, peering nearsightedly, and maybe unhappily, at the photographer.

"You read about the murder?" Reasons asked.

"Yeah. Just sounds like . . . what it is," Lucas said.

"Like a dime-a-dozen down in the Cities."

"Well—anywhere that there are a lot of street people. The reporter was getting a lot of mileage out of it."

They strolled back toward the baggage claim, Reasons still looking at the article, then at the photo again, and he said, "You wanna hear a joke about an old lady beggar and a photographer?"

"If I've got to."

"Wait a minute. I don't tell jokes good, so I got to think it out," Reasons said. He thought for a moment, then said, "There was this old lady bum, she used to push a shopping cart full of shit around this rich neighborhood. This newspaper photographer was out one day, looking for a good feature shot, and he sees her and asks if he can get a picture of her. She says, yes, and he takes a couple, and they get to talking.

"She tells him that she used to be rich, that she grew up right in that very neighborhood. She used to go to balls and big parties and she went to a fancy school, and then she inherited about a million bucks. But over the years she had a couple of bad marriages and her husbands took it all, and she didn't know how to work, and over the years, she kept going down, down, down.

"And now, here she was, in her old age, pushing a cart around the neighborhood where she used to be rich, asking people for money so she could eat. So the photographer goes back to the newspaper, and tells the story to his editor, this really sad story, and the editor says, 'Wow, that is really sad. What'd you give her?'"

"And the photographer says, 'Oh, about f-4.5 at 125.'"

. . .

LUCAS SMILED and said, "You told that all right."

"Ahh, there are guys in the office who really know how . . ." He looked up at a monitor. "They're in."

They folded their newspapers and stuffed them into a trash can. A couple of minutes later, fifteen or twenty passengers wandered in. Half of them were too young, and most of the other half too Minnesotan, too certain of what they were doing, and too worried about their luggage, to be the Russian.

Lucas was looking at a stout man in a gray suit when Reasons leaned over and asked, "You think it could be the chick?"

Lucas followed his gaze: Reasons was looking at a fortyish blonde, hair pulled back in a severe bun. Thin, intent, she was wearing a dress, with some makeup; most un-Minnesotan. And the dress, though stylish, had an undefinable foreign *something* to it—something that went back to the sixties and June Cleaver. She was carrying a nylon briefcase, holding the handle with both hands. She was nice-looking, Lucas thought, and had the same slanting eyes as his wife, who was a Finn. "You think?"

"She's the only one looking around, like she's expecting to be met. She's checked us out pretty good. She looks kind of Russian."

"You oughta know," Lucas said. With Reasons trailing behind, Lucas walked over and said, "Would you be Nadezhda Kalin?"

The woman smiled briefly, automatically: "Yes. Officer Davenport?"

"Lucas Davenport. We were told we were meeting a man."

"Well. You're not." The smile again came and went. Her English was good, but accented. She had square shoulders and there was a gap between her two front teeth, a diastema; she reminded him a bit of Lauren Hutton. "You should call me Nadya."

"I didn't get it right, did I? The Nadezhda?"

"Well. I thought, em, that you had perhaps sneezed?" She was amused.

"Sorry."

"No, no." She smiled and patted him on the arm. "Anyway, I wait for my baggage."

"We'll help you wait," Lucas said.

"We'll even help you say a little prayer," Reasons added.

"A prayer?" She looked from Reasons to Lucas.

"This airline does not always deliver the baggage with the passenger," Lucas said.

"Ah. It is the same everywhere." She laughed and patted Reasons on the chest, and Lucas could see that Reasons liked it.

THEY WAITED FOR another minute, and nothing happened with the baggage, and Nadya said to Lucas, "We must talk about my, em, em, *authority* is not the right word, because I have no authority here." Her eyes were green with flecks of amber around the pupils. "About my . . ."

She needed help. "Status," Lucas suggested.

"Yes. Status."

They talked about her status: "As far as the investigation goes, you can see everything we get, and can suggest anything you want, and I'll probably do it, as long as it's legal," Lucas said. "I mean, it's a free country, but we'd like to get this guy, the killer. He really made a mess on our dock . . ."

She looked at him oddly—she didn't quite recoil, but a line appeared in her forehead—and she said, "Thank you very much. I'm sorry for this . . . *mess.*"

"No, no, not your fault. I assume you want him caught?"

"Well, of course," she said. "What do you think?"

Lucas shrugged. "There's politics going on. That's what the FBI says. We're not exactly sure what you guys want."

The corners of her mouth dropped: "It's very simple. We would like justice."

"Oh, Jesus," Reasons said. And he added, out of the side of his mouth, *"Gavno."*

Her eyebrows went up: "You speak Russian?"

"My wife is Russian," Reasons said. "I speak three words: *gavno, Stolichnaya,* and *Solzhenitsyn.*"

The smile came again, and the corners of her eyes crinkled: "With those, you would get along very well with our intellectuals."

"Yeah, well . . ."

"You don't think we'll get justice?"

"We might get the killer," Reasons said. "Justice is out of the question."

THEY WAITED SOME more, and then the luggage started coming. Lucas watched her from the corner of his eye. She was not somebody who hit you as pretty, he decided, but if she was around for a while . . . She was like Weather that way; Weather wasn't conventionally pretty, but she was intensely attractive.

Her bag arrived, a black nylon duffel, and Reasons threw it over his shoulder. Lucas offered to carry her briefcase, but she declined, and Lucas led the way out to the city car. She climbed in the backseat, and Reasons took the wheel with Lucas in the front passenger seat.

"What first?" Reasons asked over his shoulder.

"I would like to see the body," she said. "If this is possible."

"We can do that," Reasons said. "You want to freshen up first? Check into your hotel?"

"No, I'm afraid it would be wasted, if then I went to see the body," she said.

"No problem."

THE MORGUE WAS at the University of Minnesota–Duluth medical school. They talked about the weather on the way over; in Moscow,

Nadya said, it was no different than here in Duluth. And they talked about the length of her trip: it was not so much the hours in the air, as the shift in time, she said. She would be disoriented for a while. "At home, we are nine hours ahead of your time. Right now, I am okay. At seven o'clock tonight, I will fall asleep. For sure."

"What exactly is your job back home?" Lucas asked.

"I am a police officer, a major in the Federal Security Service—like your FBI," she said. "If I help with this case, I will have some good hopes of becoming a colonel. If I don't help, I will have some good hopes of becoming a lieutenant." She smiled to show that she was joking.

"So this is a big deal." Reasons looked at her in the rearview mirror.

"Yes, big deal," she said. "What is a Dairy Queen?"

THEY EXPLAINED Dairy Queen, and then rode in silence for a bit until Lucas asked Reasons, "You gonna stay with us? Or are you gonna get pulled for this old lady?"

"I don't know. I'd like to work with you guys, but there might not be much to do. And politics gets into it. Nobody cares much about the Russian, but folks are gonna be kinda pissed about Wheaton."

"What is this?" Nadya asked, from the backseat.

"Ah, we had another murder here . . ." Reasons went on to regale her with the facts of the murder. Lucas was watching her face, the play of emotions running across them as Reasons got into the details. When he finished, Nadya touched three fingers to her lips and asked, "Does this happen often?"

"Nope. Hardly anybody ever gets killed up here. We got maybe two or three murders a year. Four in a good year."

"Only Russians and old women alcoholics," she said.

"The first Russian in memory," Reasons said. "As a matter of fact, that was the first Russian boat to come in for quite a while."

"Really," Lucas said. "I didn't know that."

"Lots of Russians back in the seventies; not many anymore," Reasons said. He looked over the seat at Nadya.

She shrugged, and said, "As far as I know, that . . . would not be connected to this death. That the boat would come here."

"So you think it was just a coincidence?" Lucas asked.

"I believe in coincidences," she said, "As long as there are not too many of them."

THE MORGUE WAS in the medical school's loading dock; a convenience, Reasons said. "You just back the ambulance up to the dock, open up the garage door, wheel the deceased over to the cooler, and put him or her inside."

They'd called ahead, and were met in the dock by the pathologist on duty, a Chinese-American man with a pleasant accent who introduced himself as Doctor Chu. He unlocked the door to the cooler, and rolled the dead man out. Oleshev was covered with a hospital sheet, and the pathologist pulled it back.

Nadya turned away, just an inch or two, a flinch, Lucas thought, and then she turned back. Oleshev looked as though he'd been carved out of a piece of chipboard. Nadya gazed at him for a moment, then dipped into her bag and took out a brown envelope, slipped out three glossy photographs, looked at the photos and then at the face. After a moment, she showed them to Lucas and Reasons. The photos didn't look exactly like the dead man, but resembled him; resembled him the way flesh resembles wood.

Lucas asked, "You know him?" Behind Nadya, Reasons's eyes cut to Lucas.

"No." To Chu she said, "It looks like him. Rodion Oleshev."

"That's not the name on his papers," Chu said.

Nadya shrugged.

"All the people from the ship agreed he was a guy named Oleg Moshalov," said Reasons, pressing just a little.

Nadya said, "Well, he's not." To Chu: "If you could make some fingerprints for me, that I could witness . . ." She dipped into her bag again and took out a stack of thin plastic envelopes.

"We've got prints . . ." Chu began.

"She'd like to witness it," Lucas said. "With her own stuff."

The pathologist nodded. "What do I do?"

She opened one of the envelopes and slipped out a sheet of plastic half the size of a dollar bill. In the center of the plastic sheet was a red square covered with a strip of peel-off film.

"You pull off the cover and roll one of the right-hand fingers in the red square," she said.

"Red Square," Chu said. To Lucas: "Get it?"

Lucas shook his head once and Nadya sighed and said, "Then you let the sheet dry for a few seconds, and we put it back in the envelope."

The pathologist said, "Slick," and took the prints. He did it quickly, expertly, and as he finished each print, Nadya lifted it to the overhead light to look through the plastic. Satisfied, she fanned each print for a moment, drying it, then slipped each plastic sheet back in its individual envelope.

"Where would you get a fingerprint kit like that?" Chu asked.

"You would have to call the consulate," Nadya said. She handed him an unused envelope. "You can have this one, if you would like. The manufacturer is named on the back, but it is in Russian. There's a phone number in St. Petersburg."

"Get my wife to translate it," Reasons said.

Nadya nodded: "The chemical on the sheet is made to . . . mmm . . . I don't know the English word, but it is, er, *compounded* to reflect light from a scanner, so that any scanner can be used to digitize the fingerprints." She used her hands when she talked, like a French woman.

"Slick," Chu said again. "Thanks."

Outside, Nadya took a breath, looked up and down the street and said, "This could be a Russian town, except for the signs. I don't mean the words on the signs, I mean the signs are everywhere. Everything is signs."

"So you want to look at the files, or what?" Reasons asked.

"No. If we could go to the hotel, I could transmit the fingerprints back to Washington, and use the toilet and maybe get clean from the trip. Then the files?"

LIKE LUCAS, Nadya was staying at the Radisson, a cylindrical building that looked like a chubby, upright tower of Pisa; the hotel was conveniently across the street from the police station. They took her all the way to her room, where Lucas explained the TV remote and the movies channel, and they showed her how to hook the modem through the hotel's phone system. They dialed into the Russian embassy's server, got the connect tone, and left her.

"We'll wait in the restaurant. Back in half an hour," Lucas said, as they went out the door.

Going back down the hallway to the elevators, Reasons said, "She said she didn't know him."

"I don't think she did," Lucas said. "She was too careful about the fingerprints."

"You saw her jump, though."

"Yeah," Lucas said. "She's no cop."

"What do you think? She's a spy?"

"I think she's probably with one of their intelligence services, and for some reason, they sent somebody who isn't used to dealing with bodies," Lucas said. They got to the elevators and Lucas pushed the up button; Reasons pushed it again just to make sure it was pushed. "She's not a clerk. She's an executive. She's been around."

"More than me," Reasons said.

"I'm not exactly a world traveler," Lucas said. "I went to Mexico a couple of years ago, on a job. I went to Europe when I was in college. That's about it."

"Europe," Reasons said. "French pussy."

"I was playing hockey," Lucas said. "All I saw was German hockey rinks and the insides of buses. I did get to see the Wall before they knocked it down."

"More'n me," Reasons said.

The elevator doors opened and they got on. Lucas pushed the button for the top floor, and Reasons pushed it again, just to make sure it was pushed. "Maybe I'll travel when I retire. The old lady would like to see Moscow."

"That's where she's from?"

"Naw. She's from some one-horse town on the Polish border. Moscow, to her . . . it'd be like seeing Manhattan the first time."

As they walked into the restaurant, a man sitting in a lounge chair with a *New York Times* looked over the paper, stood up, and asked, "Lucas Davenport?"

Lucas stopped: "Yeah?"

The man was wearing twill pants and a neat tweed jacket with a burgundy tie. He was six feet tall, military erect, sandy haired, early thirties, and pleasant, like a hopeful Xerox salesman. "I'm Andy Harmon. Barney Howard probably told you I'd look you up. I saw you going through with the lady, but couldn't catch you. I thought you'd probably come up here . . . Could I get a word with you?"

Lucas said to Reasons, "This guy's a fed. Get a booth, I'll be with you in a minute."

Lucas and Harmon drifted toward the windows facing the lake, away from other patrons. Harmon looked too young for a serious federal job; if he was not exactly apple-cheeked, the apples had only recently departed. "She give you anything interesting?"

"She said America has a lot more signs than Russia," Lucas said.

Harmon pulled at his lower lip for a couple of seconds, and then said, "That's true."

"Other than that . . ." Lucas shrugged. "We went over to the medical examiner's office and took prints off the dead guy, Oleshev. She had a fingerprint kit that makes it easy to digitize prints. She gave one of the pickup sheets to the ME and told him where he could order some more in St. Petersburg."

"Mmm."

"She's not a cop," Lucas said. "She's probably from one of the intelligence agencies that doesn't deal with bodies."

Now he was mildly interested. "How do you know that?"

Lucas explained and Harmon nodded. "We never really thought she was a cop," Harmon said. "Something happened here, and they don't know exactly what it was. She's supposed to figure it out before we do."

"Think she will?"

"She will be smart," Harmon said.

"She might be smart, but if we see everything she does, how does she plan to stay ahead of us?" Lucas asked. "There's gotta be something else."

"Mmm. She's probably got a shadow operator." He said it deferentially, as if talking to a moderately slow child.

"What's that, in English?"

"She's out here in the open, picking up everything you get. Then, even though they don't know exactly what's going on, they've probably got some ideas of their own—some conjectures, maybe some contacts who might know something. So she sends everything she gets from you back to the embassy, and her controller bounces it back to the shadow op. So he's got everything they know and everything we know . . . and maybe he stays a few steps ahead."

"What does he do if he figures it out?"

Harmon shrugged. "Takes care of it himself. Or maybe, if it doesn't jeopardize whatever they're doing here, Nadya feeds the information back to you and you make the bust."

"Well, Jesus." Lucas had never encountered anything like it.

"As for us . . . We'd like to know if they've got an organization here and what it's been doing. It could be completely commercial—tracking grain prices, that sort of thing. Then . . . maybe not."

"And I just ride along," Lucas said.

"Don't worry about it," Harmon said. "This dead guy, nobody will miss him much, except maybe his old man. He was an idiot. That's what people say . . ."

Lucas interrupted. "What people?"

Another shrug. "People. Anyway, I don't think it counts for much whether or not you get the killer. What really counts is that there might be an organization here that we should know about. The fact that she's from the SVR suggests that there is."

"The SVR is . . ."

"The Sluzhba Vneshney Razvedki, their foreign intelligence service. The FSB, the Federal'naya Sluzhba Bezopasnosti, is the national police force. That's what she says she's from." He pronounced the Russian names with relish and a sputtering dampness. "She might be quite . . . immoral, I suppose you'd call it, in your terms. If she thinks you're getting somewhere, and you're not keeping her up with it, she might try to initiate a sexual relationship with you. They're very, very well trained." Harmon's thin tongue, looking a little like a Ritz cracker, flicked over his lower lip.

Lucas nearly laughed, but suppressed the impulse and said, solemnly, "I'll take care."

"So she had nothing else? Nothing relevant, other than the signs?"

"No, we were mostly setting up a schedule. We'll show her the files when she's finished transmitting prints, and gets cleaned up. She's said she's jet-lagged and she's gonna crash pretty early."

"All right." Harmon eased away. "We'll be in touch."

"I just can't figure out . . ."

"What?"

"I can't figure out why you guys don't seem to care. I mean . . . people are getting killed."

"Honestly? Catching spies for the former Soviet Union is not exactly a good career move anymore. Costs a lot of money, disturbs the relationship, and nobody cares. So, catch a spy, you get an atta-boy and transferred to Boise, where you'll be less expensive."

"That's really . . . fuckin' great," Lucas said.

"Call me if you need anything," Harmon said. He turned away. "Anything that we got, that doesn't cost too much."

"Hey," Lucas called after him. "How was the 'signs' thing relevant?"

"Might mean she's never been here," Harmon called back. And "Good report, Davenport."

LUCAS SLID INTO the booth across from Reasons. Since the hotel was a cylinder, the restaurant, naturally, revolved. When Lucas and Harmon started talking, they were looking at the lake; when they finished, they were looking south, at right angles to the lake. When Lucas joined Reasons, they were looking down at the Civic Center complex, which included the federal building, the county courthouse, and the city hall; the port and the lake were coming up. Lucas settled into the booth and ordered a Diet Coke. "Another spy?" Reasons asked.

"Yeah, one of ours."

"Is ours better than theirs?"

Lucas waited as the barman put a glass of Coke in front of him, and then said, "I don't think so. The guy says, *'She might be immoral, in your terms. She might try to initiate a sexual relationship with you.'*"

"Really?" Reasons was impressed. "If she does, will you tell me about it? I mean, the details?"

"I'm more married than you are," Lucas said. Imitating Harmon's voice, Lucas said, *"They're very, very well trained."*

Reasons laughed merrily. "You're shitting me."

"That's what the man said." Lucas shook his head. "He also said, 'Good report, Davenport.' "

"That rhymes."

"Brilliant observation."

Reasons said, "If she can't get to you, maybe she'll try to fuck *me*. I'm a good American. If my country calls, I'd have to answer the call."

"Just don't tell her any military secrets," Lucas said. "Andy Harmon will be all over your ass."

"Maybe I couldn't help myself," Reasons said, "If she's that well trained."

AS THEY LEFT the restaurant, on the way back to Nadya's room, Lucas excused himself, took his calendar and his cell phone out of his pocket, and looked up a St. Louis phone number. He needed help.

A man answered on the third ring.

"How many Italians does it take to screw in a lightbulb?" Lucas asked.

After a moment, the man said, "You sound like a fuckin' Canadian. Is that you, Davenport?"

They talked for five minutes. When Lucas hung up, he felt a little like a spy himself.

5

NADYA WAS LOOKING GOOD.

She'd changed into a dark blue suit that went well with her blond hair and showed off her figure; she'd added a touch of lipstick and small diamond-chip earrings. Her hair, worn short, and still damp from the shower, looked artlessly windblown. As they got in the elevator to go back down, Reasons muttered to Lucas, "Christ, she wouldn't even *need* any training."

"What?" She'd heard part of it.

"How'd the prints go? When will you find out?" Lucas asked.

She said, "He's Oleshev," she said. "The fingerprints, they've already checked, there is no doubt. There wasn't much before."

"What does his father do?" Reasons asked. Distracting her from the training comment. "We've heard he's a big shot."

She was nodding. "His father is important in oil. Very important. Not so much oil itself, as, em, support machinery."

"Pumps?" Reasons suggested.

"Maybe pumps," she said. "But bigger than that. Pipelines, refineries. Systems. There is so much oil in some places in Russia, you can get it out of the ground with a stick. Getting it from the stick to Europe . . . that is the problem."

"Okay."

But she expanded: "So you see, Maksim Oleshev not only controls money, he controls workers—jobs in factories, jobs in pipeline construction. These are votes. Some people think his power could be destabilizing."

"So what's his son doing in Duluth?" Lucas asked.

"The son went his own way," she said. "He was a government official before his father came to power in oil."

"He was in the KGB," Lucas said.

She nodded. "Yes. Of course. Then in the merchant marine."

"That seems like an unlikely job change, from spy to sailor," Lucas said dryly.

She looked up at him and said, "First, he was not a spy. He was an analyst and an, *mmm*, I don't know the English. An arranger. Second, you were not in Russia in the nineties. People had no jobs. The government collapsed. The intelligence services collapsed. High, important men were selling shoes in the markets. If somebody said, 'Here is a job,' you took it. Oleshev, we think, had contacts in the merchant marine through his covert service, from being an arranger. Perhaps he . . . knew something about some of them. Anyway, he got a job. He was good at it, the crew says. He started as a third officer, which is nothing, and would have had his own ship soon."

"Really," Lucas said.

"Really. It's true." Her eyes were opaque, giving away nothing, but she smiled sweetly. "In fact . . . I will tell you some things, but if they appear on paper and I am asked, I will deny them."

"Between us, then," Lucas said.

"Yes. One line of speculation in Moscow is that Oleshev was a courier for his father, perhaps working toward some unknown agreement with American oil service companies. The Moscow government would oppose this, if they knew about it. You see, the best oil service companies are American, but the Moscow government wishes, understandably, that Russian companies begin to develop the capacity to provide these services. But how can this be done if all the contracts go to America?"

Lucas said, "But then . . . the obvious agency to kill Oleshev would be your Moscow government. The American companies wouldn't do it—they'd want Oleshev to succeed. His father wouldn't do it. And our government would probably like to see American companies get the business. So it'd be you guys. What do they call it? The SVR?"

She shook her head. The mention of the SVR didn't faze her: "Ah. But I can tell you, from the highest sources, that the SVR knows nothing. They would like to know something, because there are many people shouting at them, but they do not. And Maksim Oleshev claims that there was nothing to know; that he had no business dealings with his son. Therefore, the problem must be here."

"You believe that? He had no dealings with his son?"

She cocked her head to the side, pushed out a lip. Then, "I don't know. In Russia, the family is important. If your father has a billion dollars, why cover yourself with dirt in some old ship? But that is what Maksim says."

"So what's the Moscow speculation on the kind of problem it might be?" Lucas asked.

She ticked them off on her fingers: "One: An American thug sees a man in the dark and kills him in course of a robbery. Two: Rodion Oleshev is dealing with the Russian criminal underground, perhaps as a courier of drugs or financial instruments. There is a falling-out, and they kill him, or a rival gang kills him. Maybe Russian, maybe American. That's my favorite. Three: Maksim Oleshev is lying, and his son was working for him. Four: Something else. What, we don't know."

Reasons said, "You can probably scratch the American thug. That's a terrible place for a strong-arm robbery, down by the docks. You can't see a thing in the dark, there's no way to get out of there in a hurry, nobody has much money, and a lot of the people you might try to rob are meaner'n shit themselves."

"And he was probably shot with a silenced pistol," Lucas said. "In my whole career, I've seen about three silencers that would actually work. They're rare, here. This wasn't a street robbery."

"I agree," Nadya said. "I think, one way or another, that he was a courier, a contact person, and criminality was involved."

"The crew didn't have much to say about him," Reasons said.

Nadya frowned. "The *Potemkin* has stopped in Quebec, so that our investigators can speak to the crew members. I'll get summaries of the interrogations and give them to you."

Reasons nodded: "Okay."

Nadya said, "I would like to speak to the man who saw the killer, the American."

"So would I," said Lucas. "But he's fishing. He has a shift this afternoon. He's due in at three o'clock. He knows we'll be coming."

DULUTH POLICE HEADQUARTERS were in City Hall, a stone building that looked like a 1930s WPA post office. Along with the federal building and the St. Louis County Courthouse, it made up the civic center a block from the Radisson. They walked over, a nice afternoon, sunshine slanting down over the hill, a maple tree down the street showing a flame of autumn orange.

The detective bureau was like fifty others that Lucas had been in over his career, an undistinguished beige-painted room with a counter near the entrance, a bulletin board full of FBI "Wanted" posters, a couple of short rows of desks separated by low partitions, a twenty-four-hour wall clock, a few computers, a lot of paper. A single detective sat hunched over a newspaper, eating a sandwich from a brown paper sack. He looked up when they came in, and went back to his sandwich as Reasons led them into a side room.

"The lieutenant's gone, he's down in St. Paul at murder school. We can use his office," Reasons said. He pointed them at chairs around a conference table, and added, "I'll be right back."

He was back in a minute with a file folder, which he gave to Nadya. "Anything you want, we'll Xerox. Can I get you some coffee?"

"A cup would be good," she said. She looked at the file: "Thin."

"Not much to work with," Reasons agreed. "You've probably already seen most of it."

"Well." She flipped through the file. "Maybe I'll get some sleep tonight."

LUCAS SETTLED INTO an unused desk, paging through a copy of *Trailer Boat* magazine that had been sitting under a telephone. Reasons took a cup of coffee into Nadya, and he could hear them talking, and Reasons laughed once. Reasons came out, put his hands on the edge of a desk, backed his feet away, and did fifty quick push-ups. The sandwich-eating detective said, "If your feet ever slip out when you're doing that, you're gonna break your teeth on the edge of the desk."

"I'm quicker'n that," Reasons said.

"Okay. Your problem, as long as it's not my desk," said the other man. "I don't want any tooth marks on it."

Ten minutes after Nadya started reading, another detective wandered in, carrying a briefcase. He stopped when he saw Lucas.

Reasons said, "Davenport. BCA."

Lucas said, "Your desk? Sorry, we're just waiting."

He stood up and moved to the guest chair next to Reasons, and the second detective ambled over to his desk, said, "Take the magazine if you want, I'm all done with it." Then he sat down, sighed and said, "What a day."

"Talk to a bum?" asked Reasons.

"Talked to fifteen of them," the detective said. "Nobody knows what happened. They kept asking me if somebody was killing bums."

"We gonna lose it?"

"I don't know. Probably."

"Better you than me," Reasons said.

The detective nodded toward the lieutenant's office. "Is that the . . ."

"Russian. Yeah."

The detective whistled and said, "I thought they all wore them things like my ma. You know, the babushkas."

"She's probably got one hidden somewhere," Reasons said.

"What's happening with the old lady?" Lucas asked. "I saw the story in the paper."

"If you read the paper, you probably know more than I do, 'cause I haven't read it yet," the detective said. "But . . ."

He dipped into his briefcase and took out a manila file and passed it to Lucas. Inside was a sheaf of photos of the crime scene and the dead woman. The detective turned back to Reasons. "By the way, Chick Daniels is looking for you. He knows all about the Russian and the BCA guy . . . Davenport?"

"Davenport," Lucas said. "Who is Chick Daniels?"

"Reporter for the *News Tribune.*"

"Mmm." Lucas looked at one of the photos and then held it up to the detective. "Is this the way she looked? Is that neck right?"

"That's the way she looked. Almost cut her head off."

"I've never seen that before," Lucas said. "The cut goes all the way around."

"Sliced right through the whole front half of her neck, arteries, veins, and all."

"Maybe you got a nut," Lucas said.

The two detectives regarded Lucas for a moment, then the no-name detective said, "That's what I'm afraid of. We got a nut and he's gonna do it again." Pause. "Fuck."

NADYA WOUND UP Xeroxing a half dozen sheets from the Oleshev murder file, then she and Lucas headed for the port. Reasons opted to go home: "I already talked to the guy three times. If you get anything new, call me up."

Nadya settled into the Acura, lifted an eyebrow at the video screen on the dashboard, but left it without comment; Lucas followed the on-screen map through the maze of streets around I-35, and made it down to Garfield Avenue. At the TDX terminal, they found the entrance, a tiny white door in the otherwise faceless tower. Inside, they found a small two-man office, everything with a patina of dust. A man sat with his back to them, typing on a manual typewriter that sat on a government-style gray metal desk with a broken leg set on a two-by-four block. Lucas hadn't seen a typewriter like it in twenty years. The man didn't turn when they came in. He said, "Chris called, he wants you to call back."

"Wrong guys," Lucas said.

Then man turned from the typewriter: "Ah . . . you must be the state police guy."

Lucas nodded, introduced himself and Nadya. "Are you Harry Kellogg?"

"No, no, Harry doesn't work here, he works for the port. He's supposed to be here to meet you . . ." They heard a truck outside and the guy said, "That's probably him."

They went back outside, and found a portly, red-faced man in a yellow hard hat, just climbed out of his red-and-black GMC pickup. He shook hands with Lucas, and nodded at Nadya.

"I didn't see much. I just finished filling the number-two hold and I walked out to the bow to have a cigarette—can't have one right by the hold because there's dust in the air, and you could have an explosion," Kellogg said. "So I light up and I look over the bow. I wasn't sure what I was seeing, because . . . I don't know, I haven't seen that many dead people, and I didn't expect to see one there. I mean, it took a few seconds. Then I saw this other guy, not exactly running, but he was in a hurry, moving off into the dark. Into the weeds way back there . . . and I realized the guy on the ground was probably dead, or maybe unconscious. I yelled and the one guy started running away, and that's the last I saw of him. The dead guy was just layin' there. I ran down to the gangway and down to my truck and got my baseball bat and ran down to the dead guy. I used my cell phone and I called the ambulance . . ."

"The guy who ran away . . . you didn't see him shoot the dead man, you didn't see a gun?"

"No. And the thing is, I never even heard the shots, even though we were on deck not more than a couple of hundred feet away. There was some noise, you know, but it's not loud, the hold filling up. The cops, the police, said there were a bunch of shots, but I didn't hear a thing. Neither did the crew."

"So then what?"

"So then nothin'. The cops came and looked all over the place, and picked up the dead guy, and took a statement from me. Looked around in the weeds."

"You didn't see anybody in the weeds."

"No, I never did. The thing is, I had a couple of cigarettes—I had one about fifteen minutes before, and I went up to the bow and there was nobody in sight. The whole thing happened in that fifteen minutes. Then . . ." He glanced at Nadya and colored a bit.

"What?" Lucas asked.

"The Russian guys . . . this was years ago, mostly, we don't see many Russians anymore. The thing is, it used to be that every time a Russian boat came in, you'd see carloads of girls coming out here. They'd go on the boat and you know, take care of the guys. Sometimes, when we were loading, and there was a lot of dust and guys banging around, they'd get a blanket and go out in the weeds. I don't think there were any women aboard, but . . . there might have been some guys down in the weeds earlier in the night."

"Did you see any women at all?"

"No, I didn't. I just thought, with the weeds all crushed down . . . sometimes you'd see that. But that was years ago."

"Okay," Lucas said.

"How many of the crew did you see? Up on the deck?" Nadya asked.

"Just the captain and the loader, the guy who was helping with the loading. The rest of them were all asleep."

"So you don't think somebody from the crew might have met Oleshev on the dock . . ."

Kellogg was shaking his head: "No. The guy I saw ran away, and there was no way to get back past me on the boat. As soon as the cops got here, they sealed off the boat so nobody could come or go. I was here all that time, and pretty soon, all of the crew was up, when they heard the commotion, the sirens and all. The captain did a head count, and they were all accounted for. Nobody came or went. Besides, the guy I saw didn't look like a Russian."

" 'Didn't look like a Russian,' " Nadya repeated.

Kellogg shook his head. "The crew are blue-collar guys. Beefy, strong guys. Gorillas. The guy I saw was small. I think he was small. He looked . . . you know, thin. He had on that long coat and the Russian guys, you never saw them in long coats. They wore jackets. Leather jackets, or just regular cloth jackets, or rain suits, but I never saw one in a long coat. This looked . . . old-fashioned."

. . .

THEY TALKED a few minutes more, but Kellogg had nothing else that was relevant. They said good-bye and walked down to the end of the slip where Lucas had parked the Acura.

"Where was this weeds place, where Jerry thought there was a chase?" Nadya asked.

"Over here . . ." Lucas took her out into the weeds. "Right around here. From the lake, back this far. He said you could see what looked like pathways crushed into the weeds . . . You can see where we walked this morning. Same thing."

"Mmm." She looked around. "This does not look like so good a place for sex."

"Depends on how bad you want the sex," Lucas said. "I suppose."

THE GROUND UNDERFOOT was rough, as though it had been dug over a few times, rutted by heavy equipment and trucks. Here and there were piles of broken concrete. Nadya tramped through the weeds for a few more minutes, and then said, "If there was a chase over here, who got chased? Why was Oleshev in the middle of this big concrete? He couldn't run after he was shot, that's for sure. He was shot in the heart and the head . . . Does it make any sense?"

Lucas was looking at the remnants of a broken wine bottle. He picked it up and read the label: Holiday Arbor, and below that, a price tag: $2.99. He rubbed his face and Nadya said again, "Does it make any sense?"

Lucas thought about the pictures of the old woman in the police file, and the shot of her on the street that he'd seen in the newspaper. In the police pictures, she'd been lying on her back, her arms flung out to the side, a long coat beneath her, like a black puddle in the camera's strobe light. In the newspaper pictures, she looked small, round-shouldered.

"What?" Nadya asked, her hands on her hips.

Lucas looked at the bottle. Two ninety-nine. Mary Wheaton had been a street person. Street people wore long coats on warm nights in the summer, and they drank cheap. She'd been killed in a way he'd never seen on the street, but he *had seen*. He'd been wrong when he told the Duluth cops that he'd never seen it before. He'd seen it in the movies, when the Navy SEAL sneaks up on a lazy sentry and *zut*—the neck is cut. Was it a spy thing, a military technique? He'd assumed it was simply dramatic bullshit . . .

He looked back at the fragment of wine bottle. Holiday Arbor, $2.99. The paper label on the bottle looked new, as though it hadn't been long in the weeds.

"Come on," he said to Nadya. He started walking fast toward the elevator.

"To where?" She jogged along behind him.

"Back to the morgue. The medical examiner's."

"You have an idea?" She was looking at the chunk of glass in his hand. He carried it by the sharp edges.

"Maybe," Lucas said. "We need one."

DR. CHU HAD gone home, but the night man in pathology called the campus cops, who came with the keys, and when Lucas explained what he wanted, the night man called Dr. Chu, who gave the go-ahead.

"Everything's here," the night man said. He put a box of clothing on the counter. Much of it was soaked in now-black and dried blood. "I'll get it out for you, if you want."

"That'd be good . . ."

The night man slipped on plastic gloves and took Mary Wheaton's clothing out of the box piece by piece. At the bottom was an olive-green military-style coat with a red-white-and-blue patch on the shoulder. The night man held it up and said, "That what you want to see?"

"Long green coat," Nadya said. "With a Czechoslovakian flag on the shoulder."

"Is that what that is?" Lucas looked at the coat for another minute, and then said, "I think we better call Reasons."

R E A S O N S   C A M E   D O W N , looked at the coat. "Could be," he said. He didn't sound skeptical; he sounded neutral. "What do you want to do?"

"See if we can get some prints off the piece of bottle I found, see if the prints match the old lady's. See if we can find more bottle. Try to figure out what she might have been doing over there."

"I might be able to tell you what she was doing," Reasons said. "There's a Goodwill store maybe two blocks from there. It's just about the only thing around, I mean, that's not a warehouse. This coat, this looks like something from Goodwill."

"But it wouldn't have been open in the middle of the night," Lucas said.

"No . . ."

"Is the place still open? Now?"

Reasons looked at his watch: "I think so. Let me make a call."

T W E N T Y   M I N U T E S   L A T E R , Maxine Just, the manager at the Goodwill, led them back through the store to a clothing rack, where three Czech Army coats hung from wire hangers. "We had about five of them. A surplus place up in town, caters to college kids, got a bunch of them a couple of years ago. They couldn't sell them all, and finally gave them to us. Tax write-off. We put them up for eight dollars each."

"So you sold two."

"Two or three, yeah. We got five or six."

"Do you know who you sold them to?"

Just shrugged. "People who wanted long wool coats. The wool's pretty good. Some people buy them to make rugs—they dye the wool, do these folky kind of rugs for people's cabins. College students used to buy them, when grunge was big, but they went out of style . . . I suppose they mostly went to people who couldn't afford better. Most of our clientele."

"But you wouldn't know specifically."

"No. I could ask some of our cashiers, maybe somebody would remember."

Reasons asked her to contact the cashiers, and they agreed that he would stop by in the morning to talk with them. They talked for a couple of more minutes, then said thanks to Just, and wandered back outside. The Goodwill store was a long walk from the city center, Lucas thought—he pointed it out to Reasons and asked, "How would she get down here?"

"Bus, probably. Cheap ride, by bus. I'll have the guys check with the drivers."

They were drifting back toward the cars when a dark-complected young man with a Latino accent stepped outside and called, "Excuse."

Reasons called back, "Yeah?" The young man walked across the parking lot. He was wearing worn jeans, an Iowa Wrestling sweatshirt with the sleeves cut off at the biceps, and pointed-toe black dress shoes caked with mud. He had a sterling-silver earring in his left earlobe and a small black mustache.

"Mrs. Just said you were looking for the lady with the coat?"

"Yeah."

He pointed across the street. "I see her every day, catch the bus there."

They all looked at the bus stop.

"Every morning, she get on, every night, she get off. I think she lived around there somewhere. I see her in the Dumpster in the back. When she see me, she run across the street into the bushes." He said *booshes*.

"Where would she live?" Lucas asked. But they were all looking at a small cube-shape shed across the street. "You think in the shed?"

The man shrugged. "I don't know. But every morning, every night, I see her. All summer."

"Wearing the coat."

"Two or three days only, in the coat," he said. "We only get the coats one month ago mostly."

"Could I get your name?" Reasons said. "Where do you live?"

AS REASONS TALKED to the man, Lucas and Nadya walked across the street and through a ring of knee-high weeds to the shed. The place was a plywood cube, with boarded-over windows on two sides, a windowless, padlocked door at the front. An abandoned storage shed, Lucas thought, probably for the railroad.

"How do we look in?" Nadya asked.

"Have to talk to Reasons," Lucas said. Reasons and the Latino man were walking toward them, and when Lucas asked about breaking in the shed, Reasons said, "Let me make a call."

He stepped away again. The Latino man said, "She goes around back. I never see her open this door."

Lucas and Nadya walked around to the back of the shed and found a blank wall—but the weeds next to one part of the cinder-block foundation were worn and scuffed, almost like an animal trail that went nowhere, ending at the foundation. Lucas stooped, pushed on a block, and it moved. A few seconds later, he'd pulled out four blocks, and kneeling, and cranking his head around, he could see a man-sized hole in the floor.

"Somebody's been going in and out," he said.

"You want me to go in?" asked the Latino.

"No, no—let's do it right." He pushed the block back into place.

• • •

REASONS CAME BACK with his cell phone and said, "The city engineer says it's been condemned as an eyesore. The railroad's agreed to tear it down, but just hasn't gotten around to it yet. Bacon—the city engineer—he's calling the railroad guy who knows about it, to get the okay to go inside. There's something around back?"

"Yeah, somebody's been going in and out," Lucas said. He explained about the foundation.

Reasons went around to look and then went back to his phone. When he got off, they stood around looking at the shed, and at the port, and Lucas started talking to the Latino man about Mexico, and Reasons started bullshitting Nadya about dating in Russia, and then Reasons's phone rang. He listened, nodded, and said, "Thanks."

"We can go in. If we can get in." A patrol car was rolling down the street toward them. "I called for a hammer," he said.

The patrol car pulled to the curb. A uniformed cop got out of the car, lifted a hand to Reasons, went around to the trunk, popped it, and lifted out a sledge. "What do you need broke?" he asked.

THE COP TOOK three swings to break the padlocked latch off the door; even then, the door was jammed shut. The cop went back to his car, dug around in the trunk, and returned with an eighteen-inch-long screwdriver. "When I started on the force, they called all that shit 'burglar's tools,' " Reasons said.

"Yeah, but that was a hundred years ago," the cop said.

He worked the blade of the screwdriver around the edge of the door, grunted, "Warped," and Reasons said, "Well, Jesus, don't baby it—they're gonna tear the fucking thing down."

Then the door popped, and they all clustered together and peered inside. They could see what looked like the remains of a camp: and a briefcase with paper scattered around.

"Think we can go in?" Reasons asked.

"I'm going," Lucas said. "Fuck a bunch of crime-scene weenies."

The interior had an animal smell about it: the place had been inhabited, and recently, by somebody not fastidious. A flat pad made of bubble wrap was pushed against one wall, with an army blanket on top of it. A bed, Lucas thought.

Peeking from under the briefcase, he could see one half of what looked like a wallet. He stooped, took a pencil out of his pocket, and used the pencil to drag the wallet into the open.

"What do you see?" Nadya called.

Lucas got down on his knees and pushed his face close to the wallet. "A wallet. A bunch of cards in Russian and an ID card in English that says, 'Oleg Moshalov.' "

"Sonofabitch," Reasons said.

6

WHEN REASONS SAID, "Sonofabitch," Lucas stood up and backed out of the shed, slapped his hands together to get rid of the dust, and said, "Better call your crime-scene guys."

CRIME-SCENE INVESTIGATION had somehow become the flavor-of-the-month on TV shows, but Lucas could not remember the last time that crime-scene guys had actually broken a case. They gathered evidence—blood, semen, hair, fingerprints, firearms and shells, tool marks, clothing fibers—that could be used to pin a suspect after the cops found him, but the cops had to find him first.

In the one major case in which the crime-scene people were dominant, and in which Lucas had participated, if only from the sidelines, a hot assistant county attorney and her crime-scene buddies had proven beyond doubt, from crime-scene evidence alone, that a dope dealer named Rashid al-Balah had killed a gambler named Trick Bentoin. The evidence showed that Bentoin's body had been dumped in a peat bog in the Carlos Avery state wildlife-management area north of Minneapolis.

They'd had witnesses who recounted tension between Bentoin and al-Balah over a gambling debt, and threats made by al-Balah. They had blood from the trunk of al-Balah's car, they had seeds and soil from plants that grew nowhere else but Carlos Avery, and when it was all done, they put their man away.

Then, a year or so later, the dead man showed up. He'd been in Panama, playing high-stakes gin rummy. As the Russians would say, *gavno;* and as Lucas's pal Del had wondered, "Who *did* Rashid kill and throw in a peat bog? Had to be *somebody.*"

THE CRIME-SCENE CREW arrived half an hour after Reasons called in.

Fifteen minutes before they got there, Chick Daniels from the *News-Tribune* hopped out of his car in the parking lot of the Goodwill store and Reasons said, "Here comes the press," and walked toward him. They met in the middle of the street, talked for a few minutes, then Reasons walked him across to the shed and said, "We're gonna let him have a look inside, but deny we did it."

Lucas nodded, and the reporter, a twenties-something guy with long brown hair and Labrador retriever eyes, stuck his head in the door of the shed, looked at the litter inside for a minute, then backed away and said, "Can I look at this foundation thing?" Reasons walked him around back; they looked at the foundation. Lucas heard his name mentioned and then Nadya's, mentioned and spelled.

Nadya said, "You always talk to the news before you know anything?"

Lucas nodded. "Always. *Especially* before we know anything."

"That seems operationally unsound." She was very serious.

"It might be," Lucas said cheerfully. "But see this way, we get our pictures on television."

"This is good?"

"Sure. It proves we exist."

She still looked solemn, and a bit uncertain, so Lucas said, "I'm pulling your leg. With this kind of thing, we've found that talking to the news media, especially the newspapers, doesn't hurt much. Especially if the reporter's decent. The news is gonna get out anyway, and it's better to have it accurate, than a bunch of rumors."

"What is this leg-pulling?" she asked.

AFTER THE WALK AROUND, the reporter went back to the other side of the street and got on his cell phone. "I told him he's gotta stay over there," Reasons said. "He's a pretty good guy. TV'll be here in a couple of minutes."

Ten minutes before the crime-scene crew arrived, as Lucas was looking at the sole of his shoe, wondering about the brown stuff stuck on it, the no-name detective arrived, wearing knee shorts and a golf shirt. He was carrying a black milled-aluminum flashlight.

"Great knees," Lucas said.

No-name was not in a mood for repartee. "Fuck you. Let me look."

He stood in the door of the shack and shined the flashlight across the floor. "Somebody was living here, all right. You sure it was Wheaton?"

"I don't know. Sounds like her. We got a guy saw her every day. He's over there . . ." Reasons pointed across the street, where the Latino man was sitting on the hood of an eighties Plymouth. "And for Christ's sake, don't ask for a green card until we've deposed him."

The no-name detective glanced at the Latino, then continued playing his flashlight across the interior of the shed, methodically sweeping the dirty floor and walls. Now he said, "Look at this," and he stepped inside.

Lucas looked. Eight inches to the side of the door, at head height, a nail stuck out of the wood. In the light from the flash, Lucas could see a tiny swatch of fiber hanging from the head of the nail, like hair, or short, bristly spiderwebs.

"Green. Green wool, I think," no-name said. "That fuckin' army coat. That's weird."

"What's weird?" Lucas asked.

"We *know* where she lived. We already turned the place over. What the hell was she doing down here?"

FIVE MINUTES BEFORE the crime-scene guys arrived, two TV trucks pulled up. Reasons went across the street and pushed them back fifty yards; and then, with a show of reluctance, made an on-air statement. "See? He gets on TV," Lucas told Nadya.

Then the crime-scene crew showed, two guys in golf shirts and jeans. Reasons walked over and asked, "Where in the hell have you been? Playing golf?"

"Got here fast as we could," one of the guys said. He counter-attacked. "None of you went inside, did you?"

"Of course not," Reasons said.

Lucas and no-name shook their heads. "We were waiting for you."

WHEN THE PHOTOGRAPHY was done, the crime-scene people began picking up the litter—with Lucas's urging, they started with the small paper, picking up each piece with forceps, bagging it, and passing it out the door. Most of it was cards, most of it in Russian.

There were several items of interest: an American Express platinum card under the name Zbigniew Riscin, a New York driver's license under the same name, and a receipt from the National car-rental agency at the Duluth airport for a car rented to Zbigniew Riscin. The car had been driven a hundred and seventy-five miles and returned the same day it was rented—the day that Oleshev had been murdered.

They also found a receipt, paid with the platinum card, for $145 from Spivak's Tap, in Virginia, Minnesota.

"It's about an hour up to Virginia," Reasons said. "If he went up and back, did a little driving around, it'd be about right."

"I wonder what is the Spivak's Tap?" asked Nadya.

"A tap's a bar," Reasons said. "I'll check." He got his phone out.

Next out was a Targus retractable reel with six feet of telephone cable on it; it was used to connect laptops to motel telephones, and Lucas had one just like it. There were also three different white plastic-bodied electric wall-plug adapters for U.S. and European outlets. Nadya looked at them and said, "He had a laptop."

"No laptop in here," said a crime-scene guy.

"I'd like to find a laptop," Lucas said to Nadya.

Nadya said, "Greatly," and then, "I will check with the *Potemkin*, to see if he left one in his cabin."

ALL THE MATERIAL from the hut was bagged. One of the crime-scene guys stepped to the door and said, "Look at this." He had, in his forceps, a money band, printed "$100."

"Took some money off him," Lucas said. "How many bills in this?"

The crime-scene guy said, "Five thousand, I think."

"So she got five grand, at least. Where is it?" no-name asked. "Nothing at her place. Didn't look like she was eating any better."

"Got a Kotex here," one of the crime-scene guys said from the interior. "Unused."

Lucas said, "How old was Wheaton?"

"Fifty-eight," said no-name.

"We got a problem," Lucas said. He looked across the street at the Latino perched on the car. "I think we better haul Raul up to the medical examiner's."

THEY DID THAT.

On the way, Nadya said, "So I am thinking, this woman did not kill Oleshev, but she was first to find his body. She robbed him and when the man on the boat saw her, she ran away. So we have nobody who saw the killer."

"I am thinking that, too," Lucas said, falling into her syntax. "If it was Wheaton. But they sold more coats out of that store. It might have been another woman . . ."

At the medical examiner's, they rolled Wheaton out and peeled back the body bag. Unlike Nadya, Raul didn't flinch when the body was exposed. He looked at Wheaton's face, at her open eyes, and shook his head. "Not her. This one I saw was a younger chick, man. This one I saw was maybe . . . I don't know. Wash her up, maybe forty."

"Goddamnit," said Reasons. He looked at Raul: "Can I see your green card?"

"HOW'D YOU FIGURE this out, man?" no-name asked Lucas.

Lucas explained, the whole line of indications starting from the chase through the weeds, which didn't make any sense in terms of the dead man; the small figure in a long coat, seen running away from the body; the photographs of the small street woman in the long coat, murdered the night before; the cheap wine bottle in the area of the chase through the weeds. And luck: Reasons's idea about the Goodwill store, and Raul.

"You know, it's like detective work or something," no-name marveled.

. . .

"IT'S TIME," Lucas said. "To have a beer and think it over."

"Are we breaking the investigation?" Nadya asked.

Lucas had to think for a minute: "I have to talk to you about your slang. But no, not exactly."

"More like the investigation is breaking us," Reasons said.

"If you want to have a beer and think it over, I can tell you where to have the beer," no-name said. He took out a fat cell phone, which was also a PDA, looked up a name, and pressed the button. "Barbara, babe: we need to talk. Where are you?" He listened for a few seconds, then said, "How about we meet at Duke's? Okay."

THEY SENT RAUL back to the Goodwill store, where he'd left his car, with a campus cop, and fifteen minutes later filed into Duke's Lounge, a lump of brown brick in a wilderness of on-ramps, at the south end of the city.

The place was full of neon beer signs and dark wood, with a coin-op shuffleboard game in the back. Four guys in backwards ball caps sat talking at the bar; the bartender himself sat on a stool and leaned back toward an aged Schlitz sign with a hole in it, so he could read a book in the light coming through the hole.

When they all walked in, the guys at the bar stopped talking and looked at no-name's shorts, and the bartender said, "Barb's in the back booth." At the same time, a woman in a black leather jacket stood up and said, "Here," and the guys at the bar started talking again.

Lucas, Nadya, Reasons, and no-name, who'd finally introduced himself as Larry Kelly, trooped to the back, clunking along the wooden floor. Lucas stopped to look at an old Budweiser-made print of Custer being wiped out by the Sioux at Little Bighorn.

Nadya stopped at his elbow, took in the print, and said, "Why do Americans celebrate defeats?"

Lucas shrugged. "Like what?"

"Bunker Hill, the Alamo, Custer, Pearl Harbor, the Chosin Reservoir, September eleventh—I have even seen this movie *Blackhawk Down*. It seems strange."

"You know a lot about our history," Lucas said.

"I studied it, of course. But this is not so much history as psychology."

Lucas looked at the picture for a few more seconds; in the lower right corner, an Indian was peeling the scalp off a dead cavalryman. "I don't know why we do it," he said. "But we do, don't we?"

THEY WENT ON to the back, where Kelly introduced Barbara Langersham, a woman in her early forties, dark haired, dark eyed, broken nosed. A white scar, a match for the one on Lucas's forehead, disappeared up into her hairline.

"Barbara knows all the street people," he said. "She works for Catholic Charities."

"Doesn't have a hell of a lot of Catholic charity, though," Reasons grumbled.

"It all depends on what you want, doesn't it Jerry?" Langersham said, and Lucas thought, *Oops*.

ONLY FOUR OF them could fit in the booth, so Reasons and Lucas pulled up chairs and they all ordered beer, and Kelly said, "Barbara: Mary Wheaton, you've read about it."

"Yes." She poured her beer expertly into a pilsner glass, so the head came just over the top, not too thick. "I heard her head was almost cut off."

"Yeah. Now—we think there's a possibility that whoever killed her was the same guy who killed the Russian last week. But they got the wrong woman. Was there another woman street person around here, who walked around in a long green army coat?"

"Ah . . . shoot." She thought for a moment. "I don't remember one. But I think Mary only had that coat for a day or two. I only saw her with it once. Like she just got it. I remember thinking it was too hot."

"We're looking for a woman who might have lived across the street from the Goodwill store," Lucas said. "Might have been a redhead, or sort of reddish hair, maybe forty."

"Somebody saw her?"

"Yeah, but not somebody who could give us any information," Reasons said. "He just saw her."

Langersham licked a bit of foam off her upper lip, then said, to Reasons, "You know I don't like to talk to cops."

"But you do, when you need something," Reasons said. "The fact is, this other woman is in trouble. If the killer knows he got the wrong woman . . ."

They didn't have to draw a picture. Langersham said, "There *was* another woman. I think her name was Trey, but I don't know her last name. She wasn't forty—she was more like early thirties. I suppose, when she had a little dirt on her, she could go for forty. I saw her, I don't know, a couple of weeks ago, panhandling up at Miller Hill Mall. I haven't seen her since. I did see her, earlier this summer, a couple of times, maybe three times, on the Garfield Avenue bus. This was at night, I saw the bus going by, so she might have been going out Garfield. Toward the Goodwill."

"Tray, like ashtray," Kelly said.

"I think it was Trey, like a three-card," Langersham said. "I don't think she interacted too much with the cops, or anybody, for that matter. She pretty much stayed to herself."

"Anything else?" Lucas asked. "You know if she was ever arrested . . . ?"

Langersham shook her head. "I just don't know. She was well-spoken, like she'd had some schooling. I mean, she wasn't a dropout, or anything. I think she probably took a lot of dope sometime or other; she knew all the words, and she had that doper sense of humor. She was very good at picking out guys who'd cough up a buck."

"We can look through arrest reports; try to look her up in the nickname file," Reasons said.

They sat and talked and ate potato chips for a half hour, much of the conversation between Nadya and Langersham as the men sat back and listened. Nadya was fascinated by the underage-hooker world that Langersham worked: "We have the same problems in Moscow, but we don't even know how to start with it," she said.

"Look to your religious people," Langersham said. "Cops won't work, because they're in the crime life. The only thing that attracts these kids is the belief that somebody actually cares about them."

"But not police," Nadya said.

"Not police. You can't pretend to care about them. You've actually got to care. About them, personally, one-on-one. So—recruit the religious. It'll give them something worthwhile to do, instead of shaking their beads at some bishop. You got bishops in Russia?"

"Everywhere," Nadya said. "More than anyone could need."

Langersham nodded: "That's a problem. You've got to get your religious people away from the bishops. Get them out in the streets. If everybody saved just one person . . . we'd all be saved. And it'd do wonders for both sides."

They sat in silence for a minute, and then Reasons said, "Right on. Pass the joint."

"Fuck you, Jerry," Langersham said; but she was smiling when she said it. "Your turn to buy a round."

7

TREY SAT IN a Country Kitchen in Hudson, Wisconsin, eating French toast with link sausage, reading a copy of the St. Paul *Pioneer Press*, a story out of Duluth:

Mary Wheaton lies in the county morgue, a few doors down from Rodion Oleshev, a Russian sailor—or perhaps a spy—who was executed at the TDX grain terminal two weeks ago.

Nobody has been arrested in the murders—but now a top state investigator and a Russian policewoman, teamed with Duluth police, may have forged a link between the two brutal killings.

"We believe that somebody killed Mary Wheaton to silence her," said Duluth Police Sgt. Jerry Reasons. "We believe that she may have witnessed the murder of Mr. Oleshev."

Reasons said that police have developed specific information to link the two killings, but would not elaborate. Sources at the police department, however, said that fibers found in a hut where Wheaton was believed to have lived were matched with the military coat that Wheaton was wearing when she was killed—and the hut contained papers that appeared to have been taken from the body of Rodion Oleshev.

Reasons said that he and Lucas Davenport, an agent for the state Bureau of Criminal Apprehension, and Nadya Kalin, an officer of the Russian . . .

THE STORY WENT on, but Trey's eyes had gone watery: she wasn't seeing it. The killer had come back for her, and he must have found Mary, thinking she was Trey.

For just an instant, the wary, feral, traveling Trey felt a pulse of victory: if the police knew there was a witness to the murder—and they must have known that because somebody at the grain terminal had seen her, had shouted at her—and if they thought that person was dead . . . she was safe.

Then the Annabelle Ramford lawyer brain clicked over: it wouldn't happen. Too many people knew her, and too many knew Mary. If they checked with Tony on the bus route, he would tell them that Mary hadn't lived in the hut, and that another woman had worn the coat.

The cashier at the Goodwill store who'd sold her the coat—she'd remember, too. She'd tried to wipe out the prints in the shack, but there must have been hair left behind—and if they compared the hair from the hut with Mary's hair, they'd know that there was another woman.

A live witness. They'd come looking.

TREY HAD ALWAYS viewed her life as a strange trip: strange from the time she'd been old enough to understand the concept. The last years of high school, all of college, the crack years, the traveling time, all strange. She seemed at times to be standing outside of her body, watching herself doing something crazy. A rational, coldly realistic Annabelle standing to one side, watching a mindless, pleasure-hungry

Trey fire up a crack pipe. An intelligent, skeptical, upper-middle-class lawyer watching an out-of-control freak eating discarded pizza from a garbage can on the Santa Monica Mall.

Life had always been strange, but nothing, she thought, had ever matched the strangeness of the past few days.

SQUATTING THERE in the shack, stuffing money into her backpack, scrubbing all the wooden surfaces with a rag—get rid of the fingerprints, her only thought—she'd been aware that the world had shifted. There'd been an earthquake. She was no longer a bum; she was back in the middle class, a woman of substance. A woman with liquidity.

When the cops came, their sirens seemed aimed at her hideout—but then they turned away, bumping across the rough road down to the TDX terminal. When God gave her the few minutes she needed to finish cleaning the shack, she slid beneath the floorboards, pulling her pack behind her. The pack was stuffed with money and her clothes.

The shack was on Garfield Avenue, one of the gritty working streets found on the outskirts of all industrial towns: heavy-equipment repair shops, lumberyards, warehouses, like that, all dressed in gray and grime and broken glass. Dirt roads and railroad tracks crisscrossed the area, with weeds and brush growing up between them.

Trey stayed in the weeds, like a wild animal, stuck to the shadows, heading toward town by a long, looping route. To the north, near the terminal, a dozen cop cars were scattered around the concrete ramp, roof racks flashing, and she could see men with flashlights, and she could hear people calling to one another.

When she'd gone far enough that she felt she could risk it, she crossed Garfield to the south, toward the highway overpasses coming in from Wisconsin, a wilderness of train tracks, mud, weeds. In the green army coat, with the dark blue backpack, she was invisible.

An hour after she set out, she'd crossed an I-35 overpass into Duluth proper and started up the hill above the lake. At two o'clock in the morning, she arrived at the garage where she'd once spent a few nights. The place was full of junk piled around a wrecked car, and the floor was oily, and there were rats . . . but it was out of sight and dry.

She tried to sleep: got three hours, at best, interspersed with long fantasies of having the bag taken from her. She'd never been afraid of bogeymen in the dark, not after living with the candy man. Now she had something to lose, and the fear crept around her.

At sunrise, she started out again, now with a plan. She crawled up to the top of the city, to an all-night laundromat, sat inside and washed the best clothes she had—jeans, a black Rolling Stones T-shirt, underpants, and bra. She threw in her towel and washcloth. Her shoes were okay, a pair of cheap boating sneaks she could wear without socks.

When it was all washed and dried, she repacked and started out again, downtown this time, to the ladies' room in the skyway. It was still early, and she had the place to herself. She washed in patches, at the sink, then got impatient, soaked the whole towel, retreated to one of the bathroom stalls, stripped, washed herself clean, and put on the clean clothes. The old clothes, the dirty clothes, she stuffed in the pack on top of the money. Everything went in the bag except the army coat, which was too big.

Still nobody in the rest room.

Taking a chance—if the cops caught you, they'd toss you back out on the street—she washed her hair in the rest-room sink, using hand soap from the dispenser. She patted her hair dry with paper towels and looked at herself in the mirror. She was presentable, but just barely. She looked, she thought, like a woman just back from three weeks in the wilderness. Or maybe six weeks. Or ten. But when she left the skyway restroom, she was mostly clean, and barely resembled the woman who'd gone in.

On the way down the street, she took the dirty clothes out of her pack and dropped them in a trash basket. She carried the army coat, still unwilling to give it up.

Her first stop was at a drugstore. Under the careful eye of a sales clerk, she bought deodorant, razor blades and a razor, fingernail clippers, tweezers, a hairbrush and comb, a bottle of soap, and two tubes of lipstick. She was about to check out when she caught sight of herself in a mirror on a Camel's display; she went back into the store and bought a bottle of moisturizing lotion.

The next stop was the Westerway Motel, where she'd stayed three or four times when she had the money, before she hit bottom. The place was dank, the beds were crappy, but the price was right and the showers were just as good as the showers at the Radisson. Most important, they'd let her in.

At the Westerway, she stood in the shower for fifteen minutes. She would have taken a bath, but the tub was so grimy that it frightened her. Besides, somebody had stolen the drain plug. Who in the fuck, she wondered, jabbing at the furry hole with her big toe, would steal a drain plug? Never mind. When she was thoroughly clean, she began grooming herself. Nothing she could do about her hair, she thought: she looked like a witch.

Clean, dry, nails clipped, deodorized, and moisturized, she headed downtown. Stopped at a bank, where she changed three hundreds into twenties. Passed a test, too: a woman rubbed one of the hundreds with a test pen, and they were fine. If they'd been fake, Trey thought, she'd have had a heart attack.

She would catch a cab, she thought, and head up to a sporting-goods store across the highway from the Miller Hill Mall, and buy a real pack, the kind young women sometimes traveled with. An expensive one.

On the way down the street, she passed Hair Today, and saw the sign in the window that said, "We Take Walk-Ins," and she walked in.

By noon, she had a cut and a 'do that would take her anyplace in Minnesota; she still had that burned-out, feral face, but you couldn't see that from behind.

And by two o'clock, she had a new backpack full of new clothes from the Miller Hill Mall, two delicate pearl earrings, and a selection of expensive facial creams and moisturizers.

Back at the Westerway, she gathered up the few remaining pieces of her old identity, her old pack and the coat, and carried them out to a trash can. As she was about to dump them in, she saw Mary Wheaton rattling down the street with her cart.

The coat, she thought, was perfectly good . . .

"Mary . . ."

The older woman turned and looked and kept going. Trey caught up with her: "Mary. You want my coat?"

Wheaton looked at her nearsightedly, then looked at the coat. "Who're you?"

"I'm . . . just a person. You want the coat?"

Wheaton took the coat, shook it, looked at it, and said, "You don't want it?"

"No more."

Wheaton nodded, put the coat in the cart, and rattled away without a backward glance. She and Trey had talked a dozen times, and Wheaton knew her. This time she showed no sign of recognition.

Back at the Westerway, she looked in the mirror: she was changing, she thought. She tried to spot one thing that made the difference, but finally decided it wasn't one thing—it was a haircut that looked paid for, rather than done with manicure scissors or a knife; it was a face that looked cared for, instead of desert dry and flaking; it was an uprightness.

The next morning she left the Westerway, walked downtown, and caught a cab to the airport. She didn't have a reservation, so she had to sit in the terminal for six hours, until she got a seat on a Northwest flight to Minneapolis.

She took a cab from the airport to the University of Minnesota, where she bought a used Corolla for cash from a Lebanese graduate student who seemed nothing less than grateful for the money. Not a great car, with 85,000 miles, but it would do. As soon as she got the paper on it, she'd trade up: changing $50,000 into usable money wasn't all that easy, but she knew a few tricks from her doper days.

From Minneapolis, she moved on to Hudson, Wisconsin, on the Minnesota border twelve miles from St. Paul, where she knew a motel that would take cash, and wouldn't ask to see a credit card. Again, not a great place, but she was developing a base.

The next move: an apartment in the city, a bank account, and credit card applications. She saw the applications everywhere, and took them.

SHE WAS STILL in Hudson, waiting to be approved for an apartment in suburban St. Paul, when she sat down to eat French toast and link sausages in the Hudson Country Kitchen, and opened the paper to the story from Duluth.

Mary Wheaton was dead . . .

She sat and leaked tears for a while, read the rest of the story, looked at photographs of the cops standing outside her old hut in Duluth, then firmed up and finished her breakfast.

She'd go see about the apartment, and then she'd think.

Something had to be done.

8

LUCAS WOKE WITH A START.

There was a noise somewhere, in the room. The room was dimly lit, the light coming from cracks at the sides of the blackout curtain, so it must be after dawn. He glanced at the illuminated face of the bedside clock: eight in the morning. The sound wasn't threatening, there was no intruder in the room, but what . . . ?

He groped until he found the bedside light, turned it on. The sound was coming from the telephone: not a ring, but a low, strangled jingle, as if somebody had punched the phone in the solar plexus and it hadn't gotten its voice back.

He picked it up. "Yeah?" His voice sounded like a rusty coffin hinge in a horror movie.

"You told me to call," Reasons said. "I'm just leaving my house."

He stifled the impulse to moan. "Is there any air outside?"

"What?"

"Never mind. I'll be down in the lobby in twenty minutes. Did you call Nadya?"

"Yup. She sounds like she's been up for a while."

"I have been too, I've been up for hours," Lucas said. He yawned. He'd never been an early riser. "I was doing my push-ups."

"Twenty minutes," Reasons said.

LUCAS CLEANED UP, put on a fresh shirt and sport coat, got a bottle of Diet Coke from the machine down the hall, and found Nadya and Reasons standing opposite the elevator doors in the lobby.

"Breakfast?" Reasons asked, looking at the Coke.

"Of champions," Lucas said. Then he had to explain to Nadya. "See, there was this cereal, there still is this cereal . . ."

When he was finished explaining, she didn't see why it was funny.

"Well, it wasn't, very."

"Give it up," Reasons said.

Lucas asked Nadya, "Did you hear anything about the computer?"

"No. The question is traveling through the bureaucracy."

THE RANGE IS the remnant of both an ancient sea and an ancient mountain range, more or less an hour northwest of Duluth; it's the largest iron-ore lode in the U.S. The Range runs from northeast to southwest, and sitting atop it is a string of small iron-mining cities—Virginia, Chisholm, Eveleth, Biwabik, Hibbing. The cities are cold, hardworking, blue-collar, economically depressed, and addicted to hockey.

The town of Virginia was straight up Highway 53 from Duluth, across gently rolling countryside covered with birch and aspen—some of the aspen just beginning to turn yellow—interspersed with blue-and-green-colored fir, spruce, tamarack, and occasional rigidly ordered stands of plantation pine. Lucas drove and Reasons played with the navigation system for a while, and finally said, "So what?"

"It works when you're trying to find an address," Lucas said. "Out on the open highway, it doesn't do much. Tells you what direction you're traveling."

"Does this cost extra?" Nadya asked.

"A little bit," Lucas said.

"A lot," Reasons said.

"If it doesn't help, why do you have it?"

"It looks neat," Reasons said.

Nadya yawned, and went back to the *New York Times,* while working methodically through three bottles of spring water. She'd gotten a teensy bit in the bag the night before, drinking two vodka martinis without any rest after the trip. "Help me sleep," she'd muttered as Reasons and Lucas steered her out of the elevator down to her door.

She'd complained of dehydration as they were leaving Duluth, so they stopped for the water and the newspapers, and both Reasons, with the *Star Tribune,* and Nadya, with the *Times,* took turns reading bits and pieces to Lucas. When they were finished with the paper, Reasons and Nadya began a kind of teasing chatter.

Lucas, looking between them, thought, *Hmmm.*

VIRGINIA'S DOWNTOWN SECTION was made up of five long blocks of 1900-era red-and-yellow-brick two- and three-story buildings. Inside the five blocks, as Lucas remembered them, you could find anything you needed and most of what you wanted: you could eat American or Mexican, get drunk, acquire a tattoo, wreck your car, get busted, hire a lawyer, and get your car fixed without going off the street. You could get saved by Jesus on a Wednesday evening and then walk a hundred feet across the way and get a dirty magazine; you could buy a Jenn-

Air range or a Sub-Zero refrigerator or a used paperback, a homemade quilt or a doughnut, a chain saw or an ice-cream cone or a pack of Gitanes or Players. There was an ample supply of bars, ranging from places where you'd take your aged Aunt Sally to outright dives.

Lucas had always thought it might be the best main drag in Minnesota, and maybe the whole Midwest. He'd visited the place a dozen times between eighth grade and his senior year in high school, as a hockey player, and remembered with some fondness the brutally cold nights after the games when he and a half dozen friends went out looking for underage beer and hot women. They'd never gone home dry, and, as far as Lucas knew, nobody had ever gotten laid, despite expansive and ingenious lies about close calls, about barmaids and Virginia cheerleaders.

They arrived a little before ten o'clock in the morning. He was happy to see the street was still intact.

SPIVAK'S TAP WAS halfway down the ranks from cocktail lounge to dive. They parked in front, and got out, the sun hot on their backs despite the cool air, and Nadya said, "More signs."

"What's this thing you've got for signs?" Reasons asked.

"I have nothing for signs, but there are so many," she said. "Most people here, most men, have signs on their shirts. Why do you need so many signs?"

Reasons said, "Beats the hell out of me."

Lucas looked up at the front of the bar. "This guy—his name is Spivak?"

Reasons had called the owner the night before, and told him that they were coming, but not the purpose of the visit. He said, "Right. Anthony Spivak."

Nadya asked, "He will have a toilet here, yes?" and Lucas said, "Yes," and they followed Reasons inside.

. . .

SPIVAK'S WAS an unembarrassed beer joint, with clunky plank floors, a long mahogany bar, jars of pickled eggs and pigs' feet, two dozen booths with high backs upholstered in red leatherette, an area near a jukebox where you could dance, if you were so inclined, a couple of stuffed muskies, and an old, six-foot-long painting of a plump pink nude woman behind the bar, holding a strategically placed white ostrich feather. Lucas remembered both the painting and the feather.

Spivak was sitting at the end of the bar with a spiral notebook, a calculator, and a beer. He was a broad, short man, with a square pink face, square yellow teeth, and white hair growing out of his head, ears, and nose. He had a fat nose that looked as though it had been broken a couple of times. A blond woman with tired eyes stood behind the bar, taking glasses out of a stainless-steel sink, wiping them dry with a bar towel. Two guys in ball caps and plaid shirts sat in one of the booths, talking over their beers.

When they walked in, Spivak looked up, closed the spiral notebook, and asked, "Are you the folks from Duluth?"

"Yeah." Reasons nodded. He introduced Lucas and Nadya. Lucas raised a hand and Nadya nodded.

"Come on in the back," Spivak said. They followed him past the rest rooms, which had signs that said SETTERS and POINTERS, and which had to be explained to Nadya, who then disappeared into Setters; and then into the back, where four long tables were scattered among sixteen chairs in a party room. They took a table and Spivak cleared some chairs and said, "Could I get you something—on the house?"

"Ah, no, thanks," Reasons said. "We needed to talk to you about something that happened up here last week, but we've got to wait until Nadya gets back."

"She's got an accent," Spivak said, as they settled in at the table. "Where she from?"

"Russia."

"Russia." The corners of his mouth turned down as his eyebrows went up. "Huh. She's not a cop?"

"Yeah, she is," said Lucas. "She's part of this whole . . . We'll tell you about it in a minute." He looked around: "I used to come here as a kid—it hasn't changed much. Did the can always say Setters and Pointers?"

Spivak said, "A long time ago, it used to say Bucks and Does, but then in the seventies, some Indian guys said 'Bucks' was racist, so my dad changed it."

"But bucks means . . . deer bucks, right?"

"Well, yeah, but, you know, it was the seventies, Jane Fonda, all that," Spivak said. "And we used to get quite a few guys from Nett Lake in here drinking, they worked in the mines . . ."

"Nett Lake is an Indian reservation," Reasons told Lucas, who said, "I know."

Spivak asked Lucas, "You used to come in here?"

"Yeah, playing hockey. We were always going around looking for beer afterwards."

"You probably got a few here," Spivak said. "Dad always thought that if you were old enough to skate, a little beer wouldn't hurt you. When was this?"

"Late seventies."

Spivak nodded. "I would've missed you—I was the sixties. Things were different back then . . . So are the Wild gonna do anything this year?"

THEY TALKED HOCKEY for a couple of minutes, until Nadya came back, and when she was seated, Reasons said to Spivak, using his formal cop explanatory voice, "About fifteen days ago, a Russian guy came in here and apparently got together with some people at a meeting here in your bar. We'd like to know what you remember about that."

Spivak frowned. "A Russian? I don't remember a Russian specifically."

"He was a tough-looking guy in a leather jacket, heavy five-o'clock shadow, big square head like a milk carton," Lucas said. "Looked like a mean sonofabitch."

"You were sure he was here?" Spivak asked uncertainly.

"We got an American Express card receipt from here," Reasons said. "For a hundred and forty-five dollars."

"Ohhh . . ." Spivak's eyebrows went up again, but his eyes slid away. "Yeah. Okay. In fact, they were sitting right here. There must have been five or six guys. I didn't know the guy was Russian, though."

"What'd they do?"

Spivak shrugged: "Drank. Talked. In English, not Russian. What I remember was, when they were finished, they all tossed some money in a pot and the one guy, he must've been your Russian, collected the money, and then paid with his Amex. I mean, I was thinking it was sort of a scam, somebody would get stuck with an expense account when all the guys paid for themselves."

"We need specifics," Lucas said. "Did you know any of them?"

"No. Didn't know a single one." He frowned. "That's a little unusual. This is mostly a town joint. But it happens. We get tourists, whatever. Fishermen on their way north to Canada, sometimes they meet up here."

"They were Americans," Nadya said.

"Yeah, I guess. They spoke English. They looked like they were from around here."

"Were they talking about their families, or their business, or what?" Lucas asked.

"I don't know, I didn't pay any attention. Let me think." He leaned back in his chair, closed his eyes, and tipped his head back. After a moment, he opened his eyes and said, slowly, "Okay. When I was in here, most of the time it was the Russian guy and another guy who were doing the talking. The guy in the leather jacket. The other guy was like a big lumberjack-looking guy, plaid shirt, big shoulders, red hair. The other guys, I don't know—they looked like guys. One of them had a Green Bay hat."

"What is this?" Nadya asked Lucas.

"Sports team hat," Lucas said, watching Spivak, his eyes, listening to his voice. Spivak was lying to them for some reason.

They pressed him, but the barkeep gave them nothing more. The people at the meeting were, he said, "just a bunch of guys. Didn't disturb anybody, didn't get drunk, came, drank, paid, and left. I wish I had more of them like that."

Lucas asked, "Who all was working that night. Could we get a list?"

"Well, I guess. I'd have to go back and look," he said reluctantly. "We don't use everybody every night . . ."

He checked his time cards and put together a list of phone numbers and addresses, and as he did, said, "You guys scared the shit out of me. I thought you were up here, I mean, I thought somebody had done something in the bar, that I didn't know about. You know, raped somebody out back in the parking lot, or felt somebody up in the rest room. I thought I was gonna get sued."

THEY LEFT HIM standing at the end of the bar next to his calculator and spiral notebook, and headed out.

"Well, that was weird," Lucas said, as they stood blinking in the sunshine.

"I think we are not through with Mr. Spivak," Nadya said, looking up at him.

"You guys, uh . . ." Reasons smiled, turned his hands palms up. "I missed something, right?"

"Unless he asked you while I was in the Setters," Nadya said. To Lucas: "Did he ask you what the Russian had done?"

Lucas shook his head. "No. He never did."

"Maybe he was, em, reticent," Nadya said. "But I think not."

"I think not also," Lucas said.

"Well, if you both think not, then I think not," Reasons said. He looked back at the bar door. "Want to go ask him why he didn't ask?"

"Leave it for a while," Lucas said. "Let's go talk to the rest of the employees. Maybe there'll be something else."

SPIVAK HAD GIVEN them a list of four employees who'd worked that night. They spent two hours tracking them down, and eventually found all four—three of them working at their day jobs, a fourth at home. The first three didn't work the back room, didn't specifically remember the group. The fourth one remembered.

Maisy Reynolds lived in a single-wide trailer on a country lot, what Lucas thought was probably forty acres, ten miles outside of Virginia. The lot had been cut over perhaps ten years earlier, and now showed a few fir trees spotted through new-growth aspen on the rim of the lot. The trailer sat on a concrete foundation a hundred feet back from the road; behind it was a twenty- or thirty-acre pasture with a marshy creek running along the back edge. A metal stable stood behind the trailer; a white plastic fence, made to look like a white board fence, surrounded the stable and part of the pasture. Three horses were grazing the pasture. "Horses don't like me," Reasons said.

"Do you think that could be a question of character?" Nadya asked. She was teasing him again, Lucas thought.

THE STOOP OUTSIDE the trailer door was simply four concrete blocks set in the ground. Lucas stepped up on them, knocked, and then stepped back when he heard somebody inside coming toward the door. Reynolds, a fortyish, weathered blonde in a plaid shirt, jeans, and green gum boots, opened the inside door and looked out at them.

"You don't *look* like Witnesses," she said. She was chewing on a carrot and her house smelled, pleasantly enough, of Campbell's Cream of Mushroom Soup, horse shit, and straw.

Lucas showed her his ID, told her what they wanted, and she said, "I remember the people in the back, but I don't know what they were talking about. I don't remember a Russian. What'd they do?"

"The Russian was killed down in Duluth," Lucas said. "We're trying to figure out what he did earlier in the day that might have caused . . . something to happen."

She was wide-eyed, and poked the carrot at Lucas: "I remember that from the paper. That was the guy? The paper said he was executed."

"That's the guy," Reasons said.

"My lord," she said. "I didn't see anything that would have led to *that*. You want a carrot? No? There weren't any arguments or anything, just a bunch of guys talking . . ."

"The people in the group," Nadya said. "Anything . . . ?"

Reynolds stepped outside, onto the stoop, thinking about it, crunching the carrot. "I remember one guy was really old. I mean, really old. Ninety. Jeez—maybe a hundred. He got around okay . . . I don't remember the Russian. I wasn't waiting on them, Anton was."

"Mr. Spivak?" Reasons asked. "Anthony?"

"Anton. Not Anthony. Yeah, he took care of them. Must've been special, he doesn't wait on people. Have you talked to him?"

"Did he know them?"

She paused, then said, "Listen, I don't want to get in trouble with Anton, I sorta need the job."

"All this is confidential," Lucas said.

Out in the field, a horse whinnied, and took off in a little romp, followed by a second one. Reynolds smiled, nodding at them, then turned back to Lucas, still a bit wary. "I only saw them together for a couple of minutes, but he was talking with them. I don't know if he knew them, but they were talking along. What'd he tell you?"

"He said they were just some people passing through, they came, they drank, they paid, and they left. He said he had no idea who they were."

"Hmmm," she said. Her eyes clicked to the left and she tilted her head, as if listening to music. Then, "Maybe I got the wrong impression."

"But you don't think so."

"Listen . . ."

"The guy was *executed*," Lucas said. He looked up at her, on the stoop.

She pursed her lips, tilted her head, and then said, "I got the impression that Anton knew them better than that."

"A lot better?"

"Better," she said. "Yeah. Better."

THEY TALKED FOR a few more minutes, but Reynolds had nothing specific about the group. In the car again, Reasons said, "So we go and talk to Spivak again."

From the backseat, Nadya said, "Perhaps we should wait one day. If I can get to my room, I can do some research, to see if we know him. You could do some research also."

Reasons exhaled thoughtfully, then said to Lucas, "Between you, me, and the FBI guys, we oughta be able to put a book together. If the guy was in the army, if he was ever in trouble anywhere . . ."

Lucas was waiting for a car to pass, and then pulled out onto the road; in his rearview mirror he saw Reynolds go back inside her trailer, and hoped she wouldn't call Spivak. Before they left, she'd said she wouldn't.

"I'm a little worried about the Wheaton thing," he said. "It's not a sure thing that they're connected, but it feels like a sure thing."

"They *are* connected," Nadya said. "This killing of the old woman, this wire, this is a military technique. Very well known in the Spetsnaz, in the U.S. Special Forces, in the Special Air Service, et cetera. It does not seem to me something you would find with ordinary criminals."

"I wondered about that," Lucas said. "I saw it in the movies . . ." He turned, his arm on the back of the seat. "You think a Russian did it?"

She looked out the window, then back and said, "No. I am almost certain."

"Why?"

"Because the only reason to kill the old woman would be to silence her as a witness. The only reason to silence her would be to prevent her identification of the killer. The only way she could identify the killer is if he's still here. If a Russian had done the killing, already he would be exfiltrated and this identification would not be a problem."

A tidy line of logic. "I knew that," Reasons said.

"So we do research," Lucas said.

THEY DID RESEARCH.

Nadya worked from her room, Lucas and Reasons from the detective bureau.

Spivak had been arrested twice for drunken driving, once in 1960 and once in 1961. He had been in two automobile accidents, fifteen years apart, and hadn't been charged in either. He'd been sued twice in accidents involving people who had been drinking at his bar, lost one and had the suit paid by his insurance company. He'd been sued twice more for nonpayment of suppliers' bills, although a law clerk who pulled the records at the St. Louis County Courthouse said that both times, Spivak had had a countercomplaint against the supplier, and both suits had eventually been settled.

He'd been born in St. Louis County, in 1944; his wife was also from St. Louis County, born in 1945. Spivak's father had owned the bar before him. His father and mother had both been born in Mahnomen County, his father in 1912 and his mother in 1914; Mahnomen didn't have a regular vital-records registration at the time, and the birth certificates came from a Catholic hospital, which had since burned down.

Spivak had served with the Eighth U.S. Army in peacetime Korea, from 1962 to 1964. He had been honorably discharged, though he'd received two article fifteens—administrative punishment—for drunkenness. He'd had money withheld from his paycheck in both cases, as fines.

"Ain't shit," Reasons said, when they were done. "Nothing with NCIC, nothing with the sheriff. He did a little tearing around when he was a kid, went in the army, got out, got married and had kids, and runs a bar."

"Maybe Nadya got something . . ."

She hadn't: "We can't even find his phone number," she said. She was sitting in a high-backed chair looking at her laptop. Out the window, they could see a sailboat heading north into the lake. "He is delisted."

"Unlisted," said Reasons.

"We need phone books in Russia," she said. "Your phone books are outstanding in the whole world. Your Yellow Pages. I would cry to have Yellow Pages like this in Russia."

Was she doing a tap dance, Lucas wondered, watching her eyes, or was this all there was? "So tomorrow, we go push on Spivak."

THEY'D BEEN TOGETHER all day, and nobody mentioned dinner. After they agreed to meet in the morning, Lucas took the elevator down to his room, said good-bye to Reasons, and called home and talked to Weather and Sam.

Weather said that the new garage door matched the other two perfectly, and that if he looked on page two of the *Pioneer Press*, he would see that the governor's daughter's boyfriend had been arrested for possession of a controlled substance after a party the two of them attended together, and there was a rumor around the university that the kid was taking the fall for the girl.

"Probably wind up as the highway commissioner," Lucas said.

"I just don't want you to get involved. I don't want you to have anything to do with it," Weather said. "I don't want you fixing anything."

He promised he wouldn't.

AFTER HE GOT off the phone, he went down to the lobby, bought both the St. Paul and Minneapolis newspapers, rode back up, and read them as he watched the evening news. Then, restless, he called Nadya's room to see if she wanted to get a bite. No answer.

He cleaned up a bit, went back down, drove out to the mall, and spent an hour browsing through a bookstore, and then, with a half dozen magazines under his arm, did a walk around to see what was in the place, crossed the highway to an outdoor-sports shop, where he looked at guns and fishing equipment, and finally headed back to the hotel.

He was suffering from the nothing-to-do, out-of-town blues. If there was nothing from Spivak the next day, he thought, and nothing obvious to do in the afternoon, he might zip back home for dinner. He could be back in two hours . . .

HE WAS WATCHING a *Seinfeld* rerun and reading a *Gray's Sporting Journal* when his cell phone buzzed at him:

"Lucas?" A male voice, hushed but intense.

"Yeah?"

"Listen, man, there's something weird going on here, and I don't know what the fuck to do," the words tumbling over each other. "I'm watching the guy's car, waiting for the bar to close, and it closes but he doesn't come out. All the lights go out except one in the back, and nothing's moving. So I get a plastic garbage can and I carry it over to the window and I stand on it and peek in, and the guy is standing on a six-pack of beer, bottles, with a rope around his neck and there's somebody in there with him. The guy's legs are shaking like crazy but the place has got a big fucking metal door on the back and there's no way I can kick it and if I go in through the front it'll be too late and I don't have a gun, it's back in my car . . ."

"You mean right now?" Lucas asked.

"I mean right fuckin' now. I'm still standing on this fuckin' trash can and I can see the guy standing there."

"Don't move," Lucas said. "Just hang on, I'm going on the other phone."

He had no phone numbers. He dialed 911 and when the operator came up, said, trying to remain calm and authoritative, "I'm Lucas Davenport. I'm an agent with the Bureau of Criminal Apprehension. I've got an emergency up in Virginia, and I need the telephone number of the Virginia cops right now . . ."

The operator said, "Please slow down, sir. You need the emergency number for Virginia? Can you describe the nature . . . ?"

"Give me the fuckin' number," Lucas shouted. "The emergency number for Virginia . . ."

The woman tried to calm him again and he shouted her down and she transferred him to a supervisor, while, in his other ear, the male voice was saying, "What's going on, man? You got something coming?" and then the supervisor came up and said, "Can I help you?"

In the end, he thought, it took him only a minute to get through to the Virginia cops: "I am an agent with the Minnesota Bureau of Criminal Apprehension, my name is Lucas Davenport. Anthony Spivak at Spivak's Bar is being hanged in the back room of the bar and you have to get a couple of cars there RIGHT NOW."

"Sir, tell me again who you are . . ."

The cops got something going, and ten seconds later, in the cell phone, the male voice said, "He's out, there's a guy out the back and let me see, ah holy, I'm running . . ." Then the voice went away, but Lucas could hear a clunking, wrestling sound, and the male voice shouting something, then the cell phone apparently hit the floor, and Lucas got back on the other phone and shouted, "I've got a man in the bar, I've got a man in the bar, be careful with him, he's not armed, he's my man."

The cell phone went out. Lucas dialed it, but got no answer. On the hotel phone, he shouted at the Virginia cop, "What's going on? I've lost my guy."

"We're on the scene now, sir. Can you tell me your location? You said your name is Louis?"

"Lucas Davenport. I'm in Duluth." He was trying to shout calmly. "I will be there in one hour. Call Rose Marie Roux, the commissioner of Public Safety. I will give you her home phone number and she will fill you in. I will be on my cell phone on the way up—here's the number . . ."

WHEN HE WAS off the phone, he tried his man's cell phone again, got nothing. He thought about calling Nadya, decided against it, didn't have time to pick up Reasons. He'd call him from the road. He clipped on his .45, picked up a jacket, and was at the door when the phone rang. "Shit." He went back, picked it up.

A woman's high-pitched voice asked, "Is this Lucas Davenport?"

"Yes. What is it?" He assumed it was the front desk, and he had no time for it.

"Mary Wheaton, the lady who was murdered . . . she told me about it. She told me she saw the other man murder the Russian man, the story that was in the newspaper."

The words confused him for a moment: *Who the hell was this, and why was she bothering him?* "What?"

"She saw the murder of the Russian man. She told me about it, and I thought I should call."

"Who is this?" A crank, he thought—but then, maybe not. *There had been a second woman.*

"I'm not going to tell you. For one thing, you sound mean."

"I'm in a hurry," Lucas said. "Just tell me what she told you."

"You *really* sound mean . . ."

The woman was frightened and, Lucas thought, he *did* sound mean. He took a breath, and said, "I'm sorry. You caught me at a really bad moment. What did Mrs. Wheaton tell you?"

"She said she was down by the grain elevators, in some weeds, right by the lake. Watching the lake. She was drinking, she had a bottle, and she heard a man walking toward her so she stayed hidden. The men down there can be really tough. So she was hiding down there in the weeds, and she heard some shots. She thought they were shots, but they were quiet . . ."

"She was probably right, the gun may have had a sound suppressor on it," Lucas said, as softly as he could, trying to be agreeable. He was still burning off the adrenaline from the cell-phone call. "What did she see?"

"She said one man shot the other man, and she made a noise. When she made the noise, the man with the gun saw her, and she ran away, and he chased her. She thinks he shot his gun at her and missed, and then she fell down and he caught her, and he pointed his gun and tried to shoot her, but the gun didn't work. She had a knife and she slashed at him because she was afraid that he might try to strangle her or something. He ran away and got in his car and drove off."

"Where was his car?"

There was a second of calculation, Lucas thought, and then: "She said it was over by the street, over by the Goodwill store."

"Do you know what she was drinking? What kind of bottle it was?"

More calculation: "No, she didn't say, but I imagine it was an inexpensive wine. She didn't drink so much hard liquor."

"I didn't even know she drank," Lucas said. "I thought she was more of a schizophrenic. I didn't think she had an alcohol problem."

"Oh, she drank," the woman said. "Wine, mostly. Sometimes, when she was on her meds, it made her crazy. Crazier."

"Did she tell you what the man looked like? The man with the gun?"

"He looked like a college boy, but he might have been older than that. It was dark, and she couldn't see him that well. He was blond and not really tall, but a little tall. Six feet. Strong-looking. She thought he was an American because before she cut him, he said, 'Shit,' in English, just like an American would."

"She cut him," Lucas said. "Was she sure?"

"Pretty sure. Not positive."

"Blond, strong, American. You didn't see the car, see what make it was?"

"No, uh, she didn't say anything about that."

"Anything that you can think of that she said, that might be of more use? Anything about the guy? It's really important, because he's still out there and we think he's nuts."

"She didn't say too much . . . just that thing about how the shots weren't too loud."

"Did she say what she took off the body?"

"Nothing like that," the woman said, and Lucas heard the lie in her voice.

"How did you find me?"

"I thought about where a state policeman would stay in Duluth, and called, and they switched me up to your room."

Smart enough, Lucas thought. He took the shot: "Listen, miss. We know that Mary Wheaton was killed by mistake. We know there was another woman down there. I mean, we know it was *you*. We would really like to talk to you. For your own protection. We found the place you were staying . . ."

She said, frightened, "I'm going to hang up now."

"No, no, no, wait, wait, wait. Tell me one thing. Please. Did you—did she—shit, however you want to say it, did somebody recover a computer from the dead man? And what happened to it? It could be critical."

Another pause, then: "She gave it to me. She was afraid to sell it in Duluth, because it was full of Russian. So I took it down to Minneapolis and I sold it. I needed money to get back to Los Angeles."

"Who did you sell it to?"

"A man, a young man, a student, maybe, at the university."

"What'd you do, just walk around asking people? Did you have a contact?"

"I had a contact. This is a man who . . . buys things."

"Okay. Tell me this, then. Please. I'm really not mean, I'm just anxious, I don't want you to hang up before I can ask these questions . . ."

"You sound mean," she said again. She said, "I'm outa here. I'm going to LA. Don't bother to look for me."

"I'm sorry, I'm sorry," Lucas said urgently. "Tell me, this young man, do you have a name? Can you tell me what he looks like?"

"His name is George. He is blond and he's good-looking. He has a square jaw and blue eyes and a short haircut; he puts gel in his hair. He was wearing one of those football jackets, you know, the kind that is wool with leather sleeves, red wool with white leather sleeves."

"When did you sell the computer? How long has he had it?"

"Two days . . . I sold it to him the night before last."

"Where?"

"At Moos Tower, the medical building. There's a cafeteria in the basement. He had a table. There are two or three guys who buy stuff there. Stolen stuff. In Moos Tower."

"Can you . . . ?"

"I'm going to hang up now. I'm afraid you're tracing this call."

"No, no, please . . ."

But she was gone. And maybe, he thought, to LA, where they'd never find her.

"AH, BOY . . ."

Hoping she'd call back, Lucas left the room phone open, got on his cell phone and called the duty man at BCA offices in St. Paul. "The call would have gone into the main desk, and they transferred it up to my room: see if you can pin it down. Where it came from—we need the number."

Then he made another call, and a woman answered. "Marcy? Lucas."

She was happy to hear from him. "Hey, man, you haven't called for weeks. What's going on?"

Lieutenant Marcy Sherrill was head of the Intelligence Unit for the Minneapolis police, and a protégé. He sketched in quickly what had happened, and said, "So I've got a problem. Is there any chance that you could put somebody over at the U, and see if you can figure out who this guy is? I'll come down and get him, but I need to get something started."

"I'll put somebody over there right now—it's a little late, there may not be too many people to talk to, but I can have somebody there in twenty minutes."

"Thanks, sweetie. How's the love life?"

"We gotta talk. Do you know Don Cary?"

"Yeah—but he was married the last time I checked." Lucas looked at his watch. Time was running . . .

"Not anymore," Marcy said. "His wife, you know, was a computer freak. She said, 'Fuck Minnesota,' and took off for California. He wasn't invited. The divorce was final last week."

"You might be moving on him a little too quick."

"Actually, he started mooning around here two months ago, and we've gone out for a lunch a few times. He was pretty much over her before she left . . . The marriage had been in trouble since about week one. He'd like to have a kid or two."

"He's a pretty good guy, for a lawyer. He plays a mean game of lawyer-league basketball," Lucas said. "Marcy, we gotta talk, and I gotta run, right now. I gotta."

"Keep your ass down; I'll get back."

He hung up, looked at the phone for five seconds, ten seconds, willing a call from the witness woman. Nothing; he tossed his keys up in the air, caught them, and took off, listening for the ring of the telephone until the door banged shut behind him.

9

LUCAS KEPT A police flasher in the back of the truck, spent the ten seconds necessary to stick it to the roof of the car and plug it into the cigarette lighter, and took off, running at speed up the hill, through a couple of red lights, and out the back side of Duluth toward Virginia. As soon as he got free of traffic, he called Reasons, but got his wife.

"He is not here just now," she said, in an accent much like Nadya's. "He has a cell phone . . ."

Lucas took the number and redialed. Reasons came up after three rings, and Lucas said, "We got a problem, man."

He explained, and when he was done, Reasons said, "You want me to come?"

"I don't know what you'd do. The place is overrun by cops already, but I thought you oughta know."

"Jesus, I oughta come." Reasons sounded anxious. "But my wife . . . she's been giving me some shit about being gone all the time, and I was just on my way home."

"Go home then. I'll fill you in tomorrow."

"Thanks. If *anything* more comes up, let me know."

LUCAS FUMBLED AROUND in his pocket, found the numbers he'd scribbled down for the Virginia cops, and dialed in again. As he did, he looked down at the speedometer: he was pushing the car along at ninety-five, and the car didn't like it. The Virginia cops came up and Lucas identified himself: "What happened at Spivak's? Is my guy okay?"

"I'm sorry, sir, but I can't release any information on that," the woman said. Her voice was cool, almost bored. "It's an ongoing incident. If you could call back in an hour . . ."

"Jesus Christ, was anybody hurt? I'm with the fuckin' BCA." He was talking too loud again.

"Sir, this is being recorded . . ."

"Go ahead and record it, you moron!" he shouted. "I'm trying to find out if my guy is okay. What'd you do, shoot him?"

"Sir . . ."

He hung up, tried his man's phone, and got an answering-machine recording. He dialed Rose Marie Roux at her home in Minneapolis, was told by her husband that she was at a concert with a girlfriend. "Aaron Copland, the cowboy shit. I took a pass."

Frustrated, Lucas dropped the phone on the passenger seat and concentrated on driving. But he couldn't stand it, and ten minutes later, he picked up the phone and called Virginia again. Same woman: "Sir, I've reported this incident to my supervisor. I cannot give you any information . . ."

. . .

LUCAS CLICKED OFF and pushed the car until it wouldn't push anymore, and instead, whimpered with the wind and tire noise. The side of the highway, for all practical purposes, was empty, the houses a half mile apart, and he was flying through a tunnel carved out by his not-especially-bright headlights. He got off at the first Virginia exit, throttled back to sixty as he went through town and still squealed his tires on the turn onto the main drag.

Two cop cars were parked outside Spivak's, light bars turning, a cop standing next to one of them. A silver civilian car was double-parked beside the cop cars. Probably another city car, Lucas thought. He dumped the Acura across the street from the bar, killed the engine, and headed for the bar entrance at a trot.

A cop was writing on a clipboard, using his car hood as a desktop. When Lucas started across the street, he looked up and called, "Whoa, whoa, whoa, where you goin' there?" and Lucas held up his ID and said, "BCA—you got one of my guys." He was at the door and the cop yelled, "Hey, wait a minute, buddy," and then Lucas was inside, moving through the bar into the back. The cop was behind him, and yelled, "Hey! Hey!"

Then Lucas was through the bar and past Setters and Pointers and into the back, into the party room where they'd interviewed Spivak. Three uniformed cops and two guys in civilian clothes were talking. Lucas's man, Micky Andreno, was perched on a chair to the side, legs crossed, hands cuffed. "You all right?" Lucas asked.

"I'm annoyed, not hurt," Andreno said. "But I'm *very* annoyed."

The cop who'd followed Lucas in said, "Hey, when I'm talking to you . . ."

Lucas pointed his finger at him and snarled, "Shut the fuck up. Who's running this clown factory?"

One of the men in plainclothes snapped, "I am. Who the fuck are you?"

"Who the fuck are you?"

"John Terry, I'm the chief."

"I'm a BCA agent, I work for the governor, and I'm running a double-murder investigation that was almost a triple murder if it wasn't for my guy here, and nobody in this *fuckin'* humpty police department would tell me what the hell was going on and now I find my guy all chained up and let me ask you—you caught the guy who went running out of here, right? The double murderer who went running out of here because you put the call on your fuckin' unscrambled police frequency . . ." His voice was rising and he could feel the blood in his forehead.

Andreno said, "Tell 'em, brother," which didn't help, and added, "They didn't catch him—they didn't even chase him. A guy went outside and looked around with a fuckin' flashlight."

"That's not fuckin' true," said Terry. He was a weathered sixty, maybe, with a red drinker's face and a pushed-in nose. "We've got a team looking for him."

"Yeah, *now,*" Andreno said. "By now the guy's down in the fuckin' Twin Cities shootin' pool and playing with his girlfriend's tits."

"Who the fuck are you?" Terry demanded. "You got no ID, you got no badge, you got no car, who the fuck do you think you are?"

"I'm under fuckin' cover," Andreno shouted at him. "Maybe you heard of that? And I gotta car. I just didn't want you in it."

One of the cops, trying to be reasonable, said, "The call was on the command channel . . ."

Lucas took a step back and put up his hands, palms out, as if pushing away from them. "All right, all right: let's start over. Okay? Let's start over. And let's take the cuffs off my guy, here, okay? Okay? Let's take the cuffs off."

. . .

THEY MOVED OUT to the front of the bar. One of the cops went around behind the bar and put together some Cokes and ice, and Lucas told Terry about the investigation.

". . . I got this spy here, this Russian, and we think she's got somebody working with her. So after we come up with Spivak, she says, 'Well, let's do Spivak tomorrow, after we do the paperwork.' I think, I wonder why that is? Why don't we do him today? But I go along with it, because I already called Micky in. I tell Micky to keep an eye on Spivak, just in case. So he stakes out the place, and Spivak never comes out after the place closes. Micky starts to worry about it, so he stands up on the garbage can in back and peeks into the back room . . ."

"I see Spivak standing on two six-packs of whatever . . ."

"Bud Light," Terry said.

"Whatever," Andreno said. "His knees are shaking like crazy, he's about to hang himself, and I call Lucas. I'm standing in the back, still on the phone, and I hear Lucas talking to you, and the next thing I know, the back door bangs open and this guy comes outa there like a rocket ship. I go running after him but as I go past the door I see Spivak hanging by the neck, so I gotta stop and run inside and try to lift him up by the legs so he don't strangle, and then your guys got there. About an hour later."

"Two fuckin' minutes," one of the uniformed cops said. "And we looked for the guy. We knocked on doors down there to see if anybody saw anybody tearing out of there in a hurry, or anything."

"Nobody saw anything," said another cop.

"What pisses me off," Andreno said, "Is that when your guys got here, one of them points his pistol at me and says, 'Okay, drop him,' and Spivak is going *aaagggaaaaaaghh.*"

They all looked at him for a moment and then Lucas started to laugh, and then another cop started and then the second one, and the chief rubbed his forehead and said, "Ah, for Christ's sakes."

SPIVAK WAS AT the medical center with rope burns around his neck and on his face where the rope had cut against it. He had pulled muscles in his neck and back, and had a damaged larynx. He could talk—croak—but just barely, said the cops who'd brought him in.

His wife, a short, broad woman who might have been Spivak's sister, was in the hallway outside the hospital room where Spivak was being treated, and when she saw them coming, she said, "John Terry, I don't want you talking to him. You go away."

She was frightened and angry. Terry said, "I'm sorry, Marsha, but we gotta talk to him. This is a murder investigation. Two people have been murdered . . ."

"He almost got hung," she wailed, and then she started to cry, "You almost got him killed . . ."

Two more people came around the corner, a man and a woman, both short and stocky, both in their late twenties or early thirties, both Spivaks, Lucas assumed. One of them said, "Ma, what's wrong. Ma? Is he okay?"

"He's okay," she sniffed. "The police say it's a murder investigation . . ." and she cracked again and wandered over to a chair and sat down. The young woman said, "John, what the heck is going on here?"

"Carol, you just go take care of your mom. We need to talk to your dad for a minute. We don't know exactly what happened yet, but we're working on it."

"Did you catch anybody?"

"Not yet. That's what we're working on. You go sit down and we'll talk to your dad for a minute and then you can come in."

. . .

SPIVAK WAS PROPPED up in a hospital bed, covered to the waist with a sheet, his neck wrapped in gauze, more gauze taped to the left side of his face, another blob stuck on his earlobe. When they walked in, he looked at Lucas and croaked, "What the hell?"

Lucas asked, "Did you recognize the guy?"

"No. Never saw him before." The words came out in spurts, as though each one hurt. "Tall guy. Black hair. Black eyes. Skinny. Big nose. Maybe forty. Black raincoat. Gloves. Waited in bar. Everybody gone. Asked him to leave. Pulled a gun. Made me tie rope up. Made me stand on beer bottles. Hung me. Had radio. Kicked out beer bottles when he heard cops was coming. Ran out back."

"American? Foreign?"

"American. I think. No accent. Shot me in ear."

"In the ear?" Andreno asked. "I saw blood, didn't hear no shot."

"Silencer. When I wouldn't stand on bottles. Shot my earlobe off. Bullet one inch from eye. Scared shit out of me."

"What did he want?" Lucas asked.

"Same as you. Wanted to know, who was in room."

"What'd you tell him?"

"Same as you. Don't know."

"You didn't know a single one of them?"

"No. Told you."

They went on for a while, but Spivak knew nothin' about nothin'.

Finally, Lucas said, "I'll tell you, Mr. Spivak, you're bullshitting us. There are already two people dead and you were almost a third. This guy is nuts, and he could come back if we don't catch him."

Spivak's eyes flicked away, and without looking back at Lucas, he shook his head.

. . .

THEY SPENT FIVE minutes with the family, but the family claimed they knew nothing about any meeting at the bar, and pushed the cops off and disappeared into Spivak's room.

The chief said, "This is really screwed up."

Lucas asked, "How well do you know Spivak?"

He shrugged: "Well—I think he moved here from somewhere else when he was a kid, so I've only known him since kindergarten. That's what, fifty-four years?"

"He's a good guy?" asked Andreno.

Terry nodded: "Yeah, he's okay. He's just a guy. He runs a bar. He can be an asshole, sometimes. Most of the time, he's okay."

"Goddamnit. The problem is, there's something going on with this spy shit, and I don't know what it is," Lucas said. "Spivak isn't talking, and he knows some shit . . ."

Terry nodded in agreement. "I saw him look away. I'll tell you what, maybe you scared him. I'll go in and bullshit with him when you're gone. Tomorrow morning, see what he has to say. We've known each other a long time."

"I'd keep an eye on him," Lucas said. "This guy out there, whoever he is—he's not fuckin' around."

"I'll get them to put him down in intensive care. That way, he'll be behind the nurses' station and there'll always be somebody right there. I'll have guys stop by, and we got an extra car, I'll park it out front."

"Good. Talk to him, then. Call me."

"Get this guy some ID," Terry said, tapping Andreno on the chest. "And tell him to watch his mouth. He wise-assed us so much some of the guys wanted to shoot him to stop the bullshit."

Andreno said, "You guys . . ." But Lucas waved him off.

"I gotta ask you a favor," Lucas said to Terry. "I'd like to put out a story—your newspaper, the TV, however—that you got a call from a passerby about something weird happening at Spivak's. Maybe somebody heard a scream. When you sent a car, you missed the bad guy, but a cop or a passerby saw Spivak hanging there and cut him down. Just have somebody else do what Micky did. Tell your guys to keep their mouths shut—tell the family that. I want to keep Micky a little secret."

"Gonna be tough. This is a small town," Terry said.

"If you jump right on the story, it oughta work. I'm not worried about rumors: I just don't want Micky on the TV news, where out-of-towners are gonna hear about him. These guys, these Russians, I don't think they have local sources. They won't hear the rumors."

"Do what I can," Terry said.

LUCAS HAD MET Micky Andreno on a case in St. Louis. Andreno had retired early from the St. Louis Police Department, had a decent pension and a part-time job at a golf course, and, in his middle-fifties, was good undercover. He looked more like an Italian grocer than a cop. Lucas had used him twice before, on minor lookout jobs.

They found an all-night diner out on the highway, got a booth in the back where they could talk, and ordered cheeseburgers. Andreno said, half laughing, "Hell of a night."

"I'm sorry about this," Lucas said. "I never thought you'd get tangled up in anything rough."

"Hey, I like it," Andreno said. "I'm having a good time. I'm just sorry I got busted so fast. I could use an ID. If I'd had an ID, it would have cooled things out a lot quicker."

"I'll get you something," Lucas said. "When did you get here?"

"Flew in at noon. Rented a van."

"Nothing going on until this?"

"Hard to tell. Must've been two hundred people in and out of the bar. Any one of them could have been talking to Spivak that I couldn't see."

"Nothing we can do about that," Lucas said.

"One thing: the guy who hanged Spivak. Spivak said tall and thin and dark haired. I don't think tall. And he didn't look especially thin, either. I don't know about the hair. I couldn't see him when he was inside and only got a quick shot when he came banging out of there. But . . ."

Lucas nodded. "Spivak is bullshitting us. About a guy who tried to hang him."

"It's a goddamn good thing I didn't go chasing this asshole, if he really had a silencer on the gun. Don't want to go running after any pro fuckin' executioners with nothing in your hand but your dick."

"You had your dick in your hand?"

The waitress came with the cheeseburgers; she had a small smile on her face, and Lucas thought she must have overheard the last question. When she was gone, Andreno said, "So. I'm headed home?" He sounded unhappy.

"No. I've got another thing for you."

"Excellent," Andreno said. He rubbed his hands together and looked around. "I like this town. This is like a town in the old country. Maybe they could use an Italian restaurant."

"They'd have to find somebody who could cook Italian food," Lucas said.

"Little wine, little checkered tablecloths, fat guy with an accordion . . ."

Lucas drifted away for a moment, then shook his head: "That fuckin' Nadya. She's fuckin' with me, Micky."

"I don't know what you're talking about, but I'd beat the shit out of her if I were you," Andreno said. "Pass the ketchup."

. . .

THOUGH IT WAS late when Lucas got back in his truck, he decided to call Andy Harmon, the FBI counterintelligence contact. Once clear of Virginia, on the highway, he found Harmon's cell-phone number in his address book. Harmon answered on the first ring, in a quiet, wide-awake voice: "Harmon."

"This is Davenport. You awake?"

"Yes."

"Are you always awake?"

"No."

"Good. I'd hate to think you went around sleepy all the time."

"Is this about something, or did you just call to chat?"

Lucas told him—the hanging of Spivak and the call from the un-known woman. He didn't mention Andreno. When he was done, Har-mon whistled: "This is turning into something."

"The big question is, do I confront Nadya? She must've sicced this hangman on Spivak. Unless it was Reasons, but I don't see Reasons being involved in any of this."

"He has a Russian wife."

"That crossed my mind, but I'll tell you: I don't believe it. From what Reasons has said, she was one of those people who got out of Russia when the getting was good. She worked for an optician in Rus-sia, and she works for an optician here."

"So it's just a coincidence . . ." Harmon said it with a brooding tone, doubt right on the surface.

"Hey, it's your call. I'm not going to spend any time with it, but if you want to check Reasons out, be my guest. My main thing is Nadya. I feel it in my bones, she set this thing up with Spivak."

"Let me make some calls. I'll talk to you in the morning. Don't do anything before then."

"What time in the morning?"

"I'll call you before nine."

"All right. But listen, Andy: people are being killed. I don't much give a shit about spies or anything you guys deal with, but I get a little pissed when people are being murdered and I can't stop it. So . . . come up with something. Or I will."

"Take it easy, okay? Take it easy. I'll call before nine o'clock."

10

SVOBODA'S BAKERY IN downtown Hibbing had a U-shaped glassed-in counter with the cash register at the bottom of the U. If a customer wanted bread, which was kept in the case to the left of the cash register, he had to walk between fifteen running feet of glazed, frosted, powdered, and jelly doughnuts, cherry, apple, and blueberry popovers, poppy-seed kolaches, six kinds of Danish including prune, apple, and apricot, and a variety of strudels, cakes, jelly rolls, and cookies.

Two small bathroom-style exhaust fans, mounted in the corners of the wall behind the cash register, blew odors from the ovens into the sales space, a mixture of yeast, dough, spice, and just a touch of sea salt. Few customers made it back to the street without a load of extra calories.

LEON WITOLD AND his wife, Wanda, arrived two minutes after the bakery opened at six in the morning. Karen Svoboda, the stay-at-home daughter, was standing at the cash register and tipped her head toward the back. The Witolds nodded at her and went on past the cash register, through the preparation and oven rooms, down a short corridor past the single rest room to a small employees' lounge. The lounge was a cube with yellowed walls and a flaking ceiling, furnished with three tippy plastic-topped tables, a dozen folding chairs from Wal-Mart, and an E-Z clean vinyl floor. The room smelled of cigarette smoke, disinfectant, and warm cookies.

Rick Svoboda, a round-faced man with steel gray hair, was pushing chairs around. When the Witolds walked in, he said, his eyes downcast, worried, "Hi, guys."

"You know what it's about?" Leon Witold asked. Leon was an accountant, a tall, thin-lipped, thin-faced man with overgrown eyebrows.

"Something serious," Svoboda said. "Marsha Spivak called last night and said Anton was in the hospital. Somebody tried to hang him—and she thinks it's the Russians."

"Oh my God," Wanda said. The blood had drained from her narrow face, and she pushed a knuckle against her teeth. "Hanged him?" she breathed.

"He's not dead, but the cops are all over the place," said Svoboda. There were footsteps in the hallway outside, and Grandpa Walther was in the doorway, ancient, shaking a little, his eyes blue as the sky. Then Grandma appeared, in a wheelchair pushed by their grandson, Carl.

Svoboda looked at Carl and then Grandpa, who said, "He's been in for five years. I've been teaching him for more than twelve."

"Aw, boy. Does Jan know?" Svoboda kept his eyes on Carl, who looked back with the flat stare of a garter snake.

"No. She turns her back on us, so we tell her nothing," Grandpa said.

"Carl's *her* kid," Svoboda said.

"I'm in," Carl said. "I don't care what Mom thinks."

"I'm not sure what the others will say," Leon Witold said.

"It doesn't matter what they say," Grandpa said. His voice had an edge of the Stalin steel. "He is in. He knows our story. He knows enough to send every one of us to prison. Some of us were younger than he is, when we got in. He's our future, and he's in."

Svoboda rubbed his face. "Oh, brother. I thought it would stop with us."

"Never stop," Grandpa said. "We have a duty."

MORE PEOPLE: Marsha Spivak, Anton's wife, a heavyset woman with a hound-dog face, a babushka over her hair, the woman who raised the alarm.

"Good to see you, good to see you," she said. "My Anton is terrible hurt, terrible hurt . . ." She'd been born in the United States, but somehow managed a middle-European accent. She'd been to church already, not to Mass, just inside the door to dab her forehead with holy water and to say a prayer for Anton. She was a Communist, all right, but of the practical sort, the just-in-case kind, who had no personal problem with Jesus.

Janet Svoboda, as round faced as her husband, blond, with a long nose that looked a little like one of her bagel sticks, came in with a pot of coffee and a tray of doughnuts. "Karen will stay at the counter," she said. "What else can I get for everybody?"

Marsha Spivak sat heavily in a folding chair, dabbed at her face, took a jelly doughnut and said, "Maybe a little milk to wash down the doughnuts?"

"Oh, sure," and Janet darted away to get a carton of milk.

Bob and Carol Spivak came in, two walking fireplugs, twin brother and sister. They both looked at Carl Walther, and then Bob stooped to kiss his mother, who burst into tears again, finished her first doughnut, and took a second.

Nancy Witold Spencer came in: "Hi, Mama." She didn't speak to her father or look at him, but he said, weakly, "Hi, Nance." She nodded, a bare acknowledgment: they'd had a financial falling-out over a loan to her dance studio.

"Everybody got a seat?" Rick asked.

Everybody had a seat; the men, in plaid cotton shirts and blue jeans, the women in jeans and pastel blouses and cardigans with the sleeves pushed up. Leon Witold, working his way through a doughnut, said, "Boy, them are good, gimme a little more of that coffee, will ya, Janet?" They were using small paper cups and she gave him a refill and he said, again, "Boy, them are good doughnuts. I gotta get down here more often."

"We could use the business," Rick Svoboda said.

"Ah, bullshit, Rick, you're richer 'n Bob Dylan." Bob Dylan had been born and raised in Hibbing, and was the local standard for obscene wealth.

"I sure wish." After arranging the chairs, Svoboda took an electronic box out of a paper sack, pulled out an antenna, and walked around checking for bugs. He didn't find any. He never had; the only thing he'd ever detected was transistor radios. "Okay, guys—Marsha called for this and she is going to tell us what happened last night."

"First things first," Leon Witold said. "I want to know about Carl, before we talk."

Grandpa Walther cleared his throat and said, "When it was time to decide, Grandma and I told him about the early days, and he was a good student. He wanted to hear. So we told him. You know Jan and Ron were breaking up, and Carl was living with us, so he began to . . . understand that something else was going on. That things were not exactly as they seemed. So, when he was far enough along, we told him: five years ago. And he is a believer. A believer on his own. A good boy. We haven't forced it on him."

Carl was nodding during this, and he said, "I made up my own mind."

They all looked at him for a moment and then Leon said, "I hope to God that's the truth, because you could hang all of us. And your mom, for that matter."

"She's not one of us," Carl said.

"But she *knows,* and anyone who knows would be in as deep as the rest of us."

"If the kid is in, he's in," said Rick Svoboda. "Can't go back now." He looked at Carl for a moment, then nodded, and turned to Marsha Spivak. "So tell us what happened with Anton."

Marsha Spivak started leaking tears again and muttered around, trying to find a start, and then she sighed and lifted her heavy head and said, "Yesterday, the police came. They knew about the meeting in the back. Anton tells me that they had a receipt from this Russian, who has so many names now that I can't keep track. Remember the Russian puts all the drinks on the American Express. So stupid. Why? Why? Why did we let him do that?"

"He wanted to put it on the card so he'd have the extra unaccountable cash to go to Wal-Mart." Svoboda said.

"But he said he had all that money . . ."

"Not his money. He had to account for it," Svoboda said. "He was chipping off a couple hundred bucks, and probably a few more here and there. The stupid thing wasn't putting it on the card—the stupid thing was keeping the receipt."

"He didn't know he was going to die," Leon Witold said. "But to get back to Anton . . ."

Marsha Spivak dabbed at her eyes: "He told them *nothing.* They went away, they knew nothing. They knew only what they had on the receipt, that the Russian paid for drinks. Anton tells them that he'd never seen anybody before, he thought they were fishermen stopping on the way to the border."

Grandpa Walther nodded. "That's reasonable, anyway."

"Of course it is." Spivak sniffed. "They went away, but then this other man came. He sat in the bar late, the last one, and when Anton says it's closing time, he says that he wants to talk, that he is from Russia. So Anton locks the door and turns out the lights and they go in the back and when Anton turns around, this man has a gun. He makes Anton throw a rope over a beam and put it around his neck, and then he makes him stand up on a six-pack of beer bottles—beer bottles! Anton says, 'No!' and the man shoots him in the ear, and Anton must stand on the beer bottles. The man wants everybody's name, but Anton, he tells him nothing. He says he knows no names. The man says he will leave him on the beer bottles. Anton says he knows no names. And then, the man has a radio and he hears the police are coming and he kicks the beer bottles out and Anton is hanging by the neck and the man goes running out, and another man comes in and lifts up Anton and then the police come and cut the rope and they take him to the hospital . . ."

She started weeping again and finally Svoboda said, "He never saw the guy with the gun before?"

"No. Never."

"It all comes back to the fuckin' Russians," Leon Witold said. "We never should have met with that guy. I hope to hell nobody here had anything to do with that murder down in Duluth." His eyes scanned across the room and stuck for a moment on Grandpa Walther.

"Don't be stupid," Nancy Witold Spencer said. "We're not operators. It must be from Russia, somehow."

"She's right," Rick Svoboda said. "There's something going on in Russia that we don't know about. The first guy didn't even know for sure who we were, how many there were, who the families were."

"He knew about *me*," Grandpa Walther said.

"You're the only one," Svoboda said. "The question is, how did this second man get to Anton? Why didn't they go back to Grandpa?"

"Maybe they will." Leon Witold said.

Marsha Spivak opened her mouth to say something, but Grandpa jumped in: "We've been thinking about this," Grandpa said, "And we do have an answer, Carl and I. There was a story in the newspaper about the Russian killed in Duluth, this accident, this . . ."

"Wasn't no accident," Leon Witold snorted.

"Whatever it was," Grandpa said impatiently. "Moshalov, Oleshev, whatever his name is, is killed. We know he did not come from an official office: he was working outside the apparat. So the apparat sends its own investigator, this Rusian policewoman. I believe she must have a shadow. The story said the state police, and the Duluth police, were cooperating with the Russian. If they went to Anton, and he told them nothing, then maybe the Russian shadow went to Anton to see if Russian interrogation might work."

"Anton tells them nothing," said Marsha Spivak.

Grandpa turned to her. "Did the police say who this other guy is, who helped Anton?"

Carol Spivak shook her head, answering for her mother. "No. They won't release his name because the crazy man is still on the loose. They say he was walking past the back of the business when the crazy man came *running* out the back, and he saw Anton hanging there, and he ran in and lifted him and then the police came."

Carl frowned: "That's sounds weird."

Grandpa Walther nodded: "We should all ask. We should all *listen*. People will be talking."

"The main problem, as I see it, is that we have cops all over the place, asking questions. Probably the FBI and the CIA, too," Rick Svoboda said. "They have Anton's name, and they must suspect something. First there's the meeting, then the Russian gets killed, then Anton gets hanged. We have to believe that they will come after him."

"He will say *nothing,*" Marsha Spivak said vehemently. Her son and daughter nodded, but Janet Svoboda said, "What if this shadow, whoever he is, catches one of you and . . . you know. What if they catch Carol, and then they call Anton and say, 'We'll cut her throat if you don't answer.' You think Anton wouldn't answer to save his daughter's life?"

They had nothing to say about that, and Carol Spivak lightly pinched her Adam's apple with two fingers, as if closing a cut.

WANDA WITOLD SAID, "The big question now is, what do we do? We have no contact with Russia, everybody was swept away. We thought it was done."

"It's not done," Grandpa insisted. "How many times do I have to tell you, the party is . . ."

"Not time to argue about that," Janet Svoboda said, cutting him off. "What do we do? Do we just sit?"

"We have no choice," Leon Witold said. "We don't know who this Russian is, and even if we did, what would we do about him? We're not operators."

"I was an operator," Grandpa said.

Leon said, with exasperation, "Grandpa, that was seventy years ago, for Christ's sake. Things have changed."

Carol Spivak said, "Why should they hurt us? Seventy years of good service for the motherland, and now things change, so we retire. So what? They can always set up another ring."

"But we're in place, and we're good at this, and they never lost a single person who they sent here," Wanda Witold said, a note of despair in her voice. "We have the shelters, we can move people in and out, we can get them down the St. Lawrence and out through the Maritimes . . . That's what they want. They'll never let go."

More silence, finally broken by the old man.

"So we talk, talk, talk, delay, delay," Grandpa said. "That's all we can do, if they come back."

THEY ARGUED SOME MORE, and came to only one conclusion: they would resume the old emergency routines. They decided they would not meet again except in the most extreme circumstances.

"I don't think they could have surveillance in place this quickly," Grandpa said, and they all looked up at the ceiling, as if for bugs. "But from now on, especially with the Spivaks, and with me, no face-to-face contact. Somebody knows us, but we don't know if they know the Witolds or the Svobodas. If the Witolds or the Svobodas need to get in touch, or we need to get in touch with them, we use cold phones and code."

Marsha Spivak dabbed at her eyes: "What's going to happen to us?" she asked Grandpa Walther.

Grandpa shook his head: "If we're careful, we should be okay. Back in the forties, and the fifties, there were some close calls, but we came through. Compared to those times, this is *nothing*. We stay calm, we deal with one fact at a time."

THEY LEFT IN ones and twos, carrying white paper bags full of doughnuts. Carl drove the Taurus station wagon. After the meeting, he felt more and more like a spy, and he watched the street with narrowed, careful eyes. Grandma rode in the passenger seat, while Grandpa sat in the back with her wheelchair. Grandma watched the street go by, and suddenly asked Grandpa, "Do you remember when we came down here to dance?"

Carl looked at her: her head was up. This was the first intelligible thing she'd said in a week.

"Every day," Grandpa said, looking out the window at storefronts. "Every day I remember: I liked the snowy nights, when we'd come down, and see the lights all along the street with the big flakes coming down. Remember that wet-wool-on-the-heating-register smell? When you'd cook your mittens to dry them out. You don't smell that anymore, everything is synthetic."

Grandma nodded, smiled, and dozed, gone again.

. . .

"WHAT'S GOING TO HAPPEN?" Carl asked after a minute.

"That's what we need to talk about," Grandpa said. "You learned something valuable today—you saw it, anyway. Groups of people have trouble deciding *anything*. They also have a tendency to panic. Sometimes, for the safety of the group, you must act in secrecy, on your own, to protect the group. You have to do it even if the group is against it, because they are too frightened or too divided. You must act! That is the thing. To act!"

"I can act," Carl said. "But I don't know what to do."

"Think," Grandpa commanded. His eyes were sparkling.

Carl thought, then said, "The only thing I can think of, is we have to . . . cauterize the wound."

Grandpa recognized the phrase—he'd used it himself, before the killings of Oleshev and Wheaton. Carl had picked it up. He was pleased.

"How do we do that?"

Carl thought again for a moment: "We could get rid of the Spivaks, all of them. Couple of problems—it'd be hard to kill four people. You'd have to do it all at once. Then, the others might figure it out. Or maybe just freak out and go to the cops. Some of them are not so . . . emotionally tough as we are."

"Good. Do you think you could do it? I mean, anyway? Handle it, technically?"

He was asking whether Carl could go through with it. "Sure. Not a problem. But I'm not sure we could control what happened afterwards."

"I'm not sure, either. Because that's so cloudy, we put it aside. The other problem is, we still don't know what's going on. I can make a phone call tonight—I might be able to find something out."

"Call who?"

"A man in Moscow. If he's still alive. He should be, he'd only be, let's see . . ." He did some quick calculation, moving his lips. ". . . about seventy. He might be able to tell us something."

"What if he can't?"

"The other possibility is that we simply sow confusion. We deliberately confuse everything, so that nobody knows what is coming from where. Except us. My Russian is still good; if we make the right phone calls, make the right threats, we could perhaps create a charade, an illusion, that this is all gang warfare."

"Boy." Carl was impressed, both by the analysis, and the fact that Grandpa could call a man in Moscow. "When would you make the call?"

Grandpa looked at his watch. "Right now. It's four o'clock in the afternoon in Moscow."

"I've got to be at school in an hour."

"That's enough time. If my friend's number doesn't work, I don't know how I'd find him."

THEY WENT OUT to a Wal-Mart, left Grandma in the car. Grandpa used a phone card from a public phone, looked at a piece of paper as he punched in a long phone number, then the card number. There was a wait, and then he blurted something in Russian, smiled at Carl, gave him a thumbs up, and then turned his back, hunched over the phone for privacy, and started talking. Carl knew no Russian; he stood with his hands in his pockets, waiting.

Grandpa was on the phone for fifteen minutes, doing a little talking, but mostly listening. When he was done, he hung up, looked at the phone for a few seconds, then turned to Carl and said, "Let's go."

On the way out, when they were clear of other customers, he said, "I love to hear the old language. You should learn to speak Russian. It's much more musical than English. A beautiful language."

"Maybe when I go to college," Carl said. "What'd the man say?"

"Bad news, I'm afraid. He says the department would do anything to find Oleshev's killer. Nobody cares about Oleshev exept Maksim Oleshev, but many people care about Maksim. There is a struggle going on in Moscow, a fight over the oil, and Maksim is a big man in the fight. Putin wants him; and Maksim wants the killer."

"That puts me in a tough spot," Carl said, grinning and wrinkling his nose.

"It's not funny," Grandpa said. "It puts all of us in a tough spot. My friend says that they would throw all of us overboard if it would make Maksim happy. Except . . . he says that they don't know exactly who we are. That is why Nadya Kalin is here."

"And we can trust him? Your friend."

Grandpa smiled and tipped his head. "Not exactly . . . trust. But. He is with the party. He is like me, he is a believer. I think he was as happy to hear from me as I was to talk to him—for him to know that there are still people out here, working."

Carl looked at his watch. "I've got to get going, get you home and get to school."

"And I've got to think," Grandpa said. "It's like a chess problem, with so many pieces. But you should be ready, because one way or another, we have to act. Don't doubt it."

"I'm ready," Carl said. "Should I come over this afternoon?"

"Yes . . . Maybe I'll have figured out something. This Kalin, and her shadow . . . they are a problem."

ON THE WAY back to Grandpa's, Grandpa said, "We need some way to communicate. Everything can be tapped, now. Cell phones, everything. We could work out a routine where you come over four or five times a day. Before school, at lunch, after school . . . but in an emergency . . ."

"Walkie-talkies," Carl said.

"What?" Grandpa focused on him.

"When I went hunting with the Wolfes last year, old man Wolfe gave us walkie-talkies," Carl said. "Everybody had one—he uses them with his construction company. You couldn't call me if I was down in Duluth . . . but around town here, you could. He said they've got a range of six or seven miles, lots of privacy channels, everything, so they'd cover the town. But they're expensive."

"How much?"

"Maybe six hundred dollars for two—I think that's what Jimmy Wolfe said. You can get them at Radio Shack."

"Get two," Grandpa said.

"Where'm I gonna . . ."

"I've got funds," Grandpa said.

"You got six hundred . . ."

"More than that. Official funds. I'll get the money, you get the radios. You'll have to show me how to work them . . ."

"Easy. Easier than a cell phone," Carl said.

"I can work a cell phone," Grandpa said. "I don't have all of it figured out, the damn thing has that terrible ring now, I pushed something wrong."

"I'll show you," Carl said.

AND JUST BEFORE Carl got out of the car, Grandpa said, "We will have to get some ammunition for the pistol."

"I know how to get it," Carl said. "I was over at Jerkin's, looking. All the pistol ammo is right behind the counter. I've got the nine millimeter spotted. If we wait 'til Jerkin's wife goes to dinner, and then we go in, and you ask him for some tire inflator, and he comes around to get it for you—I spotted that, too, it's way down at the end of automotive—I can lift it right off the shelf."

"Cameras?"

"I looked real close, didn't see any. There's a big round mirror, but it's set to show somebody at the counter what's going on in the appliance aisle. If you're over there in automotive, he won't be able to see back."

"Got it all figured out," Grandpa said.

"Figured we were gonna need some ammo, sooner or later," Carl said.

LUCAS HAD ARRANGED to meet Reasons and Nadya at nine o'clock; Harmon called back at eight o'clock, waking him out of a restless sleep.

"On Spivak, specifically, we're drawing a blank," Harmon said. "We pulled every record we could find from his army records to the credit reports and his checking account. It doesn't look like he's ever been out of the U.S. except when he was in the army. And his army record . . . he was a truck driver and sort of a fuck-up. He had almost no clearance for anything, so whatever he was doing, it wasn't espionage."

"Damnit," Lucas said. "If you could get me just one thing."

"I know. We're still looking."

"So: Should I brace Nadya, or what?"

"Your call," Harmon said. "We talked it over last night and couldn't see any reason to be subtle."

"Who's we?"

"Us guys," Harmon said.

"You said you were drawing a blank on Spivak specifically. Does that mean you're not drawing a blank on something else?"

"Yeah. We talked to some old guys, you know, from back in the fifties and sixties. There were quite a few Soviets doing hard-core espionage. Height of the Cold War, and all that. When we'd get a line on a guy, sometimes they'd figure it out and run for it. They'd fly to Chicago or Omaha and rent a car or catch a bus and then they'd disappear. The cars were usually found in Iowa, around Des Moines, or in Wisconsin, around Milwaukee. The point is, there was a big-time cell operating someplace in the upper Midwest, specifically tasked with getting their agents out of the country. We never found the cell. *Now* we see there's this longtime residential network showing up on the Iron Range, where there's this long history of radicalism, lots of eastern European immigrants, ore ships and grain ships going in and out . . . and the Canadian border's right there. It'd be a perfect spot for an exfiltration cell. Maybe that's what we've got."

"Huh. But they'd be sort of the lay-low type, right? They wouldn't get involved in murdering people."

"Depends on what the problem was. If it was a question of getting caught, I don't think murder would be off the table."

WHEN HE GOT off the phone, Lucas called BCA headquarters in St. Paul and checked with a secretary in technical services about the phone trace he'd requested the night before.

"The call came from a pay phone at Snelling and University in St. Paul," said the secretary.

"The supermarket?"

"No, it's out on the street. Outside, anyway. That's what the note says."

"Damnit." If the woman had used the supermarket phones, they might possibly get a description from a cashier or a bag boy. If the phone was on the street, finding a witness would be next to impossible. "Okay. Thanks for the check."

He called Marcy Sherrill, but her cell phone was in message mode: "Get anything on that fence? Call me—I'm on the cell phone."

REASONS WAS RUNNING LATE, and Lucas was sitting alone with Nadya in a breakfast booth. After ordering, Lucas asked her what she'd done the night before, and she said, "Shopping. There are excellent shops at this mall. Everything is cheap compared to Russia."

"You didn't talk to your shadow?"

She looked at him over her coffee cup. "Shadow?"

"You know, your shadow operative. Our FBI people said you'd have one."

She was shaking her head. "They misunderstand what is going on."

"Then why don't you tell me what's going on?"

Now she put her coffee cup down. "You are angry, and you weren't angry last night. What has happened?"

"First, tell me what's going on. What you know. Why the feds are wrong."

"The . . . feds." She worked it out. "The federals. The FBI . . . Okay. Here is what they don't understand." She leaned forward, intent now. "We don't care for two shits who killed Oleshev. We care nothing about this. Nothing. We care for one thing, that somebody take his father and Vladimir Putin and all of their friends off our backs. You have that phrase, off our backs?"

"Yes."

"So—we don't care if this murder is solved. We can't do anything, one way or the other. We have not the power. We have not the resources. We want only to get ourselves clear of the trouble. If Maksim Oleshev wants to blame your president, your FBI, your Lucas Davenport, or your Jerry Reasons for this problem . . ." She shrugged. "What is it you teach me yesterday? *Tough shit?* We don't care, as long as they go away and leave us to work. Do you understand that?"

She sounded exactly like Rose Marie Roux, Lucas thought: *Just make us look good.* He nodded, and said, "I understand what you're saying, but I don't think I believe you."

"Why is this?"

He told her what happened with Spivak. She listened, her eyes narrowing as he got into the story. He finished with, "There are only three people, Nadya, who knew that Spivak wasn't telling us what he knew— me, you, and Reasons. I didn't pull this stunt and I doubt that Reasons would have the resources, unless he's some kind of spy, too."

She thought for a moment and then said, "Well, there *are* some others . . ."

"Who?"

"Anyone Spivak talked to. If Oleshev told one of his associates that he was meeting Spivak, if Oleshev is then killed, his associates might want to know what happened. If Oleshev's killer came from Spivak."

"And he just happens to show up a few hours after we talked to him," Lucas said skeptically.

"I don't *know* what happened. If there is a shadow, I don't know it. But there are other possibilities, than a shadow for me." She stood up. "I will call now, with the e-mail. I will find out now if there is a shadow."

"And you'd tell me."

"Probably," she said. "As I say to you, I . . . we . . . don't give two shits for Oleshev. All we want to do is get clear."

As she stepped away, Lucas said, "Did you ask about the laptop?"

She stopped and turned: "I did. The captain of the *Potemkin* said Oleshev definitely had a laptop, a small silver Sony and very expensive. The man who interviewed the crew in Toronto said that some accessories . . . this is correct? Accessories?" Lucas nodded. ". . . that some accessories remain in his cabin. A CD drive with some games that plugged in with a PCMCIA card and also one of the small disk drives."

"All right. Go make your call, and then I've got another thing to talk about."

"What? Tell me now."

She came back to the booth, leaned a hip against the table, and crossed her arms as Lucas told her about the call from the woman the evening before. He concluded by saying, "She was the real witness. I'm sure of it. She put the laptop on the street."

"You can find it?"

"We're trying."

N A D Y A   W E N T   T O check with the embassy. When Reasons showed up, Lucas told him about the hassle at Spivak's, again leaving Andreno out of the equation, and about the call from the anonymous woman.

"Well, shit," Reasons said. "We've got to get more pressure out on the street. You find the laptop, we'll get a name for her. Somebody's got to know who she is."

"There's another problem for your guys," Lucas said. "There's almost no point in chasing after the Wheaton murder, if it was a mistake. You won't find any connections. There aren't any."

"Yeah." Reasons thought for a minute. Then, "I gotta talk to the boss. He's not gonna be happy."

R E A S O N S   O R D E R E D   P A N C A K E S and Lucas got a Diet Coke and a waffle, and they talked about the case and the view out toward the lake and about Nadya's ass. Nadya came back and slipped into the booth next to Lucas. She wore a very light fragrance, like apple blossoms.

She exhaled and said, "Well: they say to me that there is no shadow. But."

"But," Lucas said.

"Yes. But. But somebody else called to the embassy this morning and asked for the intelligence officer. When he got the duty officer, he asked for the shadow to be put in touch with him. This call came in twenty minutes ago." She looked from Reasons to Lucas. "This was not you?"

"Not us," Lucas said.

"What about your shadow? The FBI man you talk to—there must be one."

"I'll ask," Lucas said. He pulled his phone from his pocket. "What was his name again?"

Nadya smiled and said, "I wouldn't know that," and waved at a waitress. "But say hello for me."

LUCAS CALLED Andy Harmon again and said, "This is Davenport. I'm sitting here eating a waffle and talking to Nadya. She says hello to my shadow. She says somebody just called the Russian embassy in Washington and asked to be put in touch with Nadya's shadow. Nadya says she doesn't have one, and she wants to know if it was you guys who called the embassy. 'Cause if it wasn't, that would mean that the embassy is probably talking to the killer."

"Wasn't us," Harmon said. "It just flat wasn't us. If the embassy will give us the time the call came in, we could try to trace it."

"Just a minute," Lucas said. He turned to Nadya and said, "If the embassy can give us the time the call came in, we can trace it."

"Let me talk," she said. Lucas passed her the phone and she and Harmon talked for a minute, and she gave Harmon the name of a man at the embassy he could check with.

When she was done, Lucas took the phone back and asked, "What are the chances?"

"I don't know," Harmon said. "But we'll check it. By the way, she's lying to you about the shadow. She's got one. Be nice to find him, or identify him, anyway."

"Yeah, well . . ."

"Get back to you," Harmon said.

FOR BREAKFAST, Nadya had a bowl of strawberries with a smidgen of cream, and two cups of coffee. She was a slow eater, and they went over the case again, piece by piece, as she worked her way through the strawberries. Finally, Reasons said, "I'm gonna go talk to the boss. What are you guys doing?"

"Maybe I oughta go back to Virginia and jack up the Spivaks."

"Couldn't hurt," Reasons said.

"Then that's what I'll do," Lucas said.

NADYA WENT WITH HIM. Before they left, they both went to their rooms to check for messages, and Lucas used the break to call Andreno in Virginia. "Anything?"

"No. I just got going a couple of hours ago. Spivak's gonna be checked again this morning and then they're gonna let him out. They're gonna take him down to the police station and get a drawing of the guy who hanged him, for whatever that's worth."

"Where're you?"

"In the van across from the hospital. His son went in fifteen minutes ago, and since Spivak doesn't have a car here, I'd guess the son is picking him up."

"All right. Stay with him. I'm coming up that way with Nadya. I'm gonna jack the guy up a little. Maybe his kids, too."

LUCAS AND NADYA drove north mostly in quiet, at the start, Pink Floyd's *A Collection of Great Dance Songs* playing soft on the CD. Nadya, it turned out, was married, now separated, and had three children, two boys and a girl, one at Moscow State University, the other two in secondary school. Both her husband and her father were professors at the university—her father had, in fact, introduced her to the man who'd become her husband. Her father was a chemist, her husband did computer software research.

"I once owned a software company," Lucas told her.

Her eyebrows went up. "This is serious?"

"Sure. Davenport Simulations. We made software programs that would simulate different kinds of emergencies on police computer systems to train people to respond. You know, you have a centralized communications center, and you get two car accidents with injuries and then a shooting, all coming in at the same time, and then one of the cars you expect to send is off the air, and another one breaks down on the way to a scene, what do you do, where do you put your people? We had dozens of different scenarios. I'm out of it now, but the company still exists. I hear it's been making a bunch of money since the World Trade Center attacks. Government contracts."

"You don't look like, *mmm,* a technologist," she said. She had more questions, and Lucas found himself being thoroughly and pleasantly debriefed. When she'd finished, she said, *"Hmph."*

"Hmph, what?"

She smiled: "I would prefer to work with somebody a little stupider."

HE LAUGHED and his cell phone rang. "Yeah?"

Marcy said, "Lucas. I think we have a line on your guy. What do you want to do?"

"What do you have?"

"He's a student, majors in psychology. Name is Larry Schmidt. Twenty-four. Six years in school, hasn't graduated yet. He might be hanging around because it gives him access to his market. Handles hot electronics—mostly computer equipment and sound stuff. He's been busted twice, walked both times. He's not big, he's not small, he's just . . . profitable."

"You got enough for a warrant?"

"Absolutely. We've got three different people who name him as a fence and who tell us he sells out of his apartment."

"Get one. I can be down there . . ." He looked at his watch. "By four o'clock. I'll see you at your office."

"Do that."

NADYA SAID, "WHAT?"

"We found the guy who probably has the computer. Or had it," Lucas said.

"You will arrest him?"

"Yeah. I'm going down this afternoon."

"I will come. Maybe we should go now . . ."

Lucas said, "We're right at Virginia. We take a half hour to scare the shit out of the Spivaks, to see if that produces anything, and then we head back."

"Good," she said. "Maybe things start to move."

AT THE HOSPITAL, they were told that Spivak had already left. One of the nurses said he was apparently going to the police station. Lucas called the number he'd been given by the chief, and the duty officer said that Spivak had just left, and he thought he was headed for the bar.

The bar was open: Spivak was in the back with his son, and unhappy to see them come through the door. "What, you didn't get me killed the first time you came, so you come back," he grated. He was wearing a plastic neck collar, but his voice had improved.

"That wasn't us," Lucas said. Spivak was sitting at a table, a beer in front of him; his son had just come out of the Pointers. Lucas pulled a chair around, sat down, and faced the older man. Nadya stood, looking down at him, and his son pulled out a stool at another table. "What happened was, you took a meeting that you shouldn't have. We want to know what it was about. Are you a Russian spy? Are you selling dope? Information? What? What's going on?"

"Spy," Spivak said, recoiling. "Me. I was in the fuckin' army, I'm an American. Were you in the army? You come in here and almost get me killed by some crazy man . . ."

"Yes, yes, yes," Nadya said. "This is all very . . ." She flipped a hand, as if brushing him away. ". . . dramatic. Rehearsed. We don't need this. I think Mr. Davenport would tell you that he doesn't care about spy. What we need to know is, What did Oleshev say to you? What did he say that caused him to be killed? If you wish, we can pretend that you only overheard it."

Lucas pointed a finger at him: "You got lucky the first time, pal. Some guy walking through the alley, sees you strung up. If he hadn't been there, you'd be dead. Right now, you'd be lying in a coffin down at the funeral home. And I'll tell you: whoever killed Oleshev, he's still out there. He killed Mary Wheaton in Duluth just because he *thought* she might have seen his face. He's coming back. He's a pro, and I don't think he'll miss you twice."

"BUT I DON'T KNOW ANYTHING!" Spivak shouted. "I DON'T KNOW *ANYTHING!*"

Lucas leaned back in his chair, looking at the other man's reddened face. Nadya shook her head, looked at Lucas, and said, "He's lying. If we had him in Moscow . . ."

"Maybe we'll export him," Lucas said.

"I think you two better leave, and we should get a lawyer," the son said. "Dad, stop talking."

Lucas looked at the younger man and said, "I wasn't joking about the killer coming back. But he might figure that if your father didn't talk when he was standing on the beer bottles, that he'll never talk. He might come and get you or your sister, try to get some leverage."

The son was shaking his head: "We will be careful, and I think it's all bullshit anyway. Dad doesn't know anything. This asshole should have figured it out. If Dad knew anything, he would have told him, instead of letting himself get hanged, for Christ's sakes."

"I hope so," Lucas said. "But if I'm right, and you're wrong . . ." He looked at Nadya. "There're going to be some dead people in the Spivak family."

"Maybe all of them," Nadya said. "This man . . . perhaps you should ask your police chief to see the pictures of old Mrs. Wheaton. He nearly cut her head off, with this wire. Maybe then you'll believe."

"I don't know anything," Spivak repeated. He took a nervous hit on the beer. "Honest to God . . ."

"It's not us you're gonna have to convince," Lucas said. "You got guns? You better get some. Maybe the local cops will give you bodyguards."

Nadya shook her head, speaking to Lucas, as one sober police officer to another. "That wouldn't work. This killer, as you say, is a professional." She looked at the Spivaks, from father to son and back. "To you two, I say, and to your sister and wife, good-bye. I believe because you do not tell us what happens, some of you will be dead before I return."

They sat in silence for a moment, and then Lucas said, "Well, fuck ya. We told you."

"Good-bye," Nadya said. "I am so sad . . ."

OUTSIDE, in the street, Lucas said, "That was pretty good."

Nadya said, "Standard procedure. He will ripen in a day or two."

"If he's not dead."

"That is my worry," she said. "That I was not fooling about."

12

THEY STOPPED IN Duluth to pick up clothes, and decided to keep their rooms; they'd be gone only overnight. As they headed south, they crossed the line of a weather front coming in from the west, a thin wedge of cloud that spit rain at them for a hundred miles, and then began to dissipate as they rolled through the northern suburbs of Minneapolis and St. Paul.

On the way, Lucas called Weather and told her that they'd have an overnight guest.

"The Russian guy?" she asked.

"Not exactly."

MARCY SHERRILL AND two of her intelligence cops were waiting in a no-parking zone by a McDonald's in the Minneapolis student village called Dinkytown, just off the University of Minnesota campus.

Lucas pulled in behind them, and Sherrill got out of the unmarked car and walked back, sipping a cup of McDonald's coffee, a pretty, dark-haired woman who liked to fight.

"Where're we going?" Lucas asked, rolling his window down.

"Jesus, not even a how-do-you-do," Marcy said. She stooped to look past Lucas to Nadya and said, "You must be the Russian guy."

"Yes," Nadya said. "You are the policeman?"

"Listen," Lucas said hastily, "Is this guy going to be a problem? Larry?"

Marcy switched her eyes back to Lucas and shrugged. "I don't know. I hope so. I haven't kicked anybody's ass in a long time."

"Yeah, yeah, very macho. Is he gonna be a problem?"

"No reason to think so, but he could be a runner. I've got a couple of squads ready to roll; they'll come in right behind us and cover the outside, back and front."

"What about a hammer?"

"Got one in the car."

"So let's go."

"What's happening?" Nadya asked, as they pulled away from the curb. Her face was pink, her eyes bright.

"Gonna sneak up on this guy's apartment and knock the door down. Grab him before he can run," Lucas said. And that, Lucas thought, should have been clear enough to any real cop.

LIKE STUDENT VILLAGES everywhere, Dinkytown was a collection of old retail buildings that housed overpriced student supplies and clothing, and even older residences that had been converted to overpriced apartments that were given as little maintenance as was legally possible.

Larry, the fence, lived in a crappy green shingle-sided two-story house with a sagging front porch and four rusting mailboxes nailed to the outside wall next to the door. Marcy's sources had said that there were four apartments inside, two up and two down, and that Larry rented both the upstairs apartments. There was a connecting door between the two of them with deadbolts on both sides, and the informants said Larry hoped to use one or the other as an escape route if the cops came.

They parked down the block, sideways out of sight from the apartment. Another intelligence cop wandered down the block toward them and said, "He's still inside. His girlfriend's in there with him."

"We understand he's got those fire rope things, tied to radiators, ready to go. When we kick the door, he runs into the other apartment, locks the connecting door, goes out the window," Marcy said.

"But we've got the squads," Lucas said.

"With the best on-duty runners." Sherrill reached under her coat, pulled out a Glock, checked it, reholstered it, and said, "If everybody's ready . . ." She lifted a radio to her face, got the squads, and said, "Go."

They went down the street in a rush, Nadya trailing. They were exposed to view from an upstairs window for five seconds, and then they were on the porch, still moving quietly, careful not to bang open the outer door. A student with a backpack stood on the sidewalk across the street, gaping at them.

One of the intelligence cops, wearing soft Nike running shoes, led the way up the interior stairs, gun drawn, the hammer man right behind him; the stairway smelled of old flaking wallpaper and detergent and onions and maybe the early twentieth century. Marcy followed behind the hammer, then the third intelligence guy. The rest of them came up behind, as quietly as they could. Lucas had just crossed the top stair when the hammer man hit the door lock, and with a rush, the first few were inside and one of the cops was yelling, "Wait wait wait wait," and there was another bang as a second door went down, and a woman began screaming, "Run, Larry, run." She didn't sound frightened; she sounded excited, like a bettor at a racetrack.

Then Lucas was inside and heard a male voice saying, "Take it easy, I'm not running, take it easy, man, okay, okay . . ."

Lucas followed the sound of the voices through a bedroom, where a cop was looking up at a tall, skinny, black-haired young woman standing on a bed, wearing only semitransparent underpants. She had small cupcake breasts with brown nipples, a tattoo of a dragon around her navel, and was pierced in several places by bits and pieces of metal; she was bouncing on the bed, excited, laughing, clapping her hands.

The voices were in the next room, and when Lucas went through, he found two of the intelligence cops leaning over a blond man in white Jockey shorts who lay on the floor, his hands bent behind him. One of the cops was putting on handcuffs. "Not too tight, for Christ's sakes, I play the piano," the guy said.

"Gonna be the skin flute from now on," the cop said.

"Look at this place," Marcy said, coming in behind Lucas. "We hit the fuckin' mother lode."

Dozens of laptop computers, piles of high-end audio equipment, perhaps fifty televisions, and what appeared to be hundreds of PDAs were lined up on raw pine-board shelves along the walls.

The intelligence cops lifted Larry to his feet and they all backed into the first room, where the woman was still standing on the bed. "Get down from there," Marcy said.

"You gay?" the woman asked.

"Get off the fuckin' bed," Marcy said.

"You're getting a pretty good look," the woman said. She stuck her tongue out at Marcy, then said, "Watch this." She licked her two index fingers and then twirled them over her nipples which perked right up. "Pretty good, huh?"

"You want me to get her off?" asked the intelligence cop who'd kept her on the bed. He looked like he'd enjoy it.

"Yeah, do that," the woman said to the cop. "I need somebody to get me off."

Lucas said, "Just hose her down with Mace, put the cuffs on, and throw her into the fuckin' car."

"Hey, wait a minute," the woman said, offended. "I'm coming down." To Lucas: "Jesus Christ, I was just kidding." She hopped off the bed, picked up a shirt, and pulled it over her head. As they brought Larry out of the back room, she stepped close to him and kissed him and said, "See you around in a couple years, I guess."

"Ah, fuck you," Larry said, but he laughed.

Nadya, who'd followed well behind the entry, peered first at Larry, then at the young woman, and said, "This was very interesting." To the woman, who was buttoning her shirt, "Why do you poke so many holes in yourself?"

" 'Cause it feels so creamy," the woman said.

LARRY AND THE WOMAN, both of whom were allowed to put on jeans and boots, as soon as the cops figured they were under control, were hustled down the stairs to the squads. Lucas, Marcy, and Nadya sorted through the piles of computers and came up with four Sony Vaios. Lucas lined them up on the kitchen counter and plugged them in, then brought them up, one after the other. All four were loaded with Microsoft Word; the third one showed a Cyrillic character set.

"Excellent," Nadya said. "I will translate."

Lucas shook his head, shut down the machine. "We've got our own translators," he said, grinning at her. "They'll save you the trouble."

"You see," she said, seriously, "you do not trust me."

LUCAS CALLED ANDY HARMON, who said he was in Duluth, and who was intrigued by the computer. "Barney's gonna be happy with this. Good job, Davenport. Where are you going to take it?"

"The Minneapolis cops have it right now. We'll put it on the search warrant return, and then you guys can pick it up."

"How soon?"

"Hour?"

"Excellent."

MARCY TOOK THE COMPUTER, left another of the intelligence cops in charge of the scene, and then, back in her car, led them a mile or so to a coffee bar where they got coffee and scones.

"Tell me everything," she said. "I read the story in the *Pioneer Press,* said you were up to your ass in spies . . ."

They talked for half an hour, about spies and Marcy's love life, catching up on old times. Then Marcy got a phone call, listened for a minute, and said, "I'm on the way. Fifteen minutes."

To Lucas: "Gotta go. That was the feds. They want the computer."

On the street, Lucas said, "Stay in touch," and Marcy stood on her tiptoes and pecked him on the lips.

BACK IN THE CAR, Nadya asked, "How long—is it permitted to ask?—since you were romantic together?"

Lucas cut his eyes at her, then smiled and said, "Pretty obvious, huh? It's been a while. Three years, four years. Only lasted a month or so."

"Your wife knows about this?"

"Yes. She wasn't my wife at the time. Weather and I had been seeing each other, then we had a big problem and stopped seeing each other—actually, she stopped seeing me—and then there was the little episode with Marcy . . . and then Weather came around again."

"You're a very busy man," Nadya said.

"Didn't seem busy," Lucas said. "I like women, and I was

lonely without one around. Now I'm married, and I have kids, and I'm happy."

"Good," she said. "I'm happy that it works. My life . . ."

She looked out the window and Lucas did a U-turn in traffic, hoping that the screeching turn would distract her, that Nadya wouldn't start some goofy rambling about her problems; listening sympathetically to one woman's problems was enough.

W E A T H E R   A N D   N A D Y A got along famously. Weather was wide-eyed at the idea of a spy in the house, although Nadya said she was not a spy but a policewoman; and Nadya seemed genuinely interested in Weather's reconstructive surgery work. Weather had dozens of photographs and computer graphics of a young girl born with a deformed head, for whom Weather was planning to construct a new eye socket.

Then Sam was brought out and fed and changed, and the two women ganged up on Lucas when Weather accused him of not doing his share of the diaper changing, and Lucas excused himself, got a beer, and parked in front of the TV to sulk. A little later, the women brought Sam in, in his walker, and let Lucas watch him as he rolled around the room pulling at upholstery and trying to eat magazines.

At dinner, the discussion focused on the upper limit of a woman's ability to have babies, and the technicalities of the problem. Weather mentioned that aging men were also to blame for prenatal problems—it wasn't just older women—and again, he felt that he was being ganged up on. When the conversation drifted from obstetrics to gynecology, and stories of postmenopausal women and their hot flashes, Lucas again moved into the TV room.

He'd returned to the kitchen for another beer, when Ellen Jansen, their housekeeper, returned; she'd been out having dinner with a new beau, and Weather asked, "Well, did he kiss you good night?"

"Jesus Christ," Lucas said. "I'm going for a walk."

At seven, Weather and Nadya left for the Megamall, and didn't make it back until ten. Nadya looked at Lucas and said, "Hooters," and laughed.

At bedtime, Weather took Nadya to the guest room and showed her how to plug her laptop into the phone jack and then came back downstairs and asked, "I'm sorry; have I been neglecting you?"

"You guys . . ." But he was mildly amused. They went around and checked doors and turned off the lights, made sure Sam was okay, both kissed him and headed down the hall to their bedroom; and then Nadya called, across the house, "Lucas, are you there?"

"Yeah . . ."

He walked back toward the guest room, Weather a step behind. Nadya came around a corner, still dressed. She held a finger up, and said, "I must tell you, I have not been completely truthful."

"What?" Lucas looked at Weather, who shook her head.

"Truthful. I have not been completely."

"What, uh . . ." Weather stepped up to Lucas and put her hand on his biceps.

"I have a shadow; this I knew."

Lucas shrugged: "So did everybody else."

"This shadow, I do not know him. He was assigned by the embassy, and he was investigating beside us. This morning, I told you, a man telephoned the embassy and asked to speak to a man in intelligence. I didn't tell you that he mentioned some . . . items . . . that told us he was genuine. He spoke in Russian. He arranged to meet the shadow this evening at the Greyhouse Bus Museum in the town of Hibbing. You know this museum?"

"Never heard of it, but it's probably the Grey*hound* Bus Museum. So what happened?"

"The shadow is missing. His cell phone rings, he doesn't answer. He *always* answers. There is a strict rule that he call back every half hour with information about destination and names and he had one of these, eh, photographic telephones, but his telephone now rings without answer and he took no photographs . . ."

"When was the last time they heard from him?" Weather asked. "The last moment?"

"Tonight, as he arrived at the bus museum. Since then, nothing."

"Let me make a call," Lucas said.

She was anxious, twisting her hands. "Could you hurry? People are very worried. This shadow has a daughter, but his wife died three years ago, and everybody is worried for this man and especially the daughter."

13

JAN WALTHER HAD honey-colored hair with a few streaks of gray, a round, pink-cheeked face, and worried green eyes. She worried about everybody and everything. She worried that her son, Carl, might be gay, or into drugs. She worried that her mother would have to go to a nursing home, and about where the money would come from. And she worried most of all that she wouldn't make the weekly nut at Mesaba Frame and Artist's Supply, her store in downtown Hibbing.

The one thing she hadn't worried about much was her sex life, for, though the men came around at regular intervals—some nice, respectable guys, too—she'd firmly pushed them away and focused on the business. If a thousand dollars didn't come through the door each week, she'd be out of it.

Now the whole sex thing was coming up again. A guy who owned a steel-fabricating business, a three-year widower with a couple of kids, had come in to get a watercolor framed—a whitetail deer standing in a forest glade, its front feet in a leaf-dappled pool. He'd chatted awhile when he came back to pick it up, and then he'd stopped a couple of times, passing by, he said, just to see how things were.

She'd known him most of her life—he was three grades ahead of her in school—so they were comfortable. He hadn't asked her out yet, but he was edging up to it, and she liked him. She even liked his kids, and she wouldn't mind, after this long hiatus, getting laid again.

Which brought her back to worrying about Carl. Bill, she thought, wouldn't be too happy about a gay stepchild, if that was the situation. On the other hand, she had no reason to think Carl was gay. Maybe he was just a little slow with girls. From what she read in the papers and saw on TV, half the girls Carl's age were already sexually active, and Carl had never been on a date. He was certainly good-looking enough to attract girls, but he had that tall, willowy, clear-complected look that she'd associated with homosexuality—TV homosexuality, anyway. And *something* sexual was going on with him; she'd been bleaching the semen stains out of his shorts since he was twelve.

SHE WAS IN that questioning mood when she saw the cut on his arm. She'd come home late—she kept the place open late two nights a week, trying to make that thousand-dollar nut—and she'd heard him in the shower. A strange time to take a shower, she thought; had he been up to something?

She unpacked a sack of groceries, then heard the pipes bang as the shower was turned off. She headed into the back hall a minute later, just as Carl came out of the bathroom in Jockey shorts, carrying his clothes. He jumped when he saw her, and shied away, and that's when she saw the cut.

"Carl," she began, then frowned. "What's that on your arm?"

"Where?"

"There on your arm. What happened?"

"Oh . . ." He hid it, slid sideways into his bedroom. "We didn't want to worry you. I was helping Grandpa wash some storm windows, and one was cracked, and it broke on me and I cut myself. It's all right now."

"Let me see . . ."

"Mom, jeez . . ." But he turned his arm.

The cut was clean, but the stitch holes were still evident. "Oh, God, Carl . . ." He didn't tell his mother about a cut like this? It made her feel like a failure.

"Mom, this is what we thought would happen," Carl said. "That you'd worry. But don't worry: it's all taken care of. It's almost healed."

"You should have told me." A little angry with him.

"You'd just worry more. You already worry too much."

She knew she did. She sighed, and changed directions. "Are you taking somebody to the homecoming dance?" *And if so, would your date be female?*

"I don't know," he said. He edged deeper into the doorway, trying to escape into his room. "I don't know who to ask."

"You've got ask somebody sooner or later. You've got to bite the bullet. Don't worry, girls are never insulted by being asked. You're so good-looking, that won't be a problem anyway, believe me. You're the age where you should start."

"Well, I thought about asking Jeanne McGovern," Carl said. "She talks to me in choir quite a bit, and her brother said nobody's ever going to ask her out because she's too smart."

Jan tapped her son on the bare chest: "That's exactly the kind of girl, uh, woman, person, you know, you should ask. Smart women are a hell of a lot more entertaining than the stupid ones."

"I'm thinking about it," Carl said. "But I've been helping Grandpa out a lot . . ."

"You're over there all the time. What's going on?"

"I don't know. We just like to talk, and Grandma's so messed up, that I feel like I oughta help Grandpa out."

"You're a good boy, Carl," Jan said. "I just want you to be happy. Do ask this Jeanne girl, okay?"

"Okay, Mom."

He eased the door shut and left her standing in the hall. After a moment, she turned away, worried that something about him was being left undone; but also relieved. He wasn't gay. Probably. She'd have to check out the McGovern girl.

CARL GOT ON the walkie-talkie. He'd worked out a routine with Grandpa, both of them a little excited about the small black radios: this was like the Resistance in World War II, calling from the Underground. He beeped him, beeped him again, listened.

Grandpa picked up—"Yes"—and Carl said, "Mom came home before I got out. Call and ask if I can come over. Tell her the car's got a flat."

"Yes." Click.

The phone rang a minute later, once, twice, and then stopped. A minute after that, his mother knocked on his door. "That was Grandpa. It's late, but he says the car's got a flat and he wants to go out early tomorrow . . ."

"I can get it," Carl said. He'd already put on the camouflage shirt. He opened the door. "I left a book over there, too, I can get that."

"Jeanne McGovern," Jan said.

"Mom . . ." But he smiled at her.

HE THOUGHT ABOUT Jeanne McGovern on the way to Grandpa's. McGovern wasn't great-looking, but she had all the necessary equipment, and Carl was attracted to the freckles scattered across her face; the freckles made her seem approachable, somehow. He thought of himself playing football, basketball, baseball, hockey, all the things he didn't play, with McGovern looking on, watching him score—would a smart girl be impressed? Did a smart girl give blow jobs?

He was still working on the question when he pulled through the alley to Grandpa's, and parked. They wouldn't be taking the Chevy.

GRANDPA WAS WEARING a dark turtleneck shirt and jeans, which looked strange on him: the turtleneck over Grandpa's withered neck, the jeans flapping around his elderly ass and matchstick legs.

"Plenty of time," he said. "He won't be there for half an hour."

"Unless he's scouting it out ahead of time."

"I think he would have already done that," Grandpa said.

They went back out to the garage, got in the Taurus, and headed north across town, out past the park, the night growing deeper and darker as they got away from the main city lights.

"You actually talked to the head of intelligence at the embassy?" Carl asked.

"Yes. They were quite . . . interested."

"What did you tell them?"

"I told them the truth—that I was working with Oleshev, that we had to coordinate, that we were running an operation approved by Moscow and what the hell were they doing in going after Spivak—that they'd given him away to the Americans."

"The truth?"

Grandpa grinned: "Maybe I fictionalized it a little bit."

"Oh, yeah. A little bit."

THE ROAD WAS narrow and bumpy, and went nowhere—there was a tourist site that overlooked one of the mine pits, but that was long closed. Nothing else was out there: they saw no cars or house lights.

"If people saw us out here, they'd wonder."

"Won't be here for long," Grandpa said. He looked at his great-grandson. "When your grandfather was still alive, he used to come up here and neck with his girlfriends."

"I think Dad and Mom did, too. I probably will, if I ever get a girl-friend; Mom's been bugging me again."

"You're a man now. You should learn about women."

"Yeah, yeah." Not a conversation he wanted to have. "I know all about the birds and the bees, Grandpa, so don't lean on me, okay?"

Grandpa laughed, and then coughed. "Where's the gun?"

"Right in the back of my pants. In the belt."

"Remember what I told you about it hanging up."

"That's why I'm wearing the shirt. I was practicing with it before Mom came home."

"There are schools for these things," Grandpa said, looking side-ways out the passenger window, into the dark, remembering. "I'm try-ing to teach you the best I can, but I'm not as sharp as I used to be."

"Grandma used to say that I'm the Imperfect Weapon," Carl said. "Remember? You said you'd make me the perfect weapon."

"You'll get better. But you have to think about it. Then you have to go practice. But thinking . . . thinking is the thing. You have to imagine all the things that can happen and prepare contingencies."

"I haven't thought of everything, but I'm trying," Carl said.

"You've been doing very well. One thing I've learned in all these years is that nothing ever goes exactly as planned. You plan, and then you adapt. You've done that." After a while: "You know what Lenin said. 'One man with a gun can control one hundred without one.' What you are learning, this is critical for your life in the underground."

A bit later, he said: "I talked to Lenin once. My father took me to . . ."

"The workers' hall near the Kremlin, and it was snowing out . . ."
The story was a familiar one.

"He said, 'You'll grow up, and you'll be a soldier like your father.'
And he slapped my father on the shoulder."

"Your father had medals on his coat . . ."

"He was buried with them. He was there at the beginning . . ."

"And that was one of the great days of your life."

"Yes, it was," Grandpa said, and a tear trickled down his cheek. He
wiped it away and said, "You'll be a soldier, too. Maybe someday, you'll
tell your grandson about driving out here with *me.*"

A MINUTE LATER: "I like the walkie-talkies. That was a stroke of
genius."

Carl smiled in the dark.

THEN THEY WERE THERE. Carl swung the car into the parking
lot, the red-white-and-blue façade of the Greyhound Bus Origin Museum lit in his headlights.

"Down to the end," Grandpa grunted.

"If the cops come, they'll look at us for sure."

"Football game. It should be getting out about now. Every cop in
town will be down there."

"Hope," Carl said.

They sat in silence for a minute or two, in the dark, and then
Grandpa said, "Do it as soon as you can be safe. Even if I seem to be
agreeing with this man. I *will* seem to be agreeing. Lenin said, 'It would
be the greatest mistake to think that concessions mean peace. Concessions are nothing but a new form of warfare.' The same here. I agree, I
agree, I agree, I talk, talk, talk, and then you act, when he begins to go
to sleep."

"Yes."

"I want you to treat me like I'm a little senile. Help me out of the car, talk me around a little bit. Sit here, Grandpa, like that." A set of headlights flickered through the trees to the south. "He's coming. Remember, do it as soon as you can be safe. Control your fire, control the gun. And remember what he did with Anton. He'll have a gun of his own."

"Should we have some sort of signal, in case you want to call it off?"

Grandpa nodded. "Yes. Good thought. I'll say, 'Carl, not tonight.' If I don't say that, kill him."

THE ONCOMING CAR SLOWED, turned into the museum parking lot, hesitated, then turned toward them. The car stopped, the headlights on them for a moment, then it came on, swung out, pulled into a space about twenty feet away, stopped. The lights went out, and Carl got out of the car.

The driver's-side door on the other car opened, and a man got out. He was dressed in a black raincoat and he said, "You are . . ."

"Here to meet you," Carl said. "Anyway, my grandpa is."

"Come around the car with your hands up where I can see them." The Russian looked like a Mafia guy from television; but then, so had Oleshev.

Carl lifted his hands over his head and the other man moved closer, darkly visible in the thin security light from the museum. Carl saw that one hand hung down, long; he had the gun out. As he cleared the car, hands up, Carl said, "I'm not the one, I've got to get, uh, help Grandpa . . ."

The passenger door popped then, and Grandpa pushed it open. He croaked, "Carl? Is this the man?"

The man had moved closer and now his hand was up, at his side, the gun pointed at Grandpa's door. The car's interior light had come on when Grandpa pushed the door open, and the old man swiveled, and put his feet on the ground, his hands on his knees.

"Carl? Could you help me get up?"

"Yeah . . . Uh, he's got a gun, I think . . ."

"Of course he has a gun," Grandpa said. "Could you help me, please?"

The man was closer now, watchful, and Carl edged up the side of the car, both of his hands overhead, and he said, "I don't have any kind of a gun or anything . . ."

Grandpa tried to heave himself out of the car and stumbled, went down on the blacktop. "Ahhh . . ."

"Ah, Jesus, Grandpa."

Carl stooped to lift him; actually had to lift him, and was amazed as his great-grandfather's feathery weight. The old man might not weigh even a hundred pounds, he thought. Grandpa had him by the sleeve, steadying himself, and the other man was now only eight feet away.

"Tell me who you are," the other man said.

"I'm the man who called the embassy," Grandpa said. "I am the head of the Cherry Orchard ring."

"What? I was told that you were with Rodion Oleshev . . ."

"What'd you expect me to say? The last man you talked to, you tried to kill. We want to know what's going on—we've been working loyally for seventy years, and here you come trying to kill us."

"There hasn't been a Cherry Orchard ring since the nineteen sixties," the other man said. "We looked at the histories."

"That's one thing you're wrong about," Grandpa said. He looked at Carl. "Carl, you don't want to hear this." He pointed to the swale between the parking lot and the road. "Stand over there where you can look down the road."

"I'd like to hear it," Carl said.

"Not yet," Grandpa said. "Over there."

. . .

CARL MOVED TWENTY feet away, and Grandpa slumped back against the car. He began talking to the other man, gesturing. Carl could feel the gun pressing against his back, walked over to a curb, stood on it, then stood on his tiptoes, saw from the corner of his eye the other man glance at him, then turn back to Grandpa. Carl pulled the back of his shirt over the butt of the gun, so the butt was clear.

The other man said, "Nineteen eighty-one, we'd already lost touch with Glass Bowl." Carl could tell that he was focused on Grandpa now.

"I believe you . . ."

Carl said, "If we're going to have a long talk we should go somewhere else. Somebody's gonna come. Kids'll be coming down here to neck after the game."

"The game?" the other man said.

"Football," Grandpa said. "You probably saw the lights when you came into town."

Carl stepped toward them. "Grandpa?"

"We should talk some more," Grandpa said to the other man. He glanced toward Carl, but he never said the words. "You should know that we are not interested in Russia, per se. We are Communists, and we are proud of it, and the party will come back. When that happens, we'll be waiting."

"The party," the other man said contemptuously. "The party is . . ."

They never found out what the party was, because Carl, in one smooth motion, lifted the gun from his belt, leveled it, and fired a single shot through the back of the other man's head. The other man dropped straight down and his gun clattered on the blacktop.

"Good," Grandpa said. He smiled and rubbed his hands together. "Quick now, put him in the back. And get that gun. We'll find a place . . ."

Carl dragged the man to the back of the Taurus, popped the hatch, picked him up, and threw him inside. They took one minute to look at the other man's car: took the keys, took a briefcase, looked in the trunk. The trunk was empty. Carl scooped up the other man's gun.

"Move, move," Grandpa said.

Carl hurried around the car, got inside, pulled the door shut. "I know where there's a hole in the mine fence. We could throw him off the side. He's in a black raincoat, they might not find him, you know, for a long time."

"Good as anything, if we can get there with a car," Grandpa said.

"We can get close enough," Carl said. Grandpa was touching his own face, looking at his fingers. "What?"

"I don't know."

They were backing out, then out to the road. Carl risked flicking on the interior lights, looked at Grandpa. "Oh, Jesus, you've got blood all over your hair. Must've come out of the guy."

"I need, I need . . ." Grandpa scuffed open the center console, got out a travel pack of Kleenex, and began wiping his hair. "Just drive."

They were moving again, down the dark roads. Grandpa said, "Much farther?"

"A minute. Did he tell you anything?"

"Yes. They don't know who we are. Not our names. They only know the Spivaks, and they're not sure about them. But this Oleshev called *me*. So there must be an Oleshev group that has my name, and an official group that has the Spivaks' names."

"It wasn't possible to make a deal?"

"No. He had seen our faces, he'd seen this car, he would have seen more before he left. He no longer had to make a deal; he had the information he wanted. He had to be erased. When in doubt, erase."

Carl, nodded, eased his foot off the gas, and said, "This is close. It's right up over that hump, by the curve sign."

"I don't see anybody. We must be quick."

Carl pulled to the side, got out, popped the hatch, grabbed the other man by the back of his raincoat. He dragged him up through the bushes, the other man a dead weight, his feet bouncing over the loose rock. Once away from the car, the night was almost perfectly dark. This wouldn't work. Carl let go of the body, found his way back to the car.

Grandpa: "What?"

"Isn't there a flashlight in here?"

"Glove compartment."

Grandpa fished out a cheap plastic flashlight, tried it, got a thin, pale light. "Will this work?"

"Have to," Carl said.

"Hurry."

Carl took the flashlight, went back to the body. Took the man by the collar, dragged him to the break in the chain-link fence, then across. The Rust-Hull mine was an open-pit mine, with vertical rock walls hundreds of feet high. Carl, like most kids, knew it reasonably well; and knew he didn't want to fall in.

The flashlight worked just well enough to pick out the ground a few feet ahead, and then the downslope that led to the vertical wall of the pit. He pulled the man down the slope, braking him on the steeper parts, onto a shelf. He edged up to it, then peered over the side of the shelf with the flashlight. He could see nothing at all. Nothing but air.

He pulled the body around, ready to launch it over the edge, and as he did, the man moaned.

Carl was so startled that he dropped the man's collar, staggered backwards, and nearly went over the edge himself. "Whoa," he muttered. He took the gun out of his belt, shined the flashlight on the man's face. His eyelids flickered in the light. Carl leveled the pistol and shot the man between the eyes.

"Jesus." He should have checked to make sure the man was dead; but now, there was no question. He was dead, and in another ten seconds, he was over the edge. Carl listened for a thump, heard nothing, and scrambled back to the car.

"Done?"

"Done." Carl put on the safety belt and started the car. "You cleaned up?"

"Good as I can," Grandpa said. He looked stressed now, and even older than he usually did. "I think I got some on my shirt . . . I didn't even notice when it happened, the noise, the flash . . . it's all over me."

"Back home in five minutes."

"All over me," Grandpa said, scrubbing at his hands with the last of the Kleenex. "All over me . . ."

CARL DIDN'T GET home until after midnight. Jan Walther was ready for bed, and came out to see him. "It's late," she said. "Your homework?"

"Done. Did it in study hall," Carl said, hand on his bedroom doorknob.

"Still have to get up early. What kept you?"

"Ah, you know Grandpa. He doesn't sleep so well anymore. He wanted to talk."

She smiled and said, "Okay, big guy. But get some sleep. You have to be *in* school in less than eight hours."

"No problem," said the Imperfect Weapon.

He never dreamed about the dead: he dreamed of girls in varying states of nakedness, of black cars street-racing in LA, of himself posed in a shadowed hallway somewhere with a pistol, muzzle upraised as he slid along the hall, back to the wall . . .

Carl still dreamed a child's dreams.

14

AFTER HIS EXPERIENCE with the cops in Virginia, Lucas decided not to take a chance on the Hibbing police. Instead, he called the head of the BCA's northern office in Bemidji, asked him to be the intermediary, waited ten minutes, then took the call from the Hibbing chief of police.

"We've got a situation," he told the chief. "The FBI's involved, counterintelligence people, and the whole thing is way too complicated to talk about over the phone, but what it is, is, I need somebody to run out to the Greyhound Museum to look around. If you have a Greyhound museum."

"We've got one," the chief said. He sounded sleepy, but cooperative. "I can get a car up there in five minutes. Are my boys going to run into anything?"

"Tell them to take care," Lucas said. "We're talking about a killer.

He's done two people that we know of, that Russian over in Duluth and the old lady a few days later."

"Holy smokes, I been reading about it. All right, I'll get somebody up there—hell, I'll get my pants on and go up there with them. Can I call you back?"

"I'll be sitting here," Lucas said. "Call no matter what."

WEATHER SAID, "I want to know how this comes out, but I've got to go to bed. I'm working early."

"Be up as soon as I can," Lucas said. "Whatever happens, we won't go back to Duluth tonight. It's too late, and there'd be nothing to do."

"I am very worried," Nadya said.

Lucas raised his eyebrows and said, "Well . . . you guys didn't have to have a shadow. We told you that."

"A shadow was convenient for everybody," Nadya said. "If all this trouble was an artifact of the past, we could leave it. If not, we could settle it with your FBI, informally. The shadow could act in ways that you, perhaps, could not, with your TV and newspapers . . ."

"I'll leave you two to work it out," Weather said. She yawned, kissed Lucas on the forehead, and disappeared back up the stairs.

THE HIBBING CHIEF, Roy Hopper, called back twenty minutes later. "We found a running back from the high-school football team in the backseat of his dad's car with his girlfriend. The boy didn't have his pants entirely on. Hope this doesn't turn out to be a distraction."

"Distract from what?" Lucas asked.

"He's rushing for better than a hundred yards a game so far this season . . ."

"Chief . . ."

". . . and we found an empty car, doors unlocked, nothing inside but a cell phone on a charging cord. We ran the plates. It's a rental from Avis at Duluth International. Checked out a week and a half ago to a Martin Johnson."

"Hang on," Lucas said.

He repeated the information to Nadya, who said, "That is surely the car, do you think? I don't know the name. Is this policeman near the cell phone?"

Lucas to Hopper: "Where's the cell phone?"

"Still here, in the car."

"Tell him, I will call," Nadya said. She ran upstairs, got a calendar, ran back down, and punched a number into Lucas's cell phone. A minute later, the chief said, "It's ringing."

"Oh my god," Nadya said. "I must call in. I must call."

"Better treat that area as a crime scene, Chief," Lucas said. "We'll be back up there at the crack of dawn, or nine o'clock, whichever is later."

When Lucas got off the phone, he said to Nadya, "Call in, and then get a few hours of sleep. I've got an Ambien if you need one. I'll get you up at five-thirty, we'll get out of here at six."

Nadya nodded and started dialing. Lucas was at the bottom of the stairs, headed up, when she called after him, "I'm thinking I'm not liking this Minnesota too much."

"It ain't Minnesota," Lucas said. "Minnesota's just fine."

LUCAS WAS UP at five forty-five, groggy until he got out of the shower, which he shared with Weather; she got his blood moving, anyway. Weather didn't have to shave, so she was dressed and downstairs first, having stopped to knock on Nadya's door.

When Lucas got downstairs, Weather said, "Nadya's up. She's repacking. I'll put some coffee in a thermos. You want some peanut-butter toast?"

"That'd be great. I'm sorry about the quick turnaround. Gotta make a couple of calls." He called Andreno, talked with him for a moment; then called Andy Harmon, who sounded as though he'd been up for hours, and filled him in on the shadow.

"Interesting," Harmon said. "We'll get back to you."

Nadya came in, rubbing the back of her head. She had her carry-on bag, which she'd used as an overnighter, in her hand. "Are we ready?"

"You want something to eat? Cereal, or peanut-butter toast?"

She shook her head. "I just want to go."

AT SIX FIFTEEN, they were in the car. Nadya kept yawning, couldn't stop. "I have no sleep at all," she said as they backed out the driveway. She yawned and blinked. "I should have taken the pill."

Lucas braked, put the car in park, said, "Hang on," and ran into the house. A minute later, he was back and handed Nadya a sleeping mask. "We're three hours away. Crank the seat back, see if you can doze off. Any little bit will help."

She was gone before they got out of the Cities.

THE DAY WAS brilliant and warm, with a gusty wind from the south. Lucas didn't want to disturb Nadya with the radio, so they rode in silence, running just over the speed limit in light traffic.

Time to think: but not much to think about. The case was all in pieces. Andreno was keeping an eye on Spivak, though he couldn't do a full surveillance. Nevertheless, when Lucas shook Andreno out of bed at six o'clock, he said he'd taken Spivak home at one o'clock in the morning, and had seen him, off and on, in the tavern during the day and all during the evening. The only place he'd gone all day was to a hardware store, this just before noon, where he'd bought two fluorescent lightbulbs, and to a Wal-Mart, at seven twenty.

"He went inside, and I lost him for a minute or so and then I found him back in the DVDs. He got one, and then he trailed around the store some more and I got the impression he was looking for a tail, but he wasn't very good at it. So I stayed back a little and let him run, and just before he walked out, he made a phone call from the public phones. He wasn't on for more than a minute."

"That sounds like something. I'll have the feds see if they can do anything with it."

"Okay. We might be getting a little tangled up here, though," Andreno said. "The cops already got a call about my van. The chief short-stopped it, but somebody along the main drag here is getting suspicious."

"Get a different vehicle," Lucas said. "Get Spivak in the bar during the day, and trade that one in for another one. I can make a call, get you the right one."

"Do that. But don't call me back until about ten o'clock, which is when I'm going to get up."

WHOEVER HAD MET with the shadow, it wasn't Spivak. What else? The laptop was a possibility. He should hear something from the FBI during the day. The street person, the woman who called him: Was there any way to hook into her? She almost certainly had a criminal record. If they could get a single print off anything in that shack, they should be able to get a name and a mug shot and maybe some idea of where she was. He made a mental note to call Reasons and push the Duluth crime-scene people to take the shack apart. There had to be *one* print . . . And Marcy would talk to the attorney for Larry the Fence, see if they could squeeze an ID out of him. Whoever the woman was, she'd hooked into Larry in a hurry, so maybe they had a history.

TWO HOURS OUT, Lucas got off I-35 at Cloquet, finished the rest of the coffee from the thermos, and pushed on north, as Nadya continued to sleep. Lucas understood exactly: she hadn't been able to sleep all night in a good bed because she felt like she should be doing something. The next day, when she was actually doing something—heading north—she could sleep like a baby. He was the same way . . .

Thirty miles north of Cloquet his phone rang.

"Lucas . . . Andy Harmon."

Lucas glanced at Nadya. "Yeah," he said quietly. "I'm in my car, heading north to Hibbing. Nadya's with me. She's sleeping, I think."

"Okay. First, Spivak got a call yesterday evening. I can read you what he said."

"He's tapped?"

"Well . . . yeah. What the caller said was, 'Is Tom White there?' And Spivak said, 'This is Spivak's Tap. We don't have no Tom White here.' I'm reading from a transcript."

"Okay, but so what?"

"So then the caller says, 'Is this two two zero, six seven nine, seven six eight zero?' And Spivak said, "Nope. You misdialed.' Then he hung up."

Lucas waited through the pregnant pause.

After a few seconds, Harmon said, "That was almost certainly a call code. There is no two-two-zero area code. What Spivak does is add or subtract some unknown number, and comes up with a callback. He makes the callback from a clean phone, probably to another public phone somewhere."

"You said, 'Yesterday evening,' " Lucas said. "What time yesterday evening?"

"Seven twenty."

"Huh. I have reason to believe that Spivak went running out of his bar at seven twenty, drove to a Wal-Mart and bought nothing special, but made a phone call from a pay phone."

"We can check that," Harmon said. "We can check all the calls made out of the place between seven fifteen and what, eight o'clock?"

"More like seven fifteen and seven forty. My guy was pretty specific. Let me know. What happened with the laptop?"

"The laptop. There were no usable fingerpints at all. Most of the files are not encrypted, but they appear to be innocent. Tour guides and maps and so on. There are a couple of dozen encrypted files and nothing that looks like a key, so that doesn't help us. We're still going through it. There's a lot of stuff."

"All right. Check on Wal-Mart. Is there any possibility of getting a couple of FBI thugs to lean on Spivak? Maybe he isn't scared enough, because the only people talking to him are locals."

"We can send somebody around. This thing about the shadow has us worried. From what Nadya told you, about the wife dying and the child, we think it's a guy named Piotr Nikitin. He was supposed to be a middle-level guy in their Commercial Affairs Section, but everybody figured he was Intelligence."

"Why worried?"

"Well, he's a nice guy, you know? Everybody knows him. His father-in-law bought him a place out in Virginia, and he'd have a big to-do out there every May Day, you know, for the community. He called it the Dirty Rotten Commie Fest."

"The community?"

"Yes. You know, the *community.*"

"He tried to hang Spivak, for Christ's sake," Lucas said, exasperated.

"That was just part of the job," Harmon said. "You can understand that."

LUCAS COULDN'T. He got off the phone, breathing hard for a few minutes, backed off the gas. When he got pissed, the speed tended to go up, and he got speeding tickets. Nadya stirred twenty minutes after he talked with Harmon. Stirred, then twitched, moaned softly, and pushed herself up. "What time is it?"

"Nine o'clock," Lucas said. "We're almost there."

"Really?" Her face was slack with sleep. She cranked her seat upright, said, "My mouth is terrible, I have to brush it."

"McDonald's in ten minutes," Lucas said. "You can do it there. Then we'll go see if we can find Piotr."

The name didn't faze her: "I hope to," she said. "This would be well regarded in Moscow."

LUCAS TALKED TO Chief Hopper, who was at the bus museum, and got directions through town. The museum was actually out of town a bit, and looked exactly the way a bus museum should look, a triumph of function over form: a low concrete building painted red, white, and blue, with no style whatever, except perhaps existential garage.

There were three cop cars in the parking lot, and beyond them, six men on their hands and knees, crawling up the parking lot; two more men stood chatting, watching the crawlers. Lucas rolled in next to the cars, and he and Nadya got out. One of the two standing men, a square-faced forty-year-old in a ball cap, walked over and said, "Are you Davenport?"

"Yes, and Nadya Kalin, a police officer from Russia. She's here as an observer."

"Pleased to meet you," the chief said. "I'm Roy." And then to Nadya: "You look just like Miz Wedig, a third-grade teacher here in town. You could be sisters."

"But I'm a spy," Nadya said solemnly. "Mr. Davenport will tell you so."

"Well, I'm sure every big country needs spies," Hopper said cheerfully. He turned to Lucas, his smile fading. "We may have some bad news. One of the boys was scuffing around and he found some blood over there on the other side of the car. We covered it, and the sheriff's people came over and took some samples. I put my guys to crawling the lot, inch by inch. So far . . ." He dug in his pocket and pulled out a transparent plastic bag and handed it to Lucas. ". . . this is what we found."

A nine-millimeter shell was inside the bag; it was shiny, new.

"Nine millimeter," Lucas said to Nadya.

"But not from the same group of cartridges as the one that killed Oleshev," she said. "The others were tarnished, and even had some, *mmm*, I don't know the English, *green coloring* on the brass."

"That'd be your *verdigris,*" Hopper said.

"We can tell by the firing-pin mark whether it was the same gun," Lucas said. He handed the bag back to the sheriff: "If you could have that shipped right away down to the BCA crime lab, I'd appreciate it. They could get back to us overnight on the firing-pin mark."

"Good as done," Hopper said. "You want to see where the blood was?"

They walked over to look; there wasn't much but a clean spot on the blacktop. "How much blood, you think?" Lucas asked. "Bad wound?"

"I'd say pretty bad. I'd say the guy was down at least a quart."

"Shoot." Lucas looked around. "I'll tell you what. There'd be no reason to take the body except to delay the discovery. You might find it around pretty close. I imagine that they'd want to get rid of it."

"There are a few thousand square miles of woods and swamps around here, to say nothing of the pits," Hopper said. "I wouldn't hold your breath."

Nadya had been staring morosely at the clean spot on the blacktop; now she said, abruptly, "Is this all?"

"That's about all, ma'am," Hopper said.

"I will call," she said, and she walked away from them.

"She sure does look like Sally Wedig," Hopper marveled, looking after her.

NADYA CAME BACK. "They are very upset in Washington."

"So am I," Lucas said. "I don't mean to . . . get on your case when one of your countrymen has been killed, but the whole bunch of you are playing games. It's gotta stop. It's getting people killed. You need to tell me everything you know, everything they know in Moscow, and maybe I can stop it. And I don't give a shit about this spy stuff . . ."

"I don't make that decision," Nadya said. She stepped closer to him and looked up and said, "When Weather and I were shopping, she said you were a brilliant policeman because you made things happen. Make something happen."

"Like what?" Lucas asked; he was both irritated and flattered.

"Something. I don't know."

LUCAS CHECKED AGAIN with Andy Harmon. "I got the Duluth FBI guys going. They should be in Virginia by now. They'll lean on Spivak," Harmon said.

"Okay. I've got some news about your friend Piotr Nikitin. He's probably dead."

Silence, for five seconds. "You're positive?"

Lucas told him about the nine-millimeter shell, the blood, the car and the cell phone. "Probably too early to light a candle, but you might look around for a matchbook."

"Huh. I'll pass the word on. Keep me informed."

Lucas decided: "Look. Have one of the FBI guys call me on this phone when they're done with Spivak. I'm gonna give him an hour to think about it, assuming he doesn't crack, and then I'm going to bust his ass."

"On what charge?"

"Accessory to murder," Lucas said. "I don't know how long I can make it stick, but I can keep him inside for a couple of days and out of touch. That might stir up whoever else is involved with this thing."

"We must have a bad connection," Harmon said. "I missed most of what you just said. Talk to you later." And he was gone.

"What'd he say?" Nadya asked.

"He said I'm on my own," Lucas answered.

"Ah, yes, we have this formula also in Russia," she said. "If you fail, you are on your own. If you succeed, then you were not on your own, you were helped by the entire secretariat."

"Exactly," Lucas said.

LUCAS CALLED Rose Marie at the Department of Public Safety in St. Paul, and asked her to fix an arrest warrant with a state judge in Virginia, and to arrange to have a sheriff's car meet them at the bar to transport Spivak after the arrest.

"I want to take him down to Duluth, so he'll be away from home and it'll be harder for his family to see him. I'm trying to isolate him as much as I can . . ."

When he was done with Rose Marie, he called Andreno and told him to hold off on changing vans. "I'm gonna bust Spivak on accessory to murder. See if anything happens."

"What do you want me to do?"

"Watch the son. He seems to do the talking for the family. Spivak's old lady is a little too shaky for anything important. I want to know about phone calls. Exact times. The feds can figure out where they're going."

"I'm on it."

"YOU'RE MAKING something happen?" Nadya asked.

"I'm desperate," Lucas said. "I'm jumping off a cliff."

They had time to kill, and not much to do. They toured the bus museum, which was more exciting than Lucas expected but, overall, not exciting; they did encounter a tour group that had gathered from around the Midwest to make the trip to Hibbing, and an intense young man in an American-flag T-shirt pointed at an antique blue-and-white bus and whispered to Nadya, "Nineteen thirty-six Super Coach. Perfect condition."

She nodded just like she knew what the fuck he was talking about.

In the parking lot, the chief was sending his patrolmen back to work. "Nothing more," he told Lucas. "Just the one shell."

ONE OF THE Duluth FBI agents called and said, "Harmon said we should call you. We're on the way out of town. The guy has dropped into a routine: he just sits there and shakes his head and doesn't offer a thing. Hard to move him."

"You think he was coached?"

"I don't know what to think. He's pretty effective in resisting. He just doesn't venture *anything*. He just sits there and shakes his head and acts confused and mumbles. Doesn't wise-ass you, doesn't argue."

"He's at the bar?"

"He was when we left."

HIBBING WAS ABOUT twenty-five miles southwest of Virginia, and the trip north took about half an hour. They took two more calls en route. The first came from Harmon, who said the feds had come up dry on the computer. "He might have had some good stuff in there, but it's encrypted. Plain old over-the-counter encryption, but we're stuck without the key, and he probably had the key in his head. There were also some travel-related files, some expenses that he didn't bother to encrypt. Couple other things . . . I can put it on a CD if you want to see it."

"Yeah, do that. Drop it at the Radisson."

AND NADYA TOOK a call, listened for a moment, said, *"Da,"* hung up and turned in her seat to face Lucas.

"In Washington they tell me to explain one of our problems."

"All right."

"The SVR is our foreign-intelligence service. This is the successor to the KGB that you know about, where Oleshev once worked. So. Inside the SVR, the rumors say, there is an informal group that goes back to the KGB and which does not share all the goals of the new SVR. This group is called the Circle or the Ring or, sometimes, the Zero, and it is not known if there is a specific leadership and direction, or only sympathies. We think that the Circle illegally shares information with, *mmm*, nongovernmental organizations, perhaps, or with other sympathizers in the military and the Foreign Ministry and industry. These are not traitors, you understand. They are like, *mmm*, a Republican administration hires people for your Defense Department or your State Department, and these people bore into the woodwork. Then when a Democratic president is elected, these people may continue to provide sensitive information to their old Republican friends. Do you see how I mean this?"

"Yes. Goes on all the time. Some people think it's the only thing that makes government work."

"Yes, I have heard that argument. Oleshev was believed to be in contact with the Circle. Whether he was an active agent, this is not known. But this is the reason we are both so anxious and so ignorant—the Circle has resources that we do not have now. Perhaps just . . . memories. Memories that are not in files anywhere. We need to know more about the Circle, we would like to know about these memories. But we can't help, not much. Because we just don't *know*."

"Okay."

She frowned at him: "You know what I was saying?"

"Yes. Years ago, I was asked to consult on an investigation in New York City. A group of police officers had taken it upon itself to clean up the city by killing criminals. Murdering them, really. The circle of cops went very close to the top of the police department, and had a lot of sympathy. And it was working; they probably saved lives, and certainly wiped out a lot of potential misery. But it was still murder, and we had to stop it."

"Okay," she said. "This is it. This is what we deal with."

SPIVAK WAS SITTING, head down, at the end of the bar, eating a hot dog with sauerkraut when Lucas, Nadya, and two St. Louis County deputies walked in. A bartender was behind the bar, wiping glasses, and said, "Here we go." Spivak lifted his head, chewed twice, swallowed, and said, "Oh, boy, what now? I just talked to the FBI."

"We've probably got another dead man," Lucas said. "This is the third killing."

"Who?" Spivak asked. He still had bandages around his neck.

"The guy who tried to hang you, in fact. We have to stop this. We want to give you one last chance to tell us who was at the meeting with you. If you don't, I'm going to arrest you for accessory to first-degree murder. The penalty is the same as for first degree: thirty years without chance of parole. You'll never get out of Stillwater alive."

"But I don't know who they were," Spivak said, his voice rising. A piece of sauerkraut flew across the bar.

"I think we can prove that you do," Lucas said. "I'm not sure we can prove that you wanted the murders committed, but I think we can prove that you knew the people who were involved and refused to name them. That's at least obstruction of justice, and probably accessory to murder."

Spivak put his head down and stuffed the rest of the hot dog into his mouth. He chewed and chewed and finally said, "I want a lawyer."

"You can certainly have one," Lucas said. He'd gotten the arrest warrant from one of the deputies before they walked into the bar; now he took it out of his pocket and said, "Last chance."

"Lawyer."

Lucas nodded and said to one of the deputies, "Cuff him. Take the warrant with you. I want him isolated." To Spivak: "You're under arrest. You have the right to remain silent . . ."

Lucas recited the rest of the Miranda warning, asked Spivak if he understood, and Spivak said to one of the deputies, "Jesus Christ, Clark, this is just like a bunch of fuckin' Nazis or something. You've known me all your life."

"Just doing what the man says," Clark said. The other deputy said to Lucas, "We'll take him right down . . . we'll have him there in an hour."

"Can I close the bar?" Spivak asked. "Let me count the cash drawer."

"Have your bartender call your kid," Lucas said. "Starting now, you don't get any favors."

15

O N   T H E   W A Y   from Virginia to Duluth, Lucas got a call from Andreno. "The Spivak kid hotfooted it down to the bar right after you took
his old man off. He was in there for twenty minutes, then went off to
Wal-Mart and got on the phone, just like his daddy did."

"You've got the time and phone number?"

"I do."

"I want you to call this FBI guy and tell him to make it a priority."

"Maybe something begins to break," Nadya said, when he got off
the phone.

L U C A S   D R O P P E D   N A D Y A   at the hotel, then went on to the St.
Louis County Jail, so he could watch Spivak being processed. Lucas took
him all the way to the cell; left him there, alone, head down, silent, waiting for his call to his lawyer. On the way out, Lucas said, "Have a long

talk with your lawyer. Long talk. Listen to him. Unless you've done some killing yourself, there's about an eighty-percent chance you can be walking around free by this afternoon. We just need a little help."

Spivak said nothing, and on the way out, the deputy named Clark, who had ridden down to Duluth with him, said, "There's something not quite right. I've taken God only knows how many people to the lockup, and they all said *something*. Ol' Anton, it was like name, rank, and serial number."

That brought Lucas around: "You think he might have been trained? To resist?"

The deputy shook his head. "I don't know about that. But man— he didn't say *shit*."

AT THE HOTEL, Lucas found a CD waiting for him at the desk. He took it to his room, got a beer, took a shower, then popped the CD into his laptop and found a dozen files. Six were in the original Russian; six more had been translated. They included a list of housekeeping tasks on the *Potemkin*, what looked like a soccer pool, a long shopping list, and a list of Russian names with job assignments, with a note from the translator that the men on the list were members of the *Potemkin* crew. There were random notes in a file marked *Random Notes:* "McDonald's Duluth, $4.88; Taxicab, $9.60; remember Wal-Mart; boots (Red Wing insulated with 4,000 gms Thinsulate)?"

The final file had a note attached from whoever examined it: "Had to use can opener on this one. Series of triangles, circles, squares, and lines, done as vector graphics. File type unknown, forwarded to . . ."

Somebody had deleted the last word or series of words, which made Lucas smile. Probably something like *supersecret undercover computer analysis facility,* he thought. He was about to shut down the computer when he noticed the Inspiration icon on the left side of his screen. Inspiration was an outlining program made up of circles, ovals, triangles, squares, lines, and other symbols. Give it a chance, he thought, and clicked on it.

When the program was open, he called up the file on the disk, and it instantly blossomed into a series of triangles, circles, squares, and lines, just as the file note said.

"Excellent," he muttered. The FBI didn't know about Inspiration, of which there were only about a zillion copies floating around.

One problem was instantly evident: none of the triangles, circles, squares, or lines had any text attached to them. Lucas looked at them for a moment. There were four groups of symbols, each with a square at the top, falling into a more elaborate group of boxes below, attached vertically and occasionally horizontally by lines. An organizational chart, he thought. Maybe something on the ship?

He thought about it for a while longer, then called Nadya. Her room, they'd discovered, was one floor straight above his, give or take a room. She picked up the phone and he could hear music in the background, canned jazz. He said, "I got the CD from the FBI. There's not much on it, but there's a weird diagram. Do you have a list of the ship's crew? With their ranks?"

"Yes, in my laptop."

"Then come on down; or I can come up."

"I come down right away, I brush my teeth," she said.

He gave her the room number, left the laptop on, sprawled on the bed, and paged through the channels on the cable TV. Not much going on. There never seemed to be much when he was stuck in a hotel.

Reasons: he should call Reasons about arresting Spivak. He got his calendar, found Reasons's cell phone, and punched in the number.

"Reasons."

Lucas identified himself and said, "I meant to call earlier, but it slipped my mind. We busted Spivak this morning. We think Nadya's shadow might have been killed . . ." He filled him in quickly and was about to get deeper into it when Reasons interrupted: "Listen, uh, I got most of this from Nadya. I bumped into her at the hotel right after you dropped her off, I guess. I came over to see if you guys were still in town when I didn't hear from you yesterday . . . Anyway, she filled me in on the whole thing."

"Okay. Just didn't want you to feel neglected."

There was a knock at the door, and Lucas walked over to it, popped it open, found Nadya with her laptop, waved her in, and said, "I gotta go."

"Okay. Talk to you."

Lucas said, "You oughta come over for a beer this evening. We can bullshit through the whole thing again."

"Five o'clock?"

"See you then . . ." Just before he hung up, Lucas could hear the canned jazz playing behind him, the same music that had been playing behind Nadya. Then the phone clicked out and he said, "Ah, man . . ."

"What?" Nadya asked. She looked freshly showered and wide-awake.

"Nothing," he said.

H E S H O W E D H E R the diagram, and she brought up a file of names and ranks. "Okay, here is trouble," she said. "We have more people on the ship than we have boxes."

"How about officers?"

"We have more boxes than we have officers." She tapped the screen. "Besides, this chart, there are four leaders. On a ship, just one."

"What if they were watches, or shifts, or whatever they call them on a boat?"

She peered at the screen, then said, "This is possible. I would check, but I thought ships had only three shifts, not four. But I don't know this for sure."

"Hmm."

. . .

THE SHIP DIDN'T FIT, at least not all at once. Lucas went back and sprawled on the bed while Nadya looked at the files in the original Russian. When she finished, she said, "There is nothing, unless this is some kind of code. But I think it is what it seems to be. An organizational chart."

Lucas said, "How about a genealogy?"

"What?"

"You think the chart is a genealogy? A list of ancestors?"

"Of Oleshevs?"

"Or maybe the people that Oleshev was trying to contact?" He rolled off the bed and padded over to the desk, bent over her shoulder, and said, "We know Spivak's family. Do they fit anywhere? Move over."

She stood up and Lucas sat in front of the laptop. "Spivak is married and has two children, so . . ."

Lucas tapped a chart: "If these were his parents, and this is Spivak and this is his wife, and these would be the two kids . . ."

"And this line . . ." She touched the screen over his shoulder. He could smell the warm water and hormones rolling off her. "This line leads from his wife, if this is the Spivak family, to another family. So who is his wife's family?"

"That's what the FBI is for," Lucas said. He was interested now: the diagram felt right. If Oleshev had been feeling his way around a group of spies, and he knew only one or two of them . . . he might have something like this as a mnemonic. "And I've got a phone number."

HARMON CAME UP INSTANTLY, as always.

"Those files were really interesting," Lucas said. "We're running them down now. But we need some information. We need to know Spivak's wife's maiden name, and we need to know who the members of her family are. All of them."

"And how they relate," Nadya said from over his shoulder.

"Yeah. And how they relate."

"Who's there with you?"

"Nadya."

"What'd you get?" Harmon asked. "Did you get something out of the files? What?"

Lucas told him, and Harmon said he could have the information on Spivak's wife's family in an hour.

S O   T H E Y   S A T   and waited; and Lucas found that he was a little pissed. He was ninety-seven percent sure that Nadya and Reasons had been rolling around in her bed, and though it was none of his business, it seemed to push the investigation off balance. On the other hand, he'd not only slept with witnesses in the past; he'd on occasion been in bed with the principal of an investigation . . .

He had, he thought reasonably, no stance from which to complain; but it still pissed him off. Maybe because he was married now, and the opportunities were suddenly out of reach? Would he have been sniffing after Nadya if he'd been free?

He considered her, sitting on the single easy chair, reading a copy of *Golf & Travel*. She was attractive, she was his age, she smelled good, she was safe and from out of town . . .

"Silly fuckers," he mumbled at the ceiling over the bed.

"What?" Nadya asked.

"Nothing. Thinking."

"I am surprised you have such a small room," she said, tossing the magazine back on the coffee table. "They didn't have a suite when you arrived?"

"Didn't ask. Never thought about it," Lucas said.

"You never heard of the Internet hotel sites?"

. . .

SHE STARTED RAMBLING on about Price.com and the deal she
got while she was still in Moscow, and for a few seconds Lucas thought
he was losing his mind. Then the phone rang, and Harmon said, "I've
got news." For the first time, he sounded as if he might be interested in
what was going on.

"Give."

"Marsha Spivak is the daughter of Benjamin and Maud Svoboda.
Her brother, Rick Svoboda, runs a bakery in Hibbing. And there's another brother named David. Are you getting this?"

"Yeah, I'm putting it on a scratch pad," Lucas said. "So that's the
family?"

"Not quite. Janet and Rick have three daughters, Cheryl, Karen, and
Julie. David, we haven't been able to locate. And then in the Spivak line,
Marsha had Bob and Carol, and Bob has two children, Robert Jr. and
Heather."

"All right, all right. I'll see if we can fit this—"

"That's not all. Your man from Virginia called and asked us to check
that telephone call that Bob Spivak made from Wal-Mart. The phone call
lasted seven seconds—seven—and there's not a single fuckin' thing you
can say in seven seconds that isn't some sort of callback code. The call
went to Svoboda's Bakery in Hibbing."

"You gotta be shitting me."

"That's still not all. At this point, we were getting seriously interested, so we went into the vital records to see where everybody was
born. Benjamin and Maud Svoboda were both born in Mahnomen
County, Benjamin in nineteen sixteen and Maud in nineteen twenty."
Harmon was talking so fast now that he was spitting into the phone.
"Their birth certificates came from Mercy Hospital, which burned down
in nineteen twenty-eight, so there's no independent confirmation . . ."

"Wait a minute . . ."

"That's right, dude," Harmon said, a little overebullient for a fed. "Same hospital where Spivak's parents were supposedly born. Dutch and Sarah Spivak, nineteen twelve and nineteen fourteen. Dutch and Sarah went abroad twice, once in nineteen sixty-two and again in nineteen sixty-seven, both times to visit Germany and Czechoslovakia, supposedly where their parents came from. But we can't find any record of their parents."

"So it's all bullshit," Lucas said. "The birth records. The parents—"

"Were probably born in Russia. That hospital probably existed, and probably burned down, and there are probably people around whose records were destroyed. You'd never see the connection here, unless you saw these four families involved in some other way," Harmon said. "We're bustin' a Soviet-era spy ring right here in River City. They can't believe it back in Washington. Uh, is Nadya still around?"

"Yeah."

"Don't tell her all of this. We don't want anybody breaking for the door."

"I'll lead her on," Lucas said. Across the room, Nadya's eyebrows went up.

"Do that. And listen, we're out trying to find a copy of that Inspiration program. Where'd you get yours?"

"Apple store. But it was a while ago."

"Okay. We're gonna start putting this thing together here, too."

"We need to meet. I need to see you and your FBI guys. And I want to bring Nadya. And probably Jerry Reasons, because the Duluth cops have got a piece of this thing, and they're gonna be around. Reasons is coming here at five o'clock."

"We can be there. At least me and one other guy."

WHEN LUCAS GOT OFF, Nadya said, "What did he say?"

"He said we're busting a Soviet-era spy ring." He told her the rest of it, and added, "If we meet with Harmon, don't tell him I told you all this shit."

"Good. Now, does this new family fit in the chart?"

THE NEW FAMILY FIT, but only through three generations. Both the Spivaks and the Svobodas had fourth-generation children, but if the charts represented the families—and Lucas was now convinced that they did—the youngest generation wasn't on it.

"That makes sense if they are Communist-era leftovers," Nadya pointed out. "The last contact may have been in the nineteen eighties, when these children were not yet born."

"Huh."

"Which still leaves us stranded. What do we do now? Go see these Svobodas?"

"I think we've got to wait until we talk to the feds, and get Duluth up to speed. There are a couple of different ways to go . . ."

THEY TALKED IT over for a while, then Nadya went back to her room and Lucas started going through every piece of paper he had.

In ten minutes, he gave it up as pointless. He didn't think he was missing anything in the material—he just didn't have enough material. With time to kill, he tried the TV, came up dry, looked at his collection of newspapers and magazines, gave up on them, and finally went shopping. He bought a pair of walking shoes and a $400 Barbour oilcloth jacket that the salesman said was an excellent counterpoint to his blue eyes and his stonewashed Levi's. Lucas couldn't help but agree.

"When you're right, you're right," he told the salesman, looking at himself in the triple mirror.

. . .

HARMON CALLED at four forty-five and said that he had rented a conference room on the first floor; he didn't want to meet in the FBI offices, which were across the street from the hotel, because he didn't ever want to have to explain Nadya.

Lucas called Nadya and Reasons, gave them the location, and at five o'clock, met Nadya in the elevator on the way down. Reasons was already there, with Harmon and a local Duluth FBI man named Amery. Harmon shook hands with Nadya, said, "I hope everything's okay with Piotr Nikitin."

"It does not look so good," she said.

"WE NEED TO put more pressure on Spivak," Lucas said, when they were settled around the conference table. "Is there anything in the antiterrorism stuff that you could use to lean on him with?"

Harmon glanced at Amery, then looked back at Lucas and nodded. "There are some provisions under the Patriot Act that would allow us to hold him for a while, without charging him, and without access to the outside, except for an attorney. Or, we could simply bust him under federal statutes on suspicion of espionage. We can also offer him a deal: give us the rest of the ring, and the killer, and he walks. His family walks. So we have some weapons."

"I don't think we should isolate him so much," Nadya said. "Threaten, threaten, threaten, but always allow him to talk to the outside. Always with surveillance on his family and this new family, the Svobodas."

"Is everybody tapped?" Reasons asked.

"We have warrants in the process of being issued," Harmon said. "We will have taps on the whole damn group of them by tonight—and we're looking at ways to tap the Wal-Mart there in Virginia, since that seems to be their regular outside call spot. The problem there is, we'd pick up more than the target, but our lawyers are figuring a way to work it out with the court."

"We could put one of the phones out of service, so they'd always be forced to use the tapped phone," Amery said. "Technically, it's not hard, if the court says okay."

"Do they suspect yet that we're watching?" Nadya asked.

"The Spivaks are probably looking around," Harmon said.

"Here's a risk we could take," Lucas said. "You bring in some guys, and watch all of the Spivaks full-time. Then you go over, bust Spivak for espionage, and mention the genealogy that Oleshev had, about the hospital that burned down, the four families, and so on. Then arrange for Marsha Spivak or one of their kids to see Anton, in private. And track what happens. If they make phone calls, if they warn somebody . . . They'd have to do something, wouldn't they?"

Amery shrugged, and Harmon looked at Nadya, and Harmon said, "Unless they've buttoned down the whole organization."

"This they might have done," Nadya said.

"Then there wouldn't be any harm in doing it, if they feel that they can't warn anyone," Reasons said.

Harmon said, "It's a plan. What else?"

"We'll need some kind of timetable for you to put your people on, and for me to get my guy out of your way," Lucas said. "We don't want them running over each other . . ."

AT THE END of the meeting, Lucas said, "What we don't have is a rationale for the killings of Oleshev, Mary Wheaton, and Piotr Nikitin. Wheaton was probably done to eliminate a witness, but the other two don't connect."

Harmon picked it up: "We have two Russian groups trying to contact the same spy ring, and the reaction is to kill people on both sides. I don't have a tight grip on that, either."

They all looked at Nadya, who smiled and shook her head. "There are three groups represented. The Russian government is the first; then, what we believe is a criminal group or perhaps some runaway business group, is the second; and the Communists here in Minnesota is the third. Perhaps the Communists don't want to deal with anything Russian."

"So it's our Commies against your businessmen," Amery said. He squinted sideways and did a Maxwell Smart imitation. "Whatta we do next, Chief?"

Harmon was offended, cleared his throat, and said, "Anything else?"

MORE DRIFT TIME; time not even spent thinking about the case. What could be done was being done. Reasons had walked out through the front door of the hotel when the meeting ended, never looking back; and Lucas wondered if he was wrong about Nadya and Reasons.

He talked to Weather about it that night and she said, "Who cares? They're adults."

16

LIKE ANY GOOD MINNESOTAN, Lucas rarely missed the TV weather before going to bed. But he missed it that night, caught up in watching *The Hulk* on a movie channel.

The phone call came early the next day, and, as he was running out of the hotel at seven in the morning, still half asleep, the weather smacked him in the face. Fall had arrived overnight, and he could see his breath in the air as he headed for the car.

Nadya called after him, "Wait, wait, wait." Lucas had suggested that maybe she could get a ride with Reasons, but she didn't want to ride with Reasons—the sarcasm was apparently lost on her—she wanted to go right now and with Lucas. She was wearing jeans and boots she'd bought when she was shopping with Weather, and the shoestrings were flapping and she couldn't get her shirt tucked in, and she had her new Patagonia jacket pinned under her chin as she tried to dress on the run and she called, "Wait, please, wait, wait . . ."

Lucas put the light on the roof and they were out of there, up the hill, over the top, running as hard as they could for Hibbing. "It's Piotr," she said.

"I think so."

"I hope it's not Piotr. It is Piotr, isn't it? I think it must be . . ."

Lucas was not good in the morning and had had neither a Coke nor a cup of coffee. On the outskirts of Duluth, he spotted a likely-looking gas station and roared into the lot, light still flashing, got two coffees to go, jumped the line at the cash register, ran back, hopped in the car, and took off again.

Nadya started with Piotr again, then went silent, and Lucas, grumpy, was blessing the silence when she said, "So, you know that I am sleeping with Jerry. This offends you?"

"You're sleeping with Reasons?" He feigned astonishment.

"Please." She said it exactly like a New Yorker.

"None of my business," Lucas said. "You're adults."

"That's exactly what I thought," she said. More silence, but Lucas knew she wasn't going to leave it alone. Two minutes went by with sipping of coffee, views out the passenger window—trees, then more trees—and then she said, "Do you want to know why?"

"It's none of my business," Lucas repeated, but he did want to know, so he tried to keep any harshness out of his voice.

"It's because, as Jerry would say, I am horny."

"Okay," Lucas said. "Okay."

"I am separated six years now, and here I am—I am out of town where my colleagues can't see me, I am in a nice hotel with a good bed, Jerry is somewhat attractive and certainly safe, and very enthusiastic."

"That's uh . . . Jesus, it's gotta be Piotr, don't you think?"

She looked at him sideways and said, "I am sorry if this affair offends you. But I have not had so much sex in my life, and I took the opportunity."

"No. No. Like I said . . . Poor old Piotr . . ."

Two-thirds of the way to Hibbing, Lucas said, "We should call Andy Harmon." But they didn't.

CHIEF ROY HOPPER was standing on the edge of the road, bull-shitting with a couple of guys in tan Carhartt jackets, all three of them with their hands in the jacket pockets. Lucas pulled into the weeds off the tarmac and climbed out.

"There you are," Hopper called cheerfully. He turned to the other two and he said, "Top guy from the BCA, and this is his Russian friend. Nadya? Got that right?"

"Is it Piotr?" Nadya asked.

"We don't know," he said. "You got a picture?"

"Yes, I do, on my laptop, I have my laptop . . ."

"Haven't got him up yet, he's over the edge . . ."

Lucas looked around. They were in a road cut, with trees and brush all around. "Down in what?"

"Down in the pit," the chief said. When Lucas didn't react, he said, "The Rust-Hull mine pit. Biggest pit in the country."

"Grand Canyon of the north, is what they call it around here," one of the Carhartts said.

"Where is it?" Lucas asked, looking around again.

"About thirty yards that way," the other Carhartt said, tipping his head toward the north side of the road.

"Whoever it is got throwed over the side, but he hung up on a ledge maybe a hundred feet down," Hopper said. "Come on, I'll show you."

"How'd you find him?" Nadya asked as they scrambled up the road cut. She'd gotten her boots properly tied, and Lucas thought they looked cute: retro-styled brown combat boots with giant cleated soles, but only about ten inches long.

Hopper didn't answer until they got over the top, then said, "Well,

I knew you were going to ask . . . I told everybody to keep a lookout, and this morning, there were these crows flying around . . ."

"Crows."

"Sort of the all-purpose cleanup crew around here," Hopper said. "They'll eat anything."

Nadya stopped, blood draining from her face and she said, "Oh my shit."

"That's exactly right," Hopper said.

They pushed another twenty yards through light brush, and then suddenly the mine pit opened out in front of them. It wasn't the Grand Canyon, but it was big. The lowest part of it was filled with water, a good-sized lake. A pickup truck on the dry pit floor beneath them looked like a Tonka toy. "Jesus," Lucas said.

"Never seen it before?" Hopper asked.

"Never." The dirt and rock were a deep purple, or maybe magenta— he got those confused. The colored stuff must be the iron ore, Lucas supposed. They slid carefully down a slope to a rock ledge perhaps ten yards wide, where two men in firemen's uniforms were working with a winch. Lucas and Nadya stepped carefully to the edge and looked over the side.

The pit was deep enough that Lucas had no idea of exactly how deep. Hundreds of feet, anyway, and it appeared to be miles long, maybe a couple of miles across. As Hopper had said, the body was a hundred or so feet below them, arms thrown to the side, legs spread, wrapped in a black coat, faceup. Two more firemen were maneuvering a lift basket.

"You know how to rappel?" Hopper asked Lucas.

"Fuck no," Lucas asked.

"A man after my own heart," Hopper said.

LUCAS HAD BEEN on recoveries before, and they always seemed to take two hours longer than they should; but they'd arrived more than an hour into this one, so they only had to wait a half hour before the basket was winched over the lip of the cut and pulled onto the ledge.

Nadya had gone back to the truck for her laptop, and as the body came up, she opened the laptop and brought up a picture of Nikitin. The body was wrapped in a blanket.

"Want to look?" Hopper asked Nadya. "I can look for you."

"I must look," Nadya said.

Hopper nodded, and carefully unwrapped the blanket that covered the face. When he pulled back the last flap, Nadya said, "Ohhhh . . ." and turned away, put the laptop down, walked back to the fat part of the hill and tried to vomit. The crows had gotten the eyes and the other soft parts—the lips and the nose—before they'd been chased away.

Hopper said quietly, "Put some eyes on him . . ."

"It's him," Lucas said. "Could you get your guys to print him? We can send the prints back to the Russian embassy, just to make sure."

"You'll have them in a half hour."

"Thanks, Chief." Lucas went back and took Nadya by the arm. "Let's go."

"I had nothing in my stomach except some coffee," she said, dabbing at her mouth with the back of her hand. "Now my mouth tastes like acid. It's . . . Piotr, correct?"

"Yup. They're gonna print him for you. Let's get out of here."

THEY SPENT SOME time driving around; Lucas got her a bottle of Scope at a convenience store, and wound up on the main drag. Lucas asked a passerby about Svoboda's Bakery, got pointed, and they walked down together.

"Is this smart?" Nadya asked.

"We're pushing," Lucas said.

Lucas had been in dozens of bakeries like Svoboda's all over

Minnesota and Wisconsin, small-town affairs with all the baking done on the premises, the varieties of cakes a fading tale of ethnic preferences from the early-nineteenth-century settlements. Lucas wandered down between the display cases, Nadya trailing behind. He chose two poppy-seed kolaches, and Nadya got a glazed doughnut, with two cups of coffee, and they carried them to one of two round metal tables at the front of the store and looked out at the street as they ate.

The woman behind the case busied herself with another customer, and then asked cheerfully, "You folks tourists?"

"Cops," Lucas said. He sipped his coffee, and said, "They had a Russian fellow killed up here a couple days ago. Found his body down in the Rust-Hull mine this morning. Crows got to him."

"Oh my . . . God," the woman behind the case said. Her hand went to her throat.

Lucas slipped into semi-hayseed mode. "Yup. Gonna be a big deal, all right. FBI flying around like a bunch of bats. They're talking spy rings, they're talking multiple murder. Haven't seen so much screaming and yelling since I went to a goat-fuck out in South Dakota." He sipped at his coffee and squinted NYPD-like at the street.

"Well . . . did they catch anybody?" the woman asked.

"Not yet. But they will," Lucas said. He dragged his index finger across his neck. "Murder one. Federal rap."

Nadya jumped in, her accent suddenly thicker. "They will be lucky peoples if they get to court. If my people catch them . . ." She smiled at the woman behind the counter. ". . . I am Russian—then they wish for your murder one."

"She's a spy," Lucas said to the woman, tipping a thumb toward Nadya. "But she's on our side for this one." He looked at his watch. "Oops. We better get going. Don't want to keep Chief Hopper waiting. Hey: great kolaches, huh?"

.   .   .

WHEN THEY WERE back on the street, Lucas looked down at Nadya and grinned. "I hope to hell that was one of the Svobodas. I don't want to have wasted *that* act."

"You have some abilities," Nadya conceded. Then, sadly, "Now we get these fingerprints, eh? I did not know this man, but I feel sorry for his child. Not natural to lose both your parents this way. This should not happen to anybody."

Nikitin's body had been taken to the medical examiner's office. Nadya had given Hopper some of her fingerprint forms, and the prints were ready when they got there. They spent ten minutes going through his personal effects—comb, two expensive pens, a wallet, a couple of credit cards, two photos, one of a small girl and one of a Harley-Davidson motorcycle.

"Not much," Lucas said.

"He was very professional," said Nadya. "There shouldn't be much."

"Which doesn't help."

"Now what?" she asked.

"Nothing to do but push. Push Spivak, push the Svobodas, once we decide to talk to them . . . and I guess I better call Harmon now."

Nadya picked up the picture of the girl: "And I should call the embassy, send the fingerprints. Then they will have to talk to the child."

"Find out where he was staying," Lucas suggested. "Maybe he left something in his room."

She nodded: "I will do that also."

17

GRANDPA WAS BURNING with anxiety when Carl arrived after school, said, "Where have you been?"

"School . . . we had choir practice," Carl said. Grandpa's house smelled of years of spaghetti and red spaghetti sauce and mushrooms; and old cigarette smoke, cooked into the walls for decades, ending, Carl was told, just after he was born. "I heard they found the body."

Grandma, slumped in her wheelchair, mumbled something about a *good day*—did you have a good day?—and Carl patted her on the shoulder.

Grandpa said, "Yes, but we knew they would—this is just sooner than we hoped. But we've got more trouble." He took a quick turn around the living room, stopped and stooped and looked out over the couch, between the yellowed cotton curtains, to the street. "Karen Svoboda got out and made a call. The cops who were in the Duluth paper, this Davenport and the Russian Kalin, came into the bakery today and got some pastry, and then they sat in front and told Karen about find-ing the body, and about spy rings and murder charges, and the FBI com-ing in. This was no accident, that they came to the bakery."

Carl was freaked: "Man. I hope they weren't watching Karen when she called."

"She was smart," Grandpa said. "She went down to Webster's Beauty; she's got a friend who works there. She talked to the friend and then borrowed her cell phone to make the call. I don't see how they could trace that. They couldn't see her friend, couldn't see the phone, couldn't see her calling . . ."

"But they went another step," Carl said. "Is Spivak talking? Maybe this house is bugged . . ." Carl looked up at the light fixture as if a bug might be dangling there.

"I don't think it's Anton. We would have had a warning. But Mar-sha Spivak's a Svoboda, so maybe it was just more pressure. They can't talk to Anton because of the lawyers, but they talk to the Svobodas, fig-uring it will get back to the Spivaks . . ."

"We hope," Carl said. "So what do we do? Hide out?"

"No, no. We confuse, delay, run around." He took another quick lap of the living room, twisting his gnarled fists together. Not frightened, Carl thought: excited. "I'm thinking that we should send you out again."

Carl glanced at Grandma, but she seemed to be asleep. "Who?"

"Kalin. The Russian," Grandpa said. "If we get her, there'll be a question: Where does this come from? Is this more retribution for Ole-shev? Make it seem even more as though there are two Russian groups fighting it out."

Carl said, "I can't do it tomorrow night. We're singing."

"The woman is at the Radisson Hotel in Duluth. What room, I don't know. If you were there at eleven o'clock tonight, when she would be there, and if you could figure out which room she's in . . ."

"I could buy a pizza at Domino's and get my old pizza hat and de-liver a pizza to her."

Grandpa shook a finger at him. "That is excellent, if we can find out her room number."

"How do we do that?"

"We think. We *think*. We will find a way . . . but." Grandpa paused, then said, "I want you to tell me what you think about the whole idea. Of taking out Kalin. Can you do it? Does it make sense?"

Carl had no other ideas, and nodded. "Makes sense to me. Especially if we could be sure that they are confused. Like, we call them, you could speak Russian, maybe call the embassy, tell them to stay out. If the Russians are working with the FBI . . ."

"Another phone call," Grandpa said. "That could work . . . We need confusion, we need . . . something to make them go away. To look somewhere else. Something. Something."

GRANDPA GAVE GRANDMA two sleeping pills, and she was gone. "She'll wake up at two o'clock in the morning and she'll be up all night, crying half the time," Grandpa said. "I think she just hurts sometimes."

"Maybe the pills screw her up," Carl said. He looked at her face; if anything, it looked more tense asleep than it did when she was awake.

"So many pills; I'm sure you're right, but who knows which ones to stop, eh? Anyway, let's work this out . . ."

They'd had their idea; Grandpa's eyes twinkled when he outlined it to Carl, and though Carl was doubtful, Grandpa thought it might work. "Russia is forever from these people in Duluth. What do they know about Russia? It's a million miles away, that's what."

They made the call from a shopping center telephone. They wanted a busy place, inside, but not one with loud announcements. Carl had brought an old battery-powered radio, tuned to a nonstation, so they got a noisy dead-air hiss. Grandpa dialed the number with a prepaid card, nodded when he got an answer, and Carl held the radio close to the mouthpiece. Grandpa said, with a growly, put-on Russian accent, "Hello? Hello? One moment. Radisson."

Carl took the phone. "Yes, this is Foreign Ministry calling from Moscow for a Nadya Kalin. Could you forward us to her room?"

A woman at the other end said, "Yes. Just a minute."

"Wait, wait. This is five o'clock your time, correct?"

"Yes."

"Middle of the night here," Carl said. "Is she still in five sixty-two?"

"No, no, she's on the seventh floor, but, uh, we can't give out the room number on the telephone."

"What? I'm in Moscow, what . . ."

"I'm sorry, but you can get that number from Ms. Kalin. I'll put you through . . ."

The operator disappeared from the line, and a moment later, the phone started ringing and Carl hung up. "Shit."

"What?" Grandpa asked.

"Got the floor, but she wouldn't give out the room number. She's on the seventh floor."

Grandpa thought for a moment, then said, "We've got to go to Duluth."

"You're coming? What about Grandma?"

"She's asleep. We'll be back before she wakes."

THE DRIVE TO Duluth took forever. Grandpa had another plan for finding the room, but it would only work if Kalin were out. "We should try to get there when she would be eating," Grandpa said. But when Carl drove over the speed limit, Grandpa would say, "Slow, slow, we can't afford a ticket. Look at the clock, remember the miles—we will be all right with steady progress. Calculate. Always calculate."

They finally came over the top of the hill, headed into downtown, saw the Radisson ahead, pulled into the hotel parking lot.

"We could find a public phone, so we wouldn't have to use your cell phone," Carl said.

"I think one call with a cell phone, into the switchboard . . ."

"But it's the small things that kill us," Carl said. "Let me go inside and look around."

"Quickly," Grandpa said, with a small smile. Carl was *thinking*.

CARL WENT INSIDE, had a piece of luck: the check-in desk was just inside the door, and he walked on past, as though he had a room, and found the elevators. The elevators were in the central tower, so most of the area around the elevators and stairs was not visible from the desk. And there was only one person at the desk, and apparently another person in a side room . . .

And he found a pay phone, off the lobby, out of sight from the desk. He turned and went back out. "C'mon," he said.

"What?"

"I got a phone."

He took Grandpa through, the old man putting on a hobble as they walked into the lobby. They ignored the girl behind the desk, who ignored them back, and he left Grandpa with the phone. "One minute exactly," Carl said. "You've got change?"

Grandpa fumbled in his pocket, took out some quarters and dimes. "Go," he said.

Carl took the elevator to the seventh floor. Another piece of luck: not as many rooms as he'd feared. The floor was circular, curving away from him, nobody in sight. He waited, looking at his watch. One minute. The phone should be ringing. . . .

Then he heard it. He followed the sound, four rooms down. Room 745. He paused outside the room, making sure. When he was sure, he walked the rest of the way around the tower, and found nothing but silence. He came back around to 745, and the phone was still ringing. Good.

He pushed the elevator button, the door popped open, and he rode back to the lobby, walked around to the pay phone. He nodded at Grandpa, who hung up. "Yes?"

"Yes," Carl said. He took a ballpoint out of his pocket and wrote 745 on the palm of his hand.

Before they left, he tried to imagine exactly where Kalin's room was. It had been to the right out of the elevator, not the last room . . . hard to figure in a round hotel.

"Wait one more minute," he said to Grandpa. "I want to look at the stairs."

"Hurry," Grandpa muttered.

Carl had to know where the stairs went, where they came out—and after scouting them, stopped at the third floor, 345, and walked off the distance between the room and the elevator. Back in the lobby, he held up a finger to Grandpa, then he walked it off, so he knew about where Kalin's room would be overhead. He marked the position in his mind, went outside, and counted up the building. Third room from the center line, he thought. Maybe fourth. Not second . . .

But maybe he was wasting his time. The hotel seemed nearly empty, and maybe any light on the seventh floor meant that Kalin was home . . .

TIME TO KILL. They drove up the hill, spotted the Domino's just to make sure it was still there, and open, continued to the Miller Hill Mall, spent a half hour walking around the bookstore. Grandpa took a leak, they each bought a danish, and Carl found an outdoor-sports section and browsed the books on guns. Grandpa disappeared into politics.

THE HOURS DRAGGED. At nine o'clock, they couldn't stand it any more. Grandpa had argued that they should wait until after ten, but when Carl looked up and counted, there were lights on the seventh floor, three past the center line. "She's there," Carl said.

"You're sure?"

"Just about."

"Then . . ."

"Rock and fuckin' roll," Carl said.

They went out to the Domino's, waited for the pie. "Get a stinky one," Grandpa said. "Psychologically, you want her to smell it—it means you're real."

Looking out the window of the pizza joint, Carl wished he had a different car. Basically, a cooler car. An SVT Mustang Cobra would be about right; black, so it could run at night without being seen. With tinted windows, so *he* couldn't be seen. A secret box under the floorboards, right under his knees, where he could pop the gun out if a cop stopped him at a crucial point. Bap. Cop goes down, and he's on his way . . . And you wouldn't want Grandpa there; can't be cool with the old man hunched in the corner, peering out over the windowsill.

He got the pizza, olives, onions, and pepperoni, and they each ate a slice on the way back to the hotel, found a parking spot two blocks away, across a welter of streets, not far from a corner. "If it goes smooth, then I just walk back. If there's a problem, it'll be easier to lose them on foot," Carl explained. "You've got your radio, I've got mine, I can hide, you can come and get me."

"I've got the map . . ."

Carl walked around to the back of the car: right. Like he's got this black Mustang, 4.6 liter V8 punching out 390 horsepower, and he's cool, but this cop has got to pull him over, see, and the thing is, something's going on and he can't be late so he pops the cop. But don't the cops call in your license tags when they stop you? It seems like they did on *Cops* . . .

He was caught up in the fantasy, but came out of it when he had to struggle with the hatch lid. He had a piece-of-shit Taurus with about as much cool as a fuckin' baby buggy. He got the gun out of a storage bin, checked the magazine, reseated it, went back to the passenger side. Grandpa handed him a pair of light gloves, and said, "I wiped the box, it should be clean."

"Back in a minute," Carl said.

"Wait, wait." Grandpa fished under the seat, took out a single blaze-orange glove, the kind that hunters wore during deer season. "You must remember—whatever else, you must drop this in the room, you must drop it. This is part of the confusion, part of the plan. Drop the glove."

NEW GIRL BEHIND the desk. She was reading something, and when Carl sensed that she was about to look up, he looked away from her. He pushed the elevator button, but then walked up the seven floors, carrying the pizza, to make sure the stairs were clear.

On seven, he poked his head out into the corridor. Empty. He took his old pizza delivery hat out of his pocket, walked down the corridor, the pizza balanced on top of the gun, which he held horizontally. Knocked on the door. "Pizza."

Nothing. Shit, the lights were on. He knocked again. *"Pizza."*

Then a thump, and his heart sped up just a step. Somebody coming. An eye at the eyehole, blue. He stepped back a bit, to let the woman get a look at him, the flat box and the hat.

The door opened. No woman. A guy, a big guy, a great big fuckin' guy with short hair, barefoot, slacks, and a T-shirt, and then, an instant later, behind him, the woman, saying, "I didn't order a pizza . . ."

And the guy saw the gun, or at least the barrel of it. His eyes widened, and Carl—what the heck—shot him in the heart. The guy looked surprised, and then went down like a ton of bricks and the woman screamed and ran back into another room.

The Imperfect Weapon thought with a tiny splinter of his mind, *Might have known there was another room,* and went after her—strode after her, tall, movie-killer-like—it was all over but the shooting, bitch. He heard a latching sound—sounded like a gun?—and he did a quick peek at the doorway and saw her kneeling behind the bed, fumbling with something, and he brought the gun up.

And she started to turn and he saw the gun in her hand and thought *Whoa,* and the gun seemed to explode in her hand and the doorway next to his head splintered and Carl got off a shot and the woman fired again, ten feet away, hit the door, and then another shot punched through the drywall next to his head and Carl poked the gun around the door and fired twice, quickly, and heard what sounded like a piece of china exploding. He remembered the pink lamp on the nightstand where she got the gun, thought he must have hit it; another shot hit the door and Carl said, "Fuck it," and ran.

And as he ran, he dropped the orange glove Grandpa had given him. He'd forgotten about it until that minute, had held it under the pizza box, but now he'd changed his grip on the box and he saw the glove fall and thought, "Yes," and hurtling the body in front of the door, ran down the corridor, into the stairwell and down the stairs.

He was two flights down when he heard somebody, a man, shout, "Hey, hey . . ." but he kept going, averting his face from the front desk as he hurried by, and was outside before he realized he still had the pizza. He headed for the car—walking fast, trying not to catch anybody's eye, two minutes, no more—and a hundred yards out, realized he was being chased: glancing back, saw a guy in a sport coat coming fast, and the guy was running with one hand held out to his side, like there was something in it. Like a gun.

Carl ran.

Still had the pizza, though.

18

LUCAS WAS LYING on one side of the king-sized bed, copies of *Smart Money, Barron's,* and *Rolling Stone* on the other side, talking to Weather about the case—about how much longer he might be out of town, about Nadya's relationship with Reasons.

Weather said, "She told me that they were having a little fling. How could I disapprove? It's not something we haven't both done."

"I don't want to talk about that."

"Doesn't it seem a little hypocritical, though? You're so grumpy about it. I mean, look at you and Marcy—you can't say that didn't have some kind of effect inside the department. She was working for you, for God's sake. If that happened at the university, you'd have been out on your ear."

And as she said *ear,* Lucas heard a noise that made him sit up. A scream? Very faint. Where was Nadya's room? To Weather, he said, "Wait . . ." And then *boom, boom,* gunfire, a hollow sound, inside a room not far away.

"I hear a gun," he blurted into the phone. "I gotta go."

"What?"

He dropped the phone on the bed and grabbed his gun in its holster off the nightstand and slipped into his shoes without tying the laces and ran for the door and out the door and looked around, spotted the stairwell and ran that way, crashing into the stairwell. He saw the top of a man's head clattering down, a white paper hat and white shirt, turning on the landing below and he yelled, "Hey, hey," and nearly went after him; instinct pulled him into the path of the flight, but Nadya . . .

He turned and ran up, burst through the door into the corridor, saw Nadya's door open and then Nadya with a gun, in the doorway, face pale, blood on her hands, turning toward him, her gun coming up and he yelled, "No," and she shouted, "Jerry is shot, Jerry is shot."

Lucas ran to her door, saw the body on the floor and blood on Jerry's chest. Another man stepped out of his room down the hall and Lucas turned and shouted, "Get back inside and close the door," and he looked down again: Jerry's eyes were closed but he was shaking, trembling, and Lucas stepped over him into the room, punched 911 into the phone and shouted, "There's a cop shot in room seven forty-five in the Radisson, Jerry Reasons is shot. We need an ambulance and the cops."

As he went back past Nadya, he shouted, "Take care of him, the ambulance is on the way, talk on that telephone," and he plunged down the stairway, around and around, down, and out the door at the bottom and through the lobby, shouted at the girls at the desk, "Did a guy in a white shirt come through here?"

One of the girls at the desk looked as if she was about to run away, and the other one crouched slightly, and Lucas realized that he was waving his gun and he said, "I'm with the police. You've got a man shot in seven forty-five, get an elevator ready to go up. Did you see a man in a white shirt?"

"That way," one of the girls said, pointing. "He went down the hill. He was putting on a black jacket."

Lucas was outside, the cold air swatting him, but he barely noticed. Where? A siren started a few blocks away, and he ran in the direction that the woman had pointed. He could see two people, but one of them was a woman, and older; the other was a thin man in a dark jacket, looked like blond hair, walking fast, looking over his shoulder and Lucas ran after him, trying not to make too much noise. He'd worked the gap down to a hundred yards when the man saw him coming, and started running.

The fuckin' phone, Lucas thought. He'd dropped his cell phone on the bed. Stupid. He ran through the dark and the other man turned a corner, moving uphill across a vacant lot, through weeds and some bushes, past a house, and Lucas stumbled, almost lost a shoe—didn't tie his fuckin' shoes, either—and climbed over a thigh-high concrete-block retaining wall and plunged into the weeds of the vacant lot, moving fast, sand burrs ripping at his shoelaces and socks, looking uphill at a line of trees and lights in residential windows . . .

More sirens, three or four of them now. Lucas kept climbing, and realized he was losing the guy, the guy had gained ground on him. Lucas kept going, lost the guy in the darkness of a residential street, but knew which way he was going, and ran that way, saw him again—and the guy saw *him,* turned and raised his arm and Lucas saw three quick sparks and went down on his stomach, thinking, "Too late," but nothing came close, and he scrambled back to his feet and saw a man with a dog, and the man ran up on a lawn, away from him, and Lucas kept going, north, he thought, running awkwardly with his gun held in both hands out in front of him . . .

Saw the man again, again a spark—some kind of flash retarder on the pistol, Lucas thought—and the man had the hillside behind him, and Lucas raised over his head and fired two quick shots with his .45. Way too far away, but maybe, maybe it'd slow the guy down somehow. The man scrambled away, running through yards and around trees, sometimes a faint movement in the streetlights, sometimes simply absent.

Had to make him hide. If Lucas could make him stop, make him hide, make him play cat-and-mouse, he could get the Duluth cops to throw a cordon around the neighborhood, seal it up, and then start going through it yard by yard and garage by garage. If the guy kept moving, though, sooner or later he'd lose himself in the dark . . .

Lucas sprinted along the street, tired, mouth hanging open, gasping for air. He ran three miles, three times a week, but it was on the flat; so far this had been all uphill.

Now where? There: quick movement, man turning down the hill, running downhill now. Still crashing through yards, over fences. Lucas followed, but the noise was terrific as he hit stuff in the dark, bushes, branches, weeds, a can, then the guy out front of him hit a barbecue grill and it clattered across a patio and a few seconds later, a backyard light came on and Lucas saw him disappear through a hedge.

A branch caught him on the cheek and he felt the skin rip; shit. He kept going, through the lighted yard, managed to kick the lid on the barbecue, and a guy in a T-shirt on a three-season porch yelled, "Hey, what ya . . ." and Lucas was through the hedge into the next yard, between two houses, onto the next street, working back into business buildings.

Two ways to go, left or right. He ran left a few yards, saw nothing, turned back right, saw nothing, went that way, then saw the dark movement back to the left and ran after it. But he'd lost more ground. The movement this time was a hundred and fifty yards away: the guy had a definite advantage because he apparently knew where he was going, and Lucas thought, *Car. He's gotta have a car, probably close to the hotel.*

The problem was, they were both running back toward the hotel again, and there was no way to shortcut the other man. He got a stitch in his side, ran through it, turned the corner where he'd seen the movement. Nothing down the hill, but he ran that way anyway, crossed a street, was coming to another when a cop car went by, lights flashing, then suddenly pulled to a stop and Lucas came down into the street and the cop piled out of his car and screamed something at him and Lucas slowed and looked toward him and then the cop fired a shot with a pistol, and Lucas screamed, "BCA, BCA, BCA," and raised his hands and the cop screamed something and Lucas couldn't hear it, and then the cop fired again and Lucas felt something pluck at his shirt and he started running down the hill again.

A moment later, he heard the cop car coming around and he ducked around the next corner and saw, two blocks away, the last sight of the man in the black jacket, turning downhill on that block. No chance to catch him, the cop car coming, no way to outrun it.

Lucas stepped into the street, stuck his gun into his belt, lifted his hands above his head. The cop car slewed around the corner, then nearly ran across the curb into the building, and two cops jumped out, and Lucas screamed, "I'm a cop. I'm a cop with the BCA. The guy who shot Reasons—"

But the cops were screaming at him, their guns pointed, and Lucas shouted, "BCA, you dumb motherfuckers," and finally one of the cops waved a hand at his partner and said, "Put the gun on the street."

"Fuck you," Lucas yelled back. "My hands are over my head, I'm not touching the gun again, you dumb motherfuckers'll shoot me sure as shit. I'm Lucas Davenport, I'm with the state and I'm staying at the Radisson and the guy who shot Jerry Reasons just ran around that corner down there and he's gone, or he's gonna be gone by the time you assholes figure this out."

Now the two cops were confused, and another cop car pulled up and the passenger-side cop came from behind his door and said something to his partner, and they skated around the car, pistols pointed shakily at Lucas, and then one cop said, "Put your hands down and behind your back, sir. We're gonna cuff you till we find out what's going on."

Lucas tried to be calm: "The guy who shot Reasons just ran around that corner—"

"There are more people down the block; just try to be calm and put your hands down . . ."

Lucas put his hands down, and said, "If you don't get a car down there in five seconds, he's gone," and the cops said, "That's all taken care of, sir," but he didn't exactly say *sir* as if he meant it, and the driver-cop cuffed him, the other cop took the .45 out of his belt.

Lucas was talking fast. "If we go back to the Radisson, I've got my ID in my room, and I talked to a guy named Larry Kelly in your detective bureau when we found the old lady's stuff down by the tracks . . . and the Russian investigator can ID me . . . Listen, you gotta find out . . ." He stopped, took a breath: too late. "Ah, fuck, never mind."

"Never mind, what?" asked the cop who cuffed him. Lucas could tell he'd started to believe.

"Never mind trying to put more guys on the killer. He's gone. He's gone. Didn't even get a look at his fuckin' car . . ." He looked down the street, pulled around, hoping against hope that a car might zip through one of the intersections he could see. None did.

Now they believed him a little more; didn't uncuff him, but he said, "Look, let's go over to the hotel. Reasons looked pretty bad. And be careful of the .45. The safety's on, but it's still cocked and there's a round in the chamber."

He let them put him in the backseat of the squad car, and then said, "Put out a call and tell them to nail any speeders they see. I don't know what kind of car, but we're looking for a thin blond guy in a black jacket or a white shirt. He was wearing a white shirt when I saw him, but he pulled a black jacket over it."

The driver put out the call immediately; then the other guy said, "What about Reasons?"

Lucas thought about Reasons shaking and trembling on the floor of Nadya's room. Brain death. He'd seen it before, when a guy's brain was starving of oxygen. "I think Jerry . . . Jerry was hit pretty hard," Lucas said. "I called nine one one before I ran after the guy, but he was hit hard."

"You think . . ."

"Yeah, I think."

"Jesus Christ," the cop said, his eyes big. "Jesus Christ. I was just talking to him this afternoon."

THE UNIFORM COPS brought Lucas through the police lines around the hotel, everybody looking at him hard—they thought he might be a suspect—and they went up in the elevator and Nadya, in the hallway, her blouse soaked with black blood, saw them coming and said, "Lucas, why are you . . ." and then Larry Kelly, the cop who'd been leading the Wheaton murder, and who had been talking to her, turned, saw his arms pinned behind him and asked, "What's going on with you?" looking querulously behind him at the uniform cops.

"How about Jerry?" Lucas asked.

Kelly shook his head. "Didn't even bother to transport him. He's still here."

Lucas stepped forward and looked in the room: Reasons was as Lucas had left him, sprawled faceup on the carpet.

"So what about you?" Kelly said, pressing.

"Found him in the street waving a gun, so we picked him up," one of the cops said, and then, to Lucas, "Sorry," and he stepped behind Lucas and popped off the cuffs.

"Did you see the man?" Nadya asked.

"I chased him about a fuckin' mile," Lucas said, rubbing his wrists. "Then we sort of got tangled up . . ."

"What?" Kelly demanded of the uniforms, incredulity riding his voice. "You had two guys running and you busted this one?"

"Ah, there was no way for them to know," Lucas said. "They couldn't see the other guy and there I was running around in the dark, no ID. Nothing but a gun. They did okay."

"Maybe not," one of the uniformed said. He handed Lucas his .45. "I sorta let off a couple of rounds."

"Yeah." Lucas remembered. He looked down at his left shirtsleeve, put his little finger through the nine-millimeter hole.

"Ah, fuck me," the cop said, turning away.

"We can talk about it," Lucas said. "Just everybody keep their mouths shut for a while, and . . . we can talk about it."

"Go," Kelly said to the uniforms. "But don't go too far."

"What about Jerry?" one of them asked.

"Jerry's dead," Kelly said.

"Jesus, I just talked to him this afternoon."

"Most of us did," Kelly said. "Go."

"ARE YOU ALL RIGHT?" Lucas asked Nadya.

"Yes, I am all right. If Jerry hadn't been here, I would have been . . ." She tipped her head toward the doorway. And she didn't look all right; she looked scared to death; as they talked, she started to shake, and Kelly put his arm around her, squeezing her. "There is nothing between me and death, but luck and sex and coincidence."

"You believe in coincidence."

"Yes," she said, sadly.

"So what happened?"

"A man came to the door. He said he had a pizza, but I ordered no pizza. But Jerry was standing in the bedroom door and . . . he was leaving, we had been in bed already . . . and he went to the door and opened it and I came behind him to say I ordered no pizza, and the man there, *bang*. But not so loud a bang. I saw Jerry start to fall and I ran back to the bed and got his pistol and the man came to the door and I shoot at him three times, and he shoots at me two or three times and hits the lamp . . ."

"You didn't hit him?"

"No. I know the pistol well enough to fire it, but I am not intimate with it, and everything was so fast that he came to the door and I shoot, shoot, shoot, with no thinking. Then he ran, and I ran to the door, and then you came."

"Ah, brother . . ."

Kelly: "What the fuck is going on?"

"We don't know," Lucas said. To Nadya. "How good a look did you get? Could you identify him?"

She shook her head. "I see almost nothing. Nothing! I see the hat, I see the shoot, I run to get the gun and I shoot and shoot and then he was gone."

"Goddamnit."

"But," she said, holding up a finger. She turned and pointed at a blaze orange glove on the floor. "This is his glove. This belongs not to us, and I saw it when he was at the door . . . saw the orange. He must have lost it."

"We're gonna bag it, check it for DNA," Kelly said, as Lucas stepped over to look at it. It was a cheap, fuzzy, synthetic-cloth glove like the ones deer hunters used.

"You saw the guy," Kelly said to Lucas.

The phone rang and Nadya said, "I will get that," and edged around Reasons's body.

"Yes. White guy, white hat, one of those paper pizza hats, blond, I think, wearing a white shirt when I saw him first," Lucas said. "The girls down in the lobby said he was pulling on a black jacket when he went by them . . . He was carrying a pizza box. The whole fuckin' time, he was carrying a pizza box."

"All right. We'll check the pizza places, see if somebody picked up a pizza."

"Probably a dummy to cover the gun."

"Yeah, I think."

Nadya started shouting into the phone, in Russian, then she turned toward Kelly and Lucas and pointed at the phone and Lucas said, "Shit, it's somebody. You got a cell phone?"

Kelly handed him a cell phone and he called Harmon and when Harmon came up, as cool as ever, Lucas said, "We've got a phone call coming into room seven forty-five at the Radisson exactly now, and we need it traced . . . Shit."

Nadya was shaking her head, and hung up.

To Harmon, Lucas said, "You gotta trace that call. We got a big problem here . . ." He explained quickly and Harmon said, "This is a whole new thing. I'll check out guys, but I'm pretty sure that nobody that we're watching is in Duluth."

"Hang on," Lucas said.

To Nadya, "What was that all about?"

"I must call the embassy," she said. "This was a Russian, a man. He said that I should leave, or I will be killed, like Nikitin. He said this action is none of the concern of, of, *my people.* He called us the *siloviki.* This, I do not think, was an American. This *siloviki,* used this way, meaning members of the KGB, this is a new usage."

"So you're saying . . ."

"Maybe this is not the local Americans. Maybe . . . I don't know. This *siloviki,* this is a word Oleshev would have used."

"This is Harmon," he said, handing her the phone. "Tell him about it." She took the phone and stepped away.

Lucas said to Kelly, "We're gonna need the feds in a major way. This thing is out of control."

"You're saying Reasons was killed by a Russian. A *Russian* Russian. By mistake."

Lucas said, "I don't know anymore. For a pro, like you know, an international spy hit man, the guy kinda fucked up."

"I don't see that. There was no reason to think that Jerry would be here," Nadya said, the phone at her side. "Besides that, he was good enough."

"Yeah . . ." The orange glove caught his eye. "But would an international assassin wear a goddamn used blaze orange hunter's glove? Where would he even get one at this time of year?"

They thought about that for a minute, then Lucas: "Climbing down from the international intrigue for a minute . . . Has somebody gone to tell Mrs. Reasons?"

Nadya, hand to mouth: "Oh, my God." Lucas could hear Harmon's voice: "Hello? Hello?"

19

TREY PUT HER new apartment together in two long days. The apartment was off Cretin Avenue, in St. Paul, not far from St. Thomas University, in a well-kept gray-stucco building; two bedrooms, one of which she could use for an office. The rent was twelve hundred dollars a month, which was a lot, but the place felt right.

She bought used furniture for it—good used furniture, most of it from low-end antique shops—and a new bed from Sears. She squandered another two thousand dollars at four different Target stores, buying bathroom and kitchen equipment and a small but nice-looking stereo and twenty CDs, and a television. She went to a used-book store and picked up thirty paperbacks, the best books she remembered from high school and college; *To Kill a Mockingbird,* like that.

When she was done, the place looked almost like a home. All it needed was some living-in, some accumulation of detritus. Where do you buy a clamshell full of pennies and nickels? She would get it, she thought.

The day after that, at six in the evening, when she'd gotten her guts up, she drove down Summit Avenue to the brown-brick four-square house where she'd spent her teen years. There were lights on, and she drove on past, then two more times around the block. *This was necessary,* she thought. But what if they kicked her out without giving her a chance?

She'd dressed up a little bit; a nice skirt and blouse, a navy blue jacket. Her face still looked a little wild—the kind of weathering she'd had, you didn't get rid of in two weeks. Still: she was about a million percent different from the Trey of two weeks past.

She finally parked, walked through a pattern of falling leaves up the sidewalk to the screened porch, through the outer door, crossed the porch—there was an oaken porch swing, but it looked as though it hadn't been used in years. She swallowed, and rang the doorbell; rang it quickly, so she wouldn't have a chance to run.

When she heard the footsteps, she knew her father was coming. That was better: her mother was more skeptical, less given to romantic hope. She had her back to the door as he came up, and she turned just as he opened it.

"Hi, Dad," she said. "I need to talk with you."

"Annabelle . . ." He was a tall man, much balder than she remembered, older, and a little heavier. He seemed shocked.

"I don't need any money," she said. "I'm looking more for . . . information, I guess."

"Annabelle," he said again. He turned, still holding on to the doorknob. "Lucy—Annabelle is here."

After a moment, she heard her mother coming, and her father looked her over again and said, "Well, you better come in."

Her mother came out of the dining room and into the parlor. Her mother had always colored her hair, and still did—expensive coloring, the kind where they give you the touch of gray that looks almost natural. Her hair looked great, but her face no longer did: she had gotten much older, quickly. She said, "Annabelle. I . . . you look a lot better than last time."

"I've given up all that other stuff," she said. "I finally burned out. I've been working—and as I told Dad, I don't need money. I just need a little information. A little push in the right direction."

"Well, come in," her father said. "What exactly are we talking about?"

They moved into the parlor, and Annabelle perched on an easy chair while her parents faced her from a couch. "I need . . . a place to start. You know I got in trouble with the county attorney's office, but I was never brought up on any charges, I was never arrested for anything. Never had any sanctions from the bar. I've been working around, saving my money . . . I've got an apartment here and I'd like to find a job. Clerking, doing pro bono. Anything like that. I don't need much money."

Her father said, "You're really off the dope."

She nodded: "I'm absolutely clean. No dope, no alcohol. All I want is a little quiet. I want to work."

They both stared at her for a long time, and then her mother said, "It's very hard to trust you, after what you've put us through."

"I know that," Annabelle said. "I'm not asking you for money, and I'm not asking you to trust me. I'm asking you to tell me where I can go and get an office and start working. I'll go there, rent the office, or apply for the job, but I want to shortcut it. I don't want to be running around for six weeks. I want to get going."

They looked at her again, long, measuring stares, then her father said to her mother, "We need to talk somewhere." To Annabelle: "You wait here, we're going in the kitchen."

They were gone for ten minutes, and might have been arguing, Annabelle thought. She sat perched on the chair, looked at all the stuff—the detritus—that the Ramfords had accumulated in forty years of marriage. Knickknacks, paintings, pottery, photographs. Seashells full of nickels and pennies, and the odd pair of fingernail clippers.

Ten minutes, and they came back out of the kitchen. Her father sat down, her mother moved behind the couch.

"You know our suite in the Foster Building," her father said. He cleared his throat. "At the end of the fourth floor annex, that's one up from where I am, there's an empty office. One big room. We could put a desk in there, some office equipment, and a couple of chairs. You'd have access to our library and Lexis. You would not be an employee of the firm, but . . . we'd give you all our pro bono. Nobody wants to do it, and it's all over the place, and I'll pay you out of my pocket. But: you screw up just once, and I'll lock the office and I'll tell the security people to keep you out of the building."

She thought about it: not exactly what she wanted. Better in some ways, but the idea of her father looking over her shoulder every minute . . .

But then, she could handle her father, now, she thought. Because way deep down in her heart, she no longer really gave a shit what he thought. She needed the break, and as soon as she'd worked it, as soon as she was on her feet, she could move out.

"I'll take it," she said. "You won't be sorry. All I want to do is work."

NOT EVERYTHING WAS sweetness and light. They were still wary of her, still waiting for the monster to jump out of her eyes. When she left, her father said, "I'll see you tomorrow?" and it really was a question.

"I'll be waiting for you," she said.

She stopped at a supermarket on Grand, got enough food for a week, including some easy microwave one-dish stuff. As she was lying on her used couch, eating chicken-and-rice, it occurred to her that she was about six blocks from the first place she'd ever sampled crack.

Watching herself, she was amazed to find not even the slightest whisper of desire. Two weeks ago, a bottle of cheap wine was home. Now, she thought, she might be a teetotaler. Maybe. Maybe the stress of trying to get a job going would bring back all the bad stuff.

She doubted it: it seemed now, at this time and place, that all that had been scorched right out of her.

LATER THAT EVENING, before she went to bed, she again felt the barrenness of the apartment. Not an emotional thing, but a simple, physical emptiness. She needed pottery, bird feathers, milkweed hulls, pinecones, a cup full of dried-up ballpoint pens and eraserless pencils, a file cabinet full of paper about one thing or another. She needed insurance, she needed a retirement program, she needed to open an account at Fidelity. She needed quarterly reports.

Standing in her new Target nightgown, she dumped her new pack on the floor, and looked at the few pieces that fell out. All that was left of her old life. She picked up her knife. Ought to throw it, she thought. This was not a good vibe . . .

But still, a girl should have a knife.

She opened the blade and noticed the brown crusty stuff . . . "What?"

Blood? She held it next to a new Target lamp. Dried blood. She cut the guy up there in Duluth, the killer guy.

And she thought: *DNA.* Serious evidence against somebody, right there in her hand.

What to do? She was afraid of that cop, Davenport. He'd sounded so damn mean . . .

She closed the blade on the knife.

Tomorrow, an office.

The knife, she'd think about.

20

THE HOURS AFTER a cop is killed are always a nightmare: telling the family, figuring out what went wrong, deciding if some living person is to blame—and Nadya was taking a hit on the last item.

She insisted that Reasons had initiated the relationship, telling her that his marriage was essentially over. Her argument was good enough, and detailed enough, that it made the Duluth cops angrier than ever. To have one of their own killed, and thus automatically qualified for sainthood—nobody liked to see a dead cop, but on the other hand, it never hurt the budgetary process if you lost the occasional flatfoot—and to have all of that tarnished by a *Russian* and maybe even a *Commie* . . .

Lucas took some of the heat off in a quick, illegal, and private meeting with the police chief, where everybody agreed that Lucas hadn't actually been stopped, shot at, or really handcuffed while he was pursuing the killer . . . *that* wouldn't have been good for the budget.

There was also a general agreement that it wouldn't be necessary to mention the sexual liaison to the press. Reasons had actually been *guarding* Nadya when he was murdered—he had given his life to save hers.

Lucas got back to Weather, late, waking her, telling her what had happened. Nadya had moved to a new room, and Weather said she would call her.

"I can tell you she ain't asleep," Lucas said.

WHILE ALL THAT was going on, so was the chase: Duluth cops went to every pizza place in town, trying to see who might have bought the pizza. They knew it was a fresh one—Nadya said she could smell it, even after the shooting.

"Must have been a hungry sonofabitch, hanging on to the pizza when you're chasing him all over the fuckin' hill," Kelly said.

"Weird shit happens," Lucas said.

Several pizza places had customers who might have fit the vague description they had of the killer: thin, blond, black jacket or white shirt. None of those had any more details.

The women at the hotel's front desk had seen nothing but the back of the pizza-man's head.

In any case, nobody found anything: the killer was gone.

IN THE MORNING, Andreno, calling upstate from Virginia, asked, "What the fuck happened down there?"

Lucas told him, and Andreno said, "Maybe she needs a bodyguard. Somebody with a gun."

"You want the job?"

"It's either that or go home. The Spivaks are in a bunker."

"Come on down and let's talk," Lucas said. "I need some theoretical bullshit."

"I'm on my way."

• • •

LUCAS TRIED TO go back to sleep, failed, eventually got up, cleaned up, looked at the clock, and realized that Andreno could be there at any minute. He called and Andreno said, "I'm just coming into town. If I don't get lost, I'll be there in ten minutes."

Lucas called Nadya's room. She was up, dressed, and sounded like she had a cold.

"Breakfast," he said. "Ya gotta eat."

"I need advice," she said. "And I need coffee."

"I'll see you upstairs in two minutes," Lucas said.

LUCAS TOOK the elevator. It stopped two floors up—she'd changed rooms—and Nadya got on, eyes and nose puffy, and said, "Oh, God."

"Yeah." Lucas was tempted to give her a hug, but he wasn't a hugger, and she slumped in the corner, staring at the control buttons. At the top, they went into the restaurant, got a booth. The restaurant was already rotating, and they were overlooking the city but turning toward the harbor. They could see two long, low freighters standing offshore, heading into port, and another one, on the horizon, a dwindling lump.

The waitress came and they ordered coffee and Lucas asked for a waffle and bacon. The waitress left and Nadya said, "Do you think the . . . news . . . of our relationship will be successfully suppressed?"

Lucas shrugged. "I don't know. It doesn't help anybody if it gets out, but police departments are the biggest rumor mills in the world. Everybody in the department knows by now. The police reporter here, the guy we met down at that shack . . . he's no dummy. He'll probably hear about it."

"But will he print it?"

"If he does, it could hurt him with his sources in the department—

everybody would be pissed off at him. I don't think anyone would confirm it, officially, so he'd have to worry about printing rumors . . ."

Nadya took a napkin out of a napkin holder and folded it, precisely square, then folded it again. "I have to decide whether to tell my superiors what happened. If I do, it would not be good for me. If I don't, and they find out, it would be worse. But if I don't, and they don't find out, and if we get the killer . . ."

As she was talking, Lucas noticed another woman approaching their table—not a waitress, but a woman in jeans and a nylon windbreaker. She was dark haired and stocky, and she was moving quickly, beelined toward them, and Lucas said, "Uh . . ." but the woman ignored him and said to Nadya, "Are you Nadezhda Kalin?" She pronounced the name with authority and a light went on in Lucas's brain and he started to get out of the booth just as the waitress appeared with two cups of hot coffee and blocked him, and Nadya looked at the woman and said, "Yes?"

"I am Jerry Reasons's wife," the woman said, and she launched herself into the booth on top of Nadya, her fingernails flashing, and Lucas said, "Oh, shit," and the waitress with the coffee went down ass-over-coffee-cup and Nadya screamed and slashed back.

Lucas was out of the booth and grabbed Reasons around the waist and tried to pull her off Nadya, but she was strong, angry, out of control, and when Lucas got her back a foot she turned in his arms and slashed at his face with inch-long, highly polished fingernails, cut him across the nose and he grunted and lost her, and she went back after Nadya.

Nadya had gotten her feet up into the booth in front of her and kicked Reasons in the chest, and they were both screaming and waiters were running toward them, and Lucas got Reasons around the waist again and tried to pull back while avoiding the fingernails. Both women now had blood on their faces and Lucas, trying not to hurt Reasons, but at the same time hold on to her, lost her again, and she went back into the booth and Nadya picked up the silver-metal napkin holder and smashed Reasons in the forehead.

Reasons stopped, hung over Nadya for a second, and Lucas wrapped himself around her and pinned her arms, and then Nadya, now screamingly angry herself, smashed her a second time in the forehead, and Reasons went limp.

Lucas was shouting "Whoa, whoa, whoa" at Nadya, who came out of the booth with the napkin holder, looking for a third shot, and Lucas let go of Reasons with one arm, put his hand in Nadya's face, and catapulted her back into the booth.

"Whoa!" he shouted, and the combination of the shout and the impact she took at the back of the booth stopped her. Lucas pivoted away, with Reasons still wrapped up. She was conscious, but loopy, like a fighter who's been tagged hard, but not quite dropped.

The restaurant manager was running toward them and Lucas said, "I'm a state cop. Call the police, tell them to get a car up here."

Without a word, the woman turned and ran the other way. The waitress was back on her feet, holding her coffee-stained shirt away from herself, saying, "I'm really fucked up. I'm really fucked up."

"Are you burned?" Lucas asked.

"Look at my blouse. This is like three days old," she said, and Lucas decided that if she was burned, she wasn't burned badly. Lucas looked back at Nadya, said, "Stay in the booth," and pushed Reasons further away, put her in another booth, and blocked it with his body.

"Jesus . . ."

BOTH WOMEN WERE BLEEDING, and Reasons was still dazed, but neither was badly hurt. One of them started crying, and then the other. A waitress said to Lucas, "You're bleeding like crazy," and pressed a napkin to his forehead. "She must have got you with her fingernails."

A busboy was gawking at Lucas and said, "Boy, I wish I could have seen this," which made Lucas laugh despite himself.

Then the cops arrived, a sergeant and a patrolman, and trailing them, Andreno, with a look of wonderment. Lucas explained what happened to the cops, and the sergeant said, "Ah, shit," and then, "What do you want to do?"

"Could you take Mrs. Reasons home? Talk to her?"

"Well, uh, are we gonna have charges here?"

"Just a goddamn bar fight, kind of, except in a restaurant," Lucas said.

"And except that it's in a big restaurant in the middle of the morning and nobody's drunk and everybody's bleeding," the patrolman said.

"Won't do anybody any good if it gets out," Lucas said. "Why don't we just do something?"

"Disappear it?" the sergeant suggested.

"That would be good."

"We oughta call in and see what they want to do," the patrolman said cautiously. A new guy, Lucas thought.

"Why don't you call the chief directly," Lucas said to the sergeant. "Go off the record—there's been a lot of shit since last night, and we're trying to handle it. Nobody *wants* charges. What's the good of an assault charge against a woman whose husband just got murdered?"

The cop nodded, looked at Nadya and then at Reasons, and then at his partner. "I'll make the call right here. Nothing happened."

"Atta boy," Andreno said.

"Who the fuck are you?" the partner asked.

"BCA undercover," Lucas said. "Pretend you never saw him."

"What about my shirt?" the waitress asked. "It's new, it's probably ruined."

Lucas asked, "What's the biggest tip you ever got for coffee and waffles?"

"Maybe five dollars."

"Brace yourself; your ship just came in."

She nodded, looked down at her blouse, and up at Lucas: "All right. Hope it's like one of them supertankers."

. . .

THE DULUTH COPS took Reasons out, and Andreno said, "You got a cut on your nose. You need another napkin."

"That woman was like a hurricane of fingernails," Lucas said. He touched his nose, and it stung. "I hope she didn't give me something."

"You mean, like the clap?" Andreno said. He was having a pretty good time, now.

"What is this clap?" Nadya asked. She had tears running down through her makeup, and Lucas shook his head at Andreno, said, "Let's get her to her room."

ANDRENO PROVED to be expert at gently cleaning and bandaging wounds, and he did both Nadya and Lucas, using Band-Aids from Lucas's Dopp kit. "Leave them on until the blood dries—tomorrow would be good—and then wash them off. You'll still have grooves, both of you."

"I'm not leaving it on my fuckin' nose," Lucas said. "I'd rather bleed."

"What is this groove?" Nadya asked. She'd become quiet, somber after the fight.

"Fingernail cuts," Andreno said. "Nasty. I always hated to break up fights between women. When women fight, civilization goes right out the window. They don't know how to play-fight, like guys. They go right for the eyes."

"I hit her hard, with those napkins," Nadya said, with just a sliver of satisfaction.

"Yes, you did," Lucas said. "She wasn't exactly a lightweight, either. I think I fucked up my back, getting her off you."

"Two Aleves," Andreno said. "Get a couple for Nadya."

. . .

NADYA WAS RELUCTANT, but they went back to the restaurant when Andreno complained that he hadn't had breakfast. The manager looked at them with trepidation, but the waitress was right there: Lucas had given her a hundred-dollar bill. After they ordered, Andreno said, "Tell me everything. I don't know shit."

Lucas told him. Andreno was bright, and a longtime street cop. When he finished, Andreno said, "What you need is to finish those genealogies. If there are four families, somebody in the families is gonna know who the killer is."

"Spivak might know," Lucas said. "That's not doing us any good."

"I know, but the more you nail down the families, the more you bring up the possibility that they're all going to jail on spy charges. Somebody, somewhere along the line, is gonna crack."

"We haven't even talked with the Svobodas yet," Lucas said. "Put some bullshit on a woman in their shop . . ."

"The thing I keep thinking about is those birth certificates from the ancestors. The fake ones. Maybe there's some way to go through the vital records and pull everybody who makes that claim."

"I don't think they'd be computerized that far back," Lucas said. "Maybe they would. I can check."

They thought about that for a minute, then Nadya said, "Remember when we talk to this horse-woman, the one who is a barmaid at Spivak's?"

"Yeah?"

"If I remember, she said that one of the men at the table was very old. We do not have any very old people in our families. Is there a way you can look at driver's papers?"

Lucas snapped his fingers: "Good. Good thought. That's all been on the computer for a long time. Say we go back ten years, so he's likely to have a driver's license. Everything we've seen has been on the Range, so we look only at the Range cities—Virginia, Eveleth, Hibbing, Chisholm, whatever, there can't be too many people. We pull those names, and then we start pulling birth certificates."

"Another possibility," Andreno said. "How about some kind of analysis of the telephone records of the two families you already have? Who'd they call? If they're spies, and they're all hooked together, I bet there's been a long history of calling each other."

"*Mmm.* I don't know how far that stuff goes back," Lucas said. "The FBI could figure it out."

"How do we get all this stuff going?"

"Make some phone calls," Lucas said. He added, "Micky, I think you should hang around with Nadya, at least when I'm not. Maybe, when we're driving around, you oughta follow, about six cars back. See if you can spot somebody looking at us."

"How did they find us here?" Nadya asked.

"When the woman called from St. Paul, the woman from the shack, she said she figured this is the hotel we'd stay at. Maybe everybody figures that. They just call up and asked for you. If the front desk put the call through, they'd just hang up. Then they'd know where you were . . . Not that many big hotels in Duluth."

"Maybe we should move," Andreno said.

"I think so," Lucas said. "You guys, anyway. Get adjoining rooms somewhere, go in under a different name. Ask the desk to notify you if anybody asks under your real name."

"We can do that," Andreno said, looking at Nadya. "What do you think, honey?"

"What is this 'honey'?" Nadya asked.

BEFORE ANDRENO and Nadya left to find a new place, Lucas took Nadya aside and said, "Before the fight, you were wondering about telling your bosses about this . . . liaison."

"Yes."

He shook his head: "I wouldn't. If you tell them, you're in trouble. If you don't tell them, you're in a little more trouble, but what are they gonna do, shoot you? So the spread in penalty isn't that much if they find out one way or the other. But if we crack the case, and they never find out—you're gold."

She looked at him for a long time, and then asked, "Have you been in trouble much, with your agency?"

"Not with this one. I once got fired from another one, but they hired me back."

"Why did they fire you?"

"I beat up a guy. A pimp. Maybe I was too enthusiastic."

"Why'd they hire you back?"

"Couldn't live without me," Lucas said.

She looked at him for another long moment, then smiled just a little, and said, "I think maybe you were . . . this is a phrase Jerry used for some people . . . a big pain in the ass."

LUCAS HADN'T KNOWN Reasons very well—they had spent a few hours together over a couple of days, enough that Lucas knew that they would never have been good friends. But the murder hung over his head; he didn't have any trouble functioning, didn't feel any great sorrow or terrible regret for things left undone or unsaid . . . but the death hung there. For one thing, he thought he should feel worse than he did. When his friend Del had been shot in the leg the previous winter, Lucas had spent a couple of hours a day at the hospital, then more time at Del's home, had worked out with him in rehab. With Reasons, he could hardly remember what his voice sounded like. And when he stopped to think about it, *that* made him feel bad. Reasons was a mote in the eye . . .

After Nadya and Andreno left, Lucas spent the rest of the morning and afternoon harassing people in St. Paul, trying to pull people into work on a Saturday. He called up Neil Mitford, the governor's top aide, and had him wade in, asked Rose Marie Roux to call downtown and kick butt. Generating the list of licenses was not a problem, but pulling the vital records essentially had to be done by hand. He tried to get twenty people working at it.

He'd worked this out: there were more or less forty thousand people in the Range cities. According to an almanac he carried in his laptop, only about 1 percent of the American population was male and eighty years old or older. The Range might have an older population than the country as a whole, because young people had been fleeing the area for decades—still, even if there were twice as many eighty-plus males, that'd only be eight hundred. With twenty people working on it, they would have to check only forty records each.

At four in the afternoon, a young man named Joshua called and said he'd found the name of a ninety-one-year-old man named Lou Witold who showed a baptismal certificate in Mahnomen County, and a notation that his original birth certificate, issued by the Catholic hospital, had been destroyed.

"That's the guy," Lucas said.

"He's dead," Joshua said. "He died six years ago."

"That's not the guy," Lucas said. "Got anything else on him?"

"He was married to an Anne Witold, whose records were destroyed in the same fire. She's also dead."

"Okay. You said it's, uh, Joshua? Listen, Joshua, start tracking Witolds. Pull all the Witold driver's licenses from St. Louis County, and see if you can build a genealogy, okay?"

"Okay. Do you want it today?"

"Yes. Tell your supervisor that all the overtime was authorized by the governor."

"Really?"

"Really," Lucas said. "You don't want to piss off the governor, not with these reductions in force going on."

"I need the overtime," Joshua said earnestly. "I'll work as long as the computers are turned on."

"Atta boy," Lucas said; he sounded like Andreno.

THE EARLY NEWS had Reasons all over the place. First cop killed in years—died trying to save a Russian. Every news channel that Lucas looked at had bought the bodyguard line.

At five twenty, a woman named Romany called: "I've got another one of these Mahnomen-fire birth certificates, issued to a Burt and Melodie Walther. Both still alive—Burt still has a driver's license. He's ninety-two. You want me to do the genealogy thing, like Josh?"

"Yeah. This could be the guy we want . . . How's Joshua doing?"

"Let me check," she said.

Joshua came back. "Lou and Anne Witold had two children, both boys, Leon and Duane. Duane married somebody named Karen Hafner, and we have driver's licenses for them up to nineteen seventy-eight, and then no more. It's like they moved. The other kid, Leon, married a Wanda Lindsey, and they're still in Hibbing. And they've got a couple of kids, named John and Sarah, and Sarah I can't find, but John is living in Rochester—he's twenty-eight, and I don't know if he's married or not, or if he has any kids. I'm still looking."

"Keep going," Lucas said. He hung up, took his notes on Witold over to the Oleshev genealogy, and slipped it into one of the two remaining charts, three generations.

"Goddamnit," he said, looking at it. Too good to be true? They'd get a test with Bert and Melodie Walther.

He called Nadya, who'd moved to the Harbor Lodge: "What'd you tell the bosses?"

"I told them that Jerry was shot while guarding me."

"Atta girl," he said.

"That's what Micky says. 'Atta girl.'"

"We've got some new people for our genealogy," he said.

He filled her in, and she said, "We need a picture of this man," she said. "This Walther. We can show it to the woman in the aluminum house with the horses, who saw the old man at Spivak's . . ."

"Maisy Reynolds," Lucas said. "We can do that. I'll talk to the chief up there about getting a picture. What are you doing?"

"Watching a movie. *Legally Blonde.* This is a very peculiar movie."

"Actually, it's based on a true story," Lucas said. "It's kind of a documentary."

"Really?"

"True. This can be a very unusual country, sometimes."

LUCAS WAS SMILING when he hung up. Weather had made him watch *Legally Blonde,* and he'd loathed it. Then she made him watch *Legally Blonde II,* and he'd wanted to pluck out his eyeballs. The idea of *Legally Blonde* going back to the KGB, or whatever the fuck it was, as a documentary . . .

That made him laugh, and then he thought of the mote in the eye, Jerry Reasons, and he stopped laughing.

Maybe laugh tomorrow, he thought.

21

ANDRENO AND NADYA arrived at nine o'clock the next morning, Nadya still red and puffy around the eyes. She'd been having crying jags, Andreno told him, but not as often anymore. Andreno was solemn and attentive when he was beside her, but he winked at Lucas when her back was turned. Andreno was wearing a green-and-white baseball jacket with a hammerless .38 hanging in a holster under his arm. "What's happening?"

"The Hibbing cops got a picture of the old man this morning," Lucas said. "They phoned it in to St. Paul, and St. Paul e-mailed it to me. I've got it in my laptop."

"Christ, you're a computer weenie," Andreno said. "But I knew that."

"Look, here's where we're at," Lucas said. "We know that whoever's doing the shooting isn't ninety years old and is probably hooked into these families—unless the shooter is from completely outside." He looked at Nadya. "Like a shooter out of the embassy."

She shook her head: "Absolutely no."

"I buy that," Lucas said to Andreno. "The only reason to go after the Russian Mafia guy, the Russian embassy guy, *and* Nadya is that these people are trying to protect themselves from everybody. So we're looking for somebody tied into these families, but young and healthy enough to run away from me. Spivak's kids would be candidates, except that we know where they were when the killings took place."

"Maybe not the daughter . . ."

"That wasn't the daughter running from me the other night," Lucas said. "That was a guy. Anyway: it's gotta be somebody young enough to run, which means not more than my age. I'm in good shape, for my age, and I wasn't gaining on him."

"So if we look at everybody related, everybody young enough to run away from you . . ."

"Unless the families have brought somebody in," Nadya said. "They were spies. They have resources. They would have some hidden money—gold, even. They would have some criminal contacts to perform their duties."

"Yeah . . ." They all thought about it for a few seconds. "If they were moving people out of the country through Canada . . . I mean, Canada is notorious for the criminal gangs along the border, preying on Americans," Lucas said. "They work over here, go back there, and take advantage of the lack of coordination by the cops. If it's a Canadian killer, we're probably not going to find him."

"But we keep looking," Andreno said, "Because it probably isn't."

NADYA SHIFTED the subject: "Should I find Jerry's wife and try to talk with her?"

Lucas shook his head: "No. Nothing to be said."

"Always something to be said," Nadya argued.

"Nothing that would do any good," Lucas said. "Best to finish this case, and go back home."

She nodded, but with an air of doubt, and Andreno said, "If you gotta talk to her, I'll go along. Don't go sneaking over there. Cops got guns."

Nadya nodded again and changed the subject again: "What now? With this picture in your laptop?"

"We go back up to Virginia," Lucas said. "We'll talk to Maisy Reynolds—I called and told her we're coming—and show her the old man's picture. The guy I've got in the computer looks like her description, but we need her to say yes."

"What about the genealogy?" Nadya asked.

"It fits," Lucas said. "The Walther family slips right in. One difference: the oldest ones, Burt and Melodie, the ones with the weird birth certificates, are still alive. But their kids—they had a son named Thomas, who was married to a woman named Catherine—are dead. They were killed in a car accident back in the seventies. There was still a third generation, though. Thomas and Catherine had a son named Roger who married a woman named Janet. They're still around, in Hibbing."

"You still want me to trail you?" Andreno asked.

"Yeah. If Reynolds identifies the old guy as the one who was in Spivak's bar, we're gonna go jack him up. Maybe even if she can't identify him. I'd like you to get to his place before we do, find a spot on the street, and then just watch. See if anything happens after we leave."

"What about the youngest one?" Nadya asked. "The old man's . . . what? Grandson?"

"Grandson, yes. Roger," Lucas said. "After we're done with the old man, we'll look him up. Him and his wife. He's our best candidate right now."

"Are we breaking the case now?" Nadya asked.

Lucas looked at Andreno, who did something Italian with his face and shoulders, meaning, "Could be." He said, "Could be."

. . .

AND ON THE WAY down in the elevator, Nadya said, "Micky says this woman in *Legally Blonde* will be appointed to the federal appeals court by the president."

Lucas looked at Andreno, and said, "You pushed it too far." Andreno shrugged.

"You're joking me again," she said. "Why do American men joke so much? Do you ever discuss?"

ON THE DRIVE up to Virginia, Nadya again asked about going to see Raisa Reasons. "I believe there are some useful things that I could tell her."

"Listen . . . you're not really a cop, are you?" Lucas asked. "You're some kind of intelligence agent. You can tell me, because I know you're not a cop."

"Why is this?"

"Because you know some stuff that cops know, but you don't know other stuff. Daily things. What we see every day. You don't know why you shouldn't go see Reasons's wife."

"Well, why shouldn't I?"

"Are you a cop? I won't tell anybody what you say."

She thought about it for a minute, then said, "No. I'm a major with the SVR. I'm in the Counterintelligence Division."

"Now we're getting somewhere," Lucas said. "Reasons and I figured out that you weren't a cop the first time we went to the morgue, to look at Oleshev's body."

"Yes?" She may have been discomfited, but didn't reflect it. Instead, she seemed amused and interested.

"Yes. You flinched when you looked at the body. Cops your age don't flinch. They've seen two hundred bodies and are interested in

what they're going to find out, they don't really feel much about looking at another dead guy."

"Why would that tell me about talking to Raisa Reasons?"

" 'Cause you'd know it wouldn't do any good. When you've been a
cop for a while, you figure out that the best thing in domestic disputes
is distance," Lucas said. "Just simple *distance.* You get a husband and
wife breaking up, and one of them goes after the other, the one thing
that'll end the violence, end the anger, is distance. If you can't find the
other person, don't know where she is, pretty soon the violent feelings
dissipate and everybody goes back to living their lives."

"But I could tell her—"

"What's to explain? She knows what happened. What're you going
to tell her, that it didn't feel good?"

"No, I—"

"That it did feel good?"

Small smile. "No, but—"

Lucas kept interrupting: "That he really loved *her,* but their marriage
was troubled and he was lonely? That makes his death *her* fault. That he
really wasn't serious? That devalues her marriage, that he could sleep
with somebody so casually."

"Maybe tell her that I'm sorry."

"If you're sorry for *her,* that's patronizing, and it'll really piss her off.
If you're sorry about the situation, that's obvious, and she won't care
how sorry you are. None of it does any good," Lucas said. "The best
thing to do is go home, get some distance. You know the saying 'Let
sleeping dogs lie'?"

"I know it, but this dog is not sleeping," Nadya said.

"She'll be okay, when the shock wears off. The Duluth guys will
manage her, they'll take care of her, and after a while, you won't be so
important. She'll have other things to do and other things to think about.
What to do with herself."

"Without Jerry," Nadya added, the gloom settling back.

"Without Jerry, but with some money," Lucas said. "Jerry had a lot of insurance coverage. She'll be okay."

Nadya sighed and stretched and yawned and finally said, "Maybe you're right."

"Of course I am," Lucas said. "I've seen it a lot. Best thing to do: get away from it if you can."

MAISY REYNOLDS WAS two minutes out of the shower, looking good in a cowboy shirt with pearl buttons and tight riding jeans; she smelled like Irish Spring soap. "I'm getting ready to go to work. If you guys keep coming around, I'll probably get fired. They're really mad about what you're doing. About Anton."

"How long have you worked for him?" Lucas asked, as he and Nadya followed her into her trailer. The place smelled like celery and carrots and beer. She pointed them at a tiny dinette, and Nadya and Lucas settled into chairs. Lucas took his laptop out of his briefcase and set it on the tippy Formica-topped table.

"Six years. He's not a bad guy. He's paternal, I guess you'd say. A little bit cheap, but you can talk to him. He doesn't mess with your tips."

"How about his kids?"

"The son is just like his dad. The daughter's an asshole."

"But this job, it must be good enough, if you can keep horses and a nice house," Nadya ventured.

"Thank you, honey, for the 'nice house,' " Reynolds said, looking around the kitchen. "Sometimes in the winter, when we get an ice storm, I feel like I'm living in a beer can . . . You guys want some carrot juice? I got some fresh."

"No, thanks," Lucas said, grinning at her. "It's made out of vegetables."

"I would like," Nadya said. "The vegetables in your restaurants are not so good."

"Better in Russia?" Reynolds asked, interested.

"I should say so," Nadya said. "Also better in France, in Germany, in Scandinavia, in Italy, in Israel."

"I can believe that. Most of our vegetables are designed so they're cheap to ship," Reynolds said, as she took a blender pitcher from the refrigerator. "But these are fresh and old-fashioned, right out of the garden, fertilized with genuine horse shit."

Lucas brought up the photograph of Burt Walther. Walther was outside his house in Hibbing, looking toward the camera, but not at it. He seemed to be looking at a van driver, while the photo was taken from the back of the van. Lucas turned the computer toward Reynolds, who was pouring the juice. She handed a glass to Nadya, and they both looked at the photo over their glasses. Reynolds sipped and said, "Jeez, it *kinda* looks like him . . ."

Lucas had the picture up in Photoshop Elements, and he put the zoom tool on the old man's face and clicked a couple of times, enlarging it. Reynolds half crouched, looking straight at the screen, and finally said, "That's the guy. That's definitely him. Who is he?"

"Rather not say right at the moment," Lucas said. He turned the computer around and shut it down.

"Okay. Spy stuff," Reynolds said. "Is this the thing that's gonna get me fired?"

"We won't tell if you don't," Lucas said.

"This juice, it is excellent," Nadya said. "From horse shit? I should try this when I get home. We have much horse shit in Moscow."

THE WALTHERS LIVED in a small house in a working-class neighborhood of Hibbing. Most of the neighbors had gone to vinyl siding, but the Walthers had stuck with the original gray-shingle siding, with white trim gone gray and flaky with age. The small lawn was neatly kept; a sparse foot-wide flower bed, with burgundy petunias, lay along the front wall under the picture window. A detached garage leaned disconsolately away from the wind; an old bulk-oil tank stuck to the back of the house like a metal leech.

Lucas had called Andreno as they rolled into town, and was told that he'd been down the street for twenty minutes. "The old man's there— he went out to his mailbox."

When Lucas turned the corner, following the MDX's navigation system through town, he saw the blue-painted mailbox and pulled to the curb beside it. He saw Andreno's van parked up the street, where Andreno could see both Walther's house and the garage behind it.

"When I knock, stay behind me," Lucas said.

"Yes?" She said it with a question mark.

"In case he's a nutso Russian spy and comes up shooting. Knocking on doors is the most dangerous thing we do."

She stopped smiling when Lucas took his .45 out of its holster, racked a shell into the chamber, and, leaving it cocked, clicked on the safety before slipping it back in its holster.

"Let's go," he said.

BURT WALTHER WAS standing in the picture window. Lucas saw him as they started up the walk and said out of the side of his mouth, "There he is."

Walther was wearing a generic gray sweatshirt and pleated khaki pants. He had his hands in his pockets as he watched them come up the walk, and as they approached the front door, he moved toward it, opening it as they came up to the stoop. Lucas had his ID in his left hand as the door opened. Walther stuck his head out, looked at them with blue-eyed uncertainty, and said with a question mark, as Nadya had, "Yes?"

"Mr. Walther. My name is Lucas Davenport, and I'm an investigator with the state Bureau of Criminal Apprehension. We're investigating the death of a Russian seaman in Duluth, and we need to talk to you about it."

"Duluth?" The old man—and Lucas could see he was *very* old—was uncertain, unfocused; his sweatshirt was worn and pilled around the neck, and his khakis were wrinkled and worn.

"The killing of Rodion Oleshev, although he may have told you his name was Moshalov."

"His name?" The old man grappled with the concept.

Lucas thought, *Ah, shit,* and glanced at Nadya.

Then the old man rallied and said, "Come in, I suppose. I don't have any food. My wife makes cookies sometimes but we don't have any now . . ."

They followed as he tottered back inside. An aging color television was stuck in the corner of a room and an old lady was sitting in a wheelchair, staring at it. She didn't look at them.

"Mrs. Walther?" Lucas asked.

No reply. Walther said, "She's not so well, today. You want me to go to Duluth? I can't go, there's nobody to stay with Melodie . . ."

"No, no, we don't want you to go anywhere . . ."

The ensuing interview was jagged, uninformative. Walther claimed that he hadn't been to Virginia for two years. Then he agreed that he might have been, but couldn't remember exactly when, how he got there, or what he did. He didn't remember Oleshev, the Svobodas, or the Witolds. He remembered Anton Spivak, though, and Spivak's Tap, and began a wandering reminiscence of the last time he'd been to Spivak's.

He'd gone with a man named Frank, he said, after a Hibbing–Virginia football game in which Walther's son had played right guard. Lucas realized a few seconds into the account that the game had taken place in the fifties or sixties, and that he was talking about the son who'd died in the car accident. He tried to interrupt, but Walther took such great pleasure in the story—his son had picked up a fumble out of the air and had run it back for a touchdown, and it turned out that the fumbler was a Spivak, which they didn't learn until they were laughing about it in the bar—that Nadya shushed Lucas and made him listen.

When the story was finished, they tried to press on, asking about the hospital where he'd been born.

"My parents came here with a boat, the whole boat all to the same place. From New York to Minnesota on the train. They were called the Vilnius Boat, because they gathered at Vilnius for their tickets. Vilnius is in . . ." His mind wandered away. Then, "They all came over on the same boat, and then the farms failed because of the winter, and everything died. People starved and the mines were opening and the boat came to Hibbing. The whole boat. They went to work in the mines, the men."

They asked about Roger: Roger made him happy—a good boy, worked hard, he'd be a success in this life. He was studying to be an accountant at the University of Minnesota–Duluth and had a scholarship to play hockey . . .

"I thought he was thirty or forty-something," Lucas said.

The old man looked puzzled, struggled with it for a moment, then sat up, his eyes suddenly sharp, sniffed, and with a new alertness, said, "I've got to change Melodie." And it became apparent from the odor that he did—if he didn't, he said, she'd get sores.

He refused help from Nadya, said he did this every day, and he competently rolled the old woman into the bathroom and closed the door.

"This is a waste of time," Lucas said, when the door had closed. "He thinks Roger's still in college. The guy's running on one headlight."

FIVE MINUTES LATER, Walther pushed his wife out of the bathroom, now smelling of the same Johnson's baby powder that Lucas used on Sam. He parked her in front of the television set and said, "I can't go to Duluth unless we can find somebody to take care of Grandma."

"You don't remember Spivak's Tap two weeks ago?" Lucas asked.

"I remember Spivak's. Did I tell you, I told somebody, my boy played football here for Hibbing, you know—"

Lucas jumped in. "We've got to go. Is there anything we can do for your wife? The county, there might be some kind of service . . ."

"But I called them already. Are you from the county? I called them, and they said, 'Okay, they had the papers now.' I can't remember, yesterday?"

"Okay. We'll check. Mr. Walther, thanks for your help, okay?"

NADYA SMILED AND nodded and Lucas bobbed his head and fluttered his hands and a minute later they were walking back down the sidewalk. "That didn't work out," Lucas said. In the car, he picked up the phone and said, "I'll call off Andreno . . ."

Nadya held up a hand and said, "Leave Andreno for a while."

"Why? The guy . . . ?"

"Because I am a spy, I notice that the old man now knows everything we know, and we know nothing that he does. He is probably senile. But for a man who is senile, he did an excellent debriefing."

Lucas looked at the house, where the old man had taken up his post in the picture window, staring out at the lawn. "No."

"I think no also. But . . ." She shrugged. "I see a chess magazine in his bookcase."

"A chess magazine."

"This is about the contest between the world champion of chess and the IBM computer. This contest was in the summer, so the magazine is new."

"Huh. You think he bitch-slapped me?"

"What?"

"Never mind. I'll leave Andreno," Lucas said. "Couple hours can't hurt."

"So now . . ."

"Back to the genealogies. We've got the rest of the afternoon. Pick out a new target . . ."

"One more thing—this boat that his parents came on. I have heard of such things," Nadya said. "Societies that gathered people together, and they rented a boat to come to a certain, em, *colony* in the United States that was purchased in advance. Many of these were swindles and the land would be poor or too cold and the boat would be destroyed and the people would go somewhere else."

Lucas nodded. "The point being that this might not be a cover story for illegal entry. It could be real."

"Doesn't feel real; it's too unlikely. But . . . there is a ten percent chance that this hospital problem is innocent."

"You believe in coincidence."

"As long as there are not too many."

"There are getting to be too many," Lucas said.

"I think so, but I am not certain," Nadya said. "Let's find a new target. What about this Roger person, the old man's grandson?"

"My exact thought."

22

GRANDPA WATCHED THEM GO, and without turning to his wife said, "They know all of us. I'll have to do the rescue."

She said nothing; stared sightlessly at the TV screen. He turned, stepped over to her, put his hand on her head: "We had a really good run, and we can still save the others. I'm going to start it."

She seemed to nod under his hand, and he bent, kissed her forehead, glanced at his watch, went to the kitchen, opened a drawer, and took out the walkie-talkie. A van was parked up the street, one that he hadn't seen before, but not unlike one that had been parked across the street the day before—they both had dark windows, and he could feel the surveillance.

Was the house bugged as well? He thought not, because for the last three days he'd been putting telltales on the doors before he went out, a hair stuck on with a little spit, and they'd been undisturbed.

Still, there was no point in taking chances. He carried the walkie-talkie to the front hall closet, climbed inside, sat down, pulled the closet door shut, and beeped Carl. Carl, he thought, should be finishing lunch.

Two minutes later, he got a patch of static, and then, "Yeah. I'm bringing the two-by-fours."

"The inspectors came by," Grandpa said. "We passed, but they'll be back. I need to fix the door. You'll have to pick me up."

"What time?"

"Eight o'clock."

"Eight? Can it wait that long?"

"It'll have to. I'm waiting for a guy to get off work."

"Okay. I'll see you then."

"I've got a watch; call me ahead of time, though."

"Okay."

"I'm out."

"Out."

Simple voice code, a crude effort to sound like a construction site. The key was the time: Carl would add three hours to the specified time, and would come by at eleven o'clock.

A LONG WAIT. Melodie was fine in her wheelchair. Grandpa went to the kitchen, pulled out a silverware drawer, nearly dropped it, put it on the kitchen table, and felt back under the sink until he found the pistol.

The gun was old, in a way—it had been made in the 1930s—but guns hadn't changed much. He pulled the magazine, looked at the shiny new shells stacked inside, put the magazine aside and dry-fired the pistol a hundred times, aiming at a can of soup on the kitchen counter.

There was no need for great accuracy: he'd be shooting from four feet. Carl had cleaned the gun after the last use, and the cleaning oil was pungent and not at all unpleasant. The gun felt just fine; nose heavy, because of the suppressor, but he was used to the weight.

After a hundred practice snaps, he reseated the clip and put the gun back. His hand touched the second pistol, the one they'd taken from the Russian in the parking lot outside the bus museum. That was a piece of luck—they wouldn't have to find a second pistol.

At loose ends, he went back to the living room, looked at Grandma—she was asleep, he thought, her breathing imperceptible, but he touched her neck anyway, to find the artery, now so close to the skin . . . found it, and the thready beat, and felt the usual trickle of relief. Still alive.

He could work a chess problem, but the thought bored him. Big events were under way. Lives were coming to a close. He checked Grandma again and then back to the bedroom, lay on the bed and closed his eyes.

The cop, the state cop, had seemed bright and tough, and the Russian woman just as bright. He knew their types from the early days. He'd learned, though, that the young feared dementia—Alzheimer's they all called it—and he knew how to play that card. He was old enough that not only did they believe the act, they expected it. He smiled and drifted . . .

The feel and smell of the gun took him back, all the way back. He'd been a young boy in Moscow when the revolution swept through. He could remember the crowds in the streets, the excited arguments between the adults, people rushing into the house with newspapers. His father was a Bolshevik from the start; when his father died, too young, in the winter of 1921, Sergey Vasilevich Botenkov had been taken in by his old comrades, shown how to use a rifle, and had gone off to fight the Whites.

He'd been little more than a boy, but he'd done well. He was trusted. And when he was grown, when he was eighteen, he'd been sent to the Ukraine to help with the elimination of the kulak class.

He remembered one place, one city, where they'd brought the kulaks in trucks, unloaded them in the city park, hands tied behind them by the soldiers. He and the other executioners shot each one in the back of the head and let them topple into the grave; nine shots and reload, nine shots and reload. A cigarette, a bottle of tea, another truck full of the enemies of the state.

Sergey Vasilevich Botenkov lay on his bed and remembered.

And smiled.

23

THEY FOUND JAN WALTHER in the back of Mesaba Frame and Artist's Supply, doing inventory on her acrylic paints; the place smelled of paint and freshly cut wood and coffee. They'd been to her house, had been told by a neighbor that she and Roger Walther had divorced years before, and that while Roger was still around, the neighbor didn't know where.

"Good riddance, if you ask me," the neighbor said. She had the eyes of a chicken, small and suspicious. "He used to beat her, and the boy, too. More'n one time she'd be hiding a black eye. He drinks, is what does it."

If they wanted him, the neighbor said, Jan would probably know where he was: "He must be paying child support; I don't think she makes enough to support both her and the boy." She directed them to the frame store, just off Hibbing's main drag.

. . .

WALTHER WAS A BUSY, pretty woman, with the beginnings of worry lines on her forehead and at the corners of her eyes and mouth. She was wearing a pink blouse with a round-tipped collar, inexpensive beige slacks, and a matching vest, with an arty silver dangle on a chain. With a round face and ten extra pounds, she was precisely a Minnesota Scandinavian; and when they came in, a bell jingling overhead, she was happy to see them.

That didn't last.

Lucas identified himself, told her that they were investigating the murders of two Russians and a cop, and she put both hands at her throat and said, "What do you want from *me?*"

"We'd like to talk to your husband," Lucas said. "We really don't know who is doing what, but there seems to be a group of associated families up here, and he belongs to one of them. We think they may have been spies for the Soviet Union."

"The Walthers? That's ridiculous. They've been here forever. They're from German stock, not Russian . . ." But her interlaced fingers were white as chalk.

"You wouldn't know about these people, whoever they are?" Nadya asked.

"Well, sure, I know Grandpa Walther," she said. "I never knew Roger's parents. They were killed in a car accident. This spy thing . . . you're not joking? This is absolutely *ridiculous*. If this rumor gets out, you'll ruin my business . . ." Now she had tears in her eyes.

Nadya was not sympathetic. "Did Roger tell you that he was a spy?"

"No. No. Roger's not a spy. If you knew Roger . . . Roger's an *alcoholic*. A *drunkard*. He goes around in a haze. He couldn't spy on *anything*. If he'd had a gun, he'd have sold it by now, so he could buy more beer. He's about one inch from going on the street. I mean, the whole thing . . ." She looked from one of them to the other, her voice rising. "The whole thing is ridiculous."

"I understood he was an athlete in college," Lucas said. "At UMD."

She nodded. "That's his problem. That's why he's drinking. He was a big hero here in Hibbing, he was a second-stringer in Duluth, and after that . . . nobody wanted him."

Roger Walther, she said, was basically a good guy, but had never studied anything but hockey and when his eligibility was gone, he was gone. "The coaches nursed him through four years of college with a C average, and the fifth year, when he couldn't play anymore, it was nothing but big red F's," she said indignantly.

"Where does he live?" Lucas asked.

"I don't know, exactly," she said. "Virginia. I heard that he had a job somewhere, that he was working, but he hides that from me because he's afraid that I'll have the child-support people get after him. He owes me almost fifteen thousand dollars in support."

Lucas said, "We heard that he, ah, has gotten physical with you. In the past."

"He hit me a few times—that's why I eventually threw him out. I wasn't going to put up with it. He was always drunk, but that was no excuse. He says it himself—it's no excuse."

"You ever call the cops?"

"No. I threatened to, but he begged me not to. He used to hunt, and the way the law is now, if he got a ticket, he could never have a gun again. He could never hunt again. So I didn't call; I just threw him out."

"Okay." Lucas looked around. "Where's your kid?"

"He's in school," she said. "I don't want you bothering him, he's just a child. God, you'll ruin his life, too . . ."

Jan Walther knew nothing about anything, she said. Nothing about spies, nothing about the other families, although she knew the Svobodas and had been inside Spivak's, but not for years. As a final question, Lucas asked, "Is he a runner? Roger? Go out and jog and stuff?"

An incredulous look passed over her face: "Roger? Roger has a cigarette with every drink. He couldn't run around the block."

WHEN THEY LEFT, and were back at the truck, Nadya said, "Everybody lies. She was too worried, but not enough . . . amazed . . . when we asked about spying. She should have been amazed."

"Maybe," Lucas said. "We're a half hour from Hibbing . . . wanna get a late lunch? I'm starving. Then we find Roger."

THE LUNCH SERVICE was slow, and took a while; and there was roadwork on the way to Virginia, and they got hung up while a paving machine tried to maneuver across the highway. By the time they arrived at the Virginia police station, it was almost four o'clock. John Terry, the chief, said he didn't know Roger Walther, but he could check with his on-duty cops in a few minutes. He went to do that, took ten minutes, and came back: "Nobody on-duty knows him. I took a minute and went out on NCIC and they have no record of him. He's kept his nose clean."

"He's a drunk," Lucas said.

"Really a drunk, or just an alcoholic?" Terry asked. "Lots of alcoholics hold it together forever. Keep working, never drive drunk."

"He beats his wife."

"She ever charge him?"

Lucas was already shaking his head. "Okay, listen. If he's a drunk, he's drinking up here. If you could have your guys check the bars and get back to me. Somebody's got to know him."

Lucas's cell phone rang, and he said, "Excuse me," took it out, and turned away. "Yeah, Davenport."

Larry Kelly, from Duluth. "Is Nadya Kalin with you?"

"Yes. Right here."

"We'd like to get you both down here, this evening, if we could. We need to take statements. We're not trying to cover up the relationship, but we want to make it clear that Reasons was guarding her, that he'd been assigned to do that, and that the, *mmm,* emotional relationship grew out of that, uh, *closeness.*"

"I think we can do that," Lucas said. "Nadya and I will coordinate and get down there."

"Come right into the Detective Bureau. The statements are for our shooting board, and the chief and the city attorney both say that written statements will be okay."

"See you in an hour," Lucas said.

TERRY PROMISED TO have every bar in Hibbing checked by morning. Lucas gave him a cell-phone number, and he and Nadya headed for Duluth.

"What they're doing is, they're taking testimony on the shooting to make sure nothing illegal happened, and that all proper procedures were being followed," Lucas told her on the way, explaining the board. "If Reasons was assigned to guard you, then your, *mmm,* emotional involvement becomes irrelevant. He was killed in the line of duty."

"He wasn't *exactly . . .*"

"Shhh . . . " Lucas said.

24

GRANDPA FUSSED AROUND the rest of the day—shuffled out to put a bill in the mailbox, raised the red flag for the mailman, saw that the van was still there. Went out to the garage, threw a shovel in the back of the car, unscrewed the automatic light in the garage-door opener, shuffled back to the house, and didn't look at the van, still there halfway up the block. Would it ever leave? And if it did, would it be replaced by another? He saw nothing at all on the backside of the block . . .

He couldn't help watching, but he was afraid he'd be spotted if he did. Eventually, he spent a few minutes vacuuming, pushing back and forth in front of the picture window. When he was done, he propped open one of Melodie's old compact cases in the corner of the window, among a group of plants, adjusted the mirror so he could see the van, then sat on a couch opposite the television and watched the mirror.

An hour or so after the cops left, Jan Walther called, panicked about being interviewed by the police. "They think Roger is a spy. They think he was spying with the Spivaks and the Svobodas and some people named Witold. They're *crazy*," she said.

"They are crazy," Grandpa agreed. "There's nothing we can do but cooperate. Maybe we should get a lawyer."

"Not yet; I can't afford a lawyer."

She gave him everything the cops had asked her about, but in the context of a protest to a relative. Excellent. Janet had been told a little bit, back when she was still in love with Roger, had been told that the spying was a heritage thing that the families were trying to work out of . . . but that was it. If the phones were bugged, her protests would sound normal and innocent. If the tapes ever got into court, they might help influence a jury.

He watched the van the rest of the afternoon; watched as a mostly cloudy day turned gloomy and dark, and little spits of rain began trickling down the window. At a little after five o'clock, the van pulled away. The movement was so quick, and unexpected, that Grandpa almost missed it—and he knew for certain, from watching all afternoon, that nobody had gotten into it. Whoever was driving had been inside all morning and afternoon.

This was *not* paranoia; he *was* being watched.

A T S E V E N O ' C L O C K , with a steady drizzle darkening the streets, he drove slowly down to the supermarket, and then back to the house, going out one way, coming back on the other side of the block. He saw no one following, and he knew all the cars still on the street. So the watch was sporadic—the state cop and the Russian must have wanted to see if he'd panic after they talked to him. Grandpa smiled as he pulled back into the garage, just thinking about it. He'd sold them, all right.

There was, he thought as he went into the house, just the slightest possibility that they were watching from a neighbor's house . . . but then, why would they watch from the van at all? Still . . .

. . .

INSIDE, THINKING of bugs and phone taps, he said to Grandma, "Let's eat." He banged around the kitchen, heating up some spaghetti, fed her and then himself. When she was done, he cleaned her up for the fourth time that day, and parked her in front of the TV again. The History Channel had a show about World War II, the landings at Normandy. They watched it together, and he talked to his wife, and then they watched a show about ice dancing, then the local news, and finally he said, "Let's get you off to bed, sweetheart. Let's get you off to bed, okay?"

AT TEN THIRTY, he flushed the toilet and said into the walkie-talkie as the water rushed around the bowl, "Exactly at eight."

Three words. He got back two burps of static. Good. He got the silenced pistol and put it in the pocket of a black jacket, and pulled on the jacket.

At ten fifty-five, he slipped out the back door, stood in the shadows under the eaves. The rain wasn't as heavy as it had been, but the night was misty, with fog coming up from the street. He walked straight back to the garage, through the back door, pushed the button on the garage-door opener. If they were watching from the back of the house, then he was done. If they were on the other side of the street, he'd be okay. He didn't think they were there at all, but . . .

There was a figure coming up the alley, tall and thin, in a rain jacket. Carl. He gestured at the car, and Carl edged between the car and the garage wall, careful in the dark, and got in the driver's seat. "Where to? What's going on?"

"We need to talk to your father," Grandpa said. "He's up in Virginia."

"Dad? Do I have to talk to that asshole? What are we talking to him for?"

"Because he knows. And he's a drunk. The police have ways to put pressure on people, and he has to be warned. I can't call him—they may already be watching him . . . They asked about him this morning."

"What if they're watching him now?"

"They might be. But I think this whole investigation is small. They had a van watching me for two days, different vans, and now there's nobody. The police who came today seemed confused about what was going on . . ." He told Carl about the interview with Nadya and Lucas.

"So they know everybody," Carl said, when Grandpa finished.

"They know everybody, but not everything," Grandpa said.

"What are we going to do?"

"I'm working on that," Grandpa said. "I'm working on a story. A story they can believe."

"Dad's part of it? He's a drunk, he might say anything."

"I think he'll be able to handle it. I've figured out a role for him," Grandpa said.

CARL WATCHED THEIR back trail. Every time a car turned a corner behind them, he reported it. They took back roads, miles through the dark, rarely had anything in the rearview mirror.

"What did you tell your mom?" Grandpa asked.

"I told her I was going to stay over with you, that Grandma had been trying to get up at night."

"Good. As long as she doesn't call."

"She was already going to bed when I left."

Grandpa turned in his seat, looked at the long dark road behind them and said, "Enough. Let's go."

"I don't know where he is. Dad."

"I do," Grandpa said. "I had Bob Spivak find him."

. . .

ROGER WALTHER WAS living in a shack off Old 169 between Hibbing and Parkville; a shack in every sense of the word—old weathered-board siding showing streaks of moss and rot in their headlights, a tumbledown plank stoop, junk in the front and side yards—old washing machines, a junked car, a battered fourteen-foot Lund fishing boat with a thirty-year-old outboard on the back, sitting on a trailer with no wheels.

A small porch had holes where the screens should have been; there were lights in the windows behind the porch, and when Carl got out of the car, he could smell the smoke from a wood fire, the smoke being pushed down to the yard by the thin drizzle. Grandpa got out of the car and said, "Come on."

"You sure he lives here?"

"That's what Bob said."

"I don't want to talk to the sonofabitch," Carl said. "I would've kicked his ass the last time we met up, except Mom stopped me."

"I'm not asking you to come in, I'm telling you," Grandpa snarled in the dark. "This is not an option; this is an operation. We are going to try to figure out a way to put an end to this investigation."

"How're we gonna do that?" Carl asked. The windows in the front had curtains, and now a silhouetted figure parted the curtains and looked out. The silhouette looked to Carl like a woman's.

"Watch," Grandpa said.

THEY WALKED UP to the porch and as they were about to knock on the front door, it opened. A woman was there in a terry-cloth dressing gown, yellow with age; she was forty, overweight, with dark, oily skin; she smelled of bourbon and cigarettes.

"Who're you?"

"I'm Roger's grandfather and this is his son. We need to talk to him for a moment," Grandpa said.

The woman looked them over, then turned and called, "They say it's your kid and your grandpa."

"I'm coming . . ."

She stepped back from the door, and they stepped inside. The place smelled like cheap burning wood and newspaper, and baked beans. Roger came out of the back. He was a tall man, wearing black jeans and a plain white T-shirt; his hair, once blond, was going gray. He was barefoot. "What do you two want?" he asked.

"We need to talk to you for a moment. It's important, but . . ." Grandpa looked at the woman, and then back at Roger. "It's private."

Roger looked at them for a long four seconds, then asked, "Something happen to Jan?"

"No. It's about the four families," Grandpa said. "We've got a big problem."

"Fuck that," Roger said. But he turned to the woman and said, "You go on back in the bedroom. I'll be back in five minutes. You shut that door tight."

She put her hands on her hips and sighed, as if he'd just unloaded the burden of the world on her, then sullenly went back to the bedroom and slammed the door.

When the door slammed, Roger looked at Grandpa and then at Carl, and said, "Carl knows?"

"Yes," Grandpa said. He had his hand in his pocket and when he took it out, he had the silenced pistol in it.

Carl said, "What?" when he saw the pistol coming up, and Grandpa shot Roger in the heart.

Roger, looking surprised, fell down with a thump. The wooden floor echoed like a drum.

Carl said, "You shot my dad." Like a slap in the face; it staggered him.

Grandpa said, "Don't think. Go do the woman." He handed the gun to Carl. "Don't think, don't touch her, don't touch anything. Just go do it."

"You shot my fuckin' dad," Carl said, and the gun barrel drifted up toward Grandpa's waist.

"Don't point the gun at me; just take care of the woman."

"You . . . Jesus Christ." Carl stared at the old man.

Grandpa's voice turned to gravel: *"Take care of the woman."*

For a moment, everything balanced on a knife. The gun was now aiming at Grandpa's heart, and Carl took up the slack in the trigger.

"Don't think . . ."

They posed for another three seconds, then Carl suddenly turned, walked to the bedroom door, pushed it open. Grandpa heard the woman say, "What?" and then three shots, a quick *bap-bap*, and then a finishing *bap*.

Carl wandered back into the living room, a dazed look on his face. Grandpa said, "Are you all right?"

"Maybe."

"Give me the gun."

Carl handed it over. "Are you going to kill me someday?"

Grandpa was neither startled nor disturbed by the question. "No." He put the gun in his pocket and took out two black oversized garbage bags. "Help me get Roger in these things. I don't want blood in the trunk of the car."

"What's going on?" Carl asked, a pleading note in his voice.

"The cops were breaking us down—they're going to break us down. Unless we give them the shooter. We're giving them Roger."

"Why would . . . this is crazy."

"No. I can't tell you all of it. I can tell you this: from now on, you have to be a kid. You told me about maybe asking this girl to the homecoming. Tomorrow you've got to do it. You have to borrow some money from me for a sport coat and slacks, and you have to go buy them."

"What . . . ?" Crazier and crazier.

Grandpa touched Carl on the shoulder, looked straight into his eyes. "There's more on this to do . . . But listen to me now. You are the last one of us. You have to go underground, and for you, that means that you have to go back to being a kid. A child. You're an adult now, and it'll be hard, but it's critical, Carl. You have to remember what you are, but you have to play at being a high-school boy. Can you do that?"

Carl shrugged, and said, "I suppose," and a flock of tears trickled down his cheek. He didn't notice.

Grandpa pointed at Roger's body, and Carl, stunned, helped roll the body into the two bags. When they were done, there was a small blood puddle on the floor, and Grandpa cleaned it up with paper towels and water and found that he'd left a clean spot on a dirty floor.

They fixed that by dragging a welcome mat across it a few times, until it had blended. That done, Grandpa went in to look at the woman: she was dead, all right. Carl had walked the gun up her body, shooting her first in the stomach and then in the chest, with a final shot in her forehead.

Okay.

"Let's get him out to the car."

THE WORST OF IT, Carl thought, was that Roger was still warm. He could still feel his father's body, all the heat, all the still-living cells, that hadn't yet gotten the message from his father's brain, as he staggered out into the rain and put him in the back of the car. The warmth reminded him of the day he'd killed the little dog . . .

Inside, Grandpa picked up the first of the nine-millimeter shells, the one he'd used to kill Roger; the others he left. And before walking out of the house, he took a single orange hunter's glove from his jacket pocket, and threw it in a closet.

"That's like . . ." Carl started. He looked at Grandpa. "Oh, Jesus, you knew way back when I went after the Russian."

"I was ready if we needed it," Grandpa said. "Come on. We need to go through the house and find what Roger would have taken with him, running. One suitcase. One duffel bag."

They actually found a hockey duffel in a closet, and threw everything into it that Roger might have taken—his shaving gear and miscellaneous clean-up stuff, like tweezers, Band-Aids, fingernail clippers, a brush, and comb. They took the best clothes and shoes they could find; they took photographs, including a photo of Carl as a five-year-old, on a park swing being pushed by his mother, both of them laughing; they took cigarettes and a jar of quarters and some cheap jewelry and they dumped the woman's purse and took the money out, seven dollars.

They did it all hastily, throwing the stuff into the duffel; except for the photograph of Carl and his mother, which Carl put in his pocket.

WHEN THEY WERE DONE, they turned off the lights and tramped back out through the rain and got in the car. "Drive that way," Grandpa said.

Carl followed the instructions, turning this way and that. At some point, he began to cry, clutching the steering wheel in both hands, trying to stay in the middle of a narrow gravel road track while looking through both tears and the rain.

"Turn left, right after this tree," Grandpa said.

"Where are we?"

"They were logging here last summer. Starts a hundred feet back or so."

They followed a rough dirt track through the trees, down a gentle slope, around a stump; a hundred feet in, as promised, the forest suddenly ended and the headlights punched into featureless darkness. All the trees were gone. In the near foreground, Carl could see dirt chewed up by bulldozers.

Grandpa got out of the car, walked around to the trunk. "You'll have to dig," he told Carl.

Carl dug, in the light of a flashlight; Grandpa was afraid to use the headlights. They found a low spot without any nearby tree wreckage, and cut down through the sandy ground, Grandpa urging him to work faster, Carl working as fast as he could, throwing dirt, fighting through the occasional root. When he was finished, he was covered with mud.

Together, they lifted the body from the back of the car and dropped it in the hole, and threw the duffel bag on top of it. They stood there for a minute, then Grandpa pulled the pistol out of his pocket and dropped it in the hole. Grandpa shifted the light away, and said, "Fill it."

Filling the hole took only five minutes. When it was done, they stomped around on top of it, and finally dragged a shredded aspen over the raw dirt. They'd been lucky with the rain, Grandpa said; the rain would take care of the rest of it. By morning, the grave site would be invisible.

THE RIDE HOME WAS LONG, but not silent. Grandpa said, "This is the worst. This is the worst night of your life, so you never have to worry about that anymore. This is one of the worst of my life, after the death of my son. But I tell you: this is the critical step that we needed to protect the families. And your father . . . your father was a ruined man, no good for anybody. No good for your mother, no good for you. He was a ruin. His life was already over."

Carl started crying again, and said, "But he was my *dad*."

"I know, I know . . ."

AND IT WENT LIKE THAT.

At Grandpa's, they both stripped down and threw their clothing into the washing machine, and Grandpa washed their shoes in the kitchen sink and patted them dry with kitchen towels and newspapers. "They'll be fine by morning," he said. They took their clothes out of the washer and put them in the dryer, and then Carl made a bed on the couch and Grandpa gave him two of Grandma's sleeping pills.

"You need the sleep before school," Grandpa said. "These are strong and will take you down for five hours. Try to sleep."

Carl took the pills, and immediately on swallowing, was struck by the suspicion that he shouldn't have; was he part of Grandpa's plan? But the old man had turned away from him, said, "Try to sleep; try to empty your mind. Try not to cry, because if you do, your eyes will be red. And remember tomorrow, if I forget to tell you, you must ask the girl on the date to homecoming. That's important: you have to go back to being a kid."

"Okay, Grandpa. We had to do it, didn't we?"

"We had to," Grandpa said.

Grandpa hit the lights and said good night, and then Grandma's pills came on, pulling Carl straight down into a pit of darkness.

As for Grandpa, for Burt Walther, for Sergey Vasilevich Botenkov, he slept quite well.

25

LUCAS AND NADYA made their statements, and signed them. No perjury was committed, although an observer from Mars might have observed that not all possible questions had been asked.

There had been no way, the city attorney said, to completely avoid the question of a relationship between Nadya and Reasons, but the relationship had been disposed of with two questions and two short answers, which had dismissed the possibility that a personal relationship had in any way contributed to the murder.

Reasons, the attorney concluded, had been killed on the job when a professional assassin, armed with a silenced pistol, had gone to Nadya's room to kill her, and instead, had encountered Reasons, who'd died protecting Nadya. Several throats were cleared, briefcases were stuffed, and the lights turned out.

. . .

ANDRENO CALLED from Hibbing, said there was no action at Walther's house, and Lucas ordered him back to Duluth to stay with Nadya overnight.

Kelly, the cop originally assigned to the murder of Mary Wheaton, stopped to chat with Lucas on the way out the door after the statements were given. Lucas mentioned that he was looking for a drunk named Roger Walther, but that Walther had never been arrested, and was no longer living at the house listed on his driver's license.

"I'll ask around," Kelly said. "Know anything else about him?"

"Not much . . . whacked his wife a couple times, no charges. He was the local hockey hero in Hibbing, played with UMD . . ."

"Well, shit, I know a guy named Reggie Carpenter who knows every single asshole who ever got ice time up there . . . He might be able to help you out."

"Where's he live?"

"Actually, he plays piano at T-Bone Logan's Lakeside Lumber Emporium and Saloon. He oughta be there now."

"Place with a name like that, you wouldn't see many tourists," Lucas suggested.

Kelly snorted: "There never was a T-Bone Logan, it's not on the lakeside, it was built six years ago by a doctor's group from Chicago outa fake logs, never had anything to do with lumber, and they charge nine bucks for a martini which, when they bring it to you, turns out to be purple, or maroon, or some fuckin' thing. What do you think?"

A gentle drizzle was falling as they drove.

"Feel the winter coming," Kelly said.

"This isn't it, though," Lucas said. "Not yet." Sometime in September, a bone-crunching cold front usually came through, pointing at snow, if not actually delivering any. This drizzle still contained a hint of warmth.

"You ski?"

"Ah, every once in a while. I've got a place over in Sawyer County, Hayward, I got a couple of sleds . . ."

They talked snow and cabins and snowmobiles until they pulled into the bar.

T-Bone Logan's was as Kelly said, a tourist trap with log walls and, inside, axes and saws and kerosene lanterns mounted overhead, and big photos of lumberjacks in old-timey logging camps. The tabletops were made out of split pine logs with clear finishes; the place smelled of wet-sauce ribs and beans.

Carpenter, the piano player, was a Dagwood-looking man, pale, slender, balding, with cheap false teeth that tended to clack when he talked, and a sprinkling of dandruff on his black sport coat. Lucas and Kelly got beer from the bar and carried it over to the piano and waited while Carpenter finished wending his way through an overfruited version of "Stardust," Carpenter signaling his friendship to Kelly with his eyebrows.

When he finished the song, he slid over to the side of the piano bench and said, "How's it going, Officer Kelly?"

"How many telephones you got now, Reggie?"

"Just the one cell phone," Carpenter said. "Don't even have one in my house."

"You're sure?"

"Absolutely," Carpenter said, beaming at Kelly.

Kelly said to Lucas, "Reggie used to take the occasional bet."

"Ah."

"In the month of November nineteen ninety-nine, he took bets on one thousand seven hundred and fifty-six occasions," Kelly continued.

"I never would have suspected," Lucas said.

"I was just . . . a little thoughtless," Carpenter said. "So what's going on?"

"UMD hockey," Kelly said. "Do you remember a guy named Roger

Walther? Would have been a second-stringer, maybe . . . what? Twenty-some years ago?"

Carpenter frowned, tinkled the high C key a few times, then nodded, "Yeah . . . I do. He played forward, but he was a little slow with the stick, and about six feet short getting down the ice. But he could play. What'd he do?"

"Have you seen him?" Lucas asked.

"No, not for years. I think—I think, but I'm not sure—that he once was selling cars at Landry's, but that would have been years ago."

"Not since."

"Nope. What'd he do?"

"What's he like, physically?" Lucas asked. "Fast? Big? Wide? Strong?"

"About like you," Carpenter said to Lucas. "Maybe an inch shorter, a couple of pounds heavier."

"You think he might be a runner?" Lucas asked. "Like to jog, and so on?"

"I don't know. He was a college-level jock. So probably. What'd he do, anyway?"

"Thanks for your help," Kelly said. "Stick with the one phone, huh?"

THEY HAD A few drinks, and Lucas eventually got back to the hotel and slept like a rock.

The next morning, he was in the shower, feeling a little rocky from the alcohol, when the first call came in, from John Terry, the Virginia police chief.

"We got a line on Roger Walther. He's living with a woman named Kelly Harbinson just out west of town. I got an address . . ."

Lucas took the address and said, "Thanks. I'll check it out."

ANDRENO AND NADYA came over for breakfast. The rain was still falling, and they all looked out over the lake as he told them about the call; there were no boats visible at all, and no separation between lake and sky. "I'm getting pretty damned tired of driving back and forth," Lucas said. "Everything is up on the Range—I'm gonna check out of here tomorrow morning and find a place up there."

"Me also," Nadya said. "This process feels like it is coming to an end."

Andreno nodded. "Roger'll give us something. Has to. Did you see the paper this morning?"

"The *Star Tribune*," Lucas said.

"The local paper has a story from Spivak's lawyer. You're gonna take some pressure at the preliminary hearing."

"We've got enough for the preliminary," Lucas said.

"Be a pretty fucked-up trial, though," Andreno said.

"Somebody'll crack before we get to trial. I hope."

WITH THE FOCUS on Roger Walther, they all rode to Virginia together. Lucas and Andreno chatted about another case they'd worked on, in St. Louis, and they compared promotion and salary practices with Nadya. Nadya's salary was small by American standards, but she paid almost nothing for housing, medical care, insurance, or any of the other dozens of possibilities that Americans dealt with. The one problem, she said, was food. "We don't eat so much in restaurants as you do; and the food in restaurants that I can afford is not so good anyway."

"And you don't have so many signs," Lucas said.

She laughed, the first time Lucas had heard her laugh since Reasons was killed. "You are ridiculous here. When we stopped to buy gasoline, on one pump, there were twenty-two signs. On one pump!"

"I saw you counting," Lucas said.

"Stickers," Andreno said. "They're called stickers."

"But they were signs. Only, small ones."

. . .

THE RAIN HAD stopped, but everything was still damp and dripping when they arrived at Kelly Harbinson's place outside Virginia.

"What a dump," Andreno said from the backseat. He'd taken his revolver out of its holster, and he put it in his jacket pocket. "Looks like something from a cotton plantation."

"Yeah, well . . . his ex-wife said he was like one step off the street," Lucas said.

"Wish we had vests," Andreno said.

They got out, and like Andreno, Lucas put his .45 in his jacket pocket, held it in his hand. They told Nadya to wait back off the porch, and then Lucas and Andreno trooped across the wooden stoop and knocked on the screen door. The knock, Lucas thought, might have been inaudible inside: the wood was so wet and old that the knock was more of a soggy *pup-pup-pup*. There was no sound or movement from inside, and Lucas pulled the screen door open and knocked on the inside door, a little harder.

No sound, no movement. A car went by on the road, and they looked after it, but the driver was a woman and she never looked back at them.

Lucas knocked again. Nothing. "Damnit," he said.

"Let me walk around back," Andreno said.

Lucas nodded, sure that there was nobody inside. The door was solid, without an inset window, so as Andreno squished on the wet shaggy lawn around to the back, Lucas stepped over to the front window and tried to peer in. The window was dirty enough that there was a lot of reflection, and he couldn't see much—what he could see looked like a messy house, which, given the outside appearance, wasn't surprising.

Andreno came back around. "I looked in the back door, couldn't see shit."

Lucas stepped back out to the car, took his phone out, and called John Terry. "We're out at Kelly Harbinson's place. There's nobody here. You know where she works?"

"No, but I might be able to find out. Let me get back to you. Give me fifteen minutes."

They spent the fifteen minutes filling Nadya in on American search rules. "We could go in and if it became necessary, lie about it," Nadya said.

Lucas said, "That has been done, but . . . usually, when only the one investigator is around."

Andreno agreed: "As long as you got defense attorneys, better to play by the law. When you don't see an upside."

"What is this upside?"

They explained the upside to her, and she said, "Capitalism."

JOHN TERRY CALLED back and said, "I had my girl call around to Harbinsons, and she found her parents. She works at Reeves' Wine and Spirits. About ten to one, that's where she met Walther."

"Okay. You got a number?"

LUCAS CALLED THE liquor store, identified himself to the owner, Jack Reeves, and asked for Harbinson.

"I don't know where she is," Reeves said. "We're a little worried. She was supposed to be here at eight. She drinks a little, but she's pretty reliable."

"This hasn't happened before?"

"No, not really. She's been here four years . . . I mean, she's been late, but you know, it snowed and she was late six minutes. If she didn't come in soon, I was going to drive out to her place and knock on the door."

"Nobody here . . . we're out there now," Lucas said.

. . .

OFF THE PHONE, Lucas looked at the house and said, "Let's check all the windows. See what we can see."

"Maybe they took off," Andreno said.

"That's what I'm afraid of."

They walked around the left side of the house; most of the windows had Venetian blinds, and they could see through the string holes in the sides, and the corners where the blinds weren't quite straight. They saw nothing useful until they'd circled the house. From there, a blind looked into the bedroom, and they could see a pile of clothes on the floor by what must have been a closet, and more strewn in the hallway beyond.

"Goddamnit," Lucas said.

Andreno tried the front door. "It's unlocked," he said.

"Let me do this," Lucas said. He pushed the door open and called, "Hello? Anybody home?"

No answer. He pushed the door open another foot. The place was messy inside, and smelled like tomato soup and nicotine, but there was no law against any of that.

There wasn't room on the porch for Nadya, but Andreno had moved up behind Lucas and he said, "There's a butcher knife on the floor."

"Where?"

"Right there in front of the TV." There was nothing in front of the TV except an oval braided rug.

"I better check the place," Lucas said. He stepped inside, again called, "Hello?" Nothing. He went through the living room, looked into the kitchen, checked a bedroom, which was empty, the bath, empty but in disarray, then the second bedroom, where the pile of clothes sat in front of the closet.

He almost didn't see her—nothing was visible but her head. The rest of her body was buried under a pile of clothes that had been thrown across the bed. Lucas took another step: her forehead had a hole in it.

Lucas retreated, went into the kitchen, took a tissue from a box on the counter, picked up a butcher knife, dropped it on the floor in front of the television, and went back to the porch.

Andreno looked at his face and said, "What?"

"She's in there," Lucas said.

"She's dead," Nadya said.

"Yes. Shot in the forehead."

"This is nuts," Andreno said.

LUCAS CALLED TERRY BACK: "We got a problem out here, Chief. Who covers this area?"

"St. Louis County sheriff. What do you got?"

Lucas told him, and Terry said, "Jesus Christ, Davenport, you're some kind of death angel."

"Yeah, yeah . . ."

"I'll get the sheriff started, and we'll get a couple cars out there—we got a mutual aid pact. Ten minutes."

LUCAS HUNG UP and Andreno said, "Roger Walther."

"Didn't take her with him," Lucas said. "I hope somebody has a picture."

"His wife . . ."

Lucas said to Nadya: "Okay. We've got a lot of stuff to do now. We've got to put out a bulletin on this guy, and since he might have been working with somebody from Russia, we'll have to make it international. Can you call your embassy . . ."

They were making up a list of must-do tasks when they heard the first siren coming in: Lucas turned toward the siren, then back to the other two.

"We'll hit Janet Walther first, ask if she's seen him. Then hit the old man again—Nadya thinks he might have been fucking with us with the Alzheimer's act. Start the cops looking either for his car, or Harbinson's. Check the state registrations for both of them, get the tag numbers out to the highway patrol and everybody else. Get the name to the security people at the airports . . ."

"If these cells were set up to move people, then he could be hard to locate," Nadya said. "They would have protected routes out."

"I don't know—all I know is what we can do," Lucas said. He turned and looked toward the incoming cop car, and then back to Nadya. "There's something not quite right with this whole thing. You say the group wasn't active as far as you know . . . if they *were* active, would somebody have told you? Warned you off?"

"Yes. And nobody did. There would be some indication that while they wanted enthusiasm, they did not want success. I never got that. It was the other way around—that I should learn what is happening, and we should not spare ourselves. That is why Piotr is dead."

Lucas said, "I'm just not sure how far I can trust you."

"That's for you to decide," she said. "But—we are breaking this case. We will join you in the hunt for Roger Walther, and if he is running to us, we will tell you."

"You will give him back?"

She shrugged. "That's not for me to decide. He did murder a popular diplomat."

He looked at her for a long moment, and then as the cop car turned into the yard, and he saw John Terry's face in the window, he nodded and said, "Okay. For now, anyway."

26

LUCAS PUSHED RELENTLESSLY through their list. They were on the scene of the killing for two hours, handed it over first to the Virginia cops, then to a sheriff's deputy named Max Anderson. They were there long enough for an assistant medical examiner to guess that Harbinson had been dead for twelve hours, or less.

"That's just a guess based on body temp," he said. He was a young man, thin with blond shaggy hair; prematurely shabby and quite earnest. "The temperature in here is actually fairly low, and she hadn't gotten down to room temp. So . . . last night."

A SHERIFF'S TECHNICIAN SAID, "I saw that shell from the shooting down in Hibbing. The one at the Greyhound Museum. The shells we picked up back there . . ." He nodded toward the bedroom.

"They look the same to me. That's just eyeballing it, but the firing-pin depth looks about the same, and it's round, and it's off center on the primer, just a hair, like the one from the museum."

"When will we know for sure?"

"I've got digital microphotographs on my computer back at the office. If I could get these back there, I could tell you ninety-nine percent in an hour, but I'm working on the scene here . . ."

"Screw the scene. Let me get you a car," Lucas said.

TERRY, THE VIRGINIA CHIEF, came out of the bedroom and noticed Lucas looking into a front-room closet, and asked, "Everything under control?"

"No." And Lucas asked, "Did it rain all night?"

"Pretty much. Why?"

"Walther didn't take his raincoat," Lucas said, pulling a trench-coat sleeve out of the closet. "Not a bad coat, either."

"Maybe he had a rain suit."

WHEN LUCAS PULLED the coat sleeve out of the closet, Nadya looked that way from across the room. She frowned, walked to the closet, squatted, and pushed the trench coat to one side.

"What?" Lucas asked.

"Look." She pointed, and Lucas squatted beside her. A single blaze orange hunter's glove was lying in the back of the closet.

"Sonofabitch."

LUCAS CALLED ANDY HARMON. "We've broken it down. The killer was a guy named Roger Walther. That's the Walther family on the chart I gave you. We'll send you the details on him, and we've got all the local cops looking for him, but it's time you guys got in on the act. He's running, and he's got twelve hours on us, and he's probably headed for Russia down the old spy route. Could be in Canada, so somebody's got to talk to the Mounties."

"Got a picture?" the FBI man asked.

"I'll get one, and we'll scan it and send it to you. We've got a driver's-license photo that's three years old, not too good, but I'm gonna hit his wife in a few minutes, assuming she's still there and still alive, and I'll get whatever I can and send it along."

"Excellent. Excellent job, Davenport. I'll put it in my report."

Lucas hung up. "Fuckhead," he said.

"LET'S GO," Lucas told Nadya. "Let's go talk to Janet Walther."

Andreno went to get his jacket, and as he did, another car pulled off the road outside. A middle-aged woman got out with a plastic sack in her hand, and walked down toward the house and talked to a deputy parked on the road at the end of the walk.

The deputy came to the house and said to Lucas, "It's Harbinson's stepsister. Corine Maples. She's got a picture of Harbinson with Roger Walther."

"Bring her in."

THE WOMAN, DRY-EYED but nervous, asked Lucas, "Is she still here?"

"Yes. I'm afraid we can't let you in."

"No, no, I don't want to see her . . . But I have a funeral home, the name of the funeral home."

"See the guy over there?" Lucas asked, pointing to a deputy. "That's

Max Anderson; he's the deputy in charge of the scene. Give it to him. She'll be taken to the medical school first, for an autopsy, and then . . . Well, talk to Max."

"Okay," she said. "I knew Roger was bad news, the first time I met him."

"You have a photograph?"

She fumbled in her plastic bag and pulled out a photograph taken in a backyard with a wooden fence, a summer scene with a flower bed and, partly visible to one side, a plaster Virgin Mary with her hands spread over a pond the size of a garbage-can lid. Two people stood in the foreground, squinting into the sun and the camera.

"We had a barbecue and they came," Maples said.

"Does he still look like this?"

"Oh, yes. I saw them on the street two weeks ago. That picture is only two months old."

"He looks older than I expected. I thought he was right around forty."

She bobbed her head. "He is, but, he's had a pretty hard life. He smokes and he drinks and he stays out all hours. You can't drink two or three six-packs a day and not have it get to you."

"Doesn't look fat."

"No, no, he's never been fat. But he's not healthy. We tried to tell him . . ."

"We need to send this picture to the FBI," Lucas said. "If you don't mind . . ."

"He'll know it came from me," Maples said nervously. "He's still loose, with a gun."

"We'll just use the head portion," Lucas said. "And we think he's running. It's pretty unlikely that he's still around here."

"Okay . . ." But nervous.

"Do you know Janet Walther? Roger's ex-wife?"

"No. Roger wasn't from here, he was from Hibbing. I never met the family."

"Okay. Let me introduce you to Max. He'll fill you in . . ."

OUT IN THE CAR, Lucas drove silently while Nadya and Andreno chatted. Andreno noticed after a while, and said, "What?"

"That fuckin' glove," Lucas said.

"What?"

"The fuckin' glove puts it on Walther. The shells in the bedroom could have been left behind by anyone, but that fuckin' glove . . ."

"That's bad?"

Lucas said, "I run three miles most days. I try to keep it at twenty-one minutes. Some days, I run five or six."

"You're my hero," Andreno said.

"You see that picture of Walther? The guy looked like a walking heart attack. And he outran me up and down the hills of Duluth, carrying a pizza box?"

Then they all rode for a while, and finally Andreno said, "You know the old line: too many facts can fuck up a perfectly good case."

"Yeah, yeah."

"What is this?" Nadya asked.

THEY WENT TO Janet Walther's house, which was on the way into downtown Hibbing, found it—nobody home—and continued to the frame shop. An older woman in a cloth coat was talking to Walther about a frame for a photograph of her grandchildren, something under twenty-five dollars, and Walther, almost flinching away from Lucas, Andreno, and Nadya, took her to a ready-made stand and helped her choose one. The woman said twice, "You can help these other people," and she smiled and nodded at Lucas, but Walther said, "No, no, let's get this right."

When the woman was finally gone, she moved behind her counter and said, "What do you want?"

"Your ex-husband was living with a woman named Kelly Harbinson, up near Virginia," Lucas began.

"So what? I don't know what he does, and I don't care."

"We found her shot to death in her bed this morning. Roger Walther is missing. We're looking for him."

Her mouth opened and closed, and opened and closed again, as though she were having trouble breathing, and then she said, "Oh, my God."

"Have you seen him?"

"Not for weeks. He came here and asked for a loan and I told him I didn't have any extra."

"You don't know where he might be running to? Or how he might be getting there?"

She shook her head: "I have no idea. This whole spy thing is crazy, though. He's probably in a tavern in Duluth. Or here." She looked out the front window, as though she expected him to show up. Then, "Are you sure he's the one who . . . did it?"

"He was living with her, he's missing, apparently some clothing and his shaving equipment are gone . . ."

"I don't know. I just don't know."

He tried a threat: "You know that if you're hiding him, or helping him, you're an accomplice."

Now she raised her voice: "I'm not doing that! I don't like the man anymore! He's not the man I married anymore! I don't have anything to do with him!"

Lucas swerved to a new topic: "How . . . senile . . . is Burt Walther? Is he qualified to take care of his wife?"

"Burt? Burt's not senile. Burt's sharp as a tack." Her voice was sharp, at first, as though she was afraid of a trick. Then her voice softened: "Melodie has gone away, though. She was a nice woman, and she's gone now. If Grandpa couldn't take care of her, I don't know what would happen. They'd lose the house if they had to put her in a nursing home."

"Burt's not senile."

"No, he's not senile. Have you talked to him?"

OUT THE DOOR, PISSED.

Lucas said to Nadya, "You were right. The guy bullshitted me. That doesn't happen too often."

"It's because you're afraid to look at old people who are, *mmm*, mentally dying? I don't know your word, but you know what I mean," Nadya said. "This happened to my grandfather, when he lived with us, and I saw it all. Old friends would not look at him or talk to him. It is very unpleasant. Burt did not seem that way to me."

THERE WAS NO ONE at Burt Walther's house. Lucas banged on the door, and looked in the windows, and finally a neighbor came out and said, "They're not home. Can I help you with something?"

"We're police officers and we need to talk with Burt Walther," Lucas said. "Have you seen him?"

"This is their day at the doctor," the man said. "You missed them by ten minutes. They're usually gone for two hours."

"Do you know which doctor?"

"Not exactly which, but I know the clinic . . ."

AT THE CLINIC, Andreno spotted Walther's Taurus. "They're here. Want to go in after them?"

Lucas, still a little angry, thought about it, but finally shook his head.

"We can wait. Let's get lunch. No point in messing with them in public."

THEY TOOK NADYA to a Subway; she liked the sandwiches and Lucas suggested that a franchise might work in Moscow. "Probably is one," she said. "We have one of everything now."

THEY SWUNG PAST the clinic on the way back to the Walther house, and the Taurus was still there. Down on the main drag, they stocked up on newspapers—*New York Times, Wall Street Journal, USA Today, Star Tribune*—went back to the clinic parking lot, rolled down the windows, and read newspapers for half an hour. Then Andreno said, "Here they come."

A nurse was pushing Melodie Walther in a wheelchair, and helped her into the car. She and Burt Walther talked for a moment, then Burt got in the car and drove away. Lucas fell in behind and closed up. When he was close enough, he could see Burt's eyes in the rearview mirror. He hung at that distance, and Burt took them home.

At the house, Lucas pulled to the side of the alley, next to the garage. Burt came out to meet him. "Get your wife inside, then we'll talk."

"I don't . . ." His eyes unfocused.

"Can the senile shit," Lucas said. "We talked to Janet Walther. She said you're sharp as a tack."

Walther's head bobbed up and down a couple of times, and he shuffled back to the car and helped his wife out, and into a wheelchair that he'd left in the garage. He pushed her up the back walk, helped her inside, with Lucas a step behind, Andreno and Nadya trailing.

"Where's your grandson?" Lucas asked, as Walther moved inside the house.

"Are you going to arrest me?" Walther asked, through the open door.

"Maybe."

"I want a lawyer. Right now," Walther said. "Before I answer a single question."

"Your grandson may have killed the woman he lived with."

"Am I under arrest?"

"Not yet."

"Then get out of my yard," Walther said. He closed the door in Lucas's face.

"THAT WAS PRETTY rude of him," Andreno said, looking at the door.

Lucas was smiling now: "He knows where Roger is, I think. I think we're getting to them."

Lucas led the way back to the car, called Roy Hopper, the Hibbing chief, and said, "I need a favor."

"What?"

"I need you to park a car outside Burt Walther's place. The guy doesn't need to do anything—just park it there, and watch the house."

"Ah, jeez, I don't have all that many guys . . ."

"Just . . . please."

THE SHERIFF'S DEPUTIES were still at the murder scene outside Virginia. On the way back to check on progress, Lucas told Nadya, "When somebody does the lawyer thing—he wants a lawyer and he tells you that—you have to break off any questioning. That's the way it works here. You can sometimes bullshit your way around them, but if they insist, that's it. But the thing is, most of the time, it amounts to a kind of confession. You know you've got the right guy."

"That's a big deal," Andreno said. "Once you know you've got the right guy, you can come at him from all kinds of directions. Talk to his friends, relatives, everybody he knows. You can build a picture."

Nadya nodded. "I know this from my own work. Identification is perhaps more important there than here. Identification is everything."

"Ah, there's still a lot of work."

"Oh, not really," she said. "I tell you, you take the man down in the basement, where you have an old coal furnace, and you take off his shoes. Then you have one of these, *mmm,* metal cooking tools, they turn pancakes . . ."

"Spatula," Andreno said, and he glanced at Lucas.

"Spatula," she agreed. "You put this in the coals, and when it gets so hot that it is white, you start with the toes . . ."

"Jesus Christ," Andreno blurted out.

Nadya had turned away, but Lucas caught the corner of a smile.

"I think the Russian is joking us," he said to Andreno.

AT HARBINSON'S HOUSE, the lead deputy said that the body had been moved, but the crime-scene crew was still picking up bits and pieces of DNA, as well as going through all the paper in the place. "We checked with the phone company, and there were no calls out of here last night. None. We're thinking that if he's running, and he's got something sophisticated going, he should have called *somebody.*"

"Did you check to see if he has a cell phone?"

"We checked, but couldn't find one. There are only three companies up here."

"How about bills, personal stuff?"

"That's what we're looking at now. In the kitchen. We'd be happy to have your help."

"We can look for a while," Lucas said. "Nothing in Russian?"

"No."

. . .

THEY WERE STILL THERE, an hour later, when the deputy took a call, looked at Lucas, said, "Yeah, he's still here." He handed the phone to Lucas, said, "Roy Hopper, down in Hibbing."

Lucas took the phone and said, "Hi."

Hopper was breathing hard, and Lucas could hear sirens: "Bill, uh, the guy we've got sitting outside of Walther's. He just heard two shots. He's going in."

27

GRANDPA PUSHED THE door shut on the cop, and waited. Would the cop come in after him? No. Instead, the cop seemed to laugh at him, turned, and walked back toward the other two, motioned, and they all went back out toward their car.

Let him laugh. But now there was no exit, now the endgame was critical. In a way, he felt a certain satisfaction because he'd seen it coming.

He pushed Grandma into the front room, facing the TV. She lifted her head when she saw it, and her face seemed to loosen, as though she were relaxing with the familiarity of home.

Grandpa rubbed the top of her head, something he used to do when she was still with them; he would do it before he went out, a kind of good-bye and good luck and *I love you*. And he leaned forward and kissed her on the forehead and said, "I'll be back in a minute."

He went into the kitchen, got the walkie-talkie from the drawer, buzzed it. A minute passed, and he buzzed it again. If Carl wasn't home, that could be a setback. Another minute, then "Yeah?"

A growing knot in his stomach suddenly unwrapped. "Instructions. Write this."

"Let me get a pencil." A few seconds. "Okay."

"Number one. Recover this walkie-talkie before police do."

"What?" No code. Carl was confused.

"I'm going to take this walkie-talkie and put it under Mrs. Kriegler's garbage can, between the bricks they stand on, back in the alley. Get it there."

"Why—?"

"No questions. Just write. Number two. You are a child. Act like one. *You must remember! Act like a child.*"

"I don't—"

"No questions! Remember. Will you remember?"

"Yes."

"The instructions will be clear, soon enough. They were here this afternoon, and my endgame proceeds."

"Should I come over?"

"No! Not until you must. Be a child. Act like a child. And when you must come over, you will know it's time."

"Okay . . ."

"Now we need silence. Good-bye."

"Good-bye."

GRANDPA SIGHED, got his jacket and a piece of newspaper, crumbled it into a ball, put it in his pocket with the walkie-talkie. They might be watching; maybe he couldn't get rid of the walkie-talkie. He would see.

He went out the back door, shuffled down the block, around the corner, back up the alley. Hadn't seen anyone. Came up to the Krieglers' garbage can, took the walkie-talkie and the ball of paper out of his pocket, stooped, slipped the walkie-talkie between the bricks that held the can off the ground, then stood, lifted the top off the can, and tossed the ball of paper inside. Hoped any watcher would think he'd picked up the paper and was dumping it into the can. Or, if they didn't believe that, that they would look at the trash.

Continued up the alley. Thought about Carl as he shuffled along. He hadn't had enough time with the boy. He needed two more years. He wasn't ready for what Grandpa was putting on him—but then, Grandpa hadn't been ready when he was pushed out into the world, either.

Maybe that's all it would take—to be pushed into the real world.

B A C K   H O M E . Preparing the endgame, such as it was, would take only a few minutes. Before he did it, Grandpa went to his favorite chair, turned it to look out over the front lawn, closed his eyes, and remembered.

His first memory, the earliest he'd had, came from the countryside near Moscow. In the fall, he thought, because the memory was of a gray-and-tan landscape. He was standing with his father, maybe looking out a window, and a man was walking through a field not far from them. The man had a cigarette dangling from his lip, and a gun over his shoulder. His father must have known the man, because the man smiled and held up a dead rabbit, dangling the furry body by its tail . . . There were other scattered childhood memories: watching four men trying to push a car out of a muddy ditch, groaning and swearing; sitting in a cold outhouse with an older man—an uncle?—as they talked and shared space in a three-holer. He remembered looking down the holes, into the mysterious pit below. And he remembered the smell of a country kitchen, and the big round cold purple beets sitting on the counter, ready for the soup . . .

He remembered the first time he'd seen Melodie, who was a typist at the Cheka training school, and the way she'd cocked her head when she laughed . . .

He turned away from his memories of the kulaks; those were not for this day, though he couldn't repress the memory of a peasant who tried to joke with him, tried to make him laugh as a way out of execution. The man's oval, careworn face but with the jolly mobile lips as he told his joke and did a little awkward dance to accompany it . . . Didn't work.

He remembered the English lessons, the violent old man who beat the grammar into them, the long lists of words. He remembered the first time he saw Canada, the trip across the bleak prairie, on the train, the walk through the frozen farm fields from Manitoba to North Dakota, Melodie freezing in an inadequate wool coat that turned out to be mostly cotton, and leather shoes that seemed to dissolve in the snow.

The memories after that all ran together: World War II, the arrival of the children, Korea, moving operators across the border and up the lake, the victory in Vietnam followed by the growing anxiety of the post-Vietnam years, the car accident that took his children away and left him Roger.

Regrets about Roger: he'd been too harsh with him, too demanding of a boy who just didn't have the fiber for a spy's life.

He remembered scouring the newsstands for word of Afghanistan . . .

Then the collapse, and the years of silence from the motherland.

GRANDPA OPENED HIS eyes when he heard a car crunching off the road in front of the house. A police car, and his heart sank. He stood up, waiting for the cop to get out of the car. He could see the cop looking at him, but he never got out.

What was going on? Was he waiting for more to arrive?

Maybe there was still time, he only needed five minutes . . .

He hurried into the small bedroom they used as a library, found the video camera, the new tape and the cheap tripod that had come with the package. The battery he'd recharged over the last two days, and had already tested: it was fine.

The camera had been a Christmas gift ten or twelve years earlier, and he'd only used it a few times. That wasn't a problem, though, because it was a simple, inexpensive machine. He took it into the living room and set it up in front of the picture window, aimed toward Grandma. At the same time, he looked out at the cop: the cop was reading a newspaper.

Nothing but pressure? An attempt to embarrass him? Maybe he had time . . .

Grandma stirred, and he said, "Just a minute, Melodie. It'll be just a minute."

He started the camera, made sure it was running, and focused on Grandma, then walked around it, stood beside her, and said, "This is Sergey Vasilevich Botenkov, also known as Burt Walther, checking the camera."

He went back to the camera, ran the tape back, and watched himself speaking. Fine. Plenty of light from the picture window, focus was good, sound was tinny, but clear.

Ready. He went back to the bedroom, changed into dress pants, a white shirt, and a suit coat, then went back to the kitchen and got the gun he'd taken from the Russian agent in the bus museum parking lot.

He peered out the window: the cop was still reading the newspaper.

He cleared his throat and went back and stood in front of the camera, next to Grandma, the gun at his side, one hand on her shoulder, and began.

"MY NAME IS Colonel Sergey Vasilevich Botenkov, known here in the United States and Hibbing as Burt Walther. This is my last will and testament. I came here in nineteen thirty-four as part of a spy group working with the Soviet Union. I was first a lieutenant in the Cheka, a major in the NKVD, and when the Soviet Union dissolved, I was a colonel in the KGB. Since then we have been stranded, out of contact with the motherland. Melodie and I came here with three other couples. I have reason to believe that the U.S. government knows their names, but I will not mention them here, so as not to bring embarrassment upon their children.

"I was the commander of the group. Of the group, only my generation, now all dead except for Melodie and me, were intelligence agents—with two exceptions. My son worked as an agent, and my grandson; I was able to train both of them personally, as I raised my son as a good Communist, and, after he and his wife were killed in an automobile accident, my grandson, Roger. I felt the only way I could create a reliable agent was to teach them myself. The other families, and the later generations, lacked commitment and reliability.

"Our mission here in the United States was not to spy, but to move men and materials in and out of the country. We were a major support group for Soviet intelligence in the USA.

"About three weeks ago, a man came here from Russia, and told me that I was being reactivated, after a long period without contact with my department. I learned in the course of the meeting that he was part of a rogue group within the KGB that cooperated with Russian and American criminals: they were the so-called Russian Mafia.

"We are Communists, here. We are not criminals, not Mafia, and we work only for the betterment of the working class, everywhere. This man, Oleshev, threatened to reveal my name and background. We took action: my grandson, Roger, killed him at the port in Duluth, when he was about to reboard the ship that brought him here.

"During the investigation, Russia sent two investigators here: one aboveground, known as Nadezhda Kalin, as reported in the newspaper, and another, secret investigator. The covert operator tortured and threatened to kill the descendant of one of the original families. This man was innocent, and couldn't tell anyone anything because he knew nothing.

"When I learned of this, I called the embassy, got in touch with Russian intelligence, and asked to meet with this man, the secret investigator. We met, and I learned that Russian intelligence was intent on bringing us to trial—we who'd worked faithfully for them for seventy years!—for the killing of this criminal. Because the Russian embassy did not know who we were, but this Russian investigator had now seen our faces, Roger and I were forced to eliminate him as well.

"We then sent a message to the embassy: no more investigators. The embassy ignored us, and Nadya Kalin persisted. We decided to eliminate her, to make the point. Unfortunately, an American policeman intervened and was killed. This we did not intend.

"Also, at this time, it became apparent that the American police were unraveling the family names. When they had determined them all, it would become apparent that there was, ultimately, only one possible suspect in the killings, and that was my grandson, Roger. And that was the end for us. We began making preparations for this conclusion.

"Roger is now gone. We have had seventy years to perfect our transportation and reidentification techniques, and Roger is now safe, out of the country, and has a good, established identification and enough money to live upon. You will not find him.

"As for Melodie and me—we are too old to run, and Melodie is suffering from the final stages of Alzheimer's. I have therefore decided that the best way to end this is to end ourselves."

H E H E L D U P the pistol, then, and said, "I took this pistol from the Russian agent that we met in the parking lot of the Greyhound Bus Museum." He seemed to look at it for a moment, and then said, "I will finish this film after I make a phone call."

. . .

STILL ON CAMERA, he took a cell phone out of his pocket, and dialed in a number. A woman answered, "Law Offices," and he said, "Could I speak to Kurt Maisler or Kathy Stamm?"

"I'm afraid they're in a meeting . . ."

"My name is Burt Walther, and I need to talk to one of them immediately. This is literally a matter of life and death. Somebody's going to die in the next couple of minutes, and I need to talk to a lawyer."

There was a pause at the other end, a hasty "Just a moment, please," and then, "Mr. Walther? This is Kurt Maisler."

Walther said, "Kurt, I'm about to kill my wife and commit suicide . . ."

"Mr. Walther . . . !"

"No, listen. It's all very rational. But I have a last instruction. I have changed my will slightly, and it is on a videotape that the police will have. The tape is running right now. I want you to get the tape from the police, and I am directing you to show it to the TV stations. It concerns a series of killings here in which I was involved, with my grandson, Roger."

"What?"

"Just listen. I want you to give the tape to the TV stations, if you can get it from the police. I'm not sure if this will work, but I am making it my last will, and I am appointing you to administer it."

"Burt . . . !"

"Good-bye."

GRANDPA PUNCHED the power button on the cell phone, looking up at the camera, and said, "I leave everything here, my entire estate, to Janet Walther, the wife of my grandson, Roger. I swear before God that Janet knew nothing of this, nor do the descendants of any of the other families. And I am proving my sincerity with this last act."

He thought of the "swear before God" at the last second, and it amused him: he no more believed in God than he did the tooth fairy, but he wanted viewers to sympathize.

He rubbed Melodie on the head one last time, and tears started down his cheeks. He looked up at the camera, to let them see the tears, which were real enough, then kissed his wife on the forehead and said, "I will see you in heaven, my love," placed the pistol against her temple, and pulled the trigger. The blast was deafening in the small room, and he turned away from her, at the sound of the shot, so he wouldn't have to see the wreckage.

Without looking back down at her, he spoke directly to the camera, said, "Workers of the world, unite: you have nothing to lose but your chains." Then he put the muzzle of the gun to his temple, just above and a little forward of his ear.

I should've been in show business.

He pulled the trigger.

28

LUCAS STUCK THE LIGHT on the roof, and they took off. Nadya, one hand braced against the dashboard, excited, face flushed, said, "This could be the end."

"Whatever it is, it's gonna be complicated," Lucas said.

"Big question: Was it a shooting, or a gunfight?" Andreno asked.

"Only two shots; doesn't sound like much of a fight," Lucas said. "Ought to know soon now."

WITH LUCAS RUNNING HARD, passing everything on the road and blowing through stoplights, the trip to Hibbing took sixteen minutes. When they got to Walther's house, there were six cop cars outside, all their lights going. A group of gawkers stood down the street, every one of the women with their arms crossed. Jan Walther stood directly across the street with a cop.

Lucas pulled up and they all piled out and Janet Walther shouted, "What did you do to them?"

Lucas ignored her and they tramped across the small yard, nodding at cops. Roy Hopper stood in the doorway and said, "Looks like a murder-suicide. Looks like Burt shot Melodie and then himself."

Lucas was shocked: "Ah, shit. You're sure?"

"Not positive, of course, but our guy was right outside, and he says nobody came or went. He was inside in ten seconds, and found everything just like it is now. And—we think they made a movie of it. Here, step careful."

The three of them crowded inside behind him. The bodies were on the floor, uncovered, Melodie still in her chair with a spray of blood on the wall behind her, Burt facedown on the rug, a puddle of blood around his ruined head. The air in the house was suffused with the coppery odor of blood and raw meat. Hopper pointed at a camera that was aimed at the two bodies.

"Jimmy said it was still running when he came in. He let it run, and we just decided to turn it off a couple minutes ago. We were afraid something might happen and it might erase itself."

"Nobody looked at the tape?" Andreno asked.

"Not yet. We've got a crime-scene guy coming, and we want him to check the camera for prints . . . and the tape too, I guess. Goddamnit. What a mess. Oh. Forgot. Burt called his lawyer just before he did it, told him what he was going to do. The lawyer called nine one one, but by that time, Jimmy was already inside."

"We need to see the tape," Lucas said. "Get your guy to bag it, and make a copy of it, before he tries to lift any prints. I don't want him putting anything on the tape, or doing the Super Glue trick, or anything that might fuck it up."

"I'll tell him."

Nadya touched Lucas on the shoulder and said, "This tape will tell us."

"I hope."

NOTHING TO DO except get out of the way. Lucas gave Hopper his cell-phone number, asked him to call when they could move the camera, and they went back to the truck, ignoring Janet Walther, who called to them from across the street.

In five minutes, they were in a downtown café, drinking coffee, eating hamburgers and fries, not much to say.

"Is this a good time to get back home?" Lucas asked Nadya.

"You mean, weather? I think this is the best time, the early autumn. We still have the daylight, the trees begin to color. Do you think I'll go?"

"Something will come out of the tape," Lucas said. "Walther completely bullshitted me the first time, and the second time, he was the tough guy. Now this, with the camera. There'll be something."

"Maybe you oughta defect," Andreno said to Nadya.

She laughed, said, "No, I don't think. I am happy to get back."

"Too many signs here?"

Now she frowned, looking at her sandwich: "You know, it seems very hard here. Harsh. All the time, work, work, work, money, money." She turned to Andreno. "You are retired, no? You have this pension. Yet, you travel hundreds of kilometers to work on a job with no future. Why is this?"

"Better than sitting on my ass," Andreno said.

She nodded. "This is the thing. In the rest of the world—maybe not Japan, I have not been there—people enjoy sitting on their asses and talking, dancing, playing games. Here, there is no time. You are all too busy making signs."

Then Hopper called and said, "Our technical guy has popped the tape and bagged it. We're going to take it downtown and look at it."

"See you there."

THE POLICE STATION was five minutes away. They watched the tape in the chief's office, ten people crowded inside, standing, the tape running on an aging Panasonic TV out of an equally aged VCR. "This is a copy," the tech said. "I made a quick copy so there wouldn't be any screw-ups with the original, and we can run it back and forth. I watched it. It's nasty. You don't want to be here if you don't have a strong stomach."

Nobody moved, and he started the tape.

LUCAS HAD BEEN shocked when Hopper told him about the suicide: the tape dragged him further down, and he flinched away from the killing of Melodie, and Nadya dug her fingers into his arm and pressed her forehead into it, not looking, and jumped at the sound of the shot that killed her. Half the people in the room said, "Oh, Jesus," or "Ah, shit," and one woman hurried out of the room.

When Walther killed himself, Lucas watched—did Walther have a small amused smile on his face?—then closed his eyes as the body flung itself to the floor. He felt the air leaking out of him, out of the case.

The tech said, "Anybody want anything run back?"

There was a chorus of "nos" except Lucas: "Let me see the lawyer part again. When he's talking on the phone."

They watched the lawyer portion again, and then shut down the machine.

Lucas said to Hopper, "Keep the house sealed. Nobody in, nobody out, at least until I talk it over with the feds."

"Okay. What else?"

"I don't know. There might not be much more."

"What about the tape? We can't just give it to Burt's lawyer—I mean, he's a good guy, and all, but I don't see . . ."

"Hang on to it. Just hang on to it. Make him take you to court to get it—that'll take awhile, and by the time he gets it, it won't be of so much interest."

"Oh, bullshit," Andreno said. "That tape'll be hot two years from now. Fox would give its left nut to get its hands on it."

"Okay," Lucas said. "It won't be so hot for *us*."

"Ah. Now that you 'splain it that way . . ." Hopper said.

NADYA WAS STILL unsure about American jurisprudence, and Lucas and Andreno took a couple of minutes to explain some of the pragmatic aspects of it.

"Every serious criminal charge here winds up in front of a jury, if the defendant wants one," Lucas told her. "Even if we don't believe what Burt Walther said on the tape, even if he had some paid assassin from somewhere else, we have nothing from the shootings that would prove it. And the defense has the tape in which Walther not only takes responsibility, but also gives a credible explanation of who did the shooting. By committing suicide, he not only removes himself from the possibility of interrogation and cross-examination, he seems to . . . *mmm* . . . demonstrate the *sincerity* of his statement."

"Which is the big deal," Andreno said. "Here, a guy is absolutely assumed to be innocent until he's proven to be guilty beyond any reasonable doubt. What Walther did was drop a huge reasonable doubt on almost anything we could take to court."

Lucas concluded: "So unless something really radical shows up . . . there's no point in continuing the investigation. We'd never get anybody else into court."

Nadya understood perfectly: "For me, anything that would upset this tape would be unwelcome. We have now an explanation for everything. We can take this to Maksim Oleshev and say this and this and this, one-two-three, is how your son came to die. This is all that is wanted."

"So we're good," Andreno said. To Lucas: "I can hang around if you want, but I don't know what I'd do."

"Take off," Lucas said. "You can probably get a flight out tomorrow morning."

LUCAS BORROWED AN empty office from Hopper and started by calling the boss, Rose Marie Roux. They were on the phone for fifteen minutes.

At the end of the conversation, she said, "Okay. Let me talk to the governor, but I'd say that you're done. Turn it over to the feds, and to the local people, and come on back."

When he got off the phone with Roux, he called Harmon, spent another fifteen minutes filling him in. Harmon said, when Lucas was finished, "All right. The house is sealed, I'm going straight to Washington to get a crew out here. They really can't ignore it. Who knows what they'll find in that place? Who knows who went through there?"

"You should know that I'm not quite right with it," Lucas said. "If you find Roger anywhere—if you find him in Russia—I'd like to see him. I'd like to talk with him. I'd like to run around the block with him."

"I don't know what that means," Harmon said. "Is that cop talk? I don't know the jargon."

"What?" Lucas was puzzled.

" 'Run around the block . . .' "

"No, no. I mean, I'd really, actually like to run around a block with him. Or once around a track. That's what I meant."

ROUX CALLED BACK: "Where are you? In Duluth or on the Range?"

"Still in Hibbing."

"Good. The governor wants to see you, and it turns out he's in Eveleth tonight at seven o'clock. Can you get there?"

"No problem. Just up the way."

"He's at a dance at some hall up there . . . one of the ones with all the initials and you never know what they mean . . . I'll find it here somewhere . . ."

NADYA HAD MADE reservations: "I leave for Minneapolis and then Washington tomorrow at three o'clock. Micky goes at two o'clock and says he will ride me to the airport. What do you do?"

"Probably go home tonight. I've got to hang around here for a while, though. The governor wants to talk to me about something. Want to meet a governor?"

"Mmm. Well, yes." A thin line appeared on her forehead. "Do you think he will take a picture with me? With my camera?"

"Sure. He loves that kind of thing."

THEY WATCHED THE tape again, and Lucas and Nadya made a statement for an assistant county attorney about their contacts with Burt Walther. At five o'clock, they caught the local evening news. The news was spectacular. Somebody had a good source with the Hibbing cops, and the on-the-scene reporter was standing outside of the yellow-taped Walther house. He ran down the whole story: the first killing at the harbor, the Russian agent at the bus depot, Reasons, Harbinson, and finally, the Walther murder-suicide.

An interview with Jan Walther: "I don't know what is happening. I don't know what is going on. My ex-husband is gone, and I hear these rumors . . . All of this is crazy, and the police don't tell me anything . . ."

There was more from the neighbors in the street. One guy, who didn't seem to know much about the Walthers, tried to float the line about the Walthers being loners who stayed to themselves. He was immediately and thoroughly contradicted by all the Walthers' neighbors and Burt Walthers' fellow union members, who testified that he and Melodie were good people and that Burt was a stand-up guy. "All of this, the final echoes of the fall of the Soviet Union, and a spy ring, in our midst here in Minnesota, for almost seventy years," the reporter finished portentously.

Nadya said, "This is, how do you say . . ."

"Bullshit," Lucas said.

"Mostly."

THEY HAD TIME to kill. When the news was over, they checked out with Hopper and drove to Virginia, which was only a few miles from the dance the governor was attending. They rode north in comfortable quiet, chatting about this or that aspect of the case. Nadya said that if Walther were spotted anywhere within the Soviet sphere, she would personally see that Lucas was notified.

"But I think he will not be. There is no sign that he speaks Russian, yes? I would think he would run to Canada. Maybe in the west, in the mountains, where there is not so much TV. Perhaps Alaska. With a prepared identity, he would be hard to find."

"But what's he gonna do, be a drunk?" Lucas asked. "He's got no real skills that we know of. He was a car salesman for about six months . . ."

"There are no car stores in Alaska?" Nadya asked.

Andreno leaned in from the backseat. "Wal-Mart, man. Home Depot. There are all these places that hire and fire hundreds of people every day. They don't know who the fuck they are. Half of Mexico used to work for Wal-Mart."

"All right, he can get a job."

. . .

NOBODY WAS HUNGRY, but they stopped in Virginia for coffee, and helped Nadya buy two pounds of magazines for her flight to Washington. At seven o'clock, they drove to Eveleth, got lost, drove around aimlessly for a while, and eventually found the place by a process of elimination.

THE DANCE WAS an AFL-CIO affair with a polka band and an acre of sheet cake and Jell-O molds, a cash bar, and balloons on the ceilings. The polka band was hot, and the governor not only liked to dance, he was good at it.

Elmer Henderson was a willowy man, narrow shouldered, with short blond hair going gray at the temples, a man who wore handmade suits and shoes and a different Hermès tie each day. His clan was one of Minnesota's richest, and Elmer was a typical product of money: conservative, mild, polite.

But he could dance a polka about as well as anybody Lucas had seen, and when he got going, the other dancers fell back into a circle and clapped with the band, and Lucas and Nadya laughed out loud.

He was dancing with a very fat lady—also a good dancer—when he spotted Lucas and waved. Lucas waved back and a man who'd come up behind him said, "Don't interrupt him. I've got six photographers shooting their ass off for the next campaign."

Lucas turned and found Neil Mitford , the governor's chief political operator. "Heck of a dancer," Lucas said.

"Hard to believe, huh? Look at the motherfucker go . . ."

A WHILE LATER, the governor got loose and said, "Let's find a spot."

They found a spot and Lucas introduced Nadya and Andreno, and the governor nodded and said, "Rose Marie briefed me, and I see it's leaked onto TV. Is there anything in it? For us?"

Lucas shook his head. "You should stay clear on this one. If that tape gets out—and it may, there's a whole question of probate, because he made it his last will—you can't help feeling sorry for the old guy. I'd say, take the credit for doing the feds' job for them, but then say it's up to them to carry the ball the rest of the way."

"How about the Russians?" the governor asked Nadya. "You okay with this?"

"Yes. Thank you very much. I go back home tomorrow, I will ask them to send you an official thank-you for Minnesota's help."

"Excellent. Always happy to help."

Nadya held up her camera. "Is it permitted to get a picture of you? With me?"

"Absolutely."

Lucas took the picture, one of Henderson and Nadya shaking hands, and one of Henderson with his arm around her shoulder, giving her a little hug.

"Like old comrades," Lucas said.

Mitford said, nervously, "Not *comrades*, for Christ's sake."

"I've got to get back to the dance," Henderson said. He leaned into them, his head between Lucas and Nadya and said, "I really like to dance with the big fat ones. Even if I look like Jack Spratt. Not only that, Neil says you can tell that I like it, when you see it on TV. Did you know that twenty-two point four percent of Minnesota women of voting age are officially obese?"

"Plus-sized," Mitford said.

"That's what I meant." Henderson beamed. "Plus-sized."

HE LEFT THEM, and Nadya looked at Lucas and said, "What is this Jack Spratt?"

"Just a guy," Lucas said.

"Who could eat no fat," said Mitford.

"And his wife could eat no lean," Lucas continued.

When they were done, she said, "You are joking me again."

When she'd gone to the ladies' room, Mitford looked after her and asked, "You getting any of that?"

"No, I am not. I am a happily married man," he said, thinking of Jerry Reasons. If he'd been an unhappily married man, like Reasons, he might be dead.

"Looks pretty good."

"She *is* pretty good. If you put her on your staff, she'd fit right in. She'd be one of your top guys in a week."

Mitford squinted at Lucas: "What you're saying is, you wouldn't trust her any further than you could spit a rat."

"Did I say that?"

AT EIGHT O'CLOCK, they were on their way back to Duluth when Lucas's cell phone rang. Weather, he thought.

He picked it up, said hello, and found a switchboard operator from the BCA headquarters in St. Paul. "A woman called for you. She says it's urgent, life-and-death. She said she's tried your hotel room in Duluth three times, but you're never there. She's calling from public phones . . . she says she's the laptop lady."

"Ah, Jesus, is she gonna call back?"

"I told her we could probably get in touch with you, and she said she'd call back in half an hour."

"Give her this number, but tell her I'll just be getting back to Duluth and there are some cell-phone dead spots. Tell her I'll be in my hotel by nine o'clock at the latest, or she can call me here on this phone any time after about eight forty-five."

"Okay."

"Trace the call, just in case."

Lucas hung up and Andreno said from the backseat, "What?"

"The laptop lady," Lucas said. "Life-and-death."

"Jesus. Maybe she knows where Roger went."

"How?"

"Then what the fuck is life-and-death?"

29

THE DISAPPEARANCE OF Roger Walther, and the murder-suicide of Burt and Melodie Walther, fell on Jan Walther's household like a thunderclap. She heard about it from a customer, rather than the police, closed the store, and drove to Burt and Melodie's house, where she was turned back by the police.

She saw the state cop, Davenport, and tried to flag him down. She was sure that he'd seen and heard her, but he ignored her. As the police did their work, the crowd outside the house continued to grow, now fed by rumors coming out of the police department—that the Walthers were Russian spies, and that there were other spies in the community.

When she heard that, and with no luck talking to police at the scene, she went back home and found a message from Kurt Maisler, Burt Walther's attorney. She called him back, and he told her of Burt's phone call.

"What do I do?"

"Just sit tight. I understand the FBI is taking over. They'll want to talk with you, and you might want to ask for representation."

"A lawyer? I haven't done anything. I can't afford one."

"If you can't afford one, they have to appoint one for you. But I'd have a lawyer if any of this, uh, is true, these rumors about Burt."

Maisler said that the exposure of a spy ring would draw the media like flies, and after a long series of public screw-ups, the FBI was frightened to death of more bad publicity. On the rare occasion when they actually found a bad guy, they tended to tear him to bits, Maisler said. "You've got to be prepared."

She hired him. She took a check for fifty dollars to his office, promised to call him if the FBI approached her. She went back to Burt and Melodie's house, not knowing what else she could do, and found Carl waiting for her.

CARL HAD HEARD about the murder-suicide at a service station, while he was buying gas for his old Chevy. He'd hurried downtown, found the store closed, went home, found the house empty, and continued on to Grandpa's house. The cops wouldn't let him within a block, so he ditched the car and walked in through alleys and backyards, joining a group of sixty or seventy people across the street. A few of them patted him on the back, a few edged away, and a couple pointed him out for the three TV cameras on the scene.

A moment later, his mother arrived and she ran over to him and gave him a hug, and he said, "They said Grandpa and Grandma . . ."

"It's true," she said. She held on to him but looked toward the house: "They won't let us in. I'll call Roy Hopper direct, to see what's going on, but I think we should go back home."

"They're taking pictures of us," he said. He nodded, and she turned toward the TV cameras.

"I think we should go back . . ."

. . .

THE PHONE WAS ringing when they got back home. TV, she thought—but it was a friend named Lucy Parks, who worked at a rug-and-tile store down the street, and who had been one grade ahead of Janet in school. "I heard what happened. Is there anything I can do?"

"No, I don't know what to do myself—this is crazy."

"Everybody's talking about the spy business. Do you think Burt was really a spy? And Roger?"

"Burt. I don't know about Burt. But Roger—you've met Roger. That wasn't a disguise. You think he was a mastermind?"

Parks laughed. "If it was a disguise, he *was* a mastermind. Well, tell you what, honey, it's gonna be interesting. You need anything, give me a call."

Three more old friends called, and all of them offered support. She was a little amazed, because if this had been a TV story, the whole town would have turned on her; the yard would have been full of people with ropes and pitchforks.

Then the TV people arrived, trucks parking in the street, and people began banging on her door and taking pictures of her when she answered, so she stopped answering and called Maisler.

"I'll be right there," he said. He arrived ten minutes later, talked to all the media people, then knocked, and Jan let him in. "I've told them to stay off the lawn, and I called Roy Hopper direct and asked him to send a car over here. He said he would."

"Thanks." She was grateful, but wondered if his clock was running; he seemed to be enjoying himself too much to charge for it.

"If you want, I can make a statement to these people, unless you want to. They won't go away until they have something."

"If you could do it . . ."

He was happy to.

. . .

SHE WAS TRYING so hard to stay on top of the problem that she didn't notice how quiet Carl had been. When she did notice, she went back to his bedroom and knocked. No answer. "Carl?" She turned the knob and peeked in. He was sprawled on his bed, faceup, forearm over his eyes. "Are you okay? Honey?"

"Go away."

"Are you okay? You've got to come out and talk."

"Later. I just want to lie here for a while."

"You've been lying there for an hour. You should come out and eat something. I'll make some soup and sandwiches . . ."

"I'll be out in a while," he snapped.

"I'll call you when the soup's ready."

HER HORROR OF the moment, and her astonishment, were real, for the most part. But there was a part of her, a small kernel at the edge of her mind, that had known that Burt was a spy, that there were other spies connected to him, and that Roger had, when he was young, done some spy things. Had been involved.

She hadn't known when she married him—hadn't known for a few years, after Carl was born, but small parts and pieces of it started to come out when Roger began drinking. He would talk to relieve stress—and then say he couldn't talk about why he was stressed. He began hinting of bigger forces, of untellable but important issues.

She thought of it simply as self-aggrandizement in the face of a life that had started sloping downhill after his junior year in college, when it became obvious that he wouldn't be the big hockey star at UMD.

But more pieces kept coming out, and then one night, thoroughly in the bag, he simply told her: we're a family of spies. She hadn't really believed him, and had gone to Burt, and Burt had simply sat in his chair, smiling at her, and Melodie had twinkled, and they'd said, "That was all a long time ago. Best not to think about it anymore."

She'd bought that—even when it turned out that it probably hadn't been so long ago . . .

ROGER HAD CONTINUED to drink, the divorce had followed, and Burt and Melodie had come to her rescue. The previous owner of the frame shop was about to give it up and suggested that Jan, who was working the counter and enjoyed it, might want to buy the place. "It makes just about enough to support a family of two," he said. "If you work your butt off."

Burt helped with a down payment, and for the next ten years, all through elementary and junior high school, Burt and Melodie provided Carl's day care. She'd get him off in the morning, and they'd pick him up in the afternoon, be ready with snacks and dinners on nights when she had to work late. They'd take him to after-school activities, keep him busy.

They were, she thought, as much Carl's parents as she was; and that was why, she realized, Carl was lying on his bed like a log. The boy was in serious shock, the kind of shock you experience when a parent dies . . .

She hurried with the soup and sandwich.

THE NEXT FEW hours were a jumble.

The television never left. Maisler was all over the place, and not just local television, but on Fox, CNN, the major networks. She was afraid to leave the house, and instead, parked in front of the TV, nervously eating anything she could find. Other families were being interviewed, the talking heads said: the Spivaks, the Svobodas, the Witolds.

The FBI called, and made arrangements for an interview, tomorrow, first thing.

. . .

GRANDMA'S AND GRANDPA'S bodies were taken away from the house—she saw it all on TV, the bodies coming out on gurneys, in black bags—and the police didn't know when they would be released for burial.

The house was sealed, Roy Hopper told her. Nobody in, nobody out.

SHE TOOK SO many calls, talked to so many people, that she lost track of time. When she noticed that it was eleven o'clock, she realized that she hadn't talked to Carl for an hour or more. She went back to Carl's bedroom. "You've almost worn that bed out," she said.

"Yeah."

"I don't think you should go to school tomorrow," she said. "I think we can forget that."

"I'm going. If I don't go, it's like we're guilty of something."

"The TV people, Carl, I think it'd be—"

"I'm going," he said, stubbornly. "I can take it."

"We'll talk about it in the morning," she said.

He pushed himself up on his elbows. "Are you going to reopen the store?"

"I don't know. We've got to eat, so . . . we'll see."

"If you can open the store, I can go back to school."

She kissed him on the forehead. "You've been a good boy, Carl."

30

THEY WERE ON the outskirts of Duluth when the call came in. Lucas took the car to the side of the street and stopped as he answered the phone: "Lucas Davenport."

"This is the person who called you at your hotel in Duluth. I have some more information."

"You're a little late. We broke things out this afternoon. We haven't got him yet, but we know who he is—"

"No, no. You mean this Roger person? You're chasing the wrong man. The man who killed the Russian—he's a boy, really—I saw him on television tonight. He was outside the house, the spies' house, where they committed suicide."

"The house?"

"Yes. Outside the house. If you get the video they had on Channel Three tonight, he's the blond boy who is hugging the blond woman. He comes into the camera scene and she gives him a hug. He's wearing a dark jacket, but it's open, he had a T-shirt underneath. He's handsome."

Nadya whispered, "What?"

Lucas shook his head at her, then said, "Look, I'm sorry, but you're going to have to come in. You can't just tell me . . ."

"I'm not coming in. But I will tell you two things. The first thing is—"

"I don't think that'll work," Lucas said, interrupting.

"Then the killer will get away with it, because I'm not coming in. Two things, and then I've got to run, because I'm afraid you're tracing this. First, when he tried to shoot me, I cut him on the arm with my knife. Left arm. He should still show the cut, because he bled a lot and I think I slashed him pretty good. Second, I've sent you the knife in the mail. It's still got some blood on the blade and in the grooves, and it's his blood. That should get you somewhere. I mailed it this evening at the main post office, right after the five-o'clock news, so you should get it tomorrow. I sent it to your name at the criminal apprehension office."

"I don't—"

"Good-bye." *Click.*

"Goddamnit," Lucas said.

"*What?*" Nadya and Andreno asked simultaneously.

LUCAS DROPPED THEM at their hotel. Nadya said that she would cancel her flight: she would be there until they found the killer. Lucas said that wouldn't be necessary, but she insisted.

Andreno offered to cancel his flight, but had a problem—his ticket was nonrefundable, and it would cost six hundred bucks to cancel and get another.

"Take off," Lucas said. "If this is something, we pick up the kid. If it isn't, we don't. It's all over but the shoutin'."

"Well, shit, I feel like I'm running out on you," Andreno said uncertainly.

"There's not much to do," Lucas said. "If we go after him, which is still a big *if*, it might not be for a couple of days. We'll have to take local cops with us, and if I'm there, and Nadya . . . it's already overkill."

"All right. I'll take off. If you need me to cancel, call me on the cell phone."

"I think we're good," Lucas said.

L U C A S W E N T H O M E . He hurried through the dark, pushing ninety the whole way, his flasher on top of the car. The Public Safety Department cleared him through the two highway patrol troopers still working I-35.

On the way, he made phone calls:

He called Rose Marie Roux, to update her. "I'm going to need to talk to a lawyer. Tonight, if possible. See if you can get one to call me. I need to know how to handle this, if it turns out to be true."

He called Del: "You working early tomorrow?"

"Three to eleven. I think I cracked the McDonald's thing."

"Three to eleven? Meet me at my office at seven o'clock. I'm gonna want you to handle something for me. Take an hour or two."

"See you then."

H E T O O K A C A L L from John McCord, the BCA superintendent. "Why do you need a lawyer?" McCord asked. "What'd you do?"

"I haven't done anything, yet. But I gotta figure out a maneuver, and I need a guy."

"I can't get you one tonight—I tried, but he's not answering his phone. Rose Marie said you're on the way back, so I'll get him to your office the first thing. What time?"

"Eight? Seven thirty or eight?"

A moment of silence. Then, "Have you ever gotten here at eight in your life?"

"Just get the fuckin' lawyer, John."

HE CALLED JENNIFER CAREY, an ex-girlfriend who worked at Channel Three. She was also the mother of his first daughter. He called her at home.

"What's up?" she asked. "You still in Duluth? I saw some tape on you."

"That's what I'm calling about. I'm going through Hinckley right now, headed your way. I gotta see some of your film, the stuff you showed on the five o'clock. It's kind of urgent."

"Come on in," she said. "I'll go down and get it."

HE SLOWED DOWN when he got into the heavier traffic, followed I-35 through the northern suburbs, and turned west on I-95 into Minneapolis.

At Channel Three, Carey let him in the back door, so he wouldn't have to go through the ID-and-name-tag routine, kissed him on the cheek, and took him to her office. She had the clip on tape, and ran it.

"We put some time into this, almost two minutes," she said. Much of the clip consisted of old pictures of Burt and Melodie Walther, apparently collected from friends and neighbors, along with film of people gathered outside the Walther home.

". . . neighbors and a few family members gathered across the street as Hibbing police and agents of the state's Bureau of Criminal Apprehension processed the crime scene in this modest Iron Range neighborhood where Burt Walther reportedly claims a Soviet spy ring has been operating since World War Two . . ."

The tape lingered on a blond woman whom Lucas recognized as Janet Walther. A few seconds after the camera picked her up, a blond boy stepped into the scene, and she grabbed him and hugged him.

Her son? When she'd spoken of her son, she'd left Lucas with the mental picture of a child, of an elementary-age kid. This boy was high-school age, tall, slender, in good shape. Handsome, as the laptop lady said. This kid, Lucas thought, might have run him up and down those hills.

"Is this a story?" Carey asked, from the chair beside him, as Lucas leaned toward her monitor. She had excellent instincts.

"Of course. A really good one, too," he said. "I'd hold on to this tape, if I were you."

"What is it?"

"You are absolutely gorgeous when you're pregnant," Lucas said. "How many is this? Four? It really agrees with you."

"Lucas . . ."

"Could you run the tape one more time?"

H E   G O T   H O M E at eleven thirty, found Weather and the housekeeper, Ellen, in the kitchen, eating cheese crackers and drinking beer.

"I knew you guys hit the bottle when I was gone," he said, dragging his bag in from the garage. "How's Sam?"

"Sam's fine," Weather said. "Throw your dirty clothes in the wash, don't leave them on the floor."

He threw dirty clothes in the wash, caught up on the family news, told them that he might have to go back to Range in the morning.

"I thought it was all done," Weather said. "Channel Seven said that they're 'bracing for a tidal wave of federal officers.' That's a direct quote."

"I'm not quite done," Lucas said. "Had something come up . . ."

He explained as he stuck his head in the refrigerator. Lettuce and grapes. Cheese. A couple of bottles of beer. He picked up a carton of one-percent milk, opened it, tried to sneak a gulp or two, behind the cover of the open refrigerator door.

"I can make you an egg sandwich or an omelet," Weather offered. "Or we have some instant oatmeal . . . Hey! Are you drinking out of the carton?"

A SHORT, RESTLESS NIGHT. He got up with Weather, in the early red light of dawn, dressed, ate cinnamon-and-spice instant oatmeal, kissed a noisy Sam, and headed downtown.

Del was waiting at the office. "What's going on?"

"We're going to the post office to see if we can find a package with a knife in it."

He explained as they headed downtown in the Acura. "What I need from you is, I need you to walk the knife around to everybody. We need to get it photographed, we need to get it to the lab, we need to get the bloodwork going—we need to make sure that there even *is* some blood on it. I gotta head back north as soon as I talk to the lawyer. I really do need to know if there is blood on the knife before I get up there."

"So I'll walk it around," Del said. They were headed into downtown St. Paul, snarled in the early-morning rush. "I figured out the Mc-Donald's thing, but we'll need some surveillance cameras. And some auditors. Even then, it's gonna be weird."

"Tell me." And Lucas thought, *Should I really rush this thing on the kid? Maybe I should wait—but what if the kid disappears? Or somebody executes him? Or he kills himself?*

Del was saying, "There's this guy named Slattery who delivers bulk goods to the Bruins' warehouse—the food. The warehouse is the central supply center for the stores in their chain. But this guy is also delivering for other stores in the area.

"Then there's a guy named Jones who works in the warehouse. As the truck is unloaded, he zaps the cartons with a product-code reader and manually counts the cartons and enters the manual count in a computer. So then we have two records of the stuff coming in—the product code list and the hand count. But the thing is, they go through the same guy . . ."

"Jones," Lucas said. *Could the old man have been crazy enough to use his own great-grandson as an executioner? A high-school kid?*

"Yeah. Jones. You listening?" Del looked at him suspiciously.

"I'm listening."

"I know that hamburger theft isn't one of your major interests, but I've been bustin' my balls . . . "

"I'm listening," Lucas said. "Really." *And if it really was Roger, why didn't he take his fuckin' raincoat?* Lucas wondered. *It was raining like a sonofabitch.*

Del continued. "What happens, I think, is that Jones reads a box with his hand reader, but the box stays on the truck. He also adds the box to the hand count. So the box just seems to vanish."

Lucas forced himself to pay attention: "Vanish."

"Like smoke. The Bruins were looking for theft from the warehouse, or collusion between somebody in the warehouse and one of their own stores. Or, maybe, somebody just selling burgers without ringing them up, but the thefts were too big for that. Anyway, they were looking for something that happened after the burgers got to the warehouse. The thing is, the stuff never got inside."

"A fuckin' box of hamburger patties," Lucas said. "Who gives a shit? What could be in it for this guy? Jones, Slattery, whoever . . ."

"They're stealing enough for maybe a thousand sandwiches a week," Del said.

"A thousand . . ."

"Yeah. And there must be a third guy, who's running one of the Mc-

Donald's stores outside the Bruins' chain. Probably another privately owned store, and he's selling the stuff off the books. I haven't figured that out, and that's why we need surveillance."

"Still . . ."

"You paying attention?" Del was annoyed. "Your eyeballs are rolling around like a couple of fuckin' marbles."

"I'm paying attention."

"We're talking a hundred and fifty or two hundred thousand a year—they're also stealing buns, fries, the whole thing."

Now he paid a little more attention. "Two hundred thousand dollars . . . in fuckin' hamburgers?"

"Yeah. Why do you think the Bruins are so pissed? This is like a major heist, dude, and you're sittin' there pulling your weenie. I need some goddamn help."

"All right. Let's take it from the top . . . " He tried to stop thinking about Carl Walther and Roger Walther, one or the other of them running him up and down the hills of Duluth.

AT THE POST OFFICE, the superintendent of mails said that he didn't care what the problem was, they weren't getting any mail from him. "I'll get the guy who's sorting it—he ought to be just about done—and I'll have him deliver it up there first. I'll have him make a special stop. That's as far as I can go."

"Well, Jesus, we're right here. And he's right there," Lucas said.

"Hey—we're talking federal law. You ain't coming in here and taking the mail out. You're not even supposed to be here."

"We're cops," Del said.

"I know—that's the problem," the superintendent said. "You're not postal employees. See the sign?" He pointed. The sign on the wall said POSTAL EMPLOYEES ONLY.

Del said, "Next time you have a massacre, who you gonna call? A mailman?"

Lucas jumped in: "Wait, wait, wait . . . we'll just follow the truck."

THEY WOUND UP following a mail truck back through traffic to the BCA building.

"That was really helpful about the fuckin' massacre," Lucas said.

"Fuck the guy," Dell said.

"You been in that hamburger place too long."

"No shit."

THE CARRIER, a cheerful man with an out-of-fashion brown pony-tail, dumped twenty pounds of letters and cartons at the BCA mail-room, and said, "Have at it."

There were only half a dozen candidates, and one of them, wrapped in what looked like grocery-bag paper, with six feet of Scotch tape, had Lucas's name on it.

"Probably a bomb," Del said.

"Wish you hadn't said that," Lucas said.

Del pulled on a vinyl glove and picked it up. "I'll get the lab to un-wrap it, and I'll call you at your office. We oughta know in ten minutes," he said.

31

A CHUNKY MAN in a suede sport coat was looking at an NFL schedule poster outside Lucas's office; Chuck Miles, one of the state's more competent attorneys.

"Chuck: good to see you. Come on in."

Lucas took him into his office, sat him down, and explained the situation.

". . . so we have a witness who is providing us with material evidence, but we don't know who she is. How do we prove we just didn't make it all up?" Lucas asked.

"Okay. We can get an affidavit from you now, about what you know about the woman. What the witnesses up north said, about the hut she lived in, about when she called you, both times. What she said. About the computer and how that paid off. About where she called from, what she says about cutting this kid, about the knife. We specify in the affidavit that you have not looked at the kid to see if he was cut, nor have you taken any DNA from him. Then, we go look at him. If he's been cut in the right area, on the left arm, and if the DNA from the knife is his, we might get the whole thing into court, especially since we've got independent corroborating evidence of this woman's existence, in the shack. Plus, the witness from Catholic Charities who has actually seen her."

"But you're not sure we'll get it in. Into court."

Miles shook his head: "No. There are options, different approaches, possibilities. Some of it depends on what judge we get . . . But I can't guarantee anything. I can guarantee that there'll be an appeal, no matter what happens."

"How about if we use the knife to push him into a plea? Say, cooperation on the spy ring, plus a plea of guilty to something, with our agreement that there might have been an element of self-defense in the killing. And, say, we don't fuck with his mother, as long as she's not shown to be directly involved."

"Now that's something we might pull off," Miles said, brightening. "If we could offer him no more than a few years in the youthful offender lockup, until he was twenty-one, or twenty-five, plus cooperation . . . I can see a defense attorney buying that."

"Of course, we might be giving a multiple murderer four years in prison, then turning him loose to do it again."

"Life in the big city," Miles said.

THE AFFIDAVIT TOOK an hour, Lucas dictating to a secretary with Miles looking over her shoulder, and asking questions. After getting the legal angles worked through, Lucas called Harmon with the FBI, and found him in Washington. "Getting people together. We've got the Duluth guys up there holding everything down. We're sending in a counterespionage team to do the cleanup."

"You sound a little more cheerful."

"Yeah, well . . . against the odds, it became something."

"About the kid . . ."

"If it's the kid, we could probably crack him. Our interrogators could. That's if he knows something. He's the age where they're easy to manipulate," Harmon said.

"But you don't want in on the criminal investigation? I mean like, today?"

"You're going so well . . . keep going. I'll tell the local guys you're coming back."

Del called from the lab:

"Yellow-handled switchblade in a plastic bag. The package was addressed with a computer-printed address label. She made the label with a piece of typing paper Scotch taped to the package, and the evidence guy here says we're not going to get anything on her off the package, and he's willing to bet we're not going to get anything on her off the knife, either. She was pretty careful."

"How about the blood?"

"It's blood, all right. All gummy down in the grooves. We'll have it typed before you get up there, and we'll see if the kid has a blood type on record. You going right now?"

"Yup."

"Call you on the way."

"Hey, Del?"

"Yeah?"

"I'm really fascinated by that McDonald's stuff."

"Fuck you, pal."

MORE CALLS. He arranged for a search warrant and called Dannie Carson, a BCA investigator who had been working in Brainerd on an old case involving the killing of a hooker, and asked her to meet him in Hibbing. "We're gonna get some DNA evidence and look at a kid for murder," he said.

He called the Hibbing police chief, explained about the phone call from the laptop woman, the knife, the search warrant, and the need for somebody to take a DNA sample.

"You sure it's Carl? He always seemed like a pretty good kid to me," Hopper said in a worried tone.

"He was over there, giving her a hug. He looked like her. If it's not her kid, it's somebody she knows pretty well."

"Of course, it could all be bullshit, this call from the woman."

"Yeah, it could be. But I don't think so. The knife will tell us, the DNA. If you got a DNA guy handy . . ."

"We use the pathologist over at the hospital. Be on your ticket, though. He isn't cheap."

"Tell him today at two o'clock. And we'd like you to send a car along with us."

And Lucas called Nadya: "Be ready to go."

NOW THINGS WERE running: Lucas was out of the building, heading north again. Listening to Tom Petty and Mary Jane's Last Dance, Lynyrd Skynyrd, That Smell. Cop songs. Closing-in music. Fast up I-35, fast through a hundred and fifty miles of aspen and birch and cattails and pine trees and small lakes with boats . . . cutting into Duluth, the big lake opening out below him, snatching Nadya off the blacktop at her hotel, heading north up into the Range . . .

"I think this is amazing," Nadya said, when he picked her up.

"I think so, too," Lucas said. "But it feels right."

DANNIE CARSON WAS a large woman, not fat, but big as a door: wide shouldered, wide hipped, like a female tackle. She was also intensely personable, and one of the best interrogators Lucas had ever met. Sympathy gushed out of her, and not many suspects could resist it.

She met him at the Hibbing police station: "What're we doing?"

"Pick up the kid, bring him here, get him a lawyer. Look at his arm. If he shows any kind of scar, we arrest him on suspicion of murder and do the DNA test. Short and sweet."

Hopper, the chief, said, "Is this the end of it?"

"Can't tell. Still don't know what happened to Roger."

"Well, things are really pretty screwed up around here—Janet Walther's pretty popular, and this guy up in Virginia . . ."

"Spivak."

"Yeah, the TV is saying the case against him is really thin and that he was even assaulted by the Russians, much less helping them."

"I'm gonna let the FBI worry about all of that," Lucas said. "I'm just gonna worry about the kid."

"The kid's in school," Hopper said. "I checked. I didn't let on why, and told the principal to keep my call under her hat."

"What is this hat?" Nadya asked.

AT TWO O'CLOCK, they headed for Janet Walther's frame shop in a three-car parade—the chief, followed by Lucas, Nadya, and Dannie Carson in Lucas's Acura, and a squad car with two cops. Walther was alone in her shop, and angry when she saw Lucas; Hopper took off his hat when they walked inside, and Nadya followed quietly behind.

"What do you want now?" Walther demanded.

"We've got a search warrant for your son," Lucas said. "A warrant to search his person for bodily injuries, and to take a blood sample for DNA studies. We came to invite you to come with us. If you don't wish to come with us, we'll leave a police officer with you, to make sure you don't try to warn Carl that we're coming."

"Carl? Carl's a child!"

"Well, he's not quite a child. You keep saying a child, but he's old enough to drive. He does drive. I've seen his driver's license and the registration for a car."

"What—" She began, and then her eyes suddenly flinched to the side, and Lucas thought she'd remembered something.

"What?"

"You said bodily injuries . . ."

"Does he have a knife cut on his arm, Mrs. Walther?"

"What do you think he did? What do you think . . . ?"

So he did, Lucas thought. He turned to the chief and nodded, and the chief nodded back. "We think he killed the Russian man in Duluth, and maybe the police officer. Possibly under the direction of Burt Walther."

"That's crazy . . ." But the fear shone from her eyes.

"Do you wish to come?" Lucas asked formally. The kid was toast, so he would be as formal as possible from now on. "We could also see that a public defender, a defense attorney, is waiting at the police station when we get there."

"At the police station . . ." Her eyes flooded with tears, and she covered her face with both hands. "At the police station . . ."

SHE RODE WITH Hopper to the high school, a huge old building famous for its art deco auditorium. They all went trooping inside, down a long hall to the office. The principal met them, went back to her desk, looked at a piece of paper and said, "He's in gym class."

The principal led them to the gym, where a teacher pointed them outside. They found a group of kids standing around, in gym shorts and sweatshirts, flags hanging from the sides of their shorts, all staring at the line of cops. The gym teacher said, "He said he was sick. He went back inside."

"When was this?" Lucas asked.

"Ten minutes ago."

Lucas looked out at the street, turned to Dannie: "Shit. He saw us coming. He's running. I hope he's running."

Hopper looked at the school, a looming brick pile with kids visible in the windows. "You don't think he could . . . oh, shit," and he started running toward the school, his two cops trailing behind.

"What, what?" Janet Walther screamed after them.

Lucas trotted after Hopper, Dannie Carson, jogging alongside, Nadya hurrying to keep up.

Nadya: "You think he's in the school? With a gun?"

"I hope not. I hope he just took off. But I don't know. We can't take a chance . . . I'm trying to think, I'm just trying to think . . ." He looked up. "The place is just so goddamn big."

32

CARL WALTHER ALMOST stopped thinking when Grandpa killed himself.

He spent the night wide awake, sprawled on the bed, looking at the clock; the next morning he felt like he had gears in his head, turning slowly, full of sand; the world was not quite in sync.

His mother fussed at him, argued that he should stay home, but he drove into school. Random images popping up as he drove: Grandpa and Grandma dead, the images imagined. His father dead, the image right there, replaying itself—the warmth of his body, his lonely grave out in the clear-cut. The woman he killed in Dad's bed; the lady vagrant on the street, the feel of the wire cutting into her neck; the Russian agents going down.

A car in front of him had a fading WWJD sticker on the back bumper: What Would Jesus Do? And he thought, What would Grandpa do? Grandpa would . . . work it. He'd play it like a chess game.

But exactly what would he *do*? In all the years they'd been together, Grandpa kept telling him *what* to think, but had never quite told him *how*.

HE WAS PLAYING flag football, still in silent, robot mode—no one at the school had said anything at all about Grandpa being a spy, although he could feel eyes following him in the hallways—when he saw the parade of cars turn the corner and pull up outside the main entrance.

The cars were almost a block away, and there were no sirens or lights, so nobody else paid any attention. But Carl noticed them, and focused, and saw his mother get out of the lead car with the chief, and he knew they were coming for him.

He walked over to the gym teacher and said, "I've got to get my medicine in my locker. I'm gonna puke, I'm really sick," and he turned and walked quickly across the playing field, inside, into the locker room, shedding clothes as soon as he was inside. He dressed in one minute, and was out the door, over a fence, down to the parking lot and into his old Chevy.

Where to go? Russia? He couldn't drive to Russia. He just needed to get loose, get away. Get a gun, he thought. Get out in the woods. He got a quick image of himself with a rifle and some pretty neat clothes, like the kind from Cabela's, and maybe a cowboy-type hat, looking through the trees; a Honda four-wheeler. A guerrilla . . .

He was rolling on teenage hormones. There was some joy in it, a little fear, lots of intensity. He had gas, he wasn't hungry yet, he had seven dollars in his pocket and he knew where he could get both food and guns and there was nobody home . . .

He went that way.

33

LUCAS HAD NEVER felt anything quite so close to panic as when they were running back toward the school. Hopper said, "You go check the locker room in case he's there. I'm gonna go pull the trigger on the emergency plan."

There had already been two school shootings in Minnesota that year, three kids dead. The thought that a cold-blooded killer, who'd already wiped out a Russian agent and a cop, and God knows who else, was loose in the school—maybe with a silenced pistol—was a possibility so grim that he could hardly bear to think about it.

He didn't argue with Hopper. Inside the door, Hopper said, "Locker room," and pointed. There were a few kids around, gawking at them, and Hopper started shouting, "Everybody go back to your classroom. Everybody back to your classroom."

Lucas ran down to the boys' locker room and inside. Dannie Carson continued on to the girls' locker room, her Glock at her side. Inside the boys', a kid was emptying a clothes basket full of towels, and he saw the urgency on Lucas's face and asked, "What?"

Lucas stepped close, one hand on his pistol, the pistol still under his jacket, and asked, quietly, "Have you seen Carl Walther?"

"Yeah, he was here two minutes ago. But I think he left . . ."

"Which way did he go?"

"I don't know, I didn't see him go, I only heard him . . ."

Lucas did a quick run through the locker room, including the showers, saw nobody else, and went back into the hallway. A gray-haired woman was walking down the hall, bouncing a basketball. Lucas said, "I'm a cop. Have you seen Carl Walther? He should have been out in the hallway just a minute ago . . ."

She said, "Uh . . ."

Overhead, a speaker burped some static, and then a man's voice said, "All teachers, we are turning lights out. All teachers, lights out."

And the gray-haired woman said, "Oh, shit. Carl? Does he have a gun?"

"We don't know. We can't find him, but he was just here. Were you walking around here?"

"No, I was in the gym . . ."

Dannie Carson came out of the girls' locker room and said, "Not there."

"The 'lights out' code means we're supposed to lock down and report in," the gray-haired woman said.

"Then do that," Lucas said. "Hurry."

THEY TORE THE school apart. Lucas ran through the weight room, checked the swimming pool, and two or three cops walked each row of the huge, elaborate auditorium; every room and cubbyhole was checked. No sign of Carl Walther. Twenty minutes after the search began, a teacher walked down to the office with a student and said, "Somebody needs to hear this."

And the kid said, "You should check the parking lot for his car," the kid said. "I saw him come in this morning. He parked right next to me."

Lucas borrowed the kid and they went out to the parking lot. On the way, the kid described the location where the car was parked—and when they got there, to the exact location, they found an empty space.

"This is mine," the kid said, pointing to an aging Volkswagen Rabbit in the next slot. "He's gone. But he was right here this morning. He's got a Chevy."

THE TENSION BACKED off a notch. There were now ten city cops and six or eight sheriff's deputies and a highway patrolman in the school. Parents were beginning to arrive outside; the kids had cell phones. Lucas found Hopper and told him about the car and Hopper said, "Maybe he's gone home. We'll get some guys moving. Nobody's seen him in here, thank God."

They'd put Janet Walther in the principal's office, and told her to stay there. Now they got her, and Lucas asked, "Where do you think Carl would go. Home?"

She was scared to death. "Don't hurt him. He's a good kid, don't hurt him . . ."

The only places she could think that he might be were at home, at the store, or possibly at Grandpa's.

Lucas, Nadya, and Carson went with Hopper first to Jan Walther's home, cleared the place, then down to the store. The store was locked, and they cleared it; at the same time, they got a call from cops clearing Grandpa's—all the doors were still sealed from the outside.

"I'll talk to the highway patrol, the roads going out," Hopper said. "He can't be far."

Janet Walther grabbed Lucas's arm: "You don't hurt him. You don't hurt him, okay. He's just scared, you're just scaring him."

"We don't want to hurt him," Lucas said sincerely. "We really don't."

. . .

THEY FOUND HIM late in the afternoon.

They found him because the story was now all over TV and radio, and a kid came in with his father. A half dozen of them were sitting around the police station when a cop stuck his head in the door and said, "There's a guy here with his kid. They say they might know where Carl Walther is . . . if we haven't found him yet."

"Bring 'em in," Hopper said.

The man's name was James Wolfe, and his kid was James, Jr., another high-school boy. Wolfe said, "Jimmy here had the idea . . . We took Carl deer hunting out of our cabin the last couple of years. And last summer, the kids were playing paint-ball games up there."

"Carl said it would be really a neat place for a war," Jimmy said.

"Where is it?" Lucas asked.

"On the Sturgeon River west of Cook. Thirty miles."

Hopper said to Lucas, "That'd explain why nobody's spotted him anywhere. Why we can't even find the car. He'd have been halfway up there before you went out and looked in the parking lot."

"Can we send somebody to check it?" Lucas asked one of the sheriff's deputies.

"Hard to find it," the elder Wolfe said. "We were talking about it on the way over. The best way would be to go into the Magnusons' place, they're one place down from us. You could walk through the woods over this little rise and look right down on the house. See if his car is there."

Lucas said to Hopper, "I'll go, I can take a couple of guys . . . We can be there in half an hour, and if it doesn't pan out . . ."

"There's one more thing," Wolfe said. "Uh, I keep a gun up there to clean up beaver and porcupines, and I think Carl knows where it is."

"He does," the younger Wolfe said. "We sorta let it out."

"You were screwin' around with it; that's what you were doing," his father said.

"What is it?" Lucas asked. "What kind of gun?"

"A Savage .223 bolt-action with a two-to-eight-power scope on it. Not a great scope, but the gun shoots really good. Inside a minute, anyway," the kid said.

"And there's ammo?"

Wolfe nodded. "A couple of boxes. Fast-expansion stuff to blow up the critters. You go back there, if you think he's dangerous . . . You best take care."

THE SHERIFF'S DEPARTMENT had a designated rapid-response team for the area, and three of them, including a sniper, were pulled in for the trip. They brought rifles and the usual assault and hostage gear. Lucas led the way out, with the elder Wolfe beside him in the Acura. Nadya insisted on going, and rode in the backseat. Dannie Carson had nothing with her but city clothes, and Lucas left her to co-ordinate in Hibbing.

On the way up to Wolfe's cabin, Wolfe asked Lucas what he thought the kid had done. Lucas said he wasn't sure. That they wanted to question him about a killing, and maybe two killings.

"I had a feeling about him—not anything like this—but I had a feeling that he'd been abused somehow. I know his mother, she's the nicest lady in the world, but I always wondered about old Burt. Burt was polite, but you couldn't help thinking he was an asshole. You know his grandson, Roger . . ."

"We're looking for him, too."

"I've been reading about it. I knew Roger pretty well and he was sort of messed up, too. Of course, his parents were killed in that car wreck, but that's not what it was—there was always something else, and I always wondered if Burt didn't have something to do with it. Not physical. Psychological."

"Well. Burt was a spy," Lucas said. "If he was recruiting family members, and they'd all grown up here where everybody's got a flag and supposed to be a good American . . . there'd be a lot of stress." He looked over his shoulder at Nadya. "Isn't that right?"

She nodded. "This is widely recognized in the community. Family stress is a very big problem."

Wolfe nodded, looking out the window. "Just . . . messed up, Roger was. Never saw the man *really* happy, except maybe at his wedding. Wonder where he is now?"

THE MAGNUSON HOUSE was a half mile down a gravel road from Wolfe's place, set in a deep patch of woods along a small muddy river. There was a chain on the gate, and they could see a long track down through the trees to where the house must be, but they couldn't see the house. "There's a spot over there where you can get in, where they cut the brush out for the power line," Wolfe said, pointing down the road. "You might scratch your car . . ."

Magnuson wouldn't care, Wolfe said, he was a good ol' boy.

The sheriff's GMC led the way through, and they stopped halfway down to Magnuson's house, at the point where the driveway came closest to Wolfe's. Lucas gathered the three deputies around him, and they went over the approach. They took a couple of flash-bangs and some tear gas, and just as they were about to start into the woods they heard a distant banging sound, metal on metal, from the direction of Wolfe's place.

"Somebody there," Wolfe said. "It's gotta be him."

"Let's go," Lucas said.

CARL HAD GOTTEN into the house with a rock through the kitchen window. He cleared out the glass, boosted himself inside, turned on the water pump and the electricity, pushed the thermostat from fifty to seventy-two, found a local station on the satellite, got the gun and a box of shells out of the hideaway.

All right. Get something to eat. He rummaged through the kitchen, found a couple of cans of Campbell's Cream of Mushroom Soup, heated it up, and sat at the kitchen table gobbling it down, the gun on the table.

The movement kept him preoccupied. Only when he put the bowl in the sink did he begin to feel alone—nobody to tell him to wash the bowl and put it away, nobody to tell where he was going, no Grandpa to talk to. No place to go, not with the cops looking for him.

In fact . . . the Chevy was outside, in plain sight. If anybody came down the drive, it would be the first thing they'd see. If the cops were looking for him, somebody could come down the drive, spot the car, and sneak away to report him, and he'd never know.

He picked up the gun, went outside, checked the garage. It was locked, but with a cheap padlock, enough to keep out kids. He looked around, found a hand-sized field stone, and beat on the lock until the hasp pulled out. He went inside, checked the four-by-four for keys—there were none, they were probably hung on the back of the book-case—and lifted the overhead door.

With the door up, he moved the Chevy inside, then went back to the house. A local news program was on. He got a Coke from the refrigerator, perched on the couch. He thought about the Honda in the garage. Maybe later, he'd go out and scout around. For the moment, he'd just see what they were saying about him. Maybe, he thought, nobody had noticed he was gone.

EIGHT HUNDRED YARDS, through second-growth timber, the ground soft and marshy underfoot. The banging continued, off and on, for the first three or four minutes of the march, and then stopped. They crossed a rise a few seconds later, and Wolfe whispered, "When you come across that next little rise, there, you can see the place."

They crossed a wet depression, and one of the sheriff's deputies whispered, "Nettles," and Lucas raised his hands over his head—he hated nettles—and warned Nadya. She nodded, and a minute later, they climbed out of the wet ground, through some scrubby maples, and looked down at Carl Walther's Chevy.

Carl was just walking out of a metal pole barn. A rifle lay on the hood of the Chevy and he picked it up, got in the car, started it, and rolled it into the pole barn.

"Broke into the pole barn to hide the car," Wolfe guessed.

"What's in there? Vehicles?"

"Yeah, there's a four-wheeler, a Honda, a boat, a couple of trailers, a couple of sleds, a John Deere Gator. I don't know if he knows where the keys for the Honda are, but . . . now that I think of it, I bet he does. I bet when they were up here screwing around with that gun, they were running the four-wheeler, too. If he got on that, he could go where we couldn't . . ."

Lucas turned to the deputies. "Everybody move carefully. We've got him. There's no point in anybody getting hurt." One of the deputies carried a radio, and Lucas said to him, "Call in, get some more people down here."

"We gonna talk to him, or what?"

"We'll stay in the woods, block the place, and wait until the other guys get here. Then we'll talk . . ."

"If we see him outside without the rifle, we could try to rush him."

"We could, but he might have something else with him—the pistol he used on Jerry Reasons," Lucas said.

The radio guy came back: "All right, I talked to Jim, and they're on the way, the whole bunch of them. Half hour."

"Let's move in close, and then wait," Lucas said. "Just close it up . . ."

Nadya stayed at his elbow, her face flushed, intent.

. . .

THE HOUSE SAT on the north side of the narrow river, with a tiny roll-out dock already pulled up on shore; a twelve-foot aluminum rowboat was turned upside down on the bank beside the dock. The house itself was surrounded by an open grassy yard that extended perhaps thirty feet on all sides, before the trees began; a few marigolds were spotted along the sidewalk to the front door. The driveway cut across the north edge of the yard, leading to the pole barn.

The sniper went with Lucas and Nadya, with Wolfe trailing. One of the other deputies took the east side of the house, the second the west side. They sat and waited. Five minutes passed, then ten.

And then Carl Walther burst from the house, running, rifle in hand, a fat cloth laundry bag over his shoulder. He went straight into the pole barn, head down.

"What's happening?" The sniper asked.

Lucas looked at the cabin roof. "You've got a satellite TV in there, don't you?" he asked Wolfe. He could see the pie-pan dish.

"Yeah."

"The fuckin' TV people saw them tearing out of the police station," Lucas said. The Honda's engine rumbled to life, and Carl backed out of the garage. The cloth bag was attached to a rack behind the seat, held in place with bungee cords. The rifle was in a plastic scabbard.

"Take the tires as soon as he's clear of the garage," Lucas said to the sniper. "Watch your guy there in the background."

The sniper spoke into his shoulder radio and then the Honda was easing out of the garage. "Take it," Lucas said.

The sniper waited another two seconds, waiting for an angle, and then took the back tire with a burst of three shots.

Carl tried to accelerate, but the tire flopped on the driveway and he jumped off the Honda, grabbed the gun, looked wildly in their direction, fired a single shot straight up in the air and then ran into the house again.

"What was that about?"

"Scared," Lucas said. He looked at his watch. "The other guys are still twenty minutes out. I'm going to call down to him. I'll move off your position, get as close as I can, and yell at him."

"What if he comes out with the gun?"

"You have to decide. I don't want him killed."

"Sure you don't want to wait?"

"I'm worried about what he's thinking in there," Lucas said. "His grandpa just killed himself."

LUCAS WORKED HIS way back into the woods, so the pole barn was between himself and the house. Wolfe stayed with the sniper, but Nadya followed Lucas.

"You can come," he said, when he saw she was coming no matter what he said, "but stay out of the way."

"A woman's voice . . . ," she said.

"You're the woman he once tried to kill. And he almost cut the head off another woman, if he's the one who killed the old lady in Duluth."

"Still. He might believe he would be safer with me."

"Just stay out of the fuckin' way, okay?"

They slipped around the corner of the pole barn, inside, out of sight. "Now just . . . just get behind the car or something," Lucas told Nadya.

She was peeking around the corner of the garage access door. The house was fifty feet away, with the Honda disabled halfway between. She didn't move, so Lucas took her by the arm and steered her toward Carl's Chevy. "Just . . . stay."

"I'm not a dog," she said.

• • •

LUCAS WENT BACK to the garage door and shouted at the house. "Carl. We need to talk with you. Put the gun away. Put the gun away. If you shoot it at us, you'll go to jail. We need to talk to you, son."

No answer. Movement on the drapes? Maybe.

"Carl . . ."

"Go away. You killed my grandpa." Lucas peeked. Definite movement on the drapes on the far corner of the house. A bedroom, maybe.

"We didn't kill your grandpa."

Nadya stepped up beside him and Lucas said, "Jesus Christ, Nadya . . ."

Nadya called, "Carl. I have just spoken to your mother. She's afraid you'll be hurt. She wants you to come home, Carl . . ."

"Go away."

Lucas: "We can't go away, son . . ."

The glass broke in the window where Lucas thought he'd seen drapes moving, and Lucas shoved Nadya, hard, and went after her, pulling her down, and a second later a bullet smashed through the metal side of the building where they'd been standing.

"Jesus . . ." He pulled at Nadya, and they scrambled behind Carl's Chevy.

Somebody yelled, "Davenport, you okay?"

"We're okay, hold your fire."

Another shot ripped through the garage, and then another, and small pieces of metal showered over the Chevy. Daylight streamed through the holes, and Lucas could see inch-long peels of the thin sheet steel where the slugs had punched through. Another shot didn't hit the garage. "He's shooting up in the woods, now," Lucas said.

Nadya, on her hands and knees behind the John Deere, shouted, "Carl, please, we are trying to help you."

Bam.

Another shot hit the garage and maybe ricocheted off one of the snowmobiles. Wolfe wasn't going to be happy.

A burst of three—one of the deputies up in the woods was shooting back.

"Hold on!" Lucas shouted. "Hold on . . . Carl, we've got the house covered. Come on, man, you haven't done anything yet . . ."

Two more shots tore through the garage. Lucas yelled, "Carl, man, you're shooting up your own car. You're shooting up your car, Carl . . ."

CARL RELOADED; he had a full load plus two for his pocket. No way out? If he could get to the garage, there was still the car, he could come flying out in the car and go the other way, they'd never think of that, he could drive out the utility access, there might be a couple of small trees and some brush in there . . . and he thought, nah, you'd never fuckin' make it.

Grandpa's image flashed up in his head: Grandpa dead. The gun's muzzle floated in front of his eyes, a few inches away. He could put the muzzle up under his chin . . . wouldn't hurt. He'd go from here and now, to nothing, with nothing in between. Be better than landing in some prison where he'd be living in a shoe box and getting fucked by some old guy.

It wasn't supposed to be like this. He was supposed to be underground, or a guerrilla fighter, or something—but not stuck on the bedroom floor of a crappy cabin with a half dozen shells and no food except six cans of soup and some peanut butter. When he saw the thing on TV, the cops suddenly speeding out of town, he'd thought they'd be coming, that he'd been spotted somehow, or the Wolfes had talked to somebody. He'd taken five minutes to throw a little camping equipment in a nylon laundry bag, along with the soup and peanut butter, but it was all bullshit, he really knew that—he didn't even have a sleeping bag, or a tent, or good clothes. He'd freeze out there at night.

The muzzle of the gun just hung there, the smell of the powder, not bad; from something to nothing, no pain, no transition . . .

Then the guy in the garage yelled, ". . . you're shooting up your own car. You're shooting up your car, Carl . . ."

A wave of rage went through him. He worked at the fuckin' pizza place every night for six months to buy that car, then he got screwed on the car, it was a piece of junk. But it was *his* car, and these *people* . . .

He picked up the gun and headed for the door.

THEN CARL CAME OUT, the front door slamming behind him. He walked, striding, angry, swift, toward the garage.

Lucas said, "Oh, shit, stay down . . ."

Carl had the rifle, held low, pointed into the gararge. He screamed, "Get away from my car, get away from my fuckin' car . . ."

Lucas pulled his pistol and shouted, "Don't come in here, put down your gun, I don't want to have to shoot you."

"Fuck you," Carl shouted back.

"Carl, don't do this," Nadya screamed.

Carl was moving across the front of the garage, and Lucas and Nadya tried to move back, so they could get around the back fender, but Lucas thought he was coming too fast, that he wouldn't make it, and braced his shoulder against the back door and pointed the .45 . . .

Boom. Carl fired the rifle, and the bullet went through the car's windshield, Lucas thought; and maybe the back window. He heard the glass crack, not shatter, but pop with a funny glass sound, and Carl was still coming and then,

Crack.

The shot came from the woods and Carl went down, screaming, lost the gun. Lucas was around the car in three quick running steps, kicked the rifle, the kid twisting in the dirt like a broken-back dog.

The sniper was running down the hill with his rifle, and Lucas yelled to the radio guy, "Call an ambulance, tell them we need an ambulance . . ."

He pushed Carl down, the kid moaning in pain, checked his belt for a gun, found nothing, picked up the rifle, carried it out of arm's reach, and put it down again.

The sniper had stopped and was talking into his shoulder microphone; Wolfe was in the woods, standing, looking down at them. Another deputy was running in from the other side of the house.

CARL STARTED CRYING. He looked very young, lying on the ground, with his slender blond face and pink cheeks. Lucas bent over him and asked, "Where are you hit, where are you hit?" and Carl began stuttering incoherently. The sniper came up and said, "I tried to take him in the butt. I was sure he was going to get you."

"Okay," Lucas said. "Help me roll him."

Another deputy came up, and Wolfe, and then the third deputy, and they rolled Carl up on one hip and Lucas saw the blood soaking into his jeans. "Let's get his jeans off, make sure it's not arterial."

Nadya helped, held Carl's hand, and Lucas noticed that she was bleeding; she had three or four small cuts on her face. She said to Carl, "You will be okay, you will be okay," and stroked his hair as a mother would.

The single, copper-jacketed bullet had penetrated the top of Carl's left buttock, angling down, then went through his right buttock and exited. Blood was flowing from all four wounds, but the flow wasn't too heavy. "I got a first-aid kit in the car; I'll bring it over," one of the deputies said. He left his rifle behind and ran off through the woods for the cars.

"Am I gonna die?" Carl asked.

"No, but you're gonna spend some time in the hospital," Lucas said. "Hell of a lot better than what you did to Oleshev or Jerry Reasons."

Carl, in pain, opened his mouth to say something, then a light came on in his eyes and he looked at Lucas and said, "I want a lawyer."

"FUCK YOU," LUCAS SAID. He stood up and said to Nadya, "What happened to you? Let me look."

She stood up and Lucas took her chin between two fingers, turned her face. "You have four small cuts, probably from glass. There may still be glass . . . here. Here's a piece." He could see a small sliver of glass protruding from one of the cuts. He caught it between the fingernails of his two index fingers, and lifted it out. Blood tricked down her face. "That's what happens when you don't behave."

"Bad?" she asked.

"Nah. You might have to have some glass picked out, but nobody'll even see the cuts after they heal up. You'll still be gorgeous."

He looked back at the kid, and Nadya walked away, back into the garage and behind the car. He turned back in time to see her pick up a long, thin piece of glass from the car's trunk. "Careful with that . . . ," he called.

She fit it between two fingers and then lightly slapped herself twice on the forehead. Blood trickled from two long new cuts, running across her fair skin into her eyebrows.

"What the fuck are you doing?"

"Politics," she said.

34

THE AMBULANCE TOOK a full half hour to get to the shooting scene. Carl had slipped into shock, and while the wounds were serious, they weren't life threatening, an EMT told them—Carl was young, in good shape, and should recover quickly. Before they took off in the ambulance, the EMT looked at Nadya's face, and found one additional small shard of glass, which he removed with a pair of tweezers.

When he'd finished, Nadya asked Lucas to take a picture of her with the blood on her face: "This I can use," she said. She posed next to the ambulance, with Carl's feet visible on a gurney, her face smeared with blood.

TWO DAYS LATER, she was gone. Lucas dropped her at Minneapolis–St. Paul International, and said, "Well: it's been real."

"What is this 'real'?"

"I mean, it's been interesting."

"I think I have been a pain in your ass," she said, smiling at him.

"Ah, well . . ."

"I'm so sorry about Jerry . . ." Her smile disappeared. "This will not go away."

"Nothing you could do. You did nothing wrong—except run into a crazy kid."

"Who thought he was working for Mother Russia." They were coming up to the security screening, and she sighed, stood on her tiptoes, kissed him on the cheek. "If you ever come to Russia . . ."

"Right."

She smiled again. "I know—you won't. But if you do . . ." She patted him on the chest. "Say good-bye to Weather for me. I like her very much. And I think she has a very good husband."

THE DAY AFTER THAT, he'd gotten comfortable with his couch again.

He was lying on it, reading *GQ*, an article about a specially spun wool used by an Italian tailor, for suits that cost six thousand dollars. He would not pay six thousand dollars for a suit under any conditions, he decided. Well. It'd have to be a *really* good suit.

He was reading about bespoke shoes when heard a car enter the driveway, and then a quick *beep* on a horn. He'd been waiting for it. He dropped the magazine, rolled off the couch, and headed out the front door. Weather was there, standing back, looking at her new red BMW 330 sedan. "It's not as good-looking as the Prelude," she fretted.

"It's *better*-looking than the Prelude," Lucas said, walking around the car. "It's just different."

"More practical," she said. "All-wheel drive and you can carry more stuff."

"I got your practical right here," Lucas said. "You don't buy a forty-thousand-dollar car to haul celery." He patted the car on the ass. "You buy it because it's an artwork. Just don't drive it through the fuckin' garage door."

She looked at the new garage door, then said, "What about Carl?"

When they'd gotten Carl to the hospital, an examination showed that a piece of the bullet jacket had fragmented off and had ripped into his sphincter muscle. That could have been serious, but a delicate operation had removed the remains of the bullet and had repaired the damage to the muscle.

"I talked to the doc about an hour ago—everything went fine. He won't be running for a while."

"Thirty years, if you have anything to say about it."

"The little asshole killed Jerry Reasons," Lucas said. "And the Russian. I have a hard time feeling any sympathy for him."

"Good-looking guy, though," Weather said. She turned back to her car. "Would blue have been better?"

A FEW MORE days went by. Weather began driving the new BMW into the driveway at fifty miles an hour, and Del got surveillance on the McDonald's truck deliveries.

The St. Louis County attorney announced that the grand jury had indicted Carl Walther on charges of first-degree murder in the killings of both Rodion Oleshev and Jerry Reasons. The feds indicted Anthony Spivak on espionage charges, and the county attorney dropped charges of accessory to murder, saying that they were redundant in light of the federal charges. In fact, he seemed pleased to get out from under the Spivak case.

Lucas heard from Harmon, unofficially, that Janet Walther was willing to talk about the espionage ring if she could make a deal for Carl.

The deal would be a tough one, though: the Duluth cops were convinced that Carl had killed Jerry Reasons, and they wanted him put away. The only problem was that they had little evidence, other than Lucas's story of chasing a man up and down the hills, and some general descriptions from the women behind the hotel desk.

On the other hand, the blood from the switchblade definitely was Carl Walther's, and Carl had definitely gone to the emergency room the night Oleshev was murdered, within a couple of hours of the murder taking place.

Carl claimed that the cut on his arm had come from a broken window in Grandpa's basement. The feds, as it happened, had spotted and processed the window, and confirmed that the blood was in fact Carl's.

Still, if they could get the knife into evidence—not a sure thing—nobody believed that the blood-on-the-window alibi would hold up.

If Duluth couldn't get Carl for killing Reasons, they would be somewhat satisfied with a life sentence on the Oleshev murder.

Yet another complication: Roger Walther was still missing. The feds said that Janet Walther was now blaming everything on him.

"JUST BETWEEN YOU and me," Harmon told Lucas, "I think perhaps the best we can hope for is to identify this entire Soviet ring and debrief all the participants. I don't think there will be much jail time—too many lawyers involved now. The cooperation of Janet Walther is critical to that end."

He was wheedling.

"That would be the best deal for you spooks," Lucas agreed. "For the rest of the world, including both Russia and the United States, the best deal would be to nail Carl Walther for murder. We've got to get him for *something* . . ."

Harmon was fifteen hundred miles away in Washington, but Lucas could almost hear the shrug. "If we can."

. . .

MORE TIME PASSED. Del nailed the McDonald's thefts, and Neil Mitford, the governor's aide, came down to shake his hand. "Fuck a bunch of Russian agents, this McDonald's thing was important."

"I oughta get a certificate or something," Del said, cutting his eyes toward Lucas, who yawned.

"You should," Mitford agreed. He took a dollar out of his pocket. "Here. It's even signed by the secretary of the treasury."

FOUR WEEKS AFTER Carl was shot, Lucas got a note from Nadya.

"Thank you very much for your hospitality; I enjoyed my time working with you," the note said. Blah-blah-blah. She sounded like an exchange student, Lucas thought. The laser-printed portion of the note seemed to have been written with the idea that carbon copies would be filed somewhere. The real meat came at the very end, handwritten in blue ink. "My fellow bureaucrats were most impressed with my wounds, so I thank you also for the photograph. Love, Nadya."

The note was signed Lt. Colonel Nadezhda Kalin.

"Our girl got a promotion," Lucas told Weather. He went around all day feeling pleased, although he didn't exactly know why.

SIX WEEKS AFTER Carl was shot, Lucas was sitting in his office, feet on his desk, reading about a series of snipings in which the victims were horses.

Somebody—some nut—would shoot the animals in the stomach, often several times, with a .22, and even if the shooting didn't kill the animal, the horse would have to be put down by a veterinarian.

Nine horses had been killed in three counties, and horse lovers were in an uproar. The governor wanted it fixed, and quick. Mitford put it this way: "In the whole universe of politically sensitive shootings, if Carl Walther and his shootings and a Russian spy ring is a three, then the horses are a nine. Right up there with the McDonald's heist."

"Horses are more important than cops getting killed," Lucas said.

"*I* wouldn't say so, but the fact is, cops get shot from time to time. Nothing you can do about it," Mitford said. "But don't fuck with horses. Or dogs. The voters'll rip your fuckin' heart out. I'll tell you, Lucas, if you can catch this guy, the governor would be really, really grateful . . ."

SO HE WAS sitting there, reading horse files, when the phone rang. He picked it up, and was told it was Kelly, the cop from Duluth.

"Guess what?"

"How many guesses?"

"Well, fuck it. I'll just tell you. The crime-scene guys finally unrolled that bubble-wrap mattress and found a fingerprint. Nice, neat, clear."

Lucas sat up: "No shit. Is there a name?"

"That's the interesting part. There *is* a name. Attached to a drunk-driving arrest there in St. Paul about nine years ago, a college student named Annabelle Ramford. We've looked her up, and she's apparently a lawyer there in St. Paul. Got a phone and everything."

"A lawyer? She's supposed to be a bum."

"Beats the shit out of me. I don't know what it means," Kelly said.

"There's a John Ramford, he's like a really bigshot lawyer downtown . . ."

"I'd call him up and ask about Annabelle, then . . . and if you could do it, the Duluth Police Department will be in your debt."

"Like I need that," Lucas said.

.   .   .

BUT AS SOON as he was off the phone, he looked up the Ramford firm in the phone book, called, and asked for Annabelle Ramford. "May I tell her who's calling?"

"*Mmm . . . No.*" He hung up and got his coat.

TEN MINUTES LATER, having dumped his car in one of the new parking ramps downtown, he was talking to the receptionist at the Ramford firm: "I would like to see Annabelle Ramford."

"May I tell her your name?"

"Just tell her it's the Bureau of Criminal Apprehension about the bubble wrap. She'll know."

The receptionist asked him to take a seat. He took a seat, picked up a copy of *Newsweek,* and in two minutes read more than he wanted to know about the cell phone industry in Finland. The receptionist said, "Ms. Ramford will see you now."

The receptionist directed him to an oak-doored elevator, which operated between two floors only. He took it up one. A stylish young woman was leaning in a doorway, and when she saw him step out of the elevator, she said, "Officer Bubble Wrap?"

"Yes." He walked down toward her. She was wearing a pale green dress that was almost jade, but had a gray tone to it; a subtle color that set off her eyes. A single strand of pearls acted as a frame for her tanned, athletic face. "My name is Lucas Davenport. I'm with the Bureau of Criminal Apprehension."

A skeptical look appeared on her face. "You're not here to see me about the Quentin case, are you? I told Judge Martin that we would not deal on that . . ."

"I don't even know what the Quentin case is," Lucas interrupted.

"Then what are you . . . bubble wrap?" She was puzzled, and waved him into her office. The office was small, cluttered with paper and yellow Post-It notes, and an unseemly amount of personal junk, Lucas thought: bric-a-brac, knickknacks, gimcracks, tchotchkes. Riffraff? No, riffraff was people . . .

He sat down and said, "I've been looking for a woman that you may know. You've at least been in touch with her. She was living on the street in Duluth, and she was a witness to a crime there, a murder. I know that she's now in St. Paul . . ." He gave her a short version of the story.

She nodded, interested. "I do the pro-bono work here," Ramford said, spreading her hand toward the clutter of paper. "I know a number of these women. But from Duluth? Why do you think I'd know . . . ?"

"Because we found your fingerprint on a piece of bubble wrap that she was using for a bed. In Duluth." Lucas was watching her eyes, and saw nothing in particular.

"*My* fingerprint?"

"Exactly. There is no doubt—if you're the same Annabelle Ramford who was arrested on a DWI about ten years back."

She smiled ruefully. "That was me. Graduation night. Boy, my father was *pissed*. But I'm sure I didn't know anybody . . ."

"So if you didn't know her, if you never met her, how did your fingerprint get on this bubble wrap?" Lucas asked.

She ran her index finger up and down her nose, thoughtfully, then looked up. "Ahhh . . . Was it a big piece of bubble wrap? Like most of a roll? Or two rolls?"

"Yes."

"Okay. And you found it around the port? Around a Goodwill store? Or do you know if she went to the Goodwill store, like if she shopped there, or something?"

Now Lucas's eyebrows went up. "Yes, the Goodwill was right across the street."

She leaned back in her chair. "Okay. We keep a boat up there," Ramford explained. "My family does. An Island Packet 38, the *Whiplash*. About, let me see, it must have been early August, I took a bunch of stuff up there. Wine, mostly. Loose bottles. I wrapped them in this big sheet of bubblewrap. I had some sailing stuff up there, old clothes, and some, two, or three, I think, old life jackets—perfectly good, you understand, but older—that I took off the boat. I knew where the Goodwill store was, so I stopped and threw the clothes and the life jackets in the Dumpster. Then I had that bubble wrap, and it was used but perfectly good, and I think I had another roll, too, and I was sure some poor person could use it, so I threw it all in. I bet that's where she got it."

"So you didn't . . ."

"No, I've never talked to a street person in Duluth. Honest," she said. "Never. Down here, a few."

Lucas was watching her as she talked, and she had the most guileless eyes he'd ever seen on an attorney. That would be worth a lot in court, he thought. When she was finished, he sighed and said, "Shoot. I was hoping you might know her."

She leaned back in her chair, and if she'd been wearing pants, might have put her feet up. "I've been reading about this whole thing in Duluth—that was you up there, wasn't it? The spy thing? I remembered the name about fifteen seconds ago."

"Yeah."

"Your case against this boy—it sucks." She smiled when she said it.

"You only say that because you're a defense attorney," Lucas said.

"You mean the prosecutors haven't told you?" she asked.

Lucas grinned back at her: "They've hinted that additional information would be welcome."

"I'll bet. Like *any* additional information." she said. "The kid have a good attorney?"

Lucas shrugged. "Public defender. So yeah, I'd guess he's probably pretty good. Why, you want it?"

"No, no. I do civil stuff," she said, hastily. "Guys beating wives, wives beating guys. The welfare department beating wives and guys out of their rightful checks . . ."

Lucas stood up, yawned, and stretched. "Poop. Listen, thanks for your time."

GOING DOWN IN the one-floor elevator, Lucas thought about Annabelle Ramford. Working for her old man's law firm, wearing her little pearls and her little green dress, worrying about "poor people" between charity benefits. Doing pro bono because it made her feel good and she didn't need the money. Her old man, he thought, was probably the kind of asshole who bought six-thousand-dollar Italian suits.

Still, there was something about Annabelle Ramford that tickled his bullshit meter. He just couldn't think what it might be.

ANNABELLE STOOD IN the window outside her office and watched him stroll away down the street. She felt a little sorry for him. The case against the Walther kid was weak. If news reports were correct, the FBI was pressuring state prosecutors to make a deal that would let the kid out in a couple of years, in exchange for information . . .

It didn't have to be that way. The whole case against Walther would come together if Davenport could find Trey.

But Trey was gone for good. Not even Annabelle would know where to find her, not now, not ever again. Davenport turned the corner, and Annabelle Ramford went back to her office, dropped three pennies and a nickel into a half clamshell, sat down behind her computer, and put the whole thing out of her mind.

OUTSIDE ON THE STREET, Lucas looked around, thought about going back to the office. He could call Kelly and tell him about

Ramford, and maybe plot a little strategy in Carl Walther's case. On the other hand, he could just go home and see Sam.

Walther had fired shots at cops, so he'd do *some* jail time. A couple of years, at a minimum. And who was to say that Carl hadn't been abused, having spent so much time with that crazy old man? The snarled-up history of the Walther spy ring was another matter, and finding an equitable resolution for that case was beyond him. Probably beyond anybody.

Lucas yawned. Whatever happened would happen. If he wanted nice neat endings, he was in the wrong business. And he'd been at the office too much, lately. He was getting stale. Worse than that, he was investigating horses.

He turned the corner, back toward the parking ramp. Better to go home and see Sam, he thought.

And he did.